DUST
TO
DUST

DUST TO DUST

A
Ludington - van der Berg Novel

M. M. Lindvall

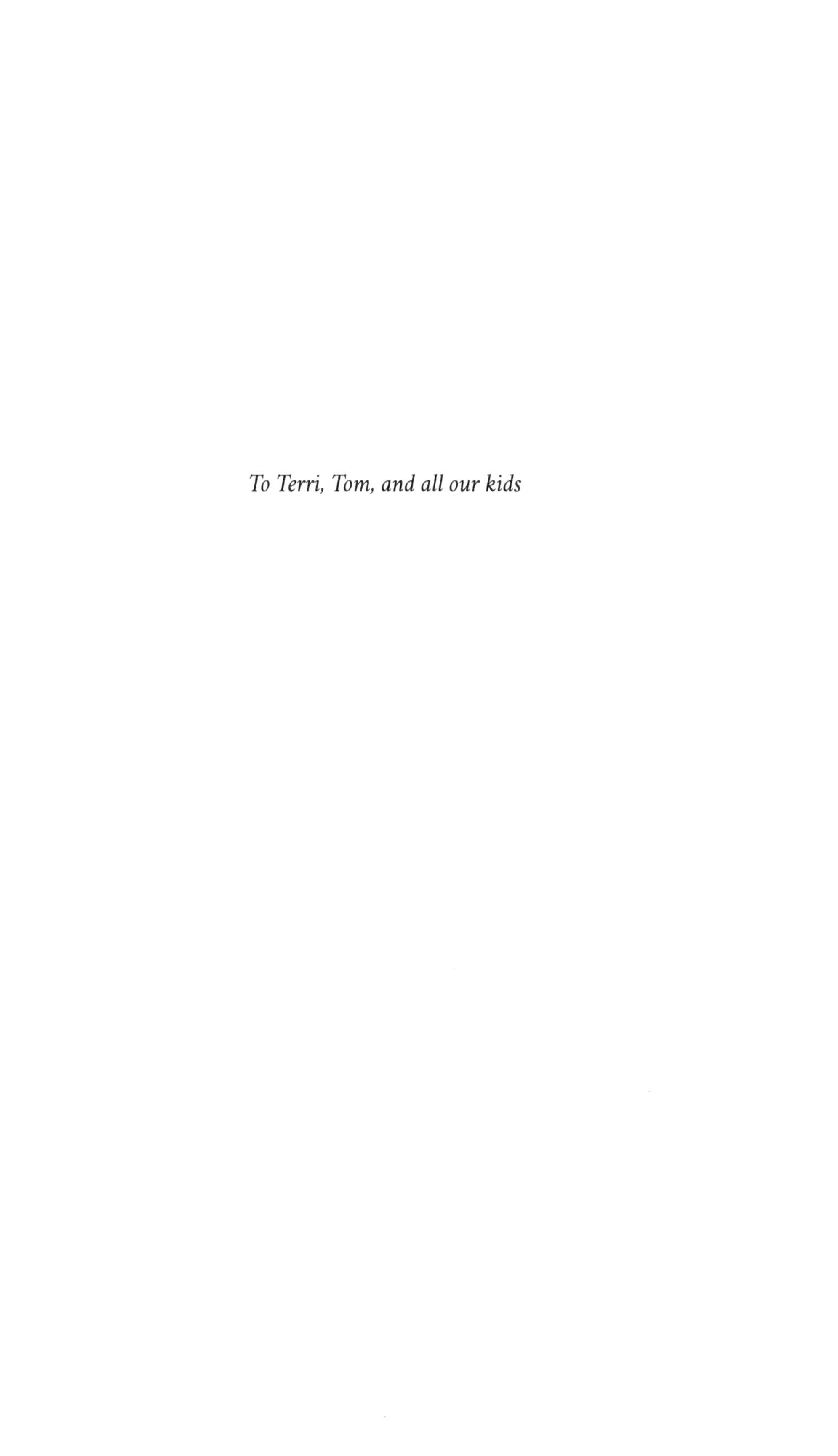

To Terri, Tom, and all our kids

Praise for Dust to Dust

"M. M. Lindvall has once again presented readers with an enthralling tale exploring not only a crime, but the mysteries behind hate and greed, the pain they inflict, and the most faithful responses possible. In this third book in the series, the characters have become literary friends who actually helped me understand life with and without grace."—M. Craig Barnes, author of *Sacred Thirst* and *When God Interrupts*

"Put together a minister, a rabbi, and a nosy church secretary and you get *Dust to Dust*, a well-plotted and supremely entertaining mystery, as the trio investigate an invaded synagogue and the death of one of its prominent congregants. This third novel in the Ludington-van der Berg series by a father-daughter writing team emphasizes character as well as plot and the warm relationship between a minister and a rabbi whose flocks share a neighborhood. Highly recommended!"—Rabbi Meir Bargeron, Congregation Achduth Veshalom

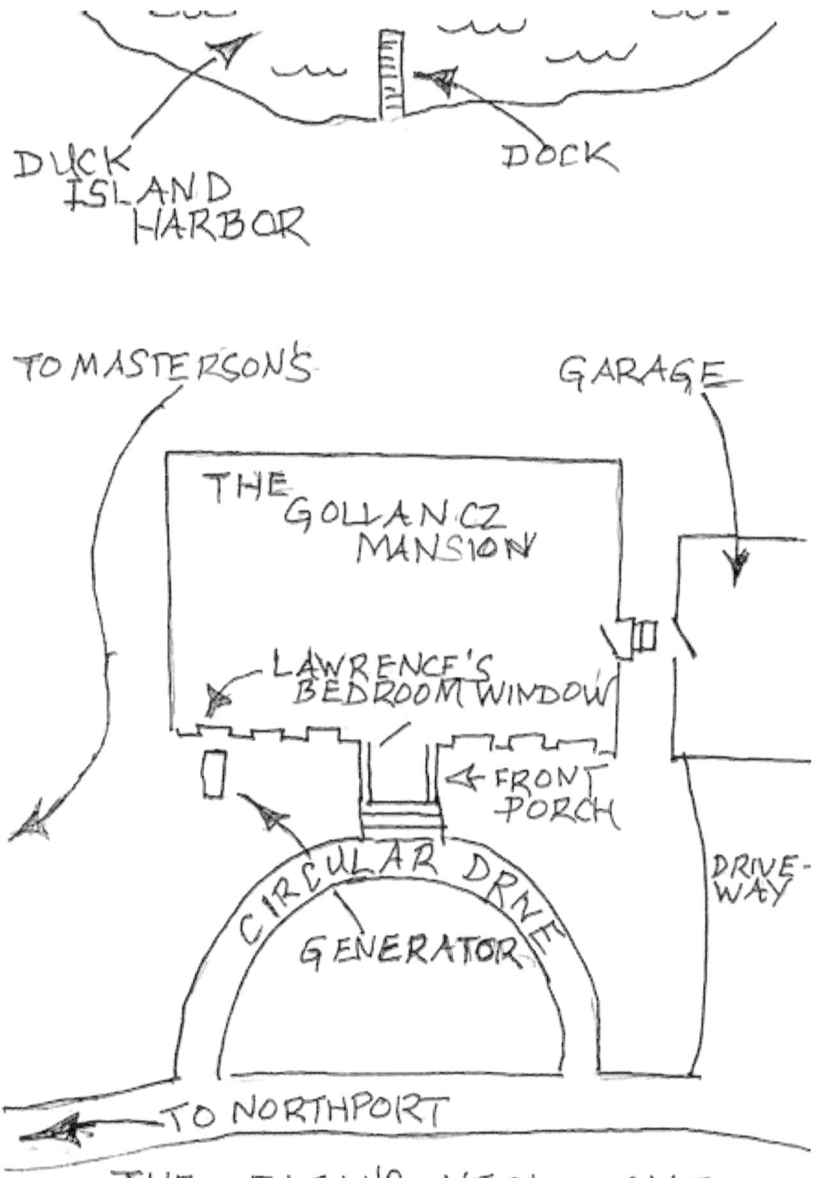

THE EATON'S NECK HOME
OF
LAWRENCE GOLLANCZ

Chapter One

Monday

Seth Ludington's iPhone didn't ring, but he heard it. It was lying on the oak of his bedside bureau and vibrated loudly enough to awaken him at 7:34 on a Monday morning in late August. Monday was his day off, and he always turned his ringer off Sunday night when he went to bed. Every member of Old Stone Church knew Monday was their pastor's day off. They had entered into an unspoken covenant not to disturb him on Mondays, save for occasions of death, or perhaps impending death. Imminently impending death.

It had roused his wife as well. Fiona turned to him, lifted her head to rest it on her right arm, and said, an edge of anxiety in her voice, "Who on earth could be calling at this hour?" They both knew that phone calls at odd hours often brought unhappy news. "You'd best take it."

Ludington jacked himself up in bed and pushed back the forelock of the rather too-long dark hair that was forever falling over his eyes. Just as he reached for the insistent phone, he thought of the quip some wag had made when cell phones first invaded life. "Who'd have thought we'd carry a thing around in our pockets that any one of the world's six billion people" (this was said in 2000 or so) "can make ring whenever they want."

He pulled the phone free of its charger. He had recently altered his lock screen to display an especially lovely shot of Fiona holding the twins in her arms, a bare smile of victory on her freckled Scots face. Plastered over the photo was the name of the caller—"Harriet." Harriet van der Berg was the volunteer part-time church secretary at Old Stone Church. She refused the offers of remuneration Ludington occasionally floated. She knew the church could not afford to pay her and that any salary would doubtless be underwritten by her boss himself, who certainly could afford it. Both had come to understand that it was a point of pride for her.

Van der Berg was in her late seventies, within hailing distance of eighty; she lived in an unusually nice rent-controlled apartment in Yorkville and had long since purchased most everything she wanted that could be purchased. The pension from the Wall Street law firm she had served for nearly fifty years was adequate. She was quite happy with the assortment of furniture that she and Margaret had selected over their years together, mostly Williamsburg reproductions. The pieces reminded her of Margaret because Harriet knew that her partner had not much liked the stuff, but had said nothing till the dark day she died three years earlier. Harriet was equally careful with her clothes, all doggedly classic, of course. She had liked the wardrobe when she'd assembled it; she still liked it well enough. "Why alter what suits you?" And she had not gained or lost more than two pounds in thirty years.

"It's Harriet," Ludington said, as much to the universe as to his wife. The phone had stopped vibrating just as he pressed the green button, but he got her in time.

"Seth, it's Harriet telephoning. I cannot but offer my most profound apologies for placing a telephone call to you at this hour, but I decided I must do so. Upon considering it, I determined that you would surely wish to be aware of the matter at hand as soon as possible. It is indeed of some urgency."

Ludington suspected that Harriet van der Berg was the last living person who "placed" telephone calls. In the several years they had worked together at the church, but also in the course of two investigations into as many dead bodies, Ludington had grown accustomed to the woman's antique speech. In truth, he had begun to delight in it.

"Of course, Harriet. So what's up?" Much as he enjoyed it, he refused to engage in it himself.

"Upon rising this morning, I discovered that the quart bottle of reduced-fat milk I bought three weeks ago had turned sour. You know that I prefer milk—real milk—in my coffee, so I dressed hastily and set off for Grace's Market to procure a fresh quart. My point it this. In the elevator, I encountered Miriam Castle, who lives in 7A just above me. Miriam appeared quite distraught, so I inquired what might be troubling her. Well Seth, she informed me that she had just heard from her dearest friend Lena Gold that their synagogue—that would be Temple Beth Shalom up on 87th Street—had been invaded and vandalized sometime last night. She indicated that the destruction was quite horrific. Perhaps you know that Lena is secretary to their rabbi. She and I have often chatted about secretarial matters at our Manhattan Administrators of Religious Institutions gatherings. The rabbi had telephoned Lena to prevent her from going in to work this morning, and to ask her to facilitate an email communication to their congregation regarding the event."

Ludington was not aware that van der Berg was a member of any such organization as the Manhattan Administrators of Religious Institutions. Indeed, he found it curious that the woman considered herself an administrator. She kept the church books, such as they were, but administrator? Ludington sighed an "Oh no" into the phone. With most anyone else, he might have uttered a profanity.

Van der Berg continued, "I am aware that you and Rabbi Gellman are acquainted, so I thought you would doubtless wish to be in contact forthwith so that you might extend expressions of support and sympathy." Ludington had grown accustomed to the woman's frequent, though usually subtler, suggestions as to how he might best do his job. She had been a member of Old Stone all her adult life and knew the place as deeply as she loved it. The woman could not help herself—she had a controlling nature. But this direction was more direct than usual.

Though she was exactly right, of course. "I'll call Daniel." *At a decent hour,* he thought to himself. "Thank you for letting me know, Harriet. This kind of stuff is just too tragic."

Van der Berg hesitated before ending the call, but finally said, almost *sotto voce*, "Perhaps we might be of some assistance in this matter, you and I. We have become rather adept at delving into the genesis of unhappy events, have we not?"

"Harriet, the authorities will be all over this. Antisemitic vandalism. It'll get major police attention. But I'll get to Daniel right away."

"As you say, Seth." She had finally stopped calling him "Dominie," at least usually. In response, he had begun to address a woman nearly as old as his grandmother, as "Harriet." He hit the red button to end the call and turned to Fiona, who had heard only his side of the conversation. He told her what had happened at Temple Beth Shalom, but did not mention that he suspected Harriet van der Berg was bored and aching to poke her long Dutch nose into a matter that was neither her business nor his.

Chapter Two

Monday

Seth Ludington was drying himself after a quick shower when he heard his wife answering Inez's quiet query from the hallway outside their bedroom. Inez was their night nurse. She slept in the twins' room, fetched whichever one of the girls declared her hunger during the hours from ten till eight, and brought the child to Fiona to nurse.

"Astrid is doubtless starving, am I right, Inez?"

Fiona had recently decided that at eight months, it was about time to ween the girls. She was back to work at her position as a human rights lawyer at the UN, yet had still been nursing every morning before the girls departed to daycare and she to her office at the UN Plaza in east Midtown, where she would pump twice later in the day. But they had decided to keep Inez, a woman whom both had come to adore. She could bottle-feed the girls at night. Both father and mother were sharply aware of the fact that Ludington's wealth made pursuing two careers and parenting twin infants a markedly easier feat. Seth felt guilty about it; Fiona did not.

But guilt was a default reaction for Seth Ludington, though that guilt—now mostly about his embarrassing wealth—was not all that haunted him. He was often plagued by doubt. Not so much theological doubts, though the *bete gris* of spiritual skepticism sometimes did stalk him. More often, he found himself uncertain whether he was fit for the strange work called "ministry" that he had been called to, called suddenly, surprisingly, out of nowhere.

He sometimes woke up mornings wondering how he had ever ended up the pastor of a struggling little church in the Yorkville neighborhood of Manhattan. His mentor, Moze Washington, once opined to him that "doubts were the ants in the pants of faith." He could only hope that his ants would keep him moving.

Still, the money took center stage in his self-doubt. He and Fiona had decided to forego a live-in nanny. Quite affordable for them, but just too publicly ostentatious for the minister. Ludington further attempted to assuage his little guilt devil by insisting that he routinely be the one to stroll the girls to the daycare center on 87th Street that they attended in lieu of a day nanny. They loved the three-block trip up 2nd Avenue in their fore and aft stroller. Seth had so named it with nautical terminology. It was as close as he got to a boat these days. He and Fiona had first considered a side-by-side model, but had been advised that it would be too wide to navigate New York sidewalks.

Ingrid, in aft position today, vocalized as they rumbled along, the cracks and bumps of the sidewalk modulating her voice in a manner that clearly pleased both her and Astrid, the older by four minutes.

The girls no longer fussed when he left them at the Happy House of Little Ones, a name that Fiona had declared "tacky" when they settled on the place. It was quite nice, really. The staff were universally "matronly," and all spoke English, even though most of their charges spoke few words in any language. The only downside to the Happy House of Little Ones was that it was too cramped to allow stroller parking, which meant that Seth Ludington, six feet-plus tall and disconcertingly handsome, had to walk an empty double stroller down the sidewalks of Manhattan, either to the church on 82nd Street or back to their brownstone on 84th. It garnered curious looks, smiles, and the occasional comment from passers-by, especially if Seth happened to be wearing his clerical collar. "You lose something, Father?"

It being Monday and his day off, Seth was wearing neither a clerical collar nor his more customary knit tie and blue blazer. He returned to their brownstone, fully renovated at last at twice the original estimate, and worked the empty stroller down the steps to the kitchen entrance and through the door. He fixed himself another cup of coffee with their pod machine. That, too, occasioned a whiff of guilt about the plastic waste it produced. He sat down at the small table now surrounded by a pair of matching highchairs in addition to two grown-up chairs, and phoned Dan Gellman with his cell.

The rabbi picked up on the first ring, "Seth, I appreciate the call." Gellman obviously had Ludington's number in his contacts.

The two clergymen had met at a terminally boring New York fund-raiser more than a year earlier and had quickly become as good friends as their over-busy lives allowed. Both served waning congregations, diminished in both size and resources, first by the exodus from city to suburbs, more recently by a post-modern indifference to spiritual matters, or at least to any specific form of spirituality. And both men were relatively new fathers. Dan's son Zack had just turned two; Seth's twins were eight months.

"How bad is it, Dan?"

Silence…then, "Terrifying, Seth. Not just the degree of damage in the sanctuary, but the nature of it. Spray paint everywhere. Over-the-top Nazi shit." Gellman was given to occasional profanity, generally mild. Seth liked that about the man, despite having been raised with a Midwestern disdain for what his mother had named "lower-class cuss words."

"I'm coming over."

"Don't Seth. You don't want your eyes to see it. It'll always stay there."

"I'm on my way."

"Not just now, Seth. Cops are still here. Maybe later this afternoon. I suppose I would appreciate some commiseration."

Yorkville and the Upper East Side, in general, were a religious mix. When asked about it once, Ludington had said, "It's one-third R.C., one-third Jewish, one-third Protestant, and one-third nothing." In fact, the fraction of "nothing" was doubtless far greater these days. In such a diversity, clergy stuck together no matter their theological flavor.

Jews in New York were divvied up into a wondrous variety of denominations. Not as many varieties as Protestants, but they were trying. Temple Beth Shalom was Reform, set at the liberal end of the spectrum. Dan had once told Seth that the synagogue had been founded in the nineteenth century by German immigrants, most of whose great-great-grandchildren had since decamped to the suburbs or secularity, leaving a faithful remnant struggling to maintain an aging building and pay a rabbi. In other words, Old Stone Church with Torah instead of Jesus. Which was doubtless part of the reason Seth Ludington and Daniel Gellman got on so well.

Ludington spent the next hours of his day off struggling through *Dominion*, Tom Holland's magisterial history of everything. It was a gripping read, but his mind kept wandering up to Temple Beth Shalom and what he would see there. He did not have to pick the girls up from the Happy House of Little Ones until five-thirty. He had told Gellman he would be at the synagogue about four. He kept glancing at his Shinola Runwell and then at the weather forecast on his phone. Big storms were supposed to roll across the City from New Jersey sometime later in the afternoon or evening. Weather forecasters had grown increasingly apocalyptic in their rhetoric, but this bout of impending weather sounded genuinely serious. He hoped to get the girls home before any assault from the heavens. He put the book down at three-thirty, grabbed an umbrella, and set off for the short hike to the synagogue.

Temple Beth Shalom was dwarfed by the two modest pre-war mid-rise apartment buildings it was tucked between. They were not doormen buildings, but yellow brick stacks of modest one or two-bedroom apartments. Seth guessed they were rent-controlled or maybe rent-stabilized. The synagogue they flanked was a three-story pile of Neo-Romanesque red sandstone, an architectural conceit once so fashionable, but now more than a little foreboding. A large round stained-glass window with a Star of David at the center loomed over the front doors. Yellow crime scene tape stretched from one wrought iron hand railing to the other, guarding the steps leading up to the doors. Seth walked past the main entrance to the low office door at the far side of the building's facade and pressed the buzzer. He normally would have heard Lena's voice in response, but this time, it was Dan's. "Seth, I'll buzz you in." Ludington looked up at the security camera over the office door and offered a quick chest-high wave. His few years in the City had acclimated him to ubiquitous door buzzers and security cameras.

As Ludington pushed open the exterior door, Gellman rounded an inner door leading to the synagogue offices to meet him. "You know, Seth, I actually am glad you came. You can't dodge reality by not looking at it." The rabbi reached out to shake his friend's hand, then turned to mount the five steps that led to the sanctuary's side entrance. "Follow me, Seth, and gird up your loins." Rabbi Daniel Gellman was a few years Ludington's junior and a couple inches shorter. Seth had noticed that the man had spectacular posture, unlike himself. Very tall people too often learn to slouch. Gellman had reddish hair—not flaming red, closer to auburn—and blue eyes that seemed to always be dancing.

As he led Ludington toward the synagogue's sanctuary, Gellman said over his shoulder, "Cops just left. Hate crime squad. They took a million photos and dusted every square inch for fingerprints."

A desecrated holy space is somehow more horrific than a vandalized office or store, even a home. Ludington's eye went first to the slashes of black spray paint strewn across the lower reaches of the white plaster walls to either side of the large and elaborate wooden cabinet called the ark. The ark was the focal point of the medium-sized room. Rows of pews were arranged in a semi-circle facing a raised platform in the front below the ark. Several swastikas crudely drawn defaced the walls, along with a "Heil Hitler" and a "Jews to the gas." To the left of the ark was a jagged "SS." Ludington was historian enough to recognize it as the runic insignia of the Nazi paramilitary crazies most responsible for the Holocaust—the *Schutzstaffel*. He questioned whether the vandal knew such details.

The reading table on which the Torah scrolls would be unrolled on Shabbat normally sat on the raised platform Gellman had once told him was called the bima. The table was tipped over onto its side, precariously balanced on the edge of the bima. The ark was still in its place, though the curtain that normally hid the scrolls from view had been ripped down and lay on the bima's floor, torn into several pieces. The Hebrew letters carved into the wood border around the ark were mostly hidden behind black spray paint. Ludington glanced around the room, looking for what was missing. The Torah scrolls that should have been in the ark were not there. He turned to

Gellman, "Dan, the Torah scrolls?"

"In my office. He—I assume it was a 'he'—pulled them out of the ark and threw them across the front pews. Damaged, but repairable. They're all hand-written, you know. Painstaking."

Ludington could think of nothing to say. He raised his head to observe the still-lit eternal light mounted just above the ark, the sign of the Divine Presence. It was lit. Gellman saw his friend looking at it, nodded, and offered the first smile to cross his face that day. A bare and defiant smile.

He said, "It can all be repaired, of course. We have insurance. Huge deductible, unfortunately, to keep the premiums down. It'll take months to collect and do the work, though. The timing couldn't be much worse. The High Holy Days are just around the corner. The only time this place is ever close to full."

"Like Christmas and Easter at Old Stone," Ludington thought.

Gellman said, "This could push Beth Shalom right over the edge. We've been hanging on by our fingertips for years. I'm not sure we'll survive the months it's going to take to put the place back together. They're a pretty loyal bunch, but, well… they'll just find somewhere else for Rosh Hashanah and Yom Kippur. Who can blame them? And then maybe they'll not come back."

"You still worship on Saturday morning, right?" Ludington knew the answer, of course, just as he did to his second rhetorical question, "And I think I saw the High Holy Days fall midweek this year, right?"

Gellman gave his friend a quizzical look at these queries. "Of course. Why?"

"Well, Old Stone Church is sitting dark and empty all those days."

Gellman was silent for a moment. Then he raised his head to look up at the taller man, extended his hand for the second time, and said, "Thank you, Seth. Okay if I come by tomorrow?"

"Of course. Ten work for you, Dan?"

"I'll bring coffee."

* * *

Ludington was early picking up the girls at the daycare center, even though he'd had to detour home to fetch the stroller. He began to hurry as he approached the Happy House of Little Ones. The sky was growing ominously black, or more accurately, that green-black that often serves as a harbinger of ferocious weather. Then the wind suddenly kicked up, roaring down the canyon of 2nd Avenue. He held tight to the empty stroller. No lightning yet, but he heard a deep and distant baritone rumble of thunder as he wiggled the empty stroller through the door of the daycare center. He helped Mary Lou strap the girls into their seats. Together, they fixed the clear plastic rain cover in place to shield the twins from whatever might befall them on the walk home. Astrid objected to the thing, but her father insisted, handing her a favorite stuffed rabbit in consolation. He was jogging the stroller down 84th to their brownstone when the first flash of lightning lit the street bright as noon. The deafening crack was almost immediate, followed by even more wind. The rain finally arrived, a torrent assaulting northern Manhattan, just as he got his little girls through the kitchen door. Then, it lumbered east toward Long Island.

Chapter Three

Tuesday

The next morning at ten, Seth sat himself down on a too small chair at the desk by the side door to the Old Stone Parrish House. The church used to have an employee stationed at the 82nd Street entrance on weekdays to buzz visitors in, but Gloria, a diminutive and sweet-tempered woman, had not been replaced when she retired. No room in the budget. Now, a typed notice taped on the inside of the door suggesting people call one of three numbers—the church's landline, Harriet's cell, or his. The note added, "Someone will be happy to buzz you in." Often as not, that happy someone was Seth Ludington. But this morning, he had thought to spare Dan the bother of waiting at the door.

* * *

Gellman arrived at ten sharp, balancing a cardboard holder with two cups of to-go coffee. Ludington pushed the door open for him, "Morning, Dan. How you doing?"

Gellman stepped into the Parrish House lobby and said, "Meh. As you might expect. You take your coffee regular, no?" He pushed the coffees toward Ludington. "The close one is yours."

In old New York, "regular" meant with milk and sugar. Ludington had recently been working to forego the sugar part of regular, but found himself pleased at the prospect of a sweet coffee.

"Perfect," Ludington said as he extricated the classic blue and white faux-Greek paper cup from the holder. He read the words on the side of the cup aloud, "We are happy to serve you."

Gellman offered a nod in response as Ludington turned to lead his friend down the hallway toward Old Stone's sanctuary. He flipped on the lights as they entered.

"It's a beautiful space, Seth. You've done some restoration work recently, right?"

Indeed, they had. Funds to replace the steeple, put a new slate roof over the sanctuary, and repaint and rewire its interior had become available when Seth and Fiona had purchased the manse, the minister's residence the church had owned for more than half a century. The price they had offered the church was inflated, something everyone understood but never mentioned. It happened to be just the amount needed for the church repair projects. Seth and Fiona's subsequent renovation of the erstwhile manse, the century-old five-story brownstone they now owned, had exposed the first of the two dead bodies that had confronted Ludington and van der Berg in the last year. Both bodies had demanded that questions be answered.

Ludington said, "They just finished. Wrapped up painting in here a few days ago. Took the sidewalk scaffolding down last month after they finished replacing the steeple and fixing the roof." Ludington did not mention his contempt for the prefab steeple the trustees had selected to save a few dollars.

The rabbi's eye scanned the Neo-Gothic worship space, as bereft of natural light as was Temple Beth Shalom, but now with its two rows of upgraded chandeliers, much better lit. He raised his head to the hammer beam trusses that supported the peaked ceiling. His eyes next went to the row of stained glass windows that lined one side of the sanctuary, all of them narrative images. The first, toward the rear of the room, depicted a barefoot Moses gazing at his burning bush, a startled look on his face. Gellman slowly read aloud the words underneath the image, "*Nec Tamen Consumebatur.*' Latin, right? Not one of my languages."

"'Yet it was not consumed,'" Ludington translated. "The burning bush, that is."

"This tale we share. Exodus Chapter Three."

Then his eye travelled to the next three windows—the first a depiction of the Nativity, the second of Jesus welcoming the little children, the last—nearest the front of the church—of the Risen Christ, white-robed, his face kindly but solemn, index and middle fingers raised in benediction.

Gellman said, "A good Jew he was."

Ludington smiled and said, "Born a Jew, lived a Jew, died a Jew."

Gellman finally turned to the front of the sanctuary and the massive cross that hung at the front of the raised chancel, behind and over the communion table. It was an empty cross—no bloody body. He looked at Ludington and raised his eyebrows.

"I know. We can cover it somehow." Ludington understood that the cross evoked radically different emotional responses from Christians and Jews. To Christians, it was a sign of the depths of divine love for humanity. But to Jews, it was a reminder of the blood curse, the notion that Jews bore eternal culpability for the death of Jesus. This erroneous idea was a key ingredient in the poison of antisemitism, perhaps humanity's oldest hatred… and surely one of the deadliest.

Harriet van der Berg suddenly poked her curious nose into the room and announced her presence by clearing her throat rather demonstrably. The two men turned to her as she eased her way into the sanctuary and down the center aisle to where they were standing at the base of the chancel steps.

As she approached, Seth said, "Harriet, this is Rabbi Daniel Gellman, from Temple Beth Shalom. We're thinking about his congregation using our sanctuary while they clean up their own. Saturdays it would be, and High Holy Days next month. All weekdays this year."

Van der Berg said, "Session will have to approve, but they will. Capital idea, Dominie."

Ludington rolled his eyes. He knew that her note about the need for the church board's approval and her retreat to the formality of "Dominie" were purely for Gellman's benefit.

The rabbi shook Harriet's hand, which she had extended to him palm down like royalty. He turned back to Ludington and said, "We'll need to bring in an ark, of course, I mean, if that's okay. For the Torah scrolls. The ark in the synagogue is built into the wall. Anyway, it's damaged and probably too big to move. They sell portable arks. You can get 'em online."

Gellman hesitated before continuing. "But Seth, well…, you're right about the cross." He appeared awkward as he mentioned that problematic focal point at the front of the Old Stone sanctuary.

"It won't be a problem, Dan. We can rig some sort of drape or screen over it when you're in here. And you're welcome to the organ, such as it is." He shrugged his shoulders and said, "Dan, it's kind of a circle, this is. I mean, some Christians and Jews worshiped together in the early years, probably till the end of the first century. Lots of early Christians figured Jesus was a new take on being Jewish."

Gellman raised an eyebrow again, "Didn't quite work out, though."

"Nope," Ludington admitted. "But this time it'll be the same space, different times."

Gellman glanced demonstratively at his watch and said, "Insurance adjuster is coming at 11:15. Gotta meet him at the synagogue."

He turned to van der Berg and said, "Pleasure to meet you, Miss van der Berg. I understand you know our Lena."

Van der Berg nodded, "Yes indeed. You and Temple Beth Shalom are blessed with a singularly astute and industrious secretary. She is a friend to a neighbor in my building, also a member of your congregation. I encountered her yesterday and heard the news of the Gothic invasion of your synagogue."

Hearing this, Ludington assumed that Gellman had probably guessed that their two friendly and newsy admins were responsible for his having learned about the vandalism so promptly the previous morning. If Gellman was surprised to hear that his right-hand woman and the synagogue's highly competent administrator named a secretary, he did not betray it. He smiled in answer.

As Gellman began his retreat down the center aisle of Old Stone Church, his cell rang loudly, Westminster Chimes of all things. He fished it out of his blazer pocket, glanced at the screen, and shrugged his shoulders. He clearly did not recognize the caller, but answered nonetheless. He offered a "Hello," his tone rising to make the word a question.

His back was to Ludington and van der Berg as he listened to the call. He first mumbled an "Oh my God" into the phone. After another few moments, he added, "I can't believe it. He was too smart for that." Gellman nodded his head as he listened for another minute and finally said, "Of course, of course. Whenever you want. Sooner the better. I'll get back to you. And Mr. Atkins, thank you for calling. I appreciate your letting me know, horrible as this is."

He ended the call, shook his head in a gesture of incredulity, and turned back to face Ludington and van der Berg at the far end of the center aisle. He whispered one last "I can't believe it" into the silent sanctuary of Old Stone Church.

Ludington walked down the aisle toward his friend, whose arms hung loosely at his sides, one of them still holding the cell phone. "What happened, Dan?"

"Lawrence Gollancz. He's dead. Died in his sleep last night."

"I'm sorry. A friend?"

"Yes. And a pillar of the synagogue, a major pillar. In fact, he was probably the only hope for the place."

"What happened?"

Gellman, clearly shocked, spit out his answer in clipped sentences, "They're not sure yet. Died in his sleep last night. At his place out on Long Island. The cops think it was probably carbon monoxide poisoning. From one of those gas generators. Too close to an open window. Power was out because of the storm."

"Who was it that just called you, Dan?"

"His lawyer out on the Island, 'Something Atkins.' He knew about Lawrence's relationship to Beth Shalom, so he called me. Lawrence was our most generous supporter. I've got to get out there, Seth. I gotta get out there right away. They might want to do an autopsy. He grew up Orthodox, Lawrence I mean. He'd hate the idea of an autopsy. This is a disaster. I gotta get out there. Now." He paused as if suddenly realizing his dilemma, "We don't keep a car."

Seth knew that many New Yorkers, especially in Manhattan, did not own cars. Parking on the street was an endless hassle. Garage rentals were outrageous. Mass transit got you everywhere.

"I can drive you out if you want. I'd be happy to."

Gellman pulled himself together and said, "That would be great. I mean, thanks. Yes." He looked at his watch again and said. "Oh, Jeez, the insurance adjuster. Seth, I gotta go."

"When do you want me to pick you up, Dan?"

"How about one? One okay?"

"Of course. I'll pick you up at the synagogue."

Gellman strode down the church aisle, his phone still clutched in his hand, and his shoulders slumped, shaking his head.

Van der Berg went to stand next to her pastor, both of them watching the retreating rabbi.

She said, "My oh my, two great tragedies befall the synagogue, one atop the other in as many days. How extraordinary."

"Extraordinary indeed." He spoke the first word as if it were two words.

Still, without looking at him, she said, "Isn't it? Well, Seth, I must say that I find it felicitous that you, at least, will be accompanying Rabbi Gellman to the scene of this unhappy death."

Chapter Four

Tuesday

After Gellman left the Old Stone sanctuary and van der Berg retreated to her office, Ludington sat down in a front pew and phoned for his car. It could take up to an hour for the attendants to find his gray Volvo and extract it from the bowels of the parking garage. He stood, glanced quickly at the cross in front of him, and went to his own office. He passed van der Berg's cubby at a brisk pace with a wave, both movements suggesting that he had things to do and no time to chat. He sat at his desk, knowing he had to ponder the sermon he would preach in five days. But he could not dismiss the scene of Temple Beth Shalom's vandalism from his mind's eye. Dan had been right. It was carved deep into the folds of his brain, lodged there for life.

He sighed a lament at the state of the world and checked his paper calendar. It was a church version that offered not only the days and weeks, but also the Scripture readings prescribed by the lectionary for each Sunday. Presbyterians were not required to use these semi-official Bible readings, but Ludington generally did. Doing so saved him from the temptation to dodge passages that made him uncomfortable and preach only those he liked. He was in a hurry, so he emailed Harriet and told her just to note the lectionary passages in Sunday's program, whatever they were. He asked her to have the organist choose the hymns and to use the same prayers as Sunday a year ago. If Ludington didn't have the bulletin information to her by five o'clock Tuesdays, she would invariably poke her French twist head into his office and start dropping hints. Why it couldn't wait till Wednesday, or even Thursday, escaped him. But he was loath to object. The woman was an unpaid volunteer, after all, and if she wanted the thing put to bed by Wednesday noon, he had to live with it. Wednesday noon had always been print-the-program deadline at Old Stone.

As he passed her little office on his way to fetch his car, Ludington said, "Get my email?"

She called toward his retreating back, "Yes, thank you. I assume you are off to procure your automobile and drive Rabbi Gellman out onto Long Island. Most kind of you, I must say. You'll be taking your new model, the large one, I assume?"

There was the slightest accent on the word "large." Ludington guessed it meant "large enough for me to go with you." His venerable and very compact Volvo PV544 had been retired to a storage facility in the Bronx by the birth of the twins. It had been replaced by a family-friendly SUV, still a Volvo, an XC90 with plenty of room for two infant car seats, or for that matter, plenty of room for a bored and insatiably curious administrative assistant.

Ludington decided to play dumb. He turned around, struck a coy smile, and said, "See you tomorrow, Harriet."

But no sooner had he said the words that a thought occurred to him. He returned to his study, took off his blue dress shirt and tie, and fished around his office closet for a black clergy shirt, the one that had a Roman collar. He had been a minister long enough to understand that a clerical collar—especially the Roman version with its little notch of white—often got you into places barred to mere laity, places like the intensive care units of hospitals, the visitors' rooms of jails, and perhaps the scenes of tragic accidents.

Ludington double-parked in front of Temple Beth Shalom, the entrance steps to which were still festooned with yellow scene-of-the-crime tape. He glanced at his watch. One sharp. He waited ten minutes, ignoring the perturbed cabs honking at him because he was blocking their pick-up lane. He was about to call Dan when the man emerged from the synagogue's office door behind a sweaty fifty-year-old gent in a blue pin-striped suit way too heavy for a steamy late August afternoon. The two men shook hands and waved a farewell. Gellman jogged to Ludington's car—an acknowledgement that he was late—and climbed into the passenger seat.

"Sorry, Seth. That was the insurance adjuster. It's going to be a real battle. Thanks for this, the ride, I mean."

"No problem."

Seth decided that the rabbi would talk about the reason for his eagerness to get himself to the scene of Lawrence Gollancz's death when he was ready, so he asked, "How are Lilly and Zack?"

"Lilly is pretty rattled by this. As you might expect. She worries for me, and for the synagogue, of course. Zack? He's a happy story. The kid just may become more loquacious than his father. Words are coming fast, phrases and little almost-sentences. He's so pleased with himself. He asked me a question this morning, three words, 'Daddy go bye-bye?'"

Gellman pulled a proud father smile and said, "And your girls? Keeping you up at night, I imagine."

Ludington was reluctant to tell his friend that he and Fiona were still enjoying the services of a night nurse, a woman who was indeed being kept up at night, though he was not. He said, "They're not sleeping through the night quite yet, but almost."

They crossed the bridge from Manhattan to Long Island that had recently been renamed for former Mayor Koch, though most New Yorkers still called it the Queensboro. They rode in silence, the mid-day traffic lighter than usual, before Gellman broached the question raised by his eagerness to get to Eaton's Neck. "Gollancz was raised Orthodox, not ultra, just straight-up Orthodox. He drifted left in middle age, after his wife died. He moved uptown and joined Beth Shalom a decade ago. Not the obvious choice. I would have thought he'd have opted for Park Avenue Synagogue. Maybe he chose us because we're little and needed him. Anyway, Lawrence Gollancz may have died a Reform Jew, but I'm pretty sure he still would have hated the notion of an autopsy. We never discussed it, but my sense is that he would have probably wanted a prompt burial, too. Some of that Orthodox stuff—no autopsy, quick burial—gets embedded in a person."

"I can't see that there'll be a problem, I mean, with either the autopsy business or a prompt funeral. You can have the service at Old Stone if you want."

"Well, I'm not so sure, Seth, not sure about either. It's one of the reasons I want to get out there. Some medical examiners want an autopsy for any accidental death. I know it's usually so here in the City. And if they do, I assume it would take a couple days, at least. The Orthodox aim for burial by dusk of the day of death, next day at the latest. No embalming, just wash the body and a simple wooden casket. They even drill holes in the bottom of the casket. They say they do it because of what God said to Adam after he and Eve ate the apple—'...*you are dust, and to dust you shall return.*' Holes let the dust in and out, I guess. But, like I said, we never had a reason to talk about his funeral. He was a healthy sixty-something. But I loved the guy, and I want to honor what I think he would have wanted."

Ludington listened, navigating the Volvo through the labyrinthine streets of Long Island City with the aid of the car's navigation system, finally entering the eastbound Long Island Expressway. Gellman spoke as Ludington accelerated to highway speed, "You know about the jingle controversy, don't you, Seth? The *Post* ran endless stories about it."

Ludington took both the *Wall Street Journal* and the *Times*, but eschewed the tabloids. "No, don't think I do. A jingle controversy?"

"Not a jingle exactly, though that's what the papers named it. It was this little musical tune. Story goes like this. Lawrence Gollancz made his fortune selling ice cream. You know the Zesty Freeze trucks? Family business. His grandfather started it with one truck on the Lower East Side. Bought the truck and started peddling ice cream right after he got himself and his wife and kids out of Germany in the thirties, got out just in time. That one ice cream truck is now a couple hundred ice cream trucks roaming every borough of the City. They play a little tune when they come down the street to start you drooling for soft-serve. Mostly, it starts kids drooling for soft-serve and trooping around the truck when it stops. Anyway, back in the thirties, Gollancz's grandfather had hit on a popular tune of the day for his trucks to play. Well, it turns out the tune was originally associated with those black-face minstrel shows. The old man may not have known it. Even if he had, it probably wouldn't have been an issue back then. Over the years, the ice cream truck tune became iconic. Every kid in New York could hum it. Nobody remembered where it came from. Or, nobody remembered until about a year ago when somebody did. In no time, all hell broke loose. In an age fine-tuned to every hint of racism, the melody and its connection with minstrel shows and blackface was unacceptable. People started campaigning for it to be dropped. Wanted it replaced with something else."

"Seems I maybe did hear about this. I didn't make the connection to your Gollancz, though."

"Well, Lawrence was actually sensitive to the issue. That was just like him. Never wanted to do harm, even if he didn't understand exactly why something would harm somebody. Of course, he'd had no idea about the jingle's history. Anyway, he changed it right away and apologized for it, apologized publicly and profusely. You would have thought that was the end of it."

"So it wasn't?"

"Not at all. In satisfying the left, he enraged the right. Some of the media coverage spun it that way. You know—'crazy woke lefties put an end to another grand old New York tradition.'

They equated it with the pressure to get rid of the horse-drawn carriages in Central Park. One story even noted that Lawrence Gollancz was a member of a 'left-leaning synagogue in Yorkville.' That would be us."

Seth said, "Can't win for losing."

Gellman nodded, "Guess so. Anyway, things got nastier in the last couple of months. The story was all over Twitter and Facebook, crazy right-wing stuff. Some of it was flavored with antisemitism and White nationalism. And then the anonymous letters started coming, letters vilifying the poor guy for caving in to the 'radical Jewish left.'" Gellman placed the last three words in air quotes and paused before adding, "Seth, there were even death threats. Lawrence came to me to talk about it a few weeks ago. He talked to me about some of the letters and social media posts. He wasn't afraid.

Mostly, he was confused. Confused about why doing what he thought was the right thing had gotten him in trouble. Confused about why people were so furious with him."

As he listened to Gellman's tale, Ludington could not but remember van der Berg's use of the word "extraordinary" to describe the conjunction of vandalism in a synagogue one day and the sudden death of one of its members the next. He said nothing about that intersection of events to the rabbi.

But he did say, "Doing the right thing often gets people in trouble."

Chapter Five

Tuesday

Ludington took the Long Island Expressway east to Fresh Meadows, exited onto the Clearview, and then the Northern State Parkway. He got off that lovely child of Robert Moses' mid-century road-building orgy at the Northport exit. The route north to Gollancz's address, which he had punched into the Volvo's navigation system took them through Northport Village, a pretty little exurban town that lay just beyond an easy commute into the City. It was quaint in an unstudied way, with a New England feel. Not surprising, as actual New England was just a few miles across the water. The place was unexpectedly hilly. They passed a white clapboard Presbyterian Church set predictably at the intersection of Church and Main Streets. Ludington had noted that Eaton's Neck, where Gollancz had lived on weekends, was an egg-shaped peninsula, almost an island itself, poking its nose west and north into Long Island Sound. It was connected to Northport and the rest of Long Island by only one long road along a narrow strip of land that the Volvo's nav map called Asharoken.

The beach-front homes that lay to the right as they drove through Asharoken looked pricey, but then anything on the water was expensive, even if it was sandwiched between a busy road and the Sound. The Asharoken strip was flat and nearly treeless, but as they came to Eaton's Neck, they saw it to be densely forested and as hilly as Northport. Homes were set in the woods, most of them unassuming center-hall colonials and split-levels from the fifties and sixties. Ludington guessed that Eaton's Neck houses on the water would be anything but modest.

* * *

Indeed, "anything but modest" was an apt description of the house they approached as the navigation system announced, "You have reached your destination." The home that Lawrence Gollancz had lived in when escaping the City and had died in the previous night was a grand and perfectly symmetrical Victorian rectangle, late nineteenth-century, Ludington guessed. It was painted a brilliant white, its many windows set between louvered green shutters. They were the real kind that actually closed, Ludington noticed. The home was two stories with a mansard roof. To the right, close to the house, was a detached triple garage. The house was blessedly free of the turrets and gingerbread that its era had fancied. Pulling into the circular drive that led down to the entrance, they could see through the narrow slot between the house and the garage to the expanse of manicured lawn that lay on the waterfront side of the property. Its lush green sloped gracefully down to a small harbor, today a blue mirror. The several small sailboats moored in its center sat motionless. The calm after the storm, Ludington thought to himself.

He appreciated both the setting and the architecture and could not resist whispering, "Beautiful."

Gellman said, "Holy crap. I knew he had money, but…."

The bucolic scene was marred by two police cars and a single EMS ambulance parked in the circular drive that curved itself languidly before the wide, pillared main entrance porch, which was as perfectly proportioned as the house itself and set square at the center of its front facade. All three vehicles' roof lights were flashing red and blue, jarringly out of sync with each other. Yellow scene-of-the-crime tape was laced everywhere, extravagantly. The first of the police cars had "Asharoken" emblazoned on its door. Parked behind it was the EMS ambulance, then a third official vehicle, its doors declaring it to be property of Suffolk County.

As Ludington pulled up behind the third vehicle, two men in EMS uniforms wheeled a gurney covered in a white sheet out of the front door and gingerly lifted it down the broad entrance steps. They were followed by a grim-faced woman who looked to be in her forties, trim with short blond hair. She was not in uniform, but wore black dress slacks and a white polo shirt. Either a detective or medical examiner, guessed Ludington.

Gellman opened his car door the second Ludington stopped. The rabbi got out without a word and strode down the drive toward the blond woman. He laid a hand on the covered body atop the gurney as he passed it as if he were offering a blessing. Perhaps he was, Ludington thought.

Seth got out of the car himself, but decided to hang back and let Gellman take the initiative. Lawrence Gollancz had been the rabbi's friend and congregant, not his. From a distance, he caught only snippets of the increasingly animated conversation unfolding between the two. Gellman raised both hands. The woman turned to face him. In the warm, still air, he heard Gellman say, "Jewish tradition." He saw the woman turn around and point in the direction of the first-floor window farthest to the left of the front entrance. Ludington could see the open window from where he stood. A silent portable gas generator sat underneath it. As she walked past the rabbi toward the Suffolk County car, he caught the blond woman saying, "We'll see. I'll discuss it with the head ME".

Gellman jogged back up the drive to Ludington and said, "That was the Suffolk County Medical Examiner, one of them anyway, maybe an assistant. She said they usually do an autopsy for an accidental death. But this one's obvious, she said, so she's going to check. 'Jewish tradition' seems to have cut some mustard."

As Ludington and Gellman spoke, they watched the two EMS medics wheel the gurney bearing the body of Lawrence Gollancz up the sloped drive toward the open back doors of their vehicle. The gurney jostled over the Belgian block pavers of the driveway. Ludington noticed that the body it bore jostled as well, as if it were reanimated. The two medics carefully lifted the gurney up and into the back of the ambulance. One of them climbed in as well, probably to secure the gurney. The other stepped into the cab, sat behind the steering wheel, and started the engine. The Asharoken cop went to her car and pulled forward out of the circular drive to let the EMS truck and medical examiner leave without having to back up. Their flashing lights were finally and happily extinguished as they drove slowly away. No reason to hurry now.

The cop car circled back around and down the drive to park behind Ludington's Volvo. The officer in the car turned off the engine, climbed out, and approached the two men.

She introduced herself, "Officer Marge Anderson, Asharoken Police Department."

She was young, petite, maybe thirty, her dark brown hair pulled back into a no-trouble ponytail. Her brown eyes flashed intelligence.

Gellman said, "Asharoken? I thought this was Eaton's Neck?"

She said, "This hunk of the Neck is in the Village of Asharoken. So we got the call."

She looked at Ludington's clerical collar and said, half a statement, half a question, "So Mr. Gollancz was a member of your church? St. Philip Neri in Northport, I suppose."

"Actually, no. Mr. Gollancz was a member of Rabbi Gellman's congregation in Manhattan. And a close friend." He nodded toward Dan to make it clear who Rabbi Gellman was and added, "I drove the rabbi out from the City."

Satisfied as to the identity of the two men, she said, "This is just too sad. Power went out last evening all over Eaton's Neck and Asharoken. Northport too. He must have started up that gas generator to get some power back up in the house. But he put it right under his bedroom window. Carbon monoxide, you know." She shook her head slightly to indicate incredulity at such misjudgment.

Gellman shook his head slowly in agreement, "But why would he do that? I mean, you would think he'd have known about gasoline engines and carbon monoxide."

"I can only guess, but the medical examiner sees it the same way. He put the generator where he put it because the junction box for the electric is right there at that corner of the house, just beyond the window to his bedroom."

She turned and pointed to a spot to the left of the entrance at the far end of the house. Ludington could make out the metal electrical junction box where the underground service from the street came to the house. The box was set about five feet off the ground, just above a trio of mature yews shielding the foundation. The grass and mud near the corner of the house looked soggy. Ludington noted a copper drainpipe that emptied onto the ground just below the junction box, soaking the area between the corner of the house and the generator, which now lounged in guilty silence. Rain off the roof and down the drainpipe must have flooded the area in last night's deluge.

Officer Anderson looked back at the two men, "The heavy-duty power cord he used to connect the thing to the house is only about ten feet long. Feeds the power to the junction box and into the house. I mean, you just start 'em up and plug the cord into the machine at one end and the junction box on the house at the other. I know because we have one. Used it last night, just like he did. My husband got it set up."

The Andersons had clearly not used their generator "just like he did." Theirs was doubtless set a wise distance from any open doors and windows. But she said nothing.

Gellman asked Anderson the obvious second question: "So why would he leave the window open?"

She said, "Well, it was so beastly hot, even after the storm rolled through. And super humid."

The rabbi still looked mystfied. "But the AC? He must have had air conditioning. If he had power, he could have closed the window."

Ludington knew the answer to that one, "Little portable gas generators don't put out enough power to run a central air conditioning system in a house like this. It'd keep the lights on, the fridge and the TV running, your phone charged, wi-fi going, not much more."

Anderson nodded in agreement and looked at Ludington, registering surprise that a clergyman would know anything about emergency gas generators. "You're right, Father. Ours won't run our AC. But this is what does surprise me. How could the guy sleep with the thing roaring under his window all night. They're not exactly quiet. At least ours isn't."

Gellman offered an ironic half-smile, "All he had to do was take out his hearing aids. I suppose you do that at night anyway. Mr. Gollancz had a hearing loss, major hearing loss."

Ludington asked, "So, who called you, I mean who called Asharoken Police?"

"Neighbor." She turned and nodded to a high ranch situated inland and up the hill, just visible through a military-straight line of spruce trees. "He says he heard the generator still running after the power came back on this morning, a little after nine it was. He thought that was odd, so he walked over to check things out. He looked in the window and saw him lying there in bed. He turned off the generator and called 911. How do you say his name, by the way? I mean the deceased."

"*Go-launch*," Gellman said."

Anderson paused, apparently considering a point in the story she found curious. "So, I have a question for you two. How did you find out, Rabbi?"

Gellman answered, "Mr. Gollancz's lawyer called me. Late this morning. He said that Lawrence's sister had just phoned him to let him know that her brother had died."

As Anderson took this information in she paused, "I called the sister. Part of the job I hate. She came right over. You just missed her. Came with a daughter. They live here on the Island. Out on the South Fork somewhere. I found her number in his phone. It was plugged in by the bed, fully charged. I brought up his emergency contacts. They came straight here, in under an hour. They wanted in the house, but we couldn't let 'em do that. It's not a crime scene, just procedure with an accidental death."

Anderson pulled out her notebook, "Okay. Rabbi, could you tell me what you know about Mr. Gollancz."

While Gellman spoke with the cop, Ludington slipped away, making his way past the front of the house to the detached garage set conveniently close. He found a side entrance door to the garage, no more than eight feet from the side door to the house. That door was protected by a small porch supported by a pair of large and gracefully curved corbels. Ludington thought to himself, "Lawrence Gollancz certainly had fine architectural taste for a soft-serve mogul."

The door to the garage just opposite had a large mullioned window on its top half, sparkling clean like everything else about the place. Ludington peered through it into the garage. A late model black Audi A-6 was parked in the far bay. Closer to him, lying on the epoxy-sealed garage floor, was a large cardboard box, its top flaps gaping open. The near side of the box was labeled "Portable Gasoline Powered Home Generator." On the garage floor between the box and the door, there was a narrow strip of paper about a foot-and-a-half long. It looked like a purchase receipt. He jiggled the door's curving wrought-iron handle. It was locked.

He heard Officer Anderson call to him from the driveway, "Rev. Ludington, may I ask what you're doing?"

He took his hand off the garage door handle to face Anderson and offered a guilty shrug and a coy smile in answer. As he had turned to face her, he saw a pair of boots placed on the top step of the side door to the house. He had gotten a pair exactly like them a few weeks earlier in anticipation of some summer weeks in Michigan—L. L. Bean Six-Inch Duck Boots. Great boots, but he had never needed them on their trip. They rested in his closet, tissue paper still stuffed down their throats. This pair looked as new and squeaky clean as his. Their laces were loose as if the wearer had just slipped out of them. It brought to mind that putative "shortest story ever written"—six words attributed to Hemingway, though there was debate about that—"For sale, baby shoes, never worn." But, Seth thought to himself, if this pair of shoes is sitting outside his back door, Lawrence Gollancz must have worn them at least once. Then, he mumbled to himself, "Wonder if it was last night? If so, they're surprisingly clean."

Chapter Six

Tuesday

Anderson pulled her card out of a back pocket and flipped it at Gellman. It read, "Officer Marge Anderson, Asharoken Police Department." She said, "Call if there's anything. That's my cell number. Again, I'm sorry for your loss. I mean, he was your friend, right? Somebody at the department said they thought he was here weekends mostly, sometimes during the week in the summer. I'd want out of Manhattan in the summer, too. We check on houses, you know, especially ones that sit empty a lot. I checked this place a couple times. Bumped into him once. Seems like he was a good guy, kinda private. Big teddy bear." She stepped to her car, opened the door, and looked back at Gellman, "If his sister is reluctant to ID, I'll give you a call. Actually, the Medical Examiner's office probably will."

Ludington and Gellman returned to the Volvo, now parked in front of the cop car. Seth drove forward and out the drive to let Officer Anderson leave without having to back out. He pulled to the side of the road to let her pass, pretending to fiddle with the car's navigation system. Then he followed the cop's car as she left the Neck and drove down the narrow isthmus of Asharoken at exactly the speed limit. Where the strip attached itself to Long Island, Anderson pulled into the parking lot next to a tidy frame building with a curious little cupola springing from its roof. The inscription on the facia above the front door read "Asharoken Village." The headquarters of everything Asharoken, Ludington guessed. He drove on a few hundred yards and turned around in a parking lot labeled "Asharoken Beach." Then he drove back past the village offices and down the road to return to Eaton's Neck.

"What are you doing, Seth?

"Dan, it took only a few years in ministry to quicken a suspicious nature in me. It's probably a piece of me that had laid dormant, but was always there. I guess I've come to be burdened with a Calvinist's take on human nature and its potential for perfidy. In truth, I'm not a very thoroughgoing Calvinist, but I have to confess that the man's anthropology has come to ring true. Annoys me, but it's so often, well…, just realistic. I mean, vandalism in the synagogue on Sunday, sudden death of a member of the same synagogue on Monday. Coincidences do happen, of course. Probably just that. But the residue of John Calvin in me says it might be a good idea to take a quick look at that misplaced emergency generator."

"Seth, What are you thinking, specifically?"

"Not thinking anything in specific, Dan. Just human depravity in general."

Ludington pulled up to the front entrance of the Gollancz house, moving slowly in an attempt at stealth born both of caution and guilt over what he was doing. Again, guilt. Both men got out of the car, closing the doors softly. Ludington took the lead as they crossed the still-damp lawn toward the villainous generator at the far corner of the house. When he was several yards short of the machine, now resting quietly from its crime under Lawrence Gollancz's bedroom window, Ludington put his right hand out at his side, palm backward toward Gellman. The rabbi dutifully froze five feet behind him.

"Rather a muddy mess," Ludington said over his shoulder, whispering the comment even though there was no one in earshot save Gellman. He pointed to a jumble of footprints in the tangled mire of wet grass and black-brown mud surrounding the generator. They were quite distinct and clear. Ludington stepped around the machine, careful not to add any more prints, and worked his way toward the junction box into which the cord from the generator was still plugged. He could see that the wet earth and mulch at the corner of the house had also been trampled on, though these prints were much less clear. It was only too obvious that someone had disturbed the wet ground at the corner of the house, surely when plugging in the ten-foot power cord from the generator to the junction box. Ludington was careful where he stepped, staying on the grass and avoiding the muddy ground. He turned to Gellman and said, "Don't imagine it would be wise for us to make it any worse by adding ours."

Ludington moved away from the corner of the house and the junction box and looked at Gellman. He raised an arm and pointed to a set of parallel tracks about eighteen inches apart carved in the wet grass. They led from the driveway near the garage and trailed forty feet across the startlingly green lawn to where the generator still sat.

Ludington said, "The thing has a pair of wheels to make it easier to move. Looks like he must have had it in the garage, then pulled it over here to the junction box. Like Anderson said, he must have put it where he did to get it close enough for the cord to reach."

"And right under his window." Gellman shook his head in disbelief.

The men turned as they heard the approach of a person Seth guessed to be the neighbor Officer Anderson had mentioned. He had pushed his way through the row of spruce trees and coughed loudly several times to announce his advent. Ludington and Gellman saw a diminutive man who looked to be in his forties striding purposefully toward them. He was dressed in beige shorts and a dark blue polo shirt bearing the golden fleece logo of the Brooks Brothers. Ludington had always thought it looked like a dead sheep strung up. The neighbor wore a pair of Sperry Topsiders on his smallish feet. The guy was either a boater or going for a preppy vibe.

When he was some ten yards away, he called out to Ludington and Gellman in a tone that suggested he was the owner of the property they were trespassing, "Can I help you?"

When he got closer, Ludington responded, "We are-were-friends of Mr. Gollancz." Half the truth. Gesturing to Gellman, he clarified, rather formally, "This is Rabbi Daniel Gellman of Temple Beth Shalom, Mr. Gollancz's congregation in New York. We drove out from the City to... facilitate arrangements."

The man looked at Ludington's clerical collar, then at Gellman. A shadow crossed the man's face, hinting at disdain.

He said only, "I found him this morning. Saw him there in bed." He nodded toward the open window. "Yelled at him, but nothing. So I called 911. Pretty stupid. The generator, I mean."

"Thoughtful of you to check on a neighbor," said Ludington, carefully masking his irony. He extended his hand, "I'm Seth Ludington, a friend of Rabbi Gellman."

"Masterson, George Masterson. I live just up the hill." He turned and pointed at the house barely visible through the line of trees. He shook Ludington's hand but ignored Gellman.

"So, you saw him in bed and called out to him, and then you shut the machine off, I suppose."

A wariness crept into George Masterson's hostility. "Why does it matter? But for your information, I got my clothes on and walked over, and, yes, I shut it down. The damn things make a racket. Then I looked in his window. None of your business anyway. I think you two should get yourselves the hell out of here. This is private property, you know. Maybe I'll have to call the cops again."

Gellman, his emotional temperature rising, stepped forward and said, "Lawrence Gollancz was a close friend, and I am his rabbi. I have a right to be here on the day of a congregant's death".

Masterson moved closer to the rabbi. He raised an index finger as if he were about to poke it in Gellman's chest.

Ludington stepped quickly between the two men, looked at Masterson, and said softly. "I think it's time you ambled back home, sir."

They were face-to-face. For a moment, Ludington thought Masterson might shove him aside to get to Gellman. But he merely glared at the minister, his eyes even with the clerical collar, then seemed to think better of it. Without another word, he backed off, but not before muttering, "So, a priest and a rabbi were at this dead guy's house…" He smiled menacingly with his attempt at wit, turned away, and stomped back up the hill and through the line of spruce trees.

Gellman said, "Well, that was an interesting meeting, was it not?"

Ludington shook his head and turned to look at the generator and the muddy impressions encircling it. He put his hands on his hips and said, "When I first saw all those footprints, they called to mind the tale of Bell and the Dragon. Odd when Scripture drops into your head, isn't it? I imagine you know the little book as well as I. It's a marginal member of our Protestant Bibles. Tucked away in the Apocrypha, the 'hidden writings.'"

"Marginal for us too. In our Ketuvim, as we name it, kinda grade-three Torah. But I do know the footprint story." Gellman looked at the generator, mused, and said, "It stars my ancient namesake, Daniel of Lions' Den fame. Detective Daniel proves the pagan god Bel to be false."

Ludington took up the story, "Bel's devotees brought food for their ravenous deity on a daily basis, and lo and behold, it disappeared nightly from Bel's temple. So Bel must exist. But Daniel, devout diaspora Jew living amongst the heathen, says there is no Bel, and he can prove it."

Gellman finished the tale, "So my namesake sprinkles a layer of ashes around the temple courtyard, which he has locked up tight. Next morning, they discover a sea of footprints in the ashes, all of them leading to the secret door behind which the sneaky priests of Bel reside and feast nightly on Bel's victuals."

Ludington pulled a grimace and said, "So, Rabbi Gellman, the moral of the story for today—footprints just might matter."

Ludington fished his iPhone out of his pocket and stepped gingerly around the generator, moving as close as he could without trespassing into the mess of footprints in the mud. Bending his lanky frame low and holding the phone as far as he could out in front of him and a few feet off the ground, the Rev. Seth Ludington proceeded to take a dozen photos of mud and several of the generator itself.

He said, "Looks to me like there's several sets of footprints." He then stepped some six feet through the wet grass to the corner of the house and took several more shots of the less distinct impressions in the wet wood chips below the junction box.

Ludington slipped his phone back in his pocket and said to his friend, "There's one other little thing to check out before we go." He walked Gellman around the front of the house to the side porch on the far side near the garage. He drew a rag out of his back pocket, a rag he had taken from the door pocket of the Volvo a moment before, and used it to pick up both of the Duck Boots at the same time. He looked at the soles and said, "Clean as a whistle. Hold them with the rag, would you, Dan? Bottoms up." As the rabbi held Lawrence Gollancz's boots upside down, his friend held his phone a bare foot away from the boot's soles and took several more photographs.

Gellman carefully set the boots back just where they had been. Ludington then looked for and found an outdoor water spigot and a garden hose neatly coiled on a holder just to the left of the back door, not far from the small porch and the boots. The two men returned to the car and sat in silence for a moment, considering all that day and the day before had brought.

"So, Seth, I'm guessing you think something's amiss here, something the cops and the Medical Examiner are missing? You gotta tell me. I mean, what are you thinking? You and your Calvin are making me uncomfortable. Aren't you supposed to comfort people?"

"More accurately, my job is usually to comfort the discomforted and discomfort the too comfortable. Today, I'm a tad discomforted by coincidences."

Ludington pushed the button to start the Volvo and pulled gingerly up and out of the long drive. He turned right onto the road leading back to the Asharoken strip. A hundred feet down the street, a squarish black Mercedes SUV passed them, going slowly in the opposite direction. Glancing in his rear-view mirror, Ludington saw the SUV slow even more and then turn into the driveway leading to the Gollancz mansion. He thought to himself, "Mercedes G-Class. One pricey ride." What he said was, "You've got to wonder just who that might be."

Seth turned his car around and drove back toward the entrance to the Gollancz drive and parked on the street behind a row of boxwoods. He and Gellman could just see over the bushes as the SUV snuck down the driveway and stopped at the front entrance to the house. A tall, bulky woman in unflatteringly tight white Capri pants and flip-flops stepped out of the vehicle, reached into her purse, and produced what was doubtless a key. She used it to open the front door of Lawrence Gollancz's house and disappeared inside. When Ludington felt confident that she was deep inside the house, he stepped out of the Volvo. Without closing its door, he walked quietly on the grass alongside the drive to get close enough to the Mercedes to snap one more photo, this time of a rear license plate.

Chapter Seven

Tuesday

As they drove down the Asharoken strip at precisely the speed limit, Seth said, "I'm starving, Dan. You mind if we stop for a bite before we head back to the City?

"Of course, of course. Man doesn't live by coffee alone. Didn't your Jesus say something like that?"

"Something like that."

A few minutes later, Ludington turned right at the white Presbyterian Church onto Main Street in Northport, where he guessed a restaurant or two might lay in welcome. The street ended at the water, "Northport Bay," the Volvo's nav map said. It was the south end of the same body of water that Lawrence Gollancz's house faced. Ludington parked in a lot near a massive dock that jutted west and then jogged north into the bay. The two men crossed the street catty-corner to a promising restaurant they had noticed as they drove down Main Street. The eatery, set so near the water, was aptly named "Skipper's." At four in the afternoon, Skipper's was nearly empty, the lunch crowd long gone, and the dinner rush still hours away. There were two grizzled gents—actual skippers perhaps—nursing afternoon beers at the bar, but every booth and table was empty. A chipper waitress in her middle years, on duty alone, greeted them with a smile and a magnificent Long Island accent, "Anywhere you fancy, guys."

Both rooms of the restaurant were generously decorated with nautical kitsch. It evoked memories for Ludington, who had grown up around boats, not on the East Coast but on the Great Lakes. He had day-sailed and cruised with his father on the man's Tartan. The memories of those sailing excursions were among the few bright spots in his relationship with his dad. However, that same sailing vessel carried a dark memory as well, a memory of youthful transgression and callousness, long hidden and only recently confessed.

Ludington and Gellman found a booth in a back corner. The waitress, who announced herself to be Gina, brought menus offering fare well beyond mere bar food. Both men scanned the vinyl-clad pages before Gina returned. Ludington ordered a glass of sauvignon blanc and chicken Francaise. It was, he knew, how New York Italians thought the French prepared chicken. Gellman chose a beer and a hamburger with French fries. An American sandwich named for a city in northern Germany, the potatoes after a country. Cuisine travels, he thought to himself. A good thing.

After they returned the menus to Gina, Ludington leaned forward across the table as if he were about to say something to his friend. Gellman had settled back into the corner of the booth, one leg up on the seat, attempting to look relaxed. Before Ludington could speak, Gellman said, "I know something about you that you might not know I know, Seth. And we should probably talk about it."

Ludington cocked his head and raised an eyebrow, but said nothing.

"You know, of course, that Lena, our synagogue administrator, and your admin, Harriet, are buddies. They met at some religious congregation administrators' thing a while back and hit it off. Anyway, you should know that Miss van der Berg told Mrs. Gold about your several shared descents into—what shall I say?—'sleuthing.' And the loquacious Lena Gold talks to me every chance she gets, talks to me about most everything. She's a veritable font of UES news and Yorkville gossip. 'Fiction and fact from Lena's almanac,' she says. So, anyway…I know about the bones in the ash pit of your brownstone, and I've been informed of the untimely death that took place on your group tour to Scotland last summer. Rest assured, I do not know how either matter was resolved. I mean, I don't know, well…'who done it.' Miss van der Berg seems to know exactly how much she can say, to the immense chagrin of Lena Gold, of course. I only know that the cases, if you would call them that, were solved. Isn't that what they say of mysteries that are punctuated satisfactorily?"

Ludington found himself furious with Harriet, or if not furious, at least disappointed. They had made a covenant of silence about both incidents. Only a handful of people knew about the body—fifty years dead—that he had discovered in his house, and he trusted them to be discrete. The latter tragedy, the death in Scotland, had been painfully public, but his and Harriet's role in the matter had not been. Ludington had been pulled into both mysteries, in part by an unmanageable conscience, and in part by a perverse curiosity, neither of which—conscience nor curiosity—could quite rest until truth was outed. Harriet van der Berg was also both curious and conscientious, but he guessed that she was often simply also bored and ached for the thrills that surround trespassing unto the turf of untoward and unresolved death. He accepted this about her, but could not accept that she had talked about their experiences outside the circle. An uncomfortable conversation with the woman was rising on the horizon of their relationship.

Ludington did not know how to respond to Gellman's disclosure. Even if Harriet did not keep to their agreement, he felt obliged to. So he merely raised his eyebrows again. But he did not smile as he swirled his sauvignon blanc to see if it had legs.

"I understand you don't want to talk about it, Seth. But I think I also understand that it's why we just turned around and went back to Lawrence Gollancz's house to check out some footprints and the trail the generator made across his front lawn and why you took photos of mud and a license plate and a pair of boots. You have a nose for this, my friend, and I have a hunch that nose is sniffing something." Gellman took a swig of his beer and looked down into it before adding, "And the something I think you may be sniffing is starting to spoil my appetite. In fact, it's making my stomach churn."

"I'm no detective, Dan. Just a Presbyterian minister with an overdeveloped appreciation for the human potential for perversity. So, yes, some things seem off about this. Four, maybe five, things are smelly, fishy, I mean." He counted on his fingers as he reviewed the list that had been forming in his mind, "One, the man—a high-profile Jew—happened to die the day after his beloved synagogue was vandalized. Maybe a coincidence, maybe not. Two, you think he was too smart to park a gas generator under his open bedroom window. But then, in my experience, smart people often do dumb things. Three, he'd received death threats, threats about his having bowed to the so-called radical Jewish left over the jingle business. That rather links up with the antisemitic garbage smeared all over your sanctuary. Four, well…, the guy had lots of money. And five, Bell and the Dragon. I think there are several different footprints in the mud, which invites questions. I could make out two or three easily enough. Probably Masterson's for one. He would have had to step in the mud to turn the thing off. Maybe Officer Anderson, or maybe the Medical Examiner. And maybe Gollancz's, though those boots of his by the back door are so clean. Looks like he was a tidy kinda guy, so he probably washed them in the house or outside with a hose and then left them out to dry. But he did a thorough job if that's the case."

Ludington took the slightest sip of his wine. "So, rabbi, it maybe needs a look. I think we should call Anderson. Actually, I think you should call her. You were the man's friend and rabbi. I'm just the chauffeur."

Gina returned with their food, a plate in each hand, "Here you go, gents. Enjoy. Anything else I can grab for ya?" Gellman asked for A-1 Sauce. Seth looked approvingly at his chicken Francaise and said, "Looks great, Gina. Not a thing."

They ate in silence, Gellman only nibbling at his burger. Finally, he put it down and pushed the plate away. He wiped his hands on the cloth napkin and said, "Last spring, I was walking over to some restaurant on Lexington with Lawrence. We were about to cross 3rd Avenue, him and me. Not a car in sight coming down the street, but the crossing light—the stop hand—was red. Lawrence wouldn't cross the street till the little walking man went white. Pulled me back when I went to cross. I mean, it's a one-way street. Nobody coming, but he insists on waiting for the light. What kind of New Yorker does that? Tourists from the Midwest, maybe. Anyway, that's how cautious the man was. My point is this. He was the kind of guy who would read all the directions as soon as he opened the box, I mean the generator box. He'd even scan the don't-sue-us lawyer pages. He would have read the directions for that generator, Seth. And you'd think there'd be something in them about not putting the thing by an open door or window."

Ludington set his fork down and reached into his shirt pocket for his phone. "Let's see if we can find some gas generator instructions." He Googled "gas generator owner's manual."

As he scrolled through the results, Gellman said, "And Seth, Lawrence Gollancz operated a fleet of trucks. I mean, he knew way more about mechanical stuff than your average New Yorker."

Ludington turned his phone toward Gellman so the man could read what he'd found. The rabbi lifted his bifocals off his nose to read the words from page one of an online owner's manual, *"Never run your generator inside a garage, house, or near open windows or doors."* He also noticed that the drawing of the generator on the first page noted the sockets into which one plugged the cord that you then ran to the house. Power cords appeared not to be part of the generator package, but something additional that needed to be purchased.

Ludington pushed the uneaten half of his lunch, fine as it was, toward the end of the booth's table. "We need to call Anderson. Let's do it now." What he meant was, "You call Officer Anderson."

Over the rabbi's protestations, Ludington paid the check. The two men retreated across the street to a solitary bench in the little park facing Northport Bay so Gellman could make the awkward call in private. Ludington coached his friend before Gellman dialed the number the Asharoken cop had given him, "Three things, Dan—the vandalism, Gollancz's cautious and intelligent nature, and, well, the death threats. Maybe you don't need to mention his money. That's obvious. And nothing about boots and mud. Could get us in trouble if she knows we poked around."

Gellman got Anderson's voice mail and left a "call me as soon as you can" message. The two clergymen sat and contemplated the crowd of boats moored in the harbor, an even mix of sail and power vessels. Ludington spotted a Tartan like his father's. Just as he raised his arm to point it out to Gellman, the man's cell rang. He would have to ask Dan why he has chosen Westminster Chimes, so Brit and vaguely Christian.

He listened as Dan outlined their concerns to Anderson over the phone, owning them as his own and leaving his minister-driver friend out of the narrative. Ludington sensed that Gellman had not grabbed the cop's attention with his news of the synagogue's vandalism or his opinions about Lawrence Gollancz's native caution and intelligence. He said nothing about either the footprints or the boots they photographed. But Ludington could tell that Anderson's attitude changed when Gellman told her about the death threats, threats with a sharp antisemitic edge. He ended the call and turned to Ludington, "She wants to see us. Now. Right now."

They both texted their wives about returning later than they had anticipated and drove back to the building that served as police station and city hall. Anderson was waiting for them at the front door. She ushered them to a small meeting room that doubtless served various purposes. They sat at a Formica-topped folding table, Anderson on one side, the two men on the other.

"Thanks for coming in. You must have been halfway back to the City. So, Mr. Gellman, tell me about the letters you say Mr. Gollancz received. They were threatening, you said?"

"Lawrence told me about them. A few weeks ago. I never saw them. He didn't say how many he'd received. But he told me a bit about them. There are a few things I recall. All of the letters were about the jingle his ice cream trucks played." Gellman related the tale of Gollancz's family business, the controversy over the little melody the trucks broadcast while wandering the streets of New York, the subsequent press coverage, Gollancz's decision to change the iconic tune, and then the right-wing anger at his having done so.

"And some of the letters were poisonously antisemitic. Lawrence said that one of the letters—at least one—made a vague threat on his life. I forget how he told me it was worded. Something like, 'Lefty Jews like you are going to pay for caving into this crazy woke crap.' I do know that one of the letters, at least one, used some of those words – 'Jews,' 'left,' 'woke,' 'crap,' and… 'pay.'"

"Was Mr. Gollancz concerned? Did he contact authorities in the City or here on the Island?"

"I told him to, but he refused. Said crazies like this were all talk. Said he wasn't afraid."

Ludington, surprised that he had even been included in the interview, asked the pertinent questions, "Dan, did he keep the letters?" Do you know where they are?"

Anderson gave Ludington and his clerical collar an "I'll ask the questions here" look, then turned to Gellman and said, "Well, do you know if he kept them? Do you know where they might be?"

"No, I don't. I don't know if he kept them or where they might be. I do know that he never talked to anybody except me about them because he told me so, told me so emphatically. And he told me to stay quiet about it. Said he didn't want news about the letters to go public. Said it would just give these nut jobs satisfaction, thinking they had succeeded in frightening him."

Ludington, interloper though he was, dared to speak again, in as solicitously a manner as he could, "Officer Anderson, what this suggests is the possibility that maybe Mr. Gollancz did not put the generator under his bedroom window, that somebody else put it there or moved it there." He paused and added, "I'm sure you noticed all the footprints in the mud around the machine. They could be, well, important."

She drew a look that was both intrigued and perturbed. "Some of them will be mine. I went up to it to see if the machine was still warm. And some will probably be the neighbor who called it in. What's his name… Masterson. He told me he turned it off when he came over to check on Gollancz. If there are others, I'd guess they belong to Mr. Gollancz himself." She paused and said, "Don't you agree?"

She raised an eyebrow at the question she had asked and turned back to the rabbi before Ludington could respond, "At any rate, Mr. Gellman, I'd like you to make a formal statement. You can include your perspective on Mr. Gollancz's caution and intelligence, but it's the threats that matter. We'll do a verbal, and I'll type it up for you to sign. Then I'm going to put a call through to Suffolk homicide. And then you are going back to the City and you are going to leave this to us. By 'us,' I mean Suffolk homicide."

The rabbi nodded and mumbled a reluctant "of course." The minister said nothing.

Officer Anderson paused, "They'll probably be calling you, Suffolk cops, I mean. You gotta understand about Asharoken. We do speeding tickets, lost dogs, the occasional B and E. Drugs now and then. But not footprints and not murder. We definitely don't do murder in Asharoken."

Gellman looked Ludington in the eyes. The "m" word had been spoken.

Chapter Eight

Tuesday and Wednesday

They drove back into the City against the early evening traffic, arriving in just under an hour. They said little in the car, both jolted by Anderson's mention of murder, though their own questions had pointed in that direction. Ludington dropped Gellman off at his apartment building on East 86th Street, returned the car to the garage, and walked down 2nd Avenue at a brisk pace. He was eager to see Fiona and the girls before the latter's bedtime, recently pushed back to eight-thirty. He got there just in time for a goodnight kiss, actually two goodnight kisses. After handing a wiggly Astrid over to Inez, he retreated to the living room for a cordial with Fiona. He poured each of them a short Grand Marnier and added an ice cube. Then he sat down with his wife in front of the cold fireplace, knowing that she would be grilling him about his day on Long Island. Gentle as her grilling was, he confessed everything, concluding with the fact that Gellman was anticipating a possible phone call from the Suffolk County Homicide Unit.

"Seth, I give up." She said this with a wry smile. "How can it be that untoward death follows you about so doggedly?"

"Well, the first one wasn't exactly murder." He meant the skeleton in the ash pit. "And the second was only technically a murder." He meant the death in Scotland early the summer before.

"There's no such legal category as 'technical murder,'" said his lawyer wife.

"I'm still not sure you and Harriet did the right thing, in Scotland I mean."

"Seth took a sip of his Grand Marnier from the cut-crystal snifter, mate of the one in Fiona's hands, brushed a forelock out of his eyes, and said, "Nor am I. Probably never will be."

"So what are you going to do with this one, this latest untoward death?"

"Wait for the Suffolk cops to call Dan. I'm guessing they'll want to talk to him, and maybe me too."

Fiona smiled, "And then it's in their hands. Right?"

"Right," he said as he finished the last of the sweet orange liqueur. "Out of our hands."

* * *

Ludington arrived at Old Stone Church the next morning at nine sharp. Harriet van der Berg was already there, as he knew she would be. He went directly into her cramped cubicle of an office, sank his lanky frame in the spare chair, and said, "Harriet, we need to talk."

"About your foray out onto Long Island with Rabbi Gellman, I suppose." This was said hopefully.

"Not exactly." Seth Ludington disliked confrontation, as do most clergy. He understood that there were people in this world who were energized by it, but he was not one of them. He had to steel himself for it whenever it became needful, whether in ministry or life in general.

"Harriet, you told Lena Gold about the body in the ash pit of our home. And you told her about Scotland, I mean that you and I got ourselves tangled up in what happened there."

When cornered, Harriet van der Berg was not a woman to retreat. She did not lower her head in any hint at contrition. Rather, she lifted it, looked at him steadily through the lower half of her bifocals, and said, "I am proud of our work. We brought light to shine into two corners of darkness. Can I not share our successes with a friend? Culpatory details were never mentioned."

"But Harriet, we agreed to keep it to ourselves. You promised." He paused and asked, "Is 'culpatory' a word?"

"I assure you it is. It's the precise antonym of 'exculpatory.' And I can also assure you that no culpatory hints passed my lips in conversation with Lena, nor with anyone else for that matter."

"You've talked with other people?"

"I have not," she snapped. "Only Lena." She paused, seeming to strategize about where to go next in this discomforting exchange. "And I am aware that you and Harry have shared information with each other concerning these matters." She meant Harry Mulholland, Old Stone's Clerk of Session and a retired NYPD detective.

"Harriet, Harry is not exactly outside the circle. He was there, in the middle of it, in both cases." Seth winced at his own use of the word "cases." As if they were detectives. "I mean, in both matters."

The woman was brilliant at deflecting conversation. She had first offered a vague hint at scripture with her "light and darkness" line, then had thrown out an obscure word from her legendary vocabulary for him to trip over, and lastly brought up his conversations with Harry, needful as they had been.

But he was not about to retreat either. "Harriet, I'm simply disappointed that you chose to talk to a stranger about these things."

She turned, looked at her computer, saw that it had defaulted to the screen saver, a shot of her and Margaret on a Circle Line boat, with a third remarkable woman, Lady Liberty, rising in the background above and between their kerchief-clad heads. Harriet looked back to her pastor and said, "I am sorry if you think I said or did anything inappropriate, Seth."

He knew that such a qualified apology was the best he would ever get. "It's just that we have to be careful, Harriet. Please."

Having made his point as sharply as he dared, Ludington started to rise from his chair to go to his own office, when van der Berg said in a voice, low and rising, "Well…?"

He sighed, sat back down, and did what he knew he would inevitably have to do. He told her about his trek with the rabbi to Long Island. He began with a description of the grand house and its stunning setting. Then he unpacked details—the foolish placement of the generator, the muddy footprints that surrounded it, the wheel marks across the wet grass, the pair of clean boots at the back door. He shared Gellman's appraisal of Lawrence Gollancz's intelligence and caution, the visits of the hostile neighbor, and the mystery woman in the Mercedes with a key to the house. Then he told her about the death threats and, finally, Officer Marge Anderson's decision to take Rabbi Gellman's statement and contact Suffolk County Police. He did not say "homicide unit," nor did he mention that Anderson had uttered the word "murder." But he did mention the photos of mud he had taken with his phone, an action that betrayed his own suspicions.

He could almost see the wheels of Harriet van der Berg's brain whirling. "Could you distinguish the number of distinct footprints, Dominie?" The woman sometimes slipped into her antique pattern of address for him when excited.

"Two, probably more," he answered. One was surely made by the neighbor who found Gollancz and then turned the generator off, another by the local cop —she said she went near the thing—and then probably Gollancz's own prints. Or maybe not. But if they're not his, they could belong to somebody else who checked the scene out, I mean later, after he had died. During the night, or this morning. Could be somebody we don't know about, maybe even one of the ambulance guys." Ludington paused, steepled his fingers, and whispered what both were thinking, "Or they could have been made by someone who moved the machine under the window of a sleeping Lawrence Gollancz."

Van der Berg nodded, "The boots by the back door were clean, you say? Here's a key question, Seth. Could he have washed them if his house was without power? That is to say, does the water work when you lose electrical service? If his home's electrical power was being supplied by this supplemental source you call a portable gas generator, would he have had access to water in order to wash them so thoroughly?"

Ludington found himself again agog at the woman's mind. He pulled out his phone, Googled Harriet's question, and discovered the answer was easy to find. He summarized, "If the house is served by a public water service, yes, he would have had water. If the house is on a private well that was powered by electricity, maybe."

Van der Berg nodded sagely, clearly proud of herself, "Another matter to investigate." She was not finished. "Seth, could I look at the photographs you made with your mobile phone?" He took his cell out of the pocket of his blue blazer and let her scroll through the shots of muddy footprints surrounding the generator.

She studied them carefully, tilting her head back slightly to view them through the bottoms of her half-glasses. "As you have observed, it would appear that these impressions were made by diverse footwear." She used her fingers to zoom in close on a shot that included the side of the deadly generator and said, "But I must say that these merest snapshots of footprints may be less than adequate." She handed his phone back and said, "On *Magnum PI*, they sometimes make molds of footprints. Or perhaps it was *Hawaii Five-0*." She thought for a moment. "Or maybe it was *Murder She Wrote*. Margaret was a fan of them all. They run together in my memory. Such castings are more precise than photos, I would surmise."

The wheels of Seth Ludington's mind had also been turning as he rehearsed the tale of his Tuesday on Long Island for the second time. He admitted her point about photos versus castings, "I'm sure you're right, Harriet. And muddy footprints and a very clean pair of boots by Lawrence Gollancz's back door do indeed ask your water source question."

He rose to leave, guessing that van der Berg would probably do more than merely reflect on the matter of the availability of water when Gollancz's power went out. He smiled and said, "Real work to do," and stepped the few feet to his adjacent office, as commodious as hers was not. He sat in the swivel chair at his desk and wondered if those two suspicious deaths that he and van der Berg had plumbed together had perhaps led them both to imagine murder where there was only a tragic accident and credible coincidence. Maybe he ought to start checking his curiosity at the door. It was perhaps out of hand again.

He had a day job, after all, and a sermon to preach in four days. He had already given Harriet the prescribed lectionary texts for the coming Sunday so she could begin to prepare the worship program, but he had not yet given her a sermon title. He reached for his worn Westminster Study Bible sitting on the corner of his desk atop his church planning calendar. It noted the several passages of Scripture assigned for the coming Sunday. He saw that the Gospel reading was from the middle of the sixteenth chapter of Matthew's Gospel. He recognized the seven verses—Peter's famous confession of who he finally understood Jesus to be. No way to mangle that passage into a sermon exploring antisemitism. Then, he saw that the Old Testament reading for the day was from the first and second chapters of Exodus. If memory served, it was the tale of the enslavement of Israel by a pyramid-building Egyptian pharaoh, his decision to murder every male child born to an Israelite woman, and then the baby Moses' famous escape in a basket floating down the Nile. It was a long lection; he might have to edit it a bit.

Antisemitism had often been called "the world's oldest hatred." This episode from the second book of the Bible was arguably that hatred's first iteration in history. A sermon that simply reminded the Old Stone congregation of that long and tragic tale would be faithful to the text, the first chapter of the long story.

Just as he made a decision to preach from Exodus 1:8 to 2:10, he heard Harriet exclaim in a voice that was clearly meant for him to hear, "Well, well, well."

Ludington called back in an equally loud voice, "Well, what, Harriet?"

Harriet van der Berg entered his office, a too-proud "aha" look spread across her face, and announced, "Well, I was also able to do some research regarding the ability of a portable gasoline generator to power a well pump. In summary, this is what I learned—you convert horsepower to watts by multiplying the constant value 746 with the horsepower. Thus, if you have a 1.5 horsepower pump, the machine's corresponding wattage would be 1119 watts. A generator needs to provide twice that level of power to start and run the pump. With the example above, one would need a generator rated at least 2238 watts. I noted that Mr. Gollancz's model, as pictured in one of your photographs, is rated at a lower wattage. Thus, it would be insufficient to start and run a typical well pump."

Ludington, no longer surprised by either the woman's brilliance or her ability to discover minutia on the internet, merely nodded and said, "So, we need to know if Gollancz's house was on city water or on a well."

"And we need to investigate the assorted footprints you photographed more closely."

Ludington sighed and said, "I suppose I should call Dan with this."

"That would be appropriate."

He reached for his cell, only to feel it vibrating and then emitting its Old Doorbell ringtone. "How about that. It's Dan calling us. I mean, me."

He hit the answer button, "Hey Dan. I was just about to call you."

Ludington listened for a good three minutes, van der Berg leaning as close as she could over the desk, straining to hear what the rabbi was saying.

When Gellman finished relating his three minutes of news, Ludington said, "Well, Dan, I've unearthed a set of curious details as well. We need to talk. Before you get the call from the Suffolk cops. Why don't we meet for lunch at the Lex?" It was a favorite lunch and dinner spot. Superb food, linen tablecloths, but no pretense. "You know where it is, right? Between 90th and 91st. West side of Lexington."

He ended the call, stood, and slid his phone back into his pocket. "I need to talk to Dan Gellman, Harriet. He's learned something interesting as well. I've got to run."

Harriet Van der Berg was far too well-mannered to make a move to accompany him uninvited, or even ask if she might tag along.

But Ludington could see the disappointment on her face as he left her sitting alone in his study.

Chapter Nine

Wednesday

It was early for a New York City lunch, not even twelve-thirty. The Lex would not fill up until one o'clock or later. Nero greeted Ludington at the door as if he were a lost Montenegrin cousin, "Your friend is here already. In the back." Nero knew that the L-shaped banquette tucked in the restaurant's rear corner was Ludington's favorite table. He had put Gellman there when the rabbi told the waiter whom he was meeting. Nero was even taller than Ludington and outpaced him as he strode to the rear of the long, narrow restaurant, menus in hand.

Gellman started to work his way out of the banquette to shake Ludington's hand. "Don't get up, Dan, for goodness sake." Ludington slid into the bench so that he and the rabbi were seated in the corner, ninety degrees to each other.

Gellman said, "You go first, Seth."

Ludington reviewed the matters of the mud, footprints, gas generators, water pumps, and Lawrence's Gollancz's clean L.L. Bean Duck Boots. He slipped his phone out of his jacket pocket and found the assorted shots of mud around the generator and the shot of the bottom of the boots by the back door. The two men moved to sit side-by-side. They could now zoom in on the prints for a closer look at what they had seen the day before.

Seth said, "We can guess that that tetchy neighbor made some of the prints when he turned the generator off in the morning. And Officer Anderson said she stepped near the thing when she arrived later. Masterson has pretty small feet. And so does Anderson. But you can see that there's a third set of prints, prints way bigger than the ones Masterson or Anderson surely made. You know Gollancz was a big guy, and you saw those boots by the back door, size 11. If he made those prints, his boots should have been a muddy mess. If they were, he sure did a job cleaning them up. But here's the question—how did he do it? Did he have water without electricity? Harriet researched water pumps for wells, and that generator of his would not seem to have done the job. But then, the house could be on public water. We need to find out. And then you have to ask why would he bother? Clean them up in the middle of a raging deluge, and then leave them outside. And then there's your confidence that he was too smart to plant the thing under his open bedroom window. Bottom line, Dan, the more I think about it, the less sure I am that Lawrence Gollancz put that generator under his window. You've said you judged him too savvy to do such a dumb thing. So, we need to confirm whether his boots made any of the prints. And if they did, we need to know if he had water that night. Water to clean muddy boots. If he did, no more questions. Maybe no more questions. But if he didn't have water, there are some questions, big ones."

As Ludington put his phone back in his pocket, Gellman considered the assorted muddy curiosities. "So Rev. Ludington, if I hear you right, you're suggesting that the generator could have been initially set up by Lawrence somewhere other than right under his window, but then it got moved there?" Gellman took a sip of the ice water Nero had set before him. "That would probably mean that, well…somebody not Lawrence Gollancz moved it. But Seth, if Lawrence had started it up and had it running somewhere sensible—like in the driveway maybe—how did he plug it into the junction box by his window? It's a good forty feet away. He would have needed a longer cord, right? And how would that someone-else-who-might-have-moved-it even know Lawrence had one, a generator, I mean?"

"The right questions, rabbi. How would they have known, and, yes, Lawrence would have needed a nice, long, heavy-duty cord. If so, you gotta wonder where it might be."

Nero wandered over to the table and cast the two men an inquisitive look. Ludington knew the menu by heart and ordered first—prosciutto Parma and melon with a glass of iced tea. Gellman had to study the document for a moment before opting for a cobb salad—"hold the bacon"—and a Coke.

As Nero retreated to the tiny kitchen in the rear of the restaurant, Ludington said, "And what's your news, Dan?"

"Two things. Yesterday, I called Lawrence's sister about funeral arrangements. I hadn't heard a thing from her. She said that the Medical Examiner was performing an autopsy, and the body wouldn't be released for another day or two. I asked her why they were doing an autopsy. I told her that the ME woman I spoke to at the house seemed to think they could forego it on religious grounds. Told her I didn't think it was what her brother would have wanted. She said, "I wouldn't know about that." Said that she personally had no objection to an autopsy, said that it would "set her mind at ease." Anyway, there will be—or there has already been—an autopsy. No quick Orthodox burial. I feel bad about this, Seth. Like I let him down."

"Disappointing, but Seth, this is more interesting. I finally got back to the lawyer, Lawrence's lawyer, the guy who phoned me about his death. He was calling to offer his condolences, of course, and to ask about the service, but there was more, lots more. He said that he had met with Lawrence just last week. Lawrence had asked for the meeting. He came to his office and said he wanted him to draft a new will. Atkins, that's his name, he's local, in Huntington. Well, this is it, Seth. This Atkins said that the new will he drafted makes Temple Beth Shalom the major beneficiary of his estate. Bequests to a few friends and to his family of course, but the bulk of it to the synagogue. Atkins said his old will had left most everything to his family, such as it is. There's just the sister. I gather she's somewhat younger, with a husband and a couple of kids. Somewhere out on the Island. That's his whole family."

Gellman paused, "So, I asked Atkins if he knew how much the estate would be."

Nero set a Coke in front of the rabbi and the iced tea in front of Ludington and went to attend to another table that had just been seated at the front of the restaurant.

Gellman waited till Nero was out of earshot and said, "Atkins said he couldn't be precise; he's unsure of the exact value of the ice cream truck business, but he'd guess the estate would come to something north of thirty-five million." Gellman set his cola down so hard it sloshed onto the tablecloth. They both understood that the implications of this development for a much-diminished Reform synagogue with a crumbling building were towering.

Ludington raised an eyebrow and asked the question, "So Atkins drew up the new will, and Gollancz signed it?"

"Well, yes and no, and maybe. Atkins said he spent the week doing up the new will and drove it out to Gollancz's place on Eaton's Neck last Friday. Major clients get personal service, I guess. Atkins had another appointment in Huntington, so he said he couldn't wait around for him to read it through and sign it. It's a lengthy document, he said. Lawrence told him he wanted to look it over first, then he'd sign it if everything looked okay. He's the kind who would want to do that. He was tech-savvy, but Atkins said he was leery of DocuSign. Always fussy and thorough. Lawrence also told Atkins that he was going to have to tell his sister about the change. The family was still going to inherit something, Atkins said, but nothing like thirty-five million dollars. Anyway, Lawrence told the lawyer that he thought he would read it through over the weekend, get it signed and witnessed, and then tell the sister. He said he had them all coming to his place for dinner Sunday night."

"So, Gollancz did sign his new will, right?" Ludington asked this question softly and hopefully.

"Atkins doesn't know if he did or not. That's why he called. He wanted to know if Lawrence had told me about the will and the synagogue. He asked me if he had maybe given me a copy of the new will."

"I assume he did neither, Dan. Right?"

"No, of course not. I would have told you. I knew nothing about this. I'm flabbergasted, frankly."

Nero arrived with a plate in each hand, shaved Italian ham with honeydew melon for Seth, a handsome but pork-less Cobb salad for Dan. The two men ate in silence, each offering sporadic and approving humming noises over his lunch.

Nero returned when he saw empty plates and suggested coffee and dessert. Both asked for an espresso, Ludington a double. The waiter was back in a flash with coffees and the usual gratis sambuca. A trio of coffee beans floated in each glass, wishing them health, happiness and prosperity.

Gellman gulped his coffee down in one Italian swig, Ludington sipped his American style and said, "Harriet opines there to be four motives for murder, though she's always careful to attribute the list to her late partner Margaret who gleaned it from the detective fiction she loved. Conveniently, they all start with the letter, 'L'—lust, loathing, love, and lucre."

Dan swirled his sambuca, careful not to spill any, and said, "And now we know there was a big pile of the last of the "Ls" in Margaret's list."

Seth said, "Which invites the detective's classic query."

They looked at each other and whispered in a *sotto voce* chorus, "Who benefits?"

Seth returned to Old Stone, surprised to see that Harriet was not planted in her cubicle waiting to quiz him about whatever it was that Rabbi Gellman was so eager to tell him. He sighed and said to himself, "She's put out with me, she is."

He sat at his desk, knowing he had to imagine a sermon about antisemitism. He knew that, like so many things, the topic wasn't that simple. Preaching week upon week was an uphill climb. Speaking cogently about things that were seldom simple, and doing it in seventeen minutes, was a steep uphill climb.

He decided that he would first phone Harry Mulholland, Old Stone's Clerk of Session. He was also a retired NYPD homicide detective who had found himself embroiled in both of the deaths Seth and Harriet had probed in the last year and a half. Seth hoped Harry respected him for what they had done, but he was not sure.

Harry picked up on the third ring. "Good afternoon, Pastor." Formality of address was as native to the man as formality of dress.

"Harry, I need a teeny-tiny favor from you. Just a phone call."

There was an awkward gap in Harry Mulholland's end of the conversation.

Seth almost said, "Harry, did I lose you?" Cell reception in Harry's building was sometimes spotty. But before he spoke, Harry said, "Seth, not again, I hope."

If Ludington's inklings about Gollancz's death ultimately grew legs, he would probably have to bring Harry in, but he was not ready to do so yet. "Not sure, Harry. Maybe nothing, but well…, would you run a license plate number for me? I mean, make a call and have the precinct do it? It's just that I saw something the other day. Made me a little suspicious, and I have to wonder."

Mulholland was savvy enough to ask no questions. "You're always wondering about something, aren't you, Seth? It's going to get you in trouble one of these days. What's the number?"

Ludington had already opened the photo file on his phone and found the shot of the rear end of the Mercedes SUV that had pulled into Lawrence Gollancz's drive the day before, disgorging a tall woman in too-tight Capri pants on the dead man's doorstep, a woman who possessed a key to the house.

"New York plate, I assume. I'll call or text when I get a name and address. Seth, be careful."

"Thanks, Harry. I will. Promise."

Ludington pulled a yellow legal pad out of the middle drawer of his desk. He wrote sermons on his laptop, but liked to make notes and sketch an outline on paper.

He first played with a title and jotted down "Antisemitism—It's Not Just Back Then or Over There." Too long, but maybe something else would occur to him before Harriet's non-negotiable drop-dead Sunday bulletin deadline.

At the top of the pad below the title he jotted down the moves he might make in the sermon: "1. Describe synagogue vandalism—in horrid detail. 2. Rehearse the story of Israel's bondage in Egypt, murder of Jewish babes (Passover), Moses' escape. 3. The long history of subsequent antisemitism. 4. Nature of Christian complicity. 5. Circle back to Beth Shalom. 6. What to do about it?"

It was edging toward five o'clock by the time he had settled on the too-long title. He couldn't think of anything else, so he emailed it to Harriet so she could finish up the bulletin. He wondered if she would come back to the church to do it or work from home so she could avoid him, put out with him as she was for sleuthing with Gellman over a lunch she was not invited to. He would have to talk to her about Gellman's central role in whatever might have to be done in response to their questions about Lawrence Gollancz's death. "Whatever might have to be done" was probably no more than he and Dan having a long talk with some Suffolk Country detective, should they ever call.

He fetched the girls' stroller from its spot by the 82nd Street door of Old Stone's Parish House and pushed it up 2nd Avenue to the Happy House of Little Ones. Both were generous with smiles when they saw their father. He and Fiona ate at home—spaghetti Bolognese, with some ground Italian sausage that he had browned and mixed with Rao's sauce—ostensibly from the notoriously exclusive restaurant of the same name up on 114th Street. Rumor was that people actually owned tables in the place. Fiona boiled the pasta to *al dente,* leaning over the sink and biting a piece to make sure.

After dinner and a shared wash-up in the kitchen, it was playtime with the girls. Both were now sitting up bravely and daring attempts at crawling. Ingrid still preferred to move herself across the oriental rug in the living room commando style. Astrid favored the butt scoot she had perfected weeks earlier. Seth mused that they would soon be up on all fours, then up on two, then out the door. After profuse Mommy and Daddy goodnight coos and kisses, Inez carted them off to the nursery while Fiona and Seth retreated up the stairs to their bedroom.

Fiona went to the desk in the corner of the room to catch up on some work emails. Ludington read in bed for an hour or two, still working his way through Tom Holland's *Dominion.* He was up to the eleventh century, a chapter titled "Revolution." "You don't generally think of the eleventh century as revolutionary," he thought to himself. He must have fallen asleep with the book open across his chest because it flew to the floor when he was jolted awake by the sirens. Sirens were anything but rare in Manhattan. After a while, you stopped hearing them. They were just another chord in the urban symphony that was New York. But this was different. There were so many sirens. And they were close.

Chapter Ten

Thursday

The din was indeed deafeningly close, literally alarming. Both Fiona and Seth leapt out of bed. He was still pulling on his jeans when his cell phone rang. He hopped across the room one-legged to retrieve it from his bedside, pulled it from its charging cord, and looked at the screen. It noted that the time was four thirty-eight, and the caller was Harriet van der Berg. Her second off-hours call in three days. Fiona was already on her way down the stairs to the twin's nursery a floor below. A mother's innate reaction to any alarm was to find her babies.

He took the call, of course. "Seth, it's Harriet on the line. I must offer my apologies for telephoning at an untoward hour a second time, but I am confident you would wish to know the disconcerting news at the earliest opportunity." She hesitated a split second before adding, the slightest edge to her voice, "given your friendship with Rabbi Gellman and your investigative work with him."

"What happened, Harriet? Is it Dan?"

"Well, I do not know for certain, but Lena—Lena Gold that would be, the rabbi's secretary—just contacted me by sending one of those electronic text messages on my cell phone. Seth, it's the synagogue. It appears to be ablaze. To be precise, Lena's message read, 'Synagogue on fire. Let Rev. Ludington know.'"

"Oh my God." Taking the Lord's name in vain was something Seth

Ludington never did, almost never anyway. He automatically apologized, "Sorry, Harriet. And yes, you were right to call. I can't believe this. I'll phone Dan. In fact, I think I'll go over there, to Beth Shalom I mean. He'll be there."

Ludington finished dressing and went to find Fiona. She was in the nursery, both twins in her arms. Inez was across the room warming two bottles. The girls and their night nurse had also been awakened by the sirens. Seth told Fiona about the synagogue as he scrolled through his phone contacts, looking for Gellman's number. He found it, called it, and listened to seven rings before it went to voicemail, *"Dan Gellman, sorry, but I can't pick up just now. Leave a message, and I'll get back to you."*

Ludington left a "call me, Dan" message and then hit the button to redial, hoping Gellman would see who it was and pick up. Voicemail again. He slipped the phone in his jeans pocket and said, "Fiona, I'm going over there. Dan's not picking up."

He helped Fiona and Inez settle the girls, then jogged north on 3rd Avenue toward 87th Street. 3rd Avenue, one way north, was closed at 86th Street. A pair of NYPD patrolmen were waving flashlights to detour traffic down 86th to Park. As Ludington neared 87th, all he could see of Temple Beth Shalom over the heads of the gathering crowd were flames—tongues of fire reaching forty or fifty feet into the air. Above the red-orange of fire arose great roiling billows of grey-black smoke. A dozen fire trucks occupied every lane of 3rd Avenue near the synagogue. A fleet of NYPD squad cars were clustered around the fire trucks. Disconcertingly, there was also an EMS ambulance. Littered among the gawkers and cop cars were several television news vans. A cameraman was perched atop one of them, his roof-mounted camera aimed at the conflagration that had been Temple Beth Shalom. Ludington saw a reporter threading his way through the crowd, poking his microphone in front of anybody eager for ten seconds of fame. Ludington followed in the reporter's wake, elbowing his way to the front of the crowd and then pushing behind him along its leading edge, looking frantically for Dan Gellman. He guessed that the reporter might also be looking for the rabbi.

Ludington didn't see Gellman anywhere, but he did bump into Nero, his waiter friend from the Lex Restaurant. He knew the man lived in the neighborhood and must have walked over to see what the excitement was about. "Nero, have you seen Dan Gellman? He's the guy I had lunch with today. He's the rabbi. Of this synagogue, I mean." He looked toward the fire, growing too hot for comfort even at their distance.

"No, sorry," Nero answered. He paused a moment and shook his head, "But, well, they took somebody away, somebody from inside the building, in an ambulance. A little while ago."

Seth Ludington took the Lord's name in vain for the second time and called van der Berg. "Harriet, can you contact your friend Lena and see if you can get a home phone number for Dan Gellman, or maybe a cell number for Lilly? That's his wife. I'm here at the fire. Harriet, it's bad. And I can't find him."

Ludington continued his search, threading his way through the mass of curious humanity when his phone, held hopefully in his right hand, finally dinged with a text. It was from van der Berg, ever efficient and having recently mastered the youthful art of texting. Her message listed two numbers, one noted as "home," the other as "Lilly," followed by "Seth, please keep me informed." There was a period at the end of the sentence and a comma after "Seth." Ludington called the 212 home number first and got another "can't come to the phone" message. Then he called Lilly's 917 cell number. She picked up on the first ring, her questioning "hello" betraying the fact that neither she nor her phone recognized his number.

"Lilly, it's Seth Ludington." The two couples had gone out to dinner together several times, so she knew him.

"Oh, Seth. I'm with Dan at New York Hospital. They just brought him here. Burns, some of them are bad, and smoke inhalation. They gave him meds for the pain. He's asleep now."

Before she could say anything more, Ludington veritably barked into his iPhone, "I'll be there in twenty."

He ran down 86th Street to 2nd Avenue and hailed a yellow cab. It deposited him in the circular drive of the hospital's entrance on East 68th Street, just a block from the river. After cajoling the attendant at the front for information, she said that Daniel Gellman was on his way from emergency to a room in the hospital's Weill Cornell burns unit. After some searching she came up with a room number. Ludington navigated the hospital's maze to find Gellman's room. His knock on the door—barely cracked open—was answered by a "come in." As he entered he saw Lilly Gellman, face drawn, her hand under a sheet covering her sleeping husband from his chest down. His eyes were closed, an oxygen mask lay over his mouth and nose. She slipped her hand from her husband's, rose without a word, and went to Ludington, judging him a close enough friend to rate an embrace.

Then she turned away and looked back at the man in the bed. "He's going to be okay, thank God. I mean, he's going to live. They're going to do something called a bronchoscopy to check for damage to his lungs, I guess. Smoke inhalation. Some first-degree burns on one of his hands, some second-degree on his arms and chest. So stupid, but just like him."

"What do you mean?"

"Well, the putz ran into the burning building. He ran over to the synagogue in a pair of shorts and a tee-shirt. All he had on his feet were rubber flip-flops. Seth, they started to melt, the flip-flops, I mean. One was stuck to the bottom of his foot."

"Lilly, why did he do that? Go into the synagogue, into the fire, I mean."

She looked at him with a hint of incredulity and then pointed to the chair in the corner of the room. "The Torah scrolls, of course. They were in his office. He'd put them there after the vandalism. He managed to carry two of them out in his first trip, but then he realized that our Holocaust scroll was not one of the two. He could never manage three at a time; they're pretty heavy. So he went back in again. The cops told me they tried to stop him, but he pulled free and he went in to the building again for the Holocaust scroll."

Three Torah scrolls, still bound in their purple velvet mantels, rested in the chair in the corner of a burn unit room, rescued from fire, now safe. Ludington thought to himself, "A good mother goes for her babies, a good rabbi goes for his Torah scrolls." He noticed that they smelled of smoke and wondered how many rescued Torah scrolls in history had smelled of the smoke from burned synagogues.

Dan had once told him that Temple Beth Shalom was the proud recipient of what he had named a Holocaust scroll, one of more than a thousand that had been stolen by the Nazis from synagogues, mostly in Czechoslovakia. The Nazis had stored them away in Prague, perhaps planning to display them in a "Museum for Extinct People." The Torah scrolls survived. So did the people. Some of them, anyway.

"Seth, they can't stay here. Would you take them? Keep them safe somewhere. I'd take them to our place, but I'm staying here no matter what they say. I'm not leaving him."

At this declaration of fidelity, a groan rose from the hospital bed. Lilly and Seth turned to the patient, his eyes struggling to open. Gellman saw Ludington, pulled his left hand from under the sheets, and lifted it toward his friend. It was not bandaged. Then he lay it back on top of the sheet and closed his eyes.

Lilly said, "I wasn't there. At the fire, I mean. I stayed home with Zack. The EMS guy said Dan came out of the synagogue carrying the scrolls under his arm like a running back. Not quite kosher scroll-carrying style, but okay in an emergency." She looked at her husband again. "The handles, the *atzei chaim.* They're usually wooden, but one set is silver. They must have been hot, looks like he touched something, maybe a handle with one of his hands, the one that's burned. Seth, have they got the fire out yet?"

Ludington hesitated, "I just left. They were still working to put it out." He was reluctant to tell her that it appeared to him the building would be a total loss.

"So it wasn't out when you left, was it? Seth, an NYFD arson investigator, is coming. That must mean they're guessing arson. It's going to be more antisemitic stuff. Seth, have you got a safe at your church? Could you keep them there, the scrolls, I mean? Please. Dan will want them locked away."

"Of course, of course."

Lilly looked back at her husband. "The authorities will be all over it now, the vandalism and now the fire." She paused and then said, "Seth, I know you and Dan had worries about Lawrence Gollancz's death, too. He told me, said that you thought it might not have been an accident. What I mean is, well, this could all be related."

Ludington felt an admixture of worry and rage rising in him—rage at what had been done to his friend, rage at what had been done to Temple Beth Shalom, rage at what had been done to Jews time and again across history. And worry—worry that the oldest hatred had drawn close and might lead them into the darkness from whence it rose.

He was pulled from his waxing anger and anxiety by the Old Doorbell ringtone of his cell. He saw that it was Harry Mulholland, always a perversely early riser. He took the call, noting the time as he did so. Six-forty-five. Ludington told Mulholland where he was and what had happened to Temple Beth Shalom and its rabbi. Harry took in the news in his phlegmatic "I've heard it all" cop manner. Seth could imagine the man nodding knowingly at the perversity of humanity before saying, "That license plate…. It's registered to one Irene Stark in Speonk. Out on the South Fork of the Island."

Ludington repeated both the proper and the place names aloud to make certain he had heard correctly, "Irene Stark, Speonk." He thanked Harry and ended the call.

Lilly overheard, jerked her head toward Ludington, and said, "Irene Stark. That's Lawrence Gollancz's sister, right? Dan talked to her again last night, more condolences, of course, and about the funeral."

Ludington nodded and explained the reason for the call he had just taken— the visitor he and Dan had seen at Gollancz's place, a visitor with a key.

Lilly nodded, looked at her husband, and then back at Ludington. "I'm going to have to ask Lena to find a rabbi to conduct the service for Gollancz. Dan had it all planned out, worked on it last night. They're releasing the body tomorrow morning, but there wasn't enough time to schedule it before Shabbat, so Dan had set it up for Sunday afternoon. Campbell Brothers' was picking up the body. It'll have to be there, of course."

Ludington nodded in response.

"Seth, I have a favor to ask of you. Would you follow through with them, I mean, the funeral home, Campbell's? And could you maybe check in with the rabbi when Lena gets one lined up? There are so many details to fuss with, you know that. Dan wanted it to be just so. I can send you the contact information he got for Irene Stark, the sister. Maybe you can put the rabbi in contact with her so he can say something personal in the eulogy. And Seth, would you consider going to the service yourself? Sounds odd, the Christian minister helping with the Jewish funeral, but I know Dan would be relieved to have your eye on things. He trusts you."

Ludington offered a series of three "of courses" to her litany of worries and added, "I'd be honored."

He rose, laid his hand on the unburned hand of a sleeping Daniel Gellman. He gave it a gentle pat and turned to Lilly, offering her a quick embrace which she accepted, and then the ritual "He'll be okay" whispered in her ear, though he knew no such thing.

Ludington carefully lifted one of the Torah scrolls from the chair in the corner of the room. It was indeed heavy. He was amazed that Dan had managed two of them in the same trip out of the burning synagogue. Ludington held it like an infant at first, wrapping his arms around its velvet mantel, beautifully embroidered with Hebrew script. He had just enough residual seminary Hebrew to recognize a few words. He set it back down. Realizing he could never carry all three of them, he went in search of a wheelchair. He returned in a few minutes and loaded the Torah scrolls of Temple Beth Shalom onto a loaner wheelchair. He set them as vertically as possible, the three of them in a noble row, perched on the seat and leaning against the back. As he wheeled them out of the room and down the hall of the burn unit, it struck him as emblematic— only the living leave the hospital in wheelchairs.

As Ludington rode the elevator down to the main floor, the Torah-laden wheelchair in front of him, it occurred to him that he had not offered to pray before he left the room. He almost always did so when he visited parishioners in the hospital. Most expected it; some were alarmed by it, surmising that an offer of prayer implied their prognosis was direr than they knew. So he offered a silent prayer in the Otis, a prayer for Dan, for Lilly and Zack, for Temple Beth Shalom, and for himself.

Chapter Eleven

Thursday

Beth Shalom's three Torah scrolls rested beside the Reverend Seth Ludington in the back seat of an Uber, taking him up the east side of Manhattan from New York Hospital to Old Stone Church. He had often walked these fourteen blocks of York Avenue when making pastoral calls at the hospital, but today, the treasure in his care demanded to be driven. Morning rush hour traffic meant the going was slow on one of Manhattan's few two-way streets. He had time to call Fiona and share the unhappy news about Temple Beth Shalom and its rabbi. The human rights lawyer in his wife agreed with Lilly Gellman's speculation about an antisemitic hate crime. She finished the conversation. "The vandalism and now this. The Feds are going be all over it, Seth. FBI, most likely. Means you can keep out of it."

As the cab passed 76th Street, he phoned van der Berg, "Harriet, I'm guessing you know the combination to the safe in the storage room by the sanctuary. I've no idea what it is. I've got the Torah scrolls from Beth Shalom, and I need to lock them up. Dan and Lilly Gellman want them somewhere safe. I'm on my way now. In an Uber." He then summarized what he had encountered at the fire and the hospital.

She listened, asked no questions, and said, "I'll meet you at the church in ten minutes."

The Uber driver, whose name was Mohammed, offered to help Ludington with the scrolls when they arrived at Old Stone church. He made no comment and asked no questions about carting what were obviously Jewish artifacts into a Christian church. New York cabbies saw it all.

With Mohammed's help, Seth got the scrolls in the side door of the Parish House and onto the top of the reception desk to the left. He thanked the driver and went to the church's kitchen in search of a serving cart. He returned, the thing rattling across the tile floor as he pushed it to a stop just when Harriet came through the church's side door. She looked at the cart and the scrolls lying on the reception desk and said, "Well, this surely must be the right thing to do," in a tone that suggested there might be some doubt about it in her moral calculus.

She followed Seth and the scrolls, clattering down the hallway that led toward the sanctuary and what was now known as "the storage room by the sanctuary," though Ludington guessed the architect had intended it to be a vestry in which clergy might dress—or "vest" in antique parlance—in preparation for services in the adjacent worship space. But the clergy of Old Stone had elected to vest in their offices, and the room had morphed into a repository for disused hymnals and boxes of sermons left behind by former preachers. And one needlessly large old safe.

As van der Berg spun the dial, she said, "You really ought to commit the safe's combination to memory, Seth. You are the minister, after all."

In truth, he never had occasion to access the safe. All it guarded was the church's Victorian-era silver communion ware—an immense chalice and equally unwieldy flagon, a bread plate eighteen inches across, plus piles of small plates for distributing bread and trays holding circles of tiny communion cups for the wine or grape juice, whichever was in fashion. The cups were themselves fussy little stemmed silver chalices.

The set was valuable, if only for its pounds of precious metal, but was rarely used anymore. It demanded polishing—a daunting chore—and passing the trays of tiny chalices through the pews had proven perilous to ladies' Sunday dresses and men's white shirts. One of Seth's predecessors, the late Phil Desmond, had introduced the congregation to communion by intinction, whereby worshipers came forward for the sacrament, tore bread from a common loaf, and dipped it in a modest clay chalice. Nobody much missed either the old practice of pew communion or the venerable silver, but there was no thought of selling it. However useless, it was heritage.

As Ludington set the three Torah scrolls upright in the safe to the right of the carefully stacked communion silver, it struck him that they were spiritually parallel to each other—the scrolls and the communion ware. For Jews, Torah bore the divine word spoken to humanity. For Christians, cup and plate bore the divine Word given to humanity. Both were precious and worthy of guarding in the grand old safe, even though they really belonged out in the world. Seth closed the safe's door and spun the dial.

Harriet said, "I've written the combination down for you. I think you should practice opening the safe." Ludington dutifully did so twice to satisfy her. He then stuffed the piece of paper into the back pocket of his jeans. She had written the combination on the first page of a sermon from 1954 alliteratively and rhymingly titled "The Case for Grace." They left the storage room together and walked side-by-side down the hall to their offices.

* * *

Van der Berg sat at her modest desk, Ludington sank his lanky frame in the spare chair in her office, pulled out his cell phone and said, "Harriet, the police out on Long Island need to know about the synagogue. It'll be all over the news, of course, but they may not connect Beth Shalom and the fire to Gollancz."

He dialed the number for Officer Marge Anderson that he had entered into his contacts. She had made it clear in their interview on Tuesday that homicide was not in the purview of the Asharoken PD. But she was the only cop out on the Island he knew to call.

Her "hello" was guarded. It was awkwardly early, and Ludington's number was clearly not in her contacts.

"Officer Anderson, this is Seth Ludington." He added, "the Reverend Seth Ludington" to jog her memory. "Rabbi Gellman and I spoke to you about Lawrence Gollancz the day before yesterday. You took Dan's statement about death threats Mr. Gollancz had received. You said you'd be contacting Suffolk Country detectives."

Anderson answered abruptly and defensively, "I did." She paused and said, "But I rather doubt they're going to open an investigation. The autopsy confirmed carbon monoxide, and the ME has ruled the death accidental. To tell the truth, I think they've got their hands full with gangs, guns, and fentanyl. Why are you calling, Rev. Ludington?"

"Well," he answered, "Somebody out there should know that the synagogue of which Mr. Gollancz was a member burned last night. Rabbi Gellman was seriously injured. It could be arson. You're aware of the break-in and the vandalism last Sunday night. I don't know, but, well…it could all be linked." He paused before saying, "Linked by antisemitism, maybe."

Anderson said, "It sure is out there. I mean antisemitism. More of it recently, a lot more. You and I both know that. But, Reverend Ludington, I… I mean, we—Asharoken—we have no jurisdiction in the City, and Gollancz has been ruled accidental. Yes, it worries me a little. Three maybe-crimes in a week and the three of them sorta connected. But my hands are tied. I do know this, though: if there's the slightest possibility that the synagogue was arson, the big guns will be rolling in—NYPD Hate Crimes, State Police maybe, and probably FBI. And if that happens, somebody should tell them about Gollancz. They ought to know—about the death threats, I mean—at least about that." She didn't mention muddy footprints or the veritably deaf victim judged too smart to place a gasoline generator under an open bedroom window. She paused and added, "Maybe that somebody should be me."

Ludington said that would surely be the right thing to do and that he'd call if he heard talk of arson, though it would be all over the news. After he ended the call, he whispered to himself, "The woman is one bright and curious cop."

He looked at van der Berg. "You get the gist of that?"

"I do believe I did. I surmise that a summary would be that no one is presently doing anything concerning the death of Lawrence Gollancz. This inaction is despite vile antisemitic death threats having been made to the man in recent anonymous correspondence. And then there is the fact that it appears he was planning to alter his will. So…, do we not have both loathing and lucre?"

She offered a harrumph at this and added, "Seth, you routinely prepare your sermons on Friday. But I suggest we travel to Long Island tomorrow to see what we might see. Should you agree to such an expedition, you might wish to commence with your preparation now."

Ludington did not resist either her suggestion about how he should do his job or her invitation to involve themselves in the investigation of yet another questionable death, but he did say, "Can't our foray to Long Island wait until Saturday, Harriet?"

"I think not. And this is why we dare not delay. I gave this some thought as I lay awake last night. Heavy rain is forecast for tomorrow night into Saturday morning. Such precipitation will surely be deleterious to the condition and clarity of footprints left in the mud. And I believe—as I think you do as well—that those prints demand a more scrupulous examination and documentation than the one offered in the nice little photographs you made with your mobile telephone camera. Such a closer examination must be conducted before the prognosticated deluge washes them away."

Ludington smiled and said, "You've had your eye on the weather, Harriet."
"Precisely."

Van der Berg overused that word, but it fit her personality. Fiona Ludington, like many a Brit, overused the word "lovely." It fit her personality equally well. Ludington had limited his wife to five a day, with an undisclosed penalty for exceeding that number. But his relationship with his admin did not yet permit such playfulness. He feared she might be hurt should he start counting the number of times she said "precisely" every day.

But it was his turn to pull his own detection reflections out of the closet and air them. "Miss van der Berg, there are two somethings I'd like to examine more closely out on Long Island. One is to search about for a well head, if there is one, the other is—at least I think it is—laying on Mr. Gollancz's garage floor, his locked garage." He offered a hint of a smile. "I noticed that there was a keypad to the left of the garage doors. You are adept at combinations. I do wonder what the code might be." He was not merely wondering, of course; he was hinting.

"Well, the combination could be anything, of course. A veritable infinity of numerical possibilities."

Van der Berg thought for a moment, placing a finger on her chin to signal cognition. Something was stirring her imagination. She said nothing, but could not resist asking Ludington the obvious question, "And what might you be seeking in Lawrence Gollancz's garage, if I may ask?"

He told her and said, "Well, Harriet, it seems I have a sermon to prepare right now, on Thursday of all days." He rose to go to his own office, turned back to her as he passed through the door, and added, "I'll pick you up at 9:00 sharp, Harriet. Don't be late."

As if she ever were. Facing away from her so she could not see the look on his face, he whispered to himself, "Two can play at controlling."

Chapter Twelve

Friday

Ludington pulled up to van der Berg's building at precisely 8:55, swerving deftly into the providentially open parking spot at the front entrance. Sergio, her most obsequious doorman, dashed to the car and opened the passenger door for Harriet as she emerged from the building carrying two orange five-gallon buckets labeled "Home Depot." Leaving the door of the Volvo open, Sergio went back to Harriet and said, "Miss van der Berg, please let me help you with those." She ignored him as she marched to the rear of the Volvo, calling out to Seth, "Can you perhaps open the rear compartment door of your automobile from the inside?"

Seth pushed the button to pop the hatch and watched a determined Sergio wrestle one the buckets from van der Berg and lift it into the car. She started to raise the second, but looked to the doorman for help. The buckets must be heavy. Experienced doorman that he was, Sergio knew where to find the button to close the rear hatch. He pushed it and then dashed to close the passenger door after van der Berg had seated herself in the car. As he did so, she smiled at him and mouthed, "Thank you, Sergio."

"So, what's in the buckets, Harriet?"

"Plaster of Paris, of course. And several milk jugs filled with tap water. I had one empty half-gallon milk jug that was awaiting recycling. Unhappily, I had to discard nearly a half-gallon of perfectly good low-fat milk in order to fill a second. I regret having to do that, but according to the formula on the packages of plaster of Paris, I might well need more than one gallon of fresh water."

Ludington could not but smile to himself at van der Berg's impending foray into forensic arts and crafts. He did recall her remark of two days ago about having watched some television detective make plaster molds of footprints. Seth assumed that Harriet had made this observation while obliging the viewing habits of her late partner Margaret in the latter's addiction to detective fiction, whether in books or on the little screen.

"And I have also brought a number of rags as well as several old towels. I'll need to tidy myself up after completing my work. And a cookie tray."

As they approached the Queensboro Bridge onto Long Island, van der Berg said, "So, I thought to phone Lena Gold about your garage code challenge. I did so because she had told me some weeks ago that the synagogue had recently installed a new security access system for the exterior office door. She was boasting about it. She suggested we might consider doing the same at Old Stone. She said their new system does not use one universal passcode for all users. Rather, each person who regularly and appropriately needs access to the building is given a unique code. That's what she called it, a "unique code." Substantially more secure, she said. Well, knowing that Lawrence Gollancz was an active and respected member of Beth Shalom, it occurred to me that he would have been a candidate for such a privilege. And if that be so, one might further surmise that he—like most mortals— had selected a code for the synagogue door that he routinely used for other things—a garage door, for instance." She nodded her head once and firmly to underscore what she thought to be the precision of her logic. "So as I said, I placed a phone call to Lena Gold to inquire about synagogue codes, specifically that used by Mr. Gollancz. I sensed that with all that's happened, she'd ask no questions."

Ludington was again bemused by the woman's keen octogenarian mind. He nodded knowingly at her thinking, satisfied that she had taken the bait he'd cast to her about codes.

"When I spoke with Lena late last evening, she said that—unhappily—the list of the codes was in the synagogue." Harriet paused for effect. "But Lena recalled his. One–zero–zero–one. Memorable number, and also that of his apartment building on Park Avenue. Lovely building, by the way. He had told Lena he chose it because it was easy for him to remember. Easy for her as well. We'll see if he used it for his Long Island garage door. If not, there may be other means to gain access."

Ludington winced at the notion of "other means to gain access." Opening and entering a garage that was not yours was doubtless a minor crime of some ilk, even with a code you had been given. "Other means" would surely be classified as breaking and entering. He hoped that Lawrence Gollancz was as cavalier with codes and passwords as most people, himself included. He and Fiona used the date of their wedding—six-seven-zero-eight—for every four-digit numerical code or password, phones included.

When they arrived on Eaton's Neck, Ludington drove by the Gollancz place twice to make sure no one was around. The property was secluded and not clearly visible from nearby homes. Even the closest house, that of the less-than-affable George Masterson, was largely hidden behind the row of spruce trees that had been planted too close together. After Ludington was confident no one was about, he pulled the Volvo slowly down the drive, parking it not in front of the house, but in a graveled spot to the side of the garage and away from the house.

"We should be quick about this, Harriet."

"The instructions indicate that plaster of Paris takes from twenty to thirty minutes to harden. That's as quick as I can be."

Ludington carried the two Home Depot buckets and their contents to the far corner of the house and set them down in the grass—now dry from the August heat—at a distance from the generator. The machine had not been moved, nor had it been unplugged. The fatally open bedroom window was now closed however, perhaps by the sister with a house key who had arrived just after Ludington and Gellman's visit three days earlier. It somehow seemed much longer ago than that.

"Do you need help, Harriet?"

"Hardly. You go try the code on the garage—one-zero-zero-one."

"I got it, Harriet, I got it." His anxiety about what they were doing was making him testy.

Ludington watched van der Berg carefully lay out the materials needed for her forensic project on the large bath towel she had brought along. She lined them up with precision, reread the back of one of the packages of plaster of Paris, pulled out a measuring cup from the orange bucket, and began to mix water with the white powder. Sensing that he was watching her, she turned around and looked at him, "The garage, Seth." Perhaps she was a bit edgy as well. As he walked across the lawn, he could not help but question the sagacity of this operation.

The code box for the garage was just where he remembered. He lifted the plastic lid and punched in the four-number code. He immediately heard the garage door groan as it began to roll open. "How about that?" he whispered as he ducked under the rising door. He found the control button inside the garage and pressed it to close the garage door. An old woman playing in the dirt would look odd enough to any passers-by. An open garage door would be patently suspicious. He decided not to turn on the garage lights. The natural light from the windows on the doors, plus another pair at the far side of the building, provided more than adequate illumination.

Ludington quickly found what he was looking for. He stooped down, and using the same tissue he had used to cover his fingers when he punched in the code, picked up the sales receipt that lay on the garage floor near the open box in which the portable generator had come. The receipt was from a Home Depot store in Syosset. It recorded two purchases—a generator costing eight-hundred and ninety-nine dollars, and a "Fifty-foot Generator Extension Cord 250-volt 30-amp" which had cost Lawrence Gollancz eighty-nine dollars and ninety-nine cents. Ludington set the receipt back on the spotless epoxy-sealed concrete floor, snapped a photo of it with his phone, and thought to himself, "Where might it be, that fifty-footer? And why did he buy it and not use it? And where did the ten-footer that is plugged into the box at the corner of the house come from?"

He was startled by a knock on the window of the door leading to the house. He saw van der Berg shielding her eyes as she peered in. He plucked the tissue out of his pocket and opened the door for her, noting that in one hand, she was holding the L. L. Bean Duck Boots he had seen three days earlier sitting at the side door to the house. In the other, she held one of her Home Depot buckets.

"I believe it would be prudent to make impressions of these boots, footwear apparently left outside by Mr. Gollancz on the night of this death."

She proceeded to set the cookie sheet on the garage floor and spoon out a layer of the thickening plaster of Paris into it, wait a few minutes, and then press both boots gingerly into the white plaster paste. "It'll take a moment, and I'll need to clean them off. Or perhaps you could do so. I am nearly out of the water I brought. But there is a sea of it nearby." She nodded her head toward Duck Island Harbor.

Ludington and van der Berg stood side-by-side, gazing down at the tray of hardening plaster of Paris and Lawrence Gollancz's duck boots.

Without looking at Ludington, van der Berg said, "A watched pot never boils."

"Tired cliché, Harriet. And not true. Just seems like it'll never boil."

Ludington looked at his Shinola Runwell, "It's been twenty minutes since you poured out your plaster by the generator."

Van der Berg touched the hardening plaster in the cookie tray and said, "Almost." A few minutes later, she lifted the boots and handed them to Ludington. He handled them using one of the paper towels Harriet brought along. As she stooped to check the hardening plaster of Paris in her cookie tray, Ludington said, "What I wanted to get to in this garage was the receipt I had seen on the floor the other day. It was lying next to the box the generator came in. I had to guess it was for its purchase… and maybe that of the cord to connect the thing to the house. They don't come with cords. I checked online. Well, I was right. The receipt noted the purchase of both the generator and a fifty-foot cord." Van der Berg nodded, as if his discovery merely confirmed her own thinking.

Ludington left the garage and walked as furtively as he could down the sloping lawn to the water of Duck Island Harbor. As he crossed the expansive lawn, he looked left and right for signs of a wellhead. He knew what they looked like. His parents' place in Michigan was on a well, its protruding head discretely surrounded by a circle of Adam's yews. He found Gollancz's wellhead easily enough, also camouflaged, but less well. Gollancz's was hidden behind a neat little decorative white fence between the shore and the garage, nearer to the latter. Seth moved closer to make certain he had identified it correctly. Indeed, he had. He then made his way to the small floating dock, jutting twenty feet out into Duck Island Harbor. He walked out a few feet onto it, knelt down, and dipped the boots into the saltwater, just far enough to wet the plaster of Paris-coated soles, but not the uppers. He wiped them clean with one of Harriet's rags and walked up the slight rise to the side door to the house facing the garage. As he did so, he asked himself if Lawrence could not have done what he just did if he had no running water—namely to amble down to his dock and baptize his duck boots in salt water? But in the pouring rain? Perhaps, but doubtful. He walked back up the slope and placed the boots where they had been when he had first seen them the previous Tuesday.

Van der Berg was still in the garage. He had left the door slightly ajar so he could push it open without touching the handle. As he did so, he found himself aghast that he—an ordained Presbyterian minister—was engaged in an action in which he needed to avoid leaving fingerprints.

Van der Berg said, "The castings I made of the prints by the machine should be sufficiently hardened, I think. Shall we retrieve them?"

As they walked past the front of the house, van der Berg said, "It truly is a magnificent home. So sad, all this."

They easily pried the dozen plaster impressions of footprints from what had been wet mud three days earlier, but had become hardened earth in the recent warm and dry days. They wrapped them in rags, placed them carefully into the Home Depot buckets, and returned to the garage, where they retrieved the plaster impression of Lawrence Gollancz's boots in van der Berg's cookie tray.

Ludington closed the side door to the garage, again covering his hand with a tissue and checking to make certain it locked behind him. He carried both buckets, now stuffed with plaster castings, seeming heavier than they had been before. Harriet carried the two empty milk jugs, and her collection of rags rolled up in the towel. They silently loaded their evidential booty into the back of the Volvo, climbed in, and set off for home, both breathing relief at having accomplished their work without being noticed.

As Ludington backed out Lawrence Gollancz's drive and turned onto the narrow lane that would lead him back to Asharoken Avenue, he saw a marked squad car moving equally slowly toward him. He edged as far to the right as he could to let the other vehicle pass. As it drew alongside, he recognized both the Asharoken markings on its doors and the driver, Officer Marge Anderson. She rolled her window down and stopped when she was even with Ludington. She signaled him to lower his window as well.

Ludington decided to take the initiative, "Forgot something last Tuesday. I mean, lost something when Rabbi Gellman and I were here." He gave her a "how silly of me" look.

"Find it?" she said, looking inquisitively past him at van der Berg.

"No, but it was worth a try." He was struggling to imagine what it could have been that he had lost, something worth a drive out from the City to retrieve. Fortunately she didn't ask, but said, "Reverend Ludington, do keep me in the loop. Let me know what you hear about the rabbi and arson. You do seem a curious type." She paused, offered the slightest crack of a smile, and added, "Be careful. And mind the Asharoken speed limit."

She raised her window and drove on down the narrow lane. Ludington breathed an audible sigh of relief and turned to van der Berg. She was expressionless, saying only, "One must wonder who she thought I was."

"I doubt that was a coincidence, Harriet. Somebody saw us and called."

Ludington looked past her as he made that observation and realized that they had stopped directly in front of George Masterson's high ranch house. It was neat if nondescript, clad in ubiquitous Long Island cedar shakes stained dark. A car was parked in the drive, a decades-old dark gray Ford Taurus sedan. There was a sticker on the back bumper. It read "Take America Back," in red, white, and blue caps, followed by the initials "ADL."

He pointed it out to van der Berg and said, "I doubt it's the Anti-Defamation League who wants to take America back."

Chapter Thirteen

Sunday

The Reverend Seth Ludington's antisemitism sermon was well received by the congregation of Old Stone Church. He guessed that the kudos it garnered in the greeting line after the service, thinly attended in late August, were due as much to the passion with which it was delivered as to its content. Ludington knew he tended to preach more from the head than the heart. This Sunday's message had plenty of head, but a surfeit of heart. He was angry, and his anger had climbed into the pulpit with him. Many of those in the pews shared his rage.

First, he was angry because the fire was indeed arson. Lena Gold, the synagogue admin, had called Harriet, who had then called Seth, with confirmation of what all suspected. Temple Beth Shalom—"House of Peace"—had been deliberately set ablaze.

And he was angry because Dan Gellman was in rough shape in New York Hospital. When he had visited him, he had found his friend marginally awake, heavily medicated, in pain but uncomplaining, his few words cogent, though barely. At his bedside, Lilly Gellman's worry was inverting to rage. Just like his. Ludington had decided to say nothing to them about footprints, plaster of Paris, or receipts for extension cords. Not yet. The couple's present burden was heavy enough.

And he was angry because of the bumper sticker. He had Googled the initials "ADL." What came up was, of course, the Anti-Defamation League, the world's premier organization working to combat antisemitism. Their website was a treasure trove of information, some of which had found its way into the revised version of the next day's sermon. The site included pages containing a terrifyingly long list of organizations, symbols, and poisonous tropes associated with antisemitism, racism, White nationalism, and general hatefulness. Ironically, one of the entries was for what was named "a loose-knit white-supremacist group concentrated on the East Coast of the United States using the initials ADL." The site did not speculate as to whether this "loose-knit group" had chosen the same three initials as the Anti-Defamation League out of ignorance or a deliberate and perverse irony. It did say that the three letters were sometimes thought to designate the "American Defense League," or alternatively, the "Arian Defense Legion." The entry noted that there had been "schisms in the group." As Seth read that last line, he thought to himself that haters don't easily stick together. At least, they usually don't stick together for long.

He had launched the sermon at Old Stone's eleven o'clock worship service by reminding the congregation of what they all already knew—that a nearby Jewish house of worship had burned to the ground earlier in the week just days after it had been broken into and vandalized, its walls defaced with spray-painted venom, its sacred objects cast to the ground. Arson was suspected, he told the congregation, though he did not betray the fact that he knew arson had become more than suspicion. He told the story of the synagogue's rabbi, whom he named "a good friend," a man who had risked his life to rescue the congregation's Torah scrolls, one of which was a Holocaust survivor. "He's now in the burn unit at Weill Cornell." Ludington then noted that these events were but one iteration of a rising and fetid tide of antisemitic hate in the country and around the globe. "The bad news is that it's not back then or over there; it's here and it's now. In fact, it's just a few blocks up 3rd Avenue. It may be the world's oldest hatred, but also its most present." He quickly rehearsed the familiar tale from the lectionary passage for the morning—Pharaoh's plot against the Jews, his infamous infanticide, and finally, baby Moses' escape. "Arguably the first pogrom, the first of many."

He then pivoted to the role Christianity had played in antisemitism. To make sense of that move, he had read several verses from John's Gospel in addition to the Moses story, Gospel words that spoke of "the Jews" as if they were Jesus' main antagonists. When he read the passage, he had translated the Greek as "the Judeans" rather than "the Jews." Linguistically legitimate, he opined. In the sermon, he noted that everyone in the story was a Jew, Jesus included. All of Jesus' first disciples were Jews. These "Judeans," Jesus' Jerusalem critics, were but one slice of the diverse Jewish pie of the day. He recognized that the pie metaphor was less than felicitous, but stuck with it anyway. Pies can be diverse.

He next noted that in the years after Jesus' death and resurrection, his Jewish followers had continued to attend their synagogues on the Sabbath and that those in Jerusalem still seemed to have worshiped at the Temple. Until it was destroyed by the Romans in 70 A.D., that is. He told his flock of Presbyterian Gentiles that in those early days, following Jesus was often understood to be one of a number of ways of being Jewish.

Ludington ended the sermon by telling the congregation, "Temple Beth Shalom will be invited to use this space for their Sabbath worship as long as they need it." He did not note that the Session had not yet met to extend the invitation. He knew he was prejudicing the vote by speaking of it as a done deal. He didn't care. Even though the air conditioning was again working in the sanctuary of Old Stone Church, he found himself perspiring as he stepped out of the pulpit.

The last person through the greeting line after church was Harriet van der Berg. She offered him a compliment, something she rarely did. "I have seldom seen you grow so impassioned in the pulpit, Seth." She then stepped away, turned back to him when she was halfway to the stairs leading to the Social Hall, and said, "I'll see you at Campbell's. Two o'clock." She dashed toward the head of the stairs and down to coffee hour before Seth could ask her why in the world she thought she should be in attendance at Lawrence Gollancz's service at the Frank E. Campbell Funeral Chapel that afternoon. He sensed that she had moved fast to dodge his question.

It was odd even for him to be there, but Lilly—and through her, Dan—had asked him to go. They had also asked him to touch base with the substitute rabbi Lena had found to conduct the service. Ludington had called the man and discovered he had matters well in hand. The rabbi told him that he had spoken at some length not only to Dan and Lena, but also to "Mr. Gollancz's sister from out on Long Island," whom he intimated (clergy-to-clergy) to be "a real piece of work, let me tell you."

An hour later, Seth had to leave Fiona to pay the bill at the Lex Restaurant and wheel the girls home after their rushed Sunday lunch. He went directly to Campbell's, arriving at ten before two. The venerable funeral home occupied primo real estate on Madison Avenue, a stretch filled with high-end European boutiques with buzzer doors and burly doormen to police them. Frank E. Campbell now openly served the deceased of all faiths. As well as those of none, of course. Gone were the days when most funeral parlors were denominational—Protestant, Roman Catholic, or Jewish, though New York still boasted a good many of the last. Campbell's was around the corner from Gollancz's erstwhile apartment on Park, conveniently located in the heart of the neighborhood where many of the man's acquaintances probably lived. And, of course, Gollancz had not selected Campbell's, the piece-of-work sister probably had.

Tony Spinelli, one of the ever-helpful staff, saw Ludington come in the door from Madison and gave him a quizzical look. Ludington had worked with Spinelli on several occasions, including an under-the-counter cremation of some old bones.

"Surprised to see you here, Rev. Ludington. Can I help you with something?"

Seth's answer—"I'm here for the Gollancz service, Tony"—garnered another questioning look from Spinelli.

Ludington explained, "Dan Gellman—Rabbi Gellman—is a friend, a good friend. He's in the hospital." Ludington hesitated, "You probably know that, of course. He asked me to be here. To represent him. Sort of…I guess…." Ludington didn't want to say, "He wanted me to keep an eye on things," which might imply that Tony Spinelli, Frank E. Campbell, and the fill-in rabbi were not capable of doing so.

Spinelli nodded as if this made sense and said, "Mr. Gollancz's service is in the large chapel. It's good to see you, Seth."

Jewish funerals, Ludington discovered, were comprised of most of the same elements as Protestant ones. He looked at the program he had been given when he entered the large chapel and saw that there were to be readings from Scripture, especially the Psalms, a eulogy offered by the rabbi, remembrances spoken—probably through tears and laughter—by family or friends, and, of course, prayers offered in both English and Hebrew, including the Mourners' Kaddish.

Just as in Christian services, the family was seated last and upfront, proceeding gravely down the center aisle to the places reserved for them after everyone else found a seat. Gellman had told him that Gollancz's surviving family consisted only of a sister, her husband, and their two children. Gollancz himself had been long widowed, and he and his wife had had no children.

The sister, Irene Stark, led the procession down the center aisle. She was a large and handsome woman, impeccably clad in what looked to be a black Chanel suit, fitting couture for the occasion, whether on the East End of Long Island or the Upper East Side of Manhattan Island. She was the same woman he and Dan Gellman had seen arriving at Lawrence Gollancz's house with a key in hand the day after the man's death. Processing behind her were her two children. First, a teenaged daughter, pretty, but very thin, with cropped hair dyed medium blue. She was in black as well, a short dress that displayed the great majority of her almost anorexic legs. Slouching behind her, but not beside her, was the son. He was a good-looking kid, tall and even more slender than his sister. His brown hair looked to have been freshly cut. The sleeves of his dark blue blazer were a good two inches too short, though he had managed to button the jacket over his dark burgundy tie, pulling it tight across his chest, skinny as he was. He wore a distant look that hinted not only at discomfort, but distracted anxiety. Bringing up the rear was a man in a motorized wheelchair. He looked to be in his seventies, decades older than his wife. His gray hair was cut short in a style Ludington's father had often worn and called "the Harvard cut." The man's suit, the same gray as his hair, hung loosely on him. It was clearly a back-of-the-closet artifact from a day when he was a larger man. The senior Mr. Stark looked decidedly unwell, though he controlled the joystick of the chair adroitly, easing it into the open spot that had been left for him in the front row next to his wife.

After the rabbi's eulogy, a well-crafted address doubtlessly constructed from notes made after phone conversations, he called two people forward to speak words of remembrance. The first was introduced as "a long-time business colleague," an ice cream supplier, Ludington guessed by some of his remarks. The man opened his words of remembrance with, "Larry Gollancz was a good guy, a really good guy." A string of personal anecdotes followed, some humorous, some poignant, most including words like "integrity" and "honest." His conclusion was a litany of three "I just can't believe it" exclamations. The man was clearly grieving, though he worked his way through his speech without tears.

Tears were the main point of Irene Stark's remembrance—extravagant tears that muffled whatever she might have been prepared to say. Ludington caught but a few phrases—"my big brother, my only brother," "he loved his family," and "there's no one else left." It finally became so painful to watch that the rabbi wisely rose and went to her, laid an arm around her sobbing shoulders, and escorted her back to her seat. Ludington noticed that she alone among the family was wearing a torn piece of black cloth pinned to her chest. It was, he knew, the emblematic remnant of the Jewish tradition of rending one's clothing when mourning.

Irene Stark had recovered her composure when Ludington reached her in the receiving line following the service. He was still wearing his clerical collar from the morning service. She saw both the collar and his handsome face and smiled broadly. He felt that both he and the dog collar needed an explanation, so he said, "I'm a good friend of your late brother's rabbi, Rabbi Daniel Gellman. He's unable to be here, of course. I thought I'd come in his stead… to offer condolences on his behalf. My name is Seth Ludington. I'm the minister of Old Stone Presbyterian Church."

"Presbyterian?" she exclaimed, almost shouting the word. "Why, Jack and

I were married in the Westhampton Beach Presbyterian Church. It's near our home, and it's just lovely, so quintessentially Hamptons. Jack was raised Protestant, I think." She nodded toward her husband, who had parked his chair in a corner of the room, well out of greeting line range.

Her effusiveness, in such contrast to the tears of moments earlier, was unbridled. Still grasping his hand, now rubbing the back of it, she said, "Reverend, we shall be sitting shiva these next several days. At our home in the Hamptons. You absolutely must come. We have engaged an exceptional caterer." She handed him a small card with an address in Speonk, Long Island, printed under the dates and times of shiva-sitting. He smiled in return, pulled his hand away, and said, "I'd be honored to stop by."

As he turned toward the door to leave, he saw that Harriet van der Berg was immediately behind him in the line. They had not sat together during the service. He saw her extend a hand to Irene Stark and then heard her say in a theatrically sober tone, "My name is Henrietta Berg. We have not met, but your brother and I were quite close these last years. I cared so deeply for Larry. Please do accept my very deepest condolences."

Stunned by such bald-faced lies, Ludington stared at her with open-mouthed incredulity. Harriet saw the look on his face, turned back to Irene Stark, and said, "Of course, I'd be pleased to visit as you sit shiva." She paused for a well-timed moment and added, "But unfortunately, I don't drive and have no idea how I might get myself out to Long Island."

To which Irene said, "Perhaps you could ride along with the Reverend Ludington."

She then turned to Seth, five feet away, his mouth still agape, and said, "Reverend Ludington, do you know Henrietta Berg?"

Chapter Fourteen

Monday

It was late morning of his day off when Seth Ludington picked up Henrietta Berg to drive her to the East End of Long Island so she might sit shiva with the bereaved family of her "dear friend," Larry Gollancz. Ludington pulled away from the curb, drove the few blocks to Park Avenue, and turned south toward the Queensboro Bridge without uttering so much as a "good morning." Five blocks down Park, he finally said, "You have some major chutzpah, Harriet. I mean Henrietta."

Secretly, he was pleased to have her along, though he was not about to tell her that. Ludington found himself waxing evermore anxious about his own duplicitousness in finagling this visit to the Stark family. He found a modicum of comfort in the company of an even more duplicitous companion.

Traffic thinned when the Volvo's sweet-voiced navigation lady finally freed them from the bumper-to-bumper traffic of the Long Island Expressway and deposited them onto the eastbound and aptly-named Sunrise Highway, aptly-named at least when one was driving east in the morning. Sensing that Seth was now both less distracted with driving and perhaps less put out with her, Harriet said, "I spent some hours on the internet last night researching the ADL, not the Jewish one, but those who are using the same initials and wish to take America back. From whom they wish to take it back, I can hazard a guess. To summarize…my search ultimately carried me into the bowels of

"

various social media sites, many of them quite noxious, I must say. The Take America Back iteration of ADL does not appear to maintain a website. Given their predilections, I suppose that's understandable. What I discovered was a group—mostly men, I surmise—who can barely mask their loathing of all persons who are not of Caucasian, and more specifically, European descent, especially those who do not identify themselves as Christians. Though, I gather that what they mean by 'Christian' is not any kind of trust in Jesus Christ as their Lord and Savior. I surmise that they mean 'not Jewish and not Muslim.' I must say, their postings betray scant evidence of actual churchgoing. So there you have it. Your Mr. Masterson would appear to be in communion with one of Margaret's "Ls," the loathing one."

Ludington had already come to the same conclusion. "He is not my Mr. Masterson. So Harriett, what about your collection of plaster of Paris castings? I didn't have a chance to look at them closely. Do any of them betray small feet? It looked to me as if some of the prints were smallish when I took my mud photos. I mean smaller than—I don't know—smaller than large?"

"Well, after my internet explorations, I carefully laid out our castings on an old bath towel atop my dining room table. I didn't want to scratch the finish. Margaret found it at Doyle's. Perfect condition, then and now. Well, there are indeed three sets of distinct footprints, much as you guessed. Some are quite clear, others not, but two of them were definitely made by persons with smaller feet. And one set was made by a person wearing substantially larger footwear. I plan to do some research on footwear, either online or perhaps I shall undertake a foray down to Macy's to see if I might discover the precise brands or styles of shoes or boots which made the various impressions, though I seem to have identified one of them."

She paused before saying, "Seth, I discovered a rather jolting fact, one that runs contrary to our suspicions. Some of the impressions I made from the mud around the machine—the large ones —match those I made in my cookie sheet of the boots by the back door, Mr. Gollancz's boots, one must assume. What did you call them? Duck boots? Generally worn when one shoots ducks, I suppose. The soles offer a unique pattern, fashioned much like links of chain."

She was silent for a moment, weighing evidence that ran contrary to their assumptions. "But Seth, it does invite our familiar question. If Mr. Gollancz had started up his generating machine when he lost power and thereby muddied his boots, he must have cleaned them thoroughly, which returns us to the question of the availability of water. He would have gotten mud on them no matter where he placed the generator as he had to venture into the mire near his window where the thing plugs into the...what did you name it?"

"Junction box. A lot of things are logically possible, Harriet, but not all are likely. The idea that Lawrence Gollancz cranked up the thing under his window in the midst of a deluge is quite possible, but it butts its head against several walls, walls of, well... walls of likelihood. Likelihood wall one: As we now know, his home is on a well, and with the power out, he would have had no running water to wash mud off the soles of his boots. I suppose he could have trooped down to Duck Island Harbor, but would he have done that in a downpour? Wouldn't he have waited till morning? Wall of likelihood two—and this is a formidable one: Where did the fifty-foot extension cord he bought with the generator go? And why in the world did he buy it if he wasn't going to use it? And where did the ten-footer that's there come from? And wall of likelihood three: By all reports, Lawrence Gollancz doesn't seem to have been that dumb."

Ludington paused for a moment, "But now comes your contrary, hard-as-plaster fact—a pair of size eleven duck boots exactly like the ones at the back door made prints in the mud around the generator. It just doesn't add up."

Harriet considered Ludington's walls of likelihood. She was unhappy with both the metaphor and the contrary and wall-like fact that boots just like those by the back door had left prints in the wet mud by the generator. So, as she often did when perplexed, she altered the subject slightly, "Seth, why did you specifically inquire if any of the prints were made by smaller feet?"

"I don't know that I mentioned it to you, but George Masterson is a small man, literally, and now it would seem, figuratively. Point is, he has dainty little feet. Couldn't help but notice the other day. So Harriett, when you do your research on the patterns on the soles of assorted footwear be sure you check out Top Siders. It's a brand of boat shoe. Nice ones. I have a pair. So does George Masterson. He was wearing them when he called on Dan and me by the generator Tuesday afternoon."

"I shall do so. 'Top Siders,' you say. But before you convict the man of felonious generator-moving, do remember that he told you he turned the machine off the morning he discovered it running and saw Mr. Gollancz dead in his bed, did he not? Should the prints prove to be his, he could easily have made them then, *ne'est-ce pas?*"

"Yes, he could have. Indeed, he could have."

Seth Ludington paused, sighed as he watched an exit sign for Center Moriches wiz by, and said, "And now we're off to visit the sister, a woman who is perhaps about to be partially—perhaps largely—disinherited. Gollancz's changing of his will in favor of the synagogue does rather suggest yet another of Margaret's "Ls.""

"Precisely."

Speonk revealed itself to be a pleasant village even though, as Seth observed to Harriett, its name sounded like what frogs say. It was not, however, quite "the Hamptons." Speonk was wedged between two Long Island worlds—that of middle-class suburbia to the west and the summer playing fields of the uber-wealthy to the east. But Speonk was on the water, Moriches Bay to be exact, which somewhat elevated its desirability and real estate prices. The Volvo's navigation led Seth and Harriet through a labyrinth of narrow lanes to one named "Tuthill" and the home of the family Stark. It was an attractive enough center-hall colonial, white clapboard with black shutters, though not the kind that actually close. It looked to hail from the 70s of the twentieth century, not the eighteenth. The nav map revealed that it lay near, but not on the water. There were three cars in the double driveway leading to an attached garage, and several more were pulled to the sides of Tuthill Lane.

As Seth pushed the button on what he recognized as a Ring doorbell, his mind was suddenly jogged by a memory. He had talked to his father about the one his parents had installed on their Charleston house when he and Fiona visited the previous March to show off the girls. His father had told him that they had bought three Ring doorbells, one for Charleston, one for Lyford Cay, and one for Pentwater. He had said, "I can watch who's at the front door of all three places from my phone. Fabulous invention. Everybody's getting them." Seth had thought that perhaps he and Fiona should install them on the upper and lower front doors of their brownstone, but they hadn't gotten to it yet.

The Stark's door was answered by a young woman in black jeans and a shirt that read "The Hamptons Feast," obviously a caterer assigned to answer the door. Without a hint of welcome, she said, "People are in the living room and the dining room, and in the kitchen, of course." There was an edge in her voice as she added the last room to the list. The people in the kitchen were surely in her way. Seth offered Harriett a gentleman's "after you" gesture with his right arm, directing her to the left and into the living room. As he did so, he thought to himself that he must remember to call her Henrietta.

The room was furnished in reproduction-Williamsburg. Two red leather wing chairs and a large sofa covered in Black Watch plaid had been pulled away from the center of the room and pushed against the walls to allow guests more space to move about. Four very low wooden stools were arranged in a row against the wall opposite the fireplace. Shiva stools, Seth surmised, seats that lowered mourners in imitation of grief-stricken Job. The family of the deceased was supposed to sit on them during the seven days of shiva. No one was sitting on them at the Stark shiva. The mirror above them was draped in a black cloth, another nod to Jewish tradition.

Irene Stark spied Ludington and van der Berg from the far end of the living room and dashed in their direction. She was again dressed in black, not the Chanel of the funeral, but fresh and equally elegant mourning attire. She still wore the piece of torn cloth pinned to her dress, now held in place with a large gold brooch much like the Van Cleef and Arpels piece he had given Fiona on their last wedding anniversary. She balanced a small plate of food in one hand, a large stemmed glass of white wine in the other. Seth had no idea whether alcohol was routine when sitting shiva.

"Reverend Ludington, Ms. Berg. How pleased—no, I should say honored—I am, I mean we are, that you came." She managed to pronounce "Ms." in a way that was neither "Missus" nor "Miss," and added a few decibels to underscore the "honored." Seth was afraid the woman was about to offer him a double-cheek European kiss, surely not routine when sitting shiva, but she restrained herself. She did take his hand however, holding it rather too long, before turning to Harriet-Henrietta and asking, "Tell me about you and my brother. I mean, how did you come to know Larry?" The woman could barely mask the suspicion crouching behind her question.

Before Harriet could produce more prevarication, Irene Stark, a prolix woman, answered for her, "Well, I know Larry had been lonely since Janet died, but that was—let me see—eight years ago now, or maybe it's nine. Did you perhaps find him at that synagogue of his? I heard it burned to the ground. How sad. He was becoming more Jewish these last years."

Turning to the covered mirror and the shiva stools lined up under it, she said, "That's for him. We are not so Jewish ourselves. Stark is an English name, you know. Jack's family came over on the Mayflower. About then, anyway."

She raised the plate of food in her hand, poking it under Ludington's nose. "Scones and clotted cream. So very Brit." She managed to say "very" with a mock English accent making the "r" into a "d." "You must have some. Ludington is an old English name, is it not?"

Their host finished speaking and turned to Harriet with an inquisitive look. Irene's burst dam of words had given Harriet time to devise an answer to the woman's question. "Yes, we met at temple. I'm a widow myself." This last was emotionally true. Harriet wisely wove no more detail into her "Henrietta and Larry" story. Liars often get caught in the details. She merely offered a sad smile that said, "I'm bearing up, but I miss him so."

A shadow of suspicion fell over Irene Stark's face, broken when a young girl, the daughter Ludington had seen process in with the family at the funeral, ambled over to stand near her mother. But not too near. She was sipping Diet Coke from a can through a huge, pliable straw. She wore the same short black skirt that she'd worn at the funeral, still proudly displaying her pencil-thin legs.

"May I present my daughter, Chelsea Stark. Chelsea, this is the Reverend Ludington, a dear friend of Lawrence's rabbi in New York. And this is Ms. Berg, some kind of friend of your uncle's from the City."

Chelsea nodded without taking the straw out of her mouth.

Her mother sighed, "This is all so very distressing. Such a tragic accident. I don't understand why he would place that thing directly under his bedroom window. He had just bought it. Why, he was showing it off to us just the night before. He had us for dinner, the whole family." She paused and adopted a look of long-suffering piety. "I guess we have to be thankful for that one last happy night together as a family."

Chelsea lifted her head, pulling the straw out of her mouth, offered an eye roll, and said to no one, "Yeah, happy like the war in Afghanistan."

Irene barked at her daughter, "Chelsea Irene Stark, really."

The girl guffawed, shrugged her shoulders, and walked off toward the kitchen.

Ludington was reluctant to inquire more about the recent family dinner, surely the one at which—according to his lawyer—Gollancz was planning to break the news about changes in his will.

But Van der Berg found words. She looked at Irene and asked in a wistful voice, "Did he serve his famous brisket at the dinner? He always did that so nicely."

Ludington managed to restrain his own eye-roll.

Irene screwed up her face in a way that said, "What are you talking about?" What she actually said was, "Lawrence? Cook? He had it catered like he always did." She quickly recovered from her incredulity at the notion of her brother cooking dinner and added, "It was perfectly elegant, of course. He always set a beautiful table. Or had one set."

Irene's attention abruptly turned to another visitor who approached tentatively, not wanting to interrupt. The woman, who looked to be about Irene's age, took her hand as she spoke, "Reenie, Tom, and I have to go. Let's you and I have another one of our walks later. Get you out of the house."

Irene gave the woman a peck on the cheek and said, "Thank you so much for coming, Muriel."

Ludington took the interruption as an opportunity to escape Irene Stark. He nodded his head sharply to the side, signaling van der Berg to follow him to the kitchen. As was often the case, there were more people packed into it than were in either the living or dining room. The kitchen was large, opening into a family room with a large screen television on the wall to the right. The house's second fireplace was at the far end of the room. Hanging on the wall to the right of the refrigerator in the kitchen was a beige wall phone, push button style. Ludington had not seen one in years. The phone number was noted on a slip of paper above the buttons. Seth memorized it.

Chelsea and a gangly kid in black skinny jeans Ludington recognized as her older brother were seated on stools at the high counter of the kitchen island, both staring at cell phones. As Seth edged his way through the crowd, he heard the girl say to her brother without looking away from her device, "I'm doing a YouTube series on unc's death. It's like a mystery. I mean— duh—putting the thing right under his window. Why did he do that? Super dumb. Which he was not. I already got some followers."

Without taking his eyes off his own phone, Hudson Stark said, "Chelsea Bun, screenager, social media addict, and wannabe true crime star."

"You're one to talk about addicted, Huddles."

"Don't you call me that. I told you."

"What? Addicted or Huddles? So when do you go back to that dippy school of yours? Can hardly wait."

"It's not dippy. It's Hofstra University. Not soon enough."

He rose from the stool, slid his phone into his jeans pocket, and walked away from his sister into a space off the kitchen that doubled as a mudroom and a laundry room. He opened a door in that room and stepped down a few steps into the attached garage. Before he closed it, Ludington glimpsed a black Mercedes G-Class and a dark gray sedan.

Ludington caught van der Berg's eye and said, "I'm going to offer my condolences to Mr. Stark."

He nodded toward the man sitting in a motorized wheelchair in the family room. He was staring at the expanse of the wall-mounted television screen. The sound was off, but it was tuned to some cable news outlet. Two pretty blond talking heads were silently exchanging wisdom. A woman was kneeling to speak with Stark at face level. As she rose, Jack Stark reached to take her hand, his own arm and hand moving erratically, barely under his control. When the woman left, Ludington moved to take her place. He knelt as she had and said, "I'm a friend of Lawrence's rabbi, Daniel Gellman. He is unable to be here. On his behalf, I came to offer my condolences to you and your family, Mr. Stark."

Jack Stark appeared to attempt a smile, but his face was frozen, a mask. He said in the softest of voices, "Thank you."

Ludington turned to see Irene Stark standing in the kitchen next to van der Berg. Both women were watching him. He rose from his crouch and went to say goodbye, offering Irene Stark his hand. She took it, squeezed it hard, and looked away from Ludington and toward her husband, "Parkinson's. He's in his tenth year. Just like his father."

Ludington offered a wan smile, "It can be really tough, though it varies from person to person. My wife's uncle wrestled with Parkinson's for years."

Irene Stark proffered the same saintly smile she had managed when singing her thankfulness for that one last dinner with her brother. After a moment's hesitation, as if unsure about saying what was on her mind, she spoke, "If it were only that. Disappointment is the story of my husband's life. He was a science teacher, middle school. Hated it. He was in line for appointment as the school's principal. He had taken the necessary courses in school administration, and he had seniority, but they passed him over. Then, he was diagnosed. Reverend Ludington, I must say, yet again, how very happy I am that you are here. As you might surmise, though my family has some Jewish roots, I find myself no longer at home in that tradition. Which rather leaves me and my family without—what shall I say?—without spiritual succor. I hope I do not presume when I ask if you might offer us such in our time of need."

Appearing to have said more than she had planned, Irene Stark smiled the strangest grin and pulled away from Ludington even before he could respond to her bizarre request, not that he knew what he would say. She then turned to face him directly and offered a limp hand, "Well, I do thank you and Ms. Berg for coming all this way."

When Seth and Harriet offered their farewells and a second round of condolences to Irene Stark at the front door, she gave Seth the double-cheek kiss she had held in check an hour and a half earlier. She hummed as she did so. Seth had often observed to Fiona that when engaging in European-style social cheek kisses, some people were "hummers" and some were "non-hummers." Irene Stark was a "hummer." He received both the kisses and the hum with a forced smile.

Seth and Harriet rode silently in the Volvo until they turned onto the westbound Sunrise Highway. He finally said, "Well, you pulled that off, Henrietta." She merely nodded in response. He then said what both were thinking, "Jack Stark looks to be a sad case. You know that Parkinson's is both idiopathic and idiosyncratic. Learned all this from Fiona who—typical for her—researched every square inch of it when her dad's brother was diagnosed. They don't know what causes it—idiopathic. And it's different for everyone—idiosyncratic. Sometimes mild, sometimes not. Sometimes fast, sometimes slow. No tests. They only know you've got it from the symptoms. But there are a few meds that help."

After that brief reflection on the vulnerabilities of all flesh, both fell back into a reflective silence as they wended their way out of Speonk.

Chapter Fifteen

Monday

Once on the Long Island Expressway, Harriet said in a whisper, "I have never been to a shiva reception before. I attended an Irish wake once. It was rather more boisterous. What is your impression, Seth?"

"She's an aspirer. I mean Irene Stark. She doesn't want to be Jewish. She wants to be a WASP. She wants to be a Hamptons matron, but she lives in a '70s colonial in Speonk. The furniture, the jewelry, the dresses, the scones with clotted cream, even the kids' names. I mean, Hudson and Chelsea? And the car, a Mercedes G-Class, the quintessential Hampton's I-have-arrived ride. And her curious affection for me, the old money uber-Protestant."

Van der Berg nodded. "What they call a climber."

"And the son, Hudson, he's one restless kid. He has that 'I wish I could be anywhere but here' look about him. So, well…fidgety. Chelsea seems a normal teenager with a cynical edge who's mostly trying to look grown up. And she's one with her iPhone. I heard her tell her brother she was going to do a video series on YouTube about Gollancz's death."

Van der Berg clicked her tongue, "I heard that as well. Tasteless in the extreme."

Ludington nodded in agreement and said, "Harriet, we need to find the caterer. He or she might be a witness—one we can trust, neutral and credible—to the dinner Lawrence Gollancz hosted to inform his family he was going to more or less drop them from his will. A vigilant caterer might know if it was a 'delightful evening' or the 'war in Afghanistan?' How many caterers can there be in greater Northport?"

"I am on it, Seth. As soon as we return, I am 'on it,' as they say." He could hear the eagerness in the woman's voice.

Just as they were crossing the Queensboro Bridge, Ludington's phone rang. A 212 number neither he nor his iPhone recognized popped up on the Volvo's screen. He took the call on the car's speaker.

"Reverend Ludington? This is Agent Brian O'Reilly, Federal Bureau of Investigation. Your number was given to me by Lena Gold, the administrator at Temple Beth Shalom. We have been brought in to assist with the investigation of the recent vandalism and fire at the synagogue. Mrs. Gold also told me that you are in possession of the synagogue's Torah scrolls. We need access to them. Right away. Can you arrange for that?"

"Of course, of course. I'll be at my church, Old Stone Presbyterian, East 82nd , tomorrow morning. The scrolls are there, in the church's safe."

"Nine o'clock okay, Father?"

"Yes, fine."

Van der Berg stifled a giggle, "He called you 'Father.'"

"Sounds young, doubtless Irish and R.C. All clergy are Father."

Chapter Sixteen

Monday and Tuesday

Ludington dropped van der Berg off at her building and into the care of the ever-vigilant Sergio. The doorman dashed to open the car door for her, a nanosecond after Seth pulled up. She gingerly exited the SUV, having no trouble with the height of the vehicle, turned back to Ludington, leaned over slightly to peer at him, and said, "I shall begin my caterer quest forthwith. Until tomorrow, then." She smiled a goofy smile and shut the door with a decisive slam.

Seth could not help but feel that she was enjoying this rather too much. He returned the Volvo to the garage and phoned Fiona as he walked home down 2nd Avenue, "What do you want to do about dinner, Hon?" he asked.

He knew she rather liked it when he called her "Hon," Americanism that it was. Once and again, Fiona addressed him as *"Mo Leannan."* Scots Gaelic, she said, though she spoke little of the language. He liked the obscurity of it.

"Seth, I called Inez and asked her to come a wee bit early. We can get the girls down and sneak out to eat. I made us a reservation at Lex for eight-thirty."

They arrived at the restaurant at eight-thirty sharp. It was almost empty, having dismissed the early dinner crowd to the night's program at the 92nd Street Y across the street. Without asking, Nero escorted them to the back corner booth. Ludington ordered the saltimbocca. It was pricey, but not quite the most expensive item on the menu. Though money was no issue,

"""

guilt stirred his stomach and compromised his appetite if he ordered the most expensive meal in any restaurant, even one as reasonable (for New York) as the Lex. Fiona ordered her usual grilled salmon in lemon and white wine. They added a bottle of modestly priced pinot grigio, a fit pairing for both meals.

Seth liked the heavy dose of sage that invariably ruled saltimbocca. Few dishes varied as much from chef to chef, but there was always sage and prosciutto. Saltimbocca could be made with veal or chicken, rolled into a tube, or pounded flat and sautéed in olive oil…, or maybe butter. But there was always sage and prosciutto. At least that was consistent.

"So, Lawrence Gollancz's sister is an interesting study." He wanted to talk about his shiva visit with someone in addition to van der Berg. "Harriet called her a climber. Doubtless true, but it's more than class. I think she wants into what she imagines to be the WASPY world of the Hamptons. A rather white world, of course, but it's not as Anglo-Saxon or as Protestant as she imagines. Point is, that's just not who she is. She's, well, Jewish—Jewish mother, Jewish father, raised orthodox Jewish."

Fiona nodded, speared a bit of salmon with her fork, and ate it appreciatively. Then she poured another inch of wine into both their glasses. She understood that her husband was embarking on one of his reflective rambles into some big life question. She nodded indulgently and said, "Proceed."

"Well, it invites the question of whether you can ever really invent yourself. I mean, totally invent yourself. The mantra of our age—you know, with its radical individualism and personal autonomy—is convinced you can create yourself, that you should create yourself. 'Be whatever you want to be.' It's the main thread of a million commencement addresses. 'Be a WASP if you want to be a WASP.' Just like Ralph Lauren. But people are connected, Fiona. I mean, to be human, you gotta be connected—connected to your family, to your history, to your culture, to your religion or no religion, connected to, well, everybody who shaped you. Donne was right. We aren't islands."

He took a sip of the pinot grigio. "Nice," he said, "Especially for the price." He cut another bite of the saltimbocca, swirled it in the butter sauce, and popped it in his mouth. "Saltimbocca means 'jumps into your mouth. Did you know that?"

Fiona nodded. "Yes, Seth, I did."

"Anyway, back to making yourself up. People make crummy choices all the time. Including choices about who they want to be. But whether they like it or not, those choices have been shaped by their history, their family, their culture, their religion. For good or ill, that's how it is. So, how autonomous are we? If Irene Stark wants to be a WASPY Protestant, okay, go ahead, Irene. But she would be a Protestant who was born and raised Jewish. When I came out of the Lexington Avenue subway a couple weeks ago, these two young guys dressed all Orthodox, probably Chabad, came up to me and asked ever so politely, 'Are you Jewish, Sir?' Some of the ultra-orthodox feel called to try to make secular Jews—which they thought I might be—into more observant Jews. But they don't feel called to convert gentiles, I mean, Judaism as a religion just doesn't proselytize. "I said, 'I'd be proud to be Jewish, but no, I'm not.' And the one guy said, 'Have a blessed day, my friend,' and patted me on the back. My point is that if I did convert, I'd always be a convert—a Presbyterian who became Jewish—at least in my head. Which is okay, part of my story, but that would always be who I was. And Dan told me that Jews who become Christians are still considered Jews by other Jews."

He poured himself another two inches of wine. Finding himself on a verbal roll, he said, "Did I really choose to be a minister? They say I was called. No voices in the night for me, but I'm not sure I did exactly choose it."

Fiona swirled the last bit of wine in her glass and said, "Like they say, 'You can wear different shoes, but they don't change the size of your foot.' Dad preached a sermon once, years ago. He was baptizing a bunch of babies. A big day for the Canongate Kirk, so he preached about baptism. I was maybe 13. I don't remember much from his sermons I heard in those years, but I remember something he said that day. I remember it because I hated it. He said, 'Baptism'—that would be your God-given identity—'saves us from the tyranny of having to invent ourselves.' It's haunted me ever since. Probably because I've always been afraid he was right. Let's get home, Seth."

* * *

Ludington's cell rang at nine-forty-five the next morning, Tuesday. "Hello? Father Ludington? It's Agent Brian O'Reilly. I'm at your church's door. Sign says to call this number."

Seth, who had been in his study for nearly an hour awaiting O'Reilly's arrival, said, "I'll be right down."

Agent O'Reilly was not alone, but was accompanied by a person Ludington assumed to be another FBI agent, a woman even younger than O'Reilly. O'Reilly was clearly not typically Irish. He wore a dark suit, perfectly cut, and a gray tie just the right width. He was tall, taller even than Ludington. He was very slender and Black.

He introduced himself, produced an ID card, and said, "This is Agent Willa Norton. Thank you for seeing us, Father."

Ludington was not wearing a collar, but still got the Roman Catholic—or maybe Episcopalian—form of address. He was surprised that O'Reilly had not realized that the word "Presbyterian" between words "Old Stone" and "Church" on the sign to the left of the door the man had just entered through signified an iteration of Protestant and that the great majority of Protestant clergy eschewed the patriarchal title. But then, "Presbyterian" is Greek to most people.

"Just call me 'Reverend Ludington,' or better yet, make it 'Seth.'" He extended a hand, first to O'Reilly, then to Norton.

O'Reilly smiled slightly and said, "We need to take the scrolls, the scrolls from Beth Shalom Synagogue, to the lab for some testing. As I said, we have been brought in to assist NYPD Hate Crimes with their investigations into the vandalism and fire. Rabbi Gellman and his administrator informed us that the scrolls are in your procession."

"Dan asked me to put them somewhere safe. They're precious. Not so much valuable as, well, invaluable. Follow me, if you would. I locked them up in the church safe."

He led the two FBI agents to the room off the sanctuary that housed Old Stone's giant and usually superfluous safe. Agent Norton whistled when she saw it, "What do you guys keep in there?"

Ludington said, "Old communion silver and Torah scrolls."

He spun the dial, the combination now committed to memory, pulled the lock lever down, and yanked the mighty door open. It protested with a screech.

Ludington nodded to the safe's interior, "There are three of them. One of them is pretty old and a bit fragile."

Both agents had donned black rubber gloves. "We'll be careful, Reverend Ludington. We should have them back in a week or so. Rabbi Gellman said to return them here."

Ludington stepped back to watch how the agents handled the scrolls. He felt increasingly protective of them. He offered the agents the rolling kitchen cart he had used to ferry them from the cab to the safe, but O'Reilly and Norton refused it, carrying the scrolls gingerly, one at a time, to the unmarked white van double-parked on 82nd Street. He could see that they were taking care not to touch the handles of the scrolls, even though their hands were rubber-clad. When the third scroll, which Ludington recognized as the Holocaust Scroll, had been carefully laid on the carpeted floor of the van, O'Reilly gave Ludington a document he named "a receipt" and said he would be in touch.

Standing with O'Reilly on the sidewalk as Agent Norton moved to take the driver's seat of the van, Seth decided to say something about Lawrence Gollancz. "Are you aware that a member—a pretty prominent member—of Beth Shalom Synagogue died suddenly the night after the vandalism? I know about it because Rabbi Gellman asked me to drive him out to Long Island the next day. That's where the man died. Carbon monoxide poisoning." Ludington avoided clichés like "under suspicious circumstances" even though he was increasingly suspicious of the circumstances.

"Yes. Suffolk PD gave us a call. The Suffolk County Coroner has ruled the death accidental."

O'Reilly said no more, leaving Ludington unsure whether that answer meant that they or Suffolk Homicide were investigating Lawrence Gollancz's demise or that they were not doing so. Agent O'Reilly, like most good cops, said not a word more than he had to.

Ludington was still on the sidewalk in front of Old Stone Church, watching the white van weave its way through several other double-parked cars on 82nd Street, when his cell vibrated in the vest pocket of his blazer. He fished it out to see that it was from a 631 area code—Long Island.

"Hello. This is Seth Ludington."

"Reverend Ludington, this is Officer Marge Anderson, Asharoken PD. I'm calling because of… well…, because of the vandalism and the fire at Lawrence Gollancz's synagogue in the City and those death threats you and the rabbi told us about. And now there's something else. We contacted Suffolk Homicide about the letters, but I haven't heard anything. And the ME did do an autopsy, and they have confirmed accidental death. I called and asked last Friday. I don't know if they're going anywhere with it, Suffolk County PD, I mean. Anyway, I just phoned them again about something else, something that happened over the weekend, and I thought you and the rabbi might want to know about it as well. How's he doing, by the way?"

"Still in the hospital, but improving. Putting on a good face, of course. So what is it, Officer Anderson?" What happened over the weekend, I mean?"

"Late Saturday night or early Sunday morning, somebody plastered homes on the Neck and in Asharoken, and parts of Northport too, with these antisemitic leaflets. Hung them on doorknobs and slipped them in mailboxes in the middle of the night. I did some checking, and it seems this has become a strategy for extremists. Avoids the internet. Hard to trace, and not necessarily even illegal. But with what you told me about those letters to Gollancz…well, maybe there's some sort of connection. I called Suffolk Homicide again, told them about the leaflets. They said that they'd refer it to Hate Crimes."

Ludington was silent for a moment.

"Reverend Ludington, you still there?"

"Officer Anderson, what did they say, these leaflets?"

I'll take photos of one of them, both sides and text them to you. I just thought you should know. Maybe you could mention it to NYPD or the FBI. Whoever's working on the synagogue stuff."

Ludington clenched his teeth as he zoomed into the black and red text of the leaflets in the two photos that had just pinged his phone. They were close-ups of the back and front. Red bullet points and black text offering the usual antisemitic tropes and conspiracy nonsense. The convoluted logic concluded that a "secret, international consortium of rich Jews" was "plotting to replace White Americans with lesser races." It ended with a call to the "right-thinking White Christian majority of this great country to rise up in resistance." Then, "It's high time to fight back!" No swastikas, no runic SS, no mention of George Soros or Hillary Clinton, just three letters in Gothic script on the bottom of the second page—"ADL." Ludington sighed and went back into the church and to his second-floor study.

Chapter Seventeen

Tuesday

Van der Berg had not been in her little office when Ludington arrived to meet the FBI agents. After they left, he went to his study and sat at his desk, musing. He pulled out his phone and looked again at the photos Anderson had sent him. He moved to delete them. He could not tolerate even having them exist on his phone. But then a thought came to him, and he decided to leave them be, at least for a day or two. As he slid the phone back into his jacket pocket, he heard Harriet trooping up the steps. She went not to her office, but straight into his study, entering without so much as a knock. She wore the smug smile that always betrayed some victory. She was breathless, maybe from the quick climb up the stairs to the second floor of the Old Stone Parish House, or perhaps from excitement.

She sat down in the chair in front of his desk and said, "Seth, I have found our caterer. That is to say, I have found the woman who catered Lawrence Gollancz's dinner with his sister and her family on the Sunday evening prior to his death. I had to make no fewer than nineteen phone calls—nineteen! Many of them twice, but I located her. One Shar Conlin. Delightful woman and quite loquacious. Happily so for us, I should say. She said she would be delighted to speak with us. I imagine she is the kind of person who is always delighted to speak."

"Well done, Miss van der Berg, well done." Despite her solid self-confidence, Ludington knew Harriet welcomed a dollop of praise once and again.

She dipped her head, but barely, and said, "Thank you, Seth. As I said, I found her on the nineteenth call."

Seth nodded in recognition of such considerable effort and said, "I think we should talk to her in person, not on the phone. People sometimes clam up on the phone. Face-to-face with your smiling visage, Harriet, and some good food plus a glass of wine or two, words are more likely to flow. So, another foray onto lovely Long Island. Would you call her back and tell her we'll take her to lunch? Her choice of venue. Chefs like to eat out, I imagine."

"I shall telephone her forthwith."

"Harriet, I'm going to run over to Weill Cornell and visit Dan. Lilly says he's up for it. He's getting restless, she said. I'll work on the stuff for the bulletin when I get back. Promise. Maybe Roger can pick the hymns again this week."

Roger Gretz was the church's part-time, pretty-good organist and choir director. When Ludington had first been called as Old Stone's minister, Gretz had been put out when Seth told him he liked to choose the Sunday hymns himself. "That way, I can fit them to the texts and the sermon, you know." If Roger was still carrying any chagrin over the matter, he did not betray it. But he was always pleased when Seth asked him to select the hymns.

"I shall also telephone Mr. Gretz. Should I inform him that you will be using the assigned lectionary Scripture readings for the day in order to guide his selection? And shall I tell him the subject of the sermon to better coordinate his choices?"

"Yes, I guess so. I mean the lectionary. Sure." Ludington had not looked at the texts for the coming Sunday and did not recall what they were. But haste again committed him to use them, whatever they might be. He had no idea what his sermon was going to be about. It was only Tuesday.

"While you visit Rabbi Gellman and I await the bulletin information, I plan to 'go on YouTube' as they say. We both heard Chelsea Stark declare her intention to produce a series of video presentations based on her uncle's death and to place them on that particular internet platform." She gave Seth a sly look and said, "What she makes of her uncle's death could be of interest to us, *n'est-ce pas?*"

Seth tipped his head to the side in reply, again taken aback by both the woman's dogged curiosity and her comfort with technologies more the province of the young.

Harriet said, "If she has done as she said she was going to, her video presentations should not be difficult to find. Her brother called her 'Chelsea Bun' when they spoke of her project. I am guessing he was suggesting that 'Chelsea Bun' was her social media name or address. It may well have been a parent's pet name for her when she was a child. Rather sweet, but I do wonder if either of them knows what a Chelsea bun is."

Ludington decided to cab it down the Weill Cornell. He was happy to see that Dan Gellman was no longer confined to a bed twenty-four hours a day. Seth found him sitting up in the more comfortable of the two chairs in his room in the burn unit. One of his hands was still heavily bandaged. When Ludington entered, the rabbi was poking rapidly at the screen of his cell phone with the index finger of his unbound hand.

"I had just learned to text with two thumbs, and now they take one away. It's good to see you, Seth. Sit down. Pull that chair over." He pointed with the bandaged hand to a pink fiberglass chair pushed up against the wall.

"Texting with Lilly. She's going to bring Zack for a visit later. We got permission. He's been asking about his Daddy."

Seth dragged the pink chair to a position a yard from his friend. "How you doing, Dan?"

"Honestly, pretty good. Hurts off and on, but they hand out plenty of fine meds. Docs are saying they're going to release me before the weekend. Healing well, they say, but they worry about infection. I'm so ready to be out of here. So tell me everything. What have you and the indomitable Miss van der Berg been up to while I've been lounging in bed?"

Seth outlined their discoveries carefully, most of which were already familiar to Gellman—the muddy earth by both the generator and the junction box where its cord plugged into the house, the three sets of footprints, Harriet's plaster of Paris castings, the pair of clean boots by the back door and the fact that they matched one set of prints, the lack of available water to clean them, and then the receipt on the garage floor indicating that Gollancz had purchased an extension cord forty feet longer than the one running from the generator to the house the night of his death.

Gellman took this in and said, "Curious, altogether curious. It's like working a jigsaw puzzle and having a piece or two that don't fit anywhere."

Ludington shrugged his shoulders in solidarity with his friend's mystification. He then related the tale of his and Harriet's attendance at the curious shiva, as well as his impressions of the Stark family. Then he told Dan about Marge Anderson's phone call and the antisemitic literature that had flooded Gollancz's neighborhood like a backed-up sewer—screeds signed by a bunch calling themselves the 'ADL.' Gellman's face morphed into a blank mask. Seth paused before he told Dan about the ADL bumper sticker on the rear of Masterson's Ford Taurus. When presented with that detail, Gellman closed his eyes.

So you think Masterson is some sort of Nazi? I can't help thinking about Lawrence's death, death by poisonous gas."

"Looks like he is, or something like that. You remember how cool he was toward you when I said you were Gollancz's rabbi? Wouldn't shake your hand. Then he started to come at you."

Gellman nodded and shifted the subject back to the curiosities surrounding footprints and extension cords. He said, "Lawrence's boots by the back door. No mud on them, you say. And no water to clean them." Yet they're a match for one of the sets in the mud. I mean, if somebody else put the generator under his window like we're speculating, it just doesn't figure, does it? But then there's the missing fifty-foot cord. Why buy it and not use it?"

Dan Gellman went silent, trying to work sums that didn't add up. Seth thought to himself that this modern Daniel must have some of the ancient Daniel's detective DNA in him. "I need to think about this, Seth."

Ludington noticed his friend wince as he spoke. Burn injuries are painful he knew, even when they were healing. As Seth left the room, he turned back to his friend, gave him a thumbs up, and said, "I'll shoot some Christian prayers up for you, if you don't mind."

"The more the better." As he left the room, Seth thought to himself, '*Shoot prayers?*' I mean, really, Reverend Ludington."

When he returned to Old Stone, he found van der Berg in her cubicle of an office. Without looking away from her computer monitor, she said, "Seth, you must view these video presentations. As I guessed, they were prepared by one 'Chelsea Bun.' But in truth, I found them by simply searching for 'murder mystery,' and 'gasoline generator.' YouTube has a great many such true crime videos, but I happened upon hers quite quickly. Do sit down, Seth. Sit next to me and watch. Quite interesting, I must say."

Van der Berg wiggled her mouse and hit play. Chelsea Irene Stark appeared on the screen, a microphone in her hand, clad in a beige trench coat to make her look like a noir detective and—comically and incongruously—a deerstalker on her head to make her look like Sherlock Holmes. She was standing in the aisle of some big box store in front of a display of portable gas generators, the brand names of which were blacked out.

Van der Berg said, "All of this is magnificently adolescent. The trench coat and the deerstalker mix detective tropes unforgivably."

Chelsea began to speak. "*Larry Golden was wealthy. He was also very smart. And he is dead. So here's the question that haunts his family, the very mystery we are going to probe in this series.... Why in the world would he place his brand new portable gas generator, just like this one.*" Here Chelsea made a sweeping gesture to the display behind her. "*And place it directly under the window of the bedroom of his palatial estate, the very bedroom he was sleeping in the night of a storm that cut power over all of New Jersey? Everyone knows not to do that. Carbon monoxide, you know. It says so on the box.*" Another gesture to the stack of gas generators in the store's display. "*So follow me, Chelsea Bun, as we dive deeper into the mystery of the gas generator. Episode Two coming soon.*" She signed off by sticking a meerschaum pipe in her mouth.

Harriet looked at Seth and rolled her eyes, "That was posted a week ago tomorrow."

Seth said, "She's altered names and moved it to New Jersey. None too subtle. But the storm, the generator under the bedroom window, the carbon monoxide, and more to the point, Harriet, she's thinking murder. Whether she believes it or not, somebody in the Stark family is thinking murder, even if they're just playing with the idea."

"Wait till you see Episode Two."

Van der Berg scrolled down the YouTube feed to find *"The Gas Generator Mystery, Episode Two."* The opening seconds of the video were obviously recorded during her uncle's funeral at Campbell Brothers' Funeral Home the previous Sunday. Chelsea must have held her phone close in front of her chest. It first showed Larry Gollancz's casket, then panned to the lectern from which the guest rabbi and her mother would soon speak, and then back to the closed casket. Innocuous pre-recorded organ music played softy under the visual. It was no more than ten seconds and carefully revealed no faces, only the backs of heads. Organ music and casket set the spooky mood for episode two. Chelsea then appeared on screen, still absurdly in her deerstalker and trench coat, speaking reporter-like into a microphone and standing audaciously on the expansive front lawn of her late uncle's Eaton's Neck home.

"The very night before his untimely death, Larry Golden hosted a dinner party for his brother, sister-in-law, and their two children at his New Jersey mansion. Chelsea stepped quickly to the side and out of the frame to reveal the façade of Lawrence Gollancz's Long Island house. *"In the course of that fateful evening, he disclosed the fact that he intended to alter his will away from his only family in favor of his church in Newark. As noted in Episode One, Larry Golden was an extremely wealthy man. This news did not sit well with his gathered family, who had long been anticipating that they would inherit extremely well."* Chelsea dragged out the word "extremely" and then said in a parenthetical voice, *"Larry Golden was, I should note, much older than his brother. Well, as you might imagine, the family was outraged that fateful night. In fact, one of the brother's kids, the son, left the dinner in a fury after vowing retaliation. Follow Chelsea Bun for Episode Three, in which the plot really thickens."* The meerschaum pipe was again produced and popped between unsmiling lips.

Seth sighed and said, "Chelsea Bun has rearranged the family. Made

Gollancz's sister into a brother. But more to the point, she just threw Hudson under the bus. Harriet, she threw her own brother under the bus."

113

Chapter Eighteen

Wednesday

En route to their lunchtime assignation with Lawrence Gollancz's personal chef, the eastbound Northern State was moving along well on a midweek morning in late August. Harriet did not notice the traffic—or much else, for that matter—as she had become enraptured by YouTube over the last twenty hours. She was on her phone even before she and Seth crossed the RFK Bridge onto Long Island.

"Why, Seth, look at this. YouTube offers video presentations teaching one how to speak Portuguese, and there are any number instructing one how to jumpstart your automobile should its battery die. Have you ever jumpstarted an automobile?"

Adventure always made the woman loquacious. And as with many people who lived alone, sequestered words burst the dam of solitude when she found herself in company.

"Yes, in college. On a frigid morning in Ann Arbor, after I left the headlights on overnight. That was the old PV544. You remember Inga. This was before cars turned off the lights for you if you forgot. But I didn't need YouTube. My roommate was all I needed—him, jumper cables, and his Ford Bronco."

"Well, there may be a plethora of video presentations demonstrating the practice of jumpstarting, but there is nary another from Chelsea Bun regarding what she has named 'The Gas Generator Mystery.' But I shall continue my searching."

At Shar Conlin's request, Ludington had made a twelve-thirty reservation for a table for three at the Mill Pond House Restaurant in Centerport. As he parked, they discovered that the Mill Pond House was indeed located on a mill pond, a southern finger of Centerport Harbor just west of Northport and its larger eponymous harbor. And the Mill Pond House was a house, or it appeared to have once been one, though now much expanded. As he had requested, they were seated at a water-view table.

"Linen tablecloths," said Harriet, "even for lunch. I do approve."

Seth scanned the encyclopedic menu as they waited for Shar Conlin to arrive. It naturally listed toward the sea, offering fish of vast variety and varied preparation, plus pricey steaks, more reasonable pasta dishes, and—for lunch only, he assumed—several sandwich selections.

Just as Seth decided on chicken Milanese to compare it with that served at the Lex, the smiley young hostess approached their table, followed by a woman of medium height, a tad plump, dressed in loose-fitting gray slacks and a white short-sleeved blouse. Her hair was cut just above the neck in a page boy with bangs. It did not appear to have been dyed, turning from brown to gray as it was. She was pleasantly attractive and made more so by the smile that burst over her face as she extended her hand, first to Seth and then to Harriet, both of whom had stood to welcome her.

When Harriet had called her the day before, she had explained their interest in Gollancz's next-to-the-last supper on the grounds that "her boss," as she had named Ludington, was "acting in the interest of Rabbi Daniel Gellman." She had then noted the matter of the will and added that she, "Ludington's professional assistant," would be accompanying him for the interview. The impression she had intended to make—successfully it appeared—was that she and Seth Ludington were some iteration of hired investigators. Though, of course, she had never used any such words.

"Miss van der Berg, I presume. And you must be Mr. Ludington."

As the hostess pulled the third chair away from the table for her, Shar Conlin sat, pulled the chair back to the table herself, and took the conversational initiative. This, Seth judged, was a self-possessed and confident woman. Probably a dependable witness.

"I am so very pleased to be of some assistance. Poor dear Mr. Gollancz. He would want me to help square things away. I cooked for him for—let me think—eleven years now. Not that often, maybe once a month, but more after his wife died. He was helpless in the kitchen."

When their waitress arrived and asked if they'd like to start with "something to drink," Seth selected a nice Poully-Fuisse as Shar had already declared her intention of ordering fish and a preference for white wine. She ordered first, the Mediterranean Bronzino, then Harriet, a wedge salad with blue cheese, and Seth, his predictable chicken Milanese.

When the bottle arrived, he poured Shar a generous glass and then a shorter one for himself. Harriet showed her palm when he moved the bottle in her direction. Seth guessed she wanted to make certain there would be enough Poully-Fuisse to lubricate their guest's conversation.

It soon became apparent that Shar Conlin's conversation needed little lubrication. They were only halfway through their meals, and she most of the way through her second generous pour of wine (which she pronounced "superb") when she launched into a narrative of what she named "the night of the big dinner."

"I was in the kitchen cleaning up. I had served gazpacho to start, then a spinach salad with dried cherries and blue cheese crumbles, broiled salmon with asparagus as the entrée, cold of course. Out of season, but it's what Lawrence wanted. It was a beastly hot evening. They were eating inside because of the heat, so I could hardly help hearing them." She paused and took another sip of wine. "I mean, it got loud."

Harriet nodded encouragement. Seth poured encouragement into Shar's nearly empty wine glass.

"I heard Mr. Gollancz tell them he was altering his will somewhat. I remember that last word, 'somewhat.' There were five for dinner, Lawrence of course, his sister and her husband. He's in a wheelchair. Did you know that? And then their two children, a tall skinny kid, college age, I'd guess, and a daughter, high school probably, with dyed hair, very dyed hair."

Shar was clearly relishing both the memory and the telling of the tale.

"The sister—Irene, that's her name—said, 'Altered somewhat? In what way altered somewhat?'"

The only part of his answer I could hear was 'synagogue,' but there was a lot more I couldn't quite make out. And then all hell broke loose. Yelling… 'How can you do that? It's family money, Lawrence. Our father made it.' Finally, I heard her scream, 'synagogue schminagogue.' Then I went back to the sink to wash up."

Seth guessed that last detail was an unintended confession to having had an ear plastered to the door between the dining room and the kitchen.

He said only, "This is helpful, Ms. Conlin. One question. When Mr. Gollancz spoke of the altered will, did he say he had already signed it, or did he speak of signing it in the future tense?"

"Future tense? You mean, did he say he was going to sign it, but hadn't yet? That he was going to? I don't know what he said about signing. Like I said, by then I was at the sink with the water running. What I know is they all left before the key lime pie. Homemade. Mrs. Stark and the daughter loaded her husband into their big SUV thing. The kid—I think his name is Hudson—he was pissed. I mean, the kid was pissed." Startled at the word she had just uttered, she mumbled, "Sorry," and took another sip of the Poully-Fuisse. "I mean angry." She looked at Harriet as if to apologize to a woman who was old enough to be her mother and said in a softer voice, "Well, what I mean is that he left first, left in his own car. Roared off up the driveway."

Seth ordered three double cappuccinos in lieu of dessert. He knew Harriet liked her coffee after lunch, and he thought Shar needed it, if only for the time it would take to drink it and inch into sobriety.

When he and Harriet climbed into the Volvo, he sat for a moment, staring at the calm water of Centerport Mill Pond. "Well, we learned at least two things. First, Lawrence Gollancz did exactly what he told Atkins he was going to do. He told his sister and her family that Temple Beth Shalom was going to inherit the bulk of his estate, and he did it at that Sunday night dinner. Second, it was not, to quote Irene, 'delightful.' More like Chelsea's 'war in Afghanistan.'"

He paused, tapped the steering wheel, and said, "Harriet, it's only two-thirty, and here we are out on the Island. How about we kill some more birds with this stone? Maybe we could drop in on the lawyer, What's-His-Name Atkins. And, well, I'd like to visit Eaton's Neck once again and make an unannounced call on Mr. George Masterson. I have something I'd like to show him. And there's one other little thing to check on at the Gollancz estate."

Harriet nodded, but refrained from asking either what Seth wanted to show George Masterson or what it was he wanted to look for at Gollancz's house. He would tell her when he was ready. Fifty years working for shiny-shoe Wall Street litigators had taught her when to ask questions and when not to ask questions.

* * *

Seth found Dan Gellman's number in his iPhone contacts. The rabbi picked up on the first ring. "Dan, Harriet, and I are out on the Island. We just had an interesting lunch with the caterer. Now I'm going to pay a call on George Masterson and then I'm going to sneak about the Gollancz house to check on something. But while we're out here, I thought we might pay lawyer Atkins a visit. Could you maybe help make that happen? I mean, give the guy a call and tell him—I don't know—tell him that I'm your representative or something?"

"Of course, of course. I'll phone him right now and get back to you. Man, I wish I were there doing this."

"I do, too. Dan, see if four or four-thirty works for him. We're headed out to Eaton's Neck now."

Ludington's phone rang ten minutes later as they were turning off 25A into Northport Village and towards Eaton's Neck. Gellman's name popped up on the Volvo's screen. "Seth, it's Dan. We're in luck. I told Atkins about the synagogue fire and mentioned that I'm in the hospital because of it. I said I had asked you to pay him a visit about the new will. Said I would do so myself if I weren't in the burn unit. Milked it a bit, I did. If the guy wondered why this couldn't be accomplished by a phone call or email, he didn't say so. Told me that he'd already heard about the fire and my injuries. So I said you just happened to be in Huntington, and was he maybe available this afternoon? I suggested four-thirty, and he said that'd be fine, any time before five. He sounds older. My guess is he's semi-retired. Anyway, I'll text you the address. If he was curious as to why a minister was playing surrogate for a rabbi, he said nothing."

Thanks, Dan, thanks. I'll keep you up to speed."

Ludington punched the screen to end the call and said to van der Berg, "So Miss van der Berg, let's get ourselves to Eaton's Neck and gird our loins for what will doubtless be an encounter every bit as delightful as that Sunday family dinner."

Chapter Nineteen

Wednesday

George Masterson's dark gray Ford Taurus was parked in his single-car garage, the door of which was open. As Ludington pulled up and parked behind it, the first thing both he and van der Berg noticed was that the "Take America Back ADL" bumper sticker was no longer on the rear end of the car.

"Interesting," was all Harriet said.

"I doubt his sentiments have changed, Harriet. But perhaps he's a bit more reluctant to advertise them than he was a week ago."

Seth never relished confrontation, avoiding it as often as he could, and, if unavoidable, postponing it as long as he could manage. But a rare indignation still burned in his breast, fanned hot by Dan Gellman's bandaged hand and the charred hulk of Beth Shalom, still smoldering when he had driven by that morning on his way to pick up van der Berg.

He pulled out his phone, went to his photo file, and scrolled past sweet shots of the twins sitting up on their own to find the toxic photographs of the front and back of one of the flyers the ADL had left on doors and in mailboxes all over Eaton's Neck, Asharoken, and Northport.

"Harriet, let me do this one alone. I want to, and it could be unpleasant."

Van der Berg nodded in acquiescence, but said, "You really think I cannot manage unpleasantness?"

When Masterson answered the door, he didn't seem to recognize Ludington at first. Seth wasn't wearing his clerical collar for this visit. They were separated by a screen door. The man stared through it at Ludington, but did not speak.

In a near whisper and slowly, Seth said, "We met about a week ago. I was here with your former neighbor's rabbi. His synagogue was vandalized, then burned to the ground." Then he held his phone up to Masterson's face, confronting him with the photos of the poisonous flyer. He then said, even more slowly and softly, "Could there be a connection? Look familiar?"

"I don't know what you're talking about. Get the hell off my property." With that, Masterson shut the door in Seth's face, mumbling "Jew lover" as he did so.

Ludington got back in the Volvo and wordlessly raised an eyebrow at Harriet.

He didn't drive deep into Gollancz's driveway next door. He didn't want to get too close to the house, especially not its front door. He stopped at the top of the drive, just off the road, and said to Harriet, "Won't take a minute." He walked toward the house, not on the driveway, but on the grass far to its right and well away from the house. Then he slithered along the front of the garage to a spot near the corner of the house. He saw what he wanted to see and returned to the car by the same circuitous route. He backed the still-running car out of the drive onto the road and said to Harriet, "Yep, he's got one."

"One what?"

"One Ring doorbell camera mounted by the front door."

"Don't all doorbells ring?"

"This kind does more. It takes little videos of everybody who comes to visit. Or everyone or everything that walks or drives by it. Then stores them for posterity, or as much posterity as you want to pay for."

"So, I suppose your stealth was intended to avoid being video recorded by this device."

"Well, the thing already has plenty of footage of you and me in its little brain. Probably not the best idea to leave yet another video calling card."

"But Seth, who can access these videos? Surely not just anyone."

"You can access them on the phone or computer which the thing was set up on, of course. The owner's usually."

"And he's dead."

As they drove away, Seth said, "When I saw that his sister had one of the things at her house in Speonk, I started wondering if maybe Lawrence had one as well. The sight of it at the Starks' reminded me of the technology. I know about them because my parents have three, one at each of their places. Anyway, the Starks' Ring doorbell got me thinking—Gollancz's big house, a bit secluded, often empty. Just like my mom and dad's places."

Van der Berg harrumphed, "An automated camera built into one's doorbell. I much prefer my doorman."

As they drove back along the Asharoken strip, Ludington phoned Marge Anderson. "Officer Anderson, This is Seth Ludington. So, well, I happened to be in the neighborhood, and I was wondering if you could spare me a minute."

"Just happened to be in the neighborhood, eh? Okay. I'm in my car, just leaving the station. Let's meet in the Asharoken Beach parking lot in five. I have something I should probably tell you."

She was leaning against the driver's door of her marked car when Seth and Harriet pulled in the parking lot. The place was full of moms and dads herding tired, cranky, sun-burned children back into their SUVs after a blistering afternoon at the beach. Seth and Fiona had recently ventured to an East Coast beach with their girls. Having been raised on sugar-sand Lake Michigan beaches, blessedly free of salt, horseshoe crabs, sharks, and crowds, Ludington had been unimpressed. Seth was about to suggest that Harriet again wait in the car, but she was out the door and standing beside him facing Marge Anderson before he could say anything.

He introduced her to Anderson as his administrative assistant, to which Harriet said, "He means secretary."

Anderson was bright enough to guess that she was an unlikely partner in his amateur sleuthing. She first asked after Dan Gellman.

After Seth's report on Gellman's recovery, Anderson said, "So, when you told us about the ADL bumper sticker on George Masterson's car, we decided to pay him a visit. It's illegal to put anything other than official mail in a mailbox designated as such. People do it all the time, but it's actually a federal offense. Our guess is that he's maybe our hate flyer guy, but nobody saw him doing it, so we can't press any charges, at least not yet. But I have to tell you, the guy got really spooked."

Harriet said, "Well, he's taken the bumper sticker off his car."

"I bet he did. I mean, he blanched when we talked to him, went white as a sheet. It was me and the chief."

Ludington said, "Maybe nobody saw him doing it, but people have these doorbell cameras, right?"

Anderson raised an eyebrow, "Ahead of you, Rev. Ludington. We're going to try to get access to some. People can share videos, and a bunch of folks have agreed to do so."

Seth paused, looked Anderson in the eyes, and said, "You know, Lawrence Gollancz has a Ring doorbell. It would be interesting to see if it recorded anyone who might have been around his place the night of the storm, the night he died."

Anderson looked intrigued. "Well, he can't share his stored videos, even if they're still around. And the legal process to access them without the registrant's cooperation is onerous. We're talking search warrants, subpoenas, and time. These security camera companies are particular about privacy. Unless there's an open investigation, there's just no way for quick third-party access without permission."

Harriet listened to Anderson's pessimism. She hesitated before saying, a conspiratorial edge to her voice, "One must wonder where Lawrence Gollancz's cell phone is. Officer Anderson, did you not tell Mr. Ludington and the rabbi that you used it to find his sister's phone number the morning his body was discovered? I assume you simply held the side buttons on his iPhone to access the SOS slider and the emergency numbers stored therein."

Marge Anderson offered an almost comic head jerk to signal her surprise that an antique woman, a near-octogenarian, could be so tech-savvy. She looked at Harriet van der Berg with fresh regard.

"Yes, that's exactly what I did."

Van der Berg sighed theatrically and said, "If only we had his mobile telephone. One could then perhaps access any such Ring doorbell video recordings which may exist."

The cop nodded her head in agreement.

Seth thanked Anderson as he and Harriet climbed back in the Volvo. He started the car, punched the address for Atkin's law office that Dan had texted him into the navigation system, backed carefully out of the narrow parking space, and turned right onto Asharoken Avenue. He wended his way through Northport to 25A and then made another right turn toward Huntington Village.

Though a mere six miles west of Northport, Huntington felt cosmopolitan by comparison. The nav voice led them to Charles Atkins's office, located on the second floor of a nondescript building just off New York Avenue in the downtown business district.

As Ludington parked the car, he said to van der Berg, "Harriet, there's no way I can explain your presence to Atkins. You okay sitting this one out?" As much as she ached to be there, she understood and nodded assent.

The demure brass plaque to the left of the lawyer's office's door read, "Charles Atkins, Attorney at Law." Seth was unsure whether he needed to knock before entering, so he cracked the door a few inches and called out, "Hello?"

Silver-haired and old-school, in shirt sleeves and a nautical tie on a hot summer day, Charles Atkins greeted Seth warmly, if warily. "Charles Atkins, Attorney at Law" was clearly a one-lawyer operation housed in a single, though nice-sized and graciously furnished room. There was but one desk, a yacht-sized piece of craftsman oak. There was no place for a receptionist, much less a legal assistant. After self-introductions, Atkins gestured for Ludington to sit on the leather Chesterfield couch against the wall opposite the giant desk. The lawyer sat in one of the two wing chairs on either side of the coffee table in front of the couch. Seth moved to break the ice by sharing his impression of Huntington's relative urbanity.

"You're quite right, Rev. Ludington, Huntington does feel more—well—urban, than everything to the east of us on the Island. We're the last electric stop on the North Shore line. You have to change trains from Manhattan for Northport and beyond. Adds time and trouble to the commute. So we're more of a commuter town than places east of here."

Atkins explained the solo office as semi-retirement. Dan had guessed correctly. "I had a pretty big firm in town, two partners, legal assistants, receptionist, the works. I like to practice law, but only just as much as I want. And with staff, all the HR nonsense got so tiresome. Now I get to work with only the people I want to work with. Larry Gollancz was one of them. Great guy. What does his tribe say? A mensch. I was flabbergasted by his death."

Ludington rehearsed the reason for his visit, namely the last will and testament of said Lawrence Gollancz, and that he was there on behalf of his friend, the hospitalized Rabbi of Temple Beth Shalom, a putative beneficiary. This tale of his role as representative of the rabbi of a synagogue sounded as lame to Ludington as it did when Dan had first suggested it. If Atkins was curious about it, he said nothing. Lawyers know when to ask questions and when not to. Atkins simply nodded to Ludington to continue.

Seth did so. "I understand the synagogue is a major beneficiary in the revised will you drew up on Mr. Gollancz's behalf. You may know that he had not informed the synagogue or Rabbi Gellman of his intentions. Rabbi Gellman only learned of it from your phone call after Mr. Gollancz's death. And he does not, of course, have a copy of the new will."

"Well, I drove the original over to Larry for him to review and sign the week before he died. He told me he wanted to look it through first. He would've had to have it witnessed, of course. There have to be at least two witnesses. It was a major alteration. The old will had left nearly all of his estate to the sister, with substantial bequests—quite substantial—to his nephew and niece. But you're right, the new will made the synagogue the largest beneficiary by far. Significant, but more modest bequests to the family. I have a duplicate copy here, but unsigned and unwitnessed, so it means nothing."

"Did Mr. Gollancz indicate to you exactly when he planned to sign it?"

"No. He just said he planned to tell his sister about the change. He was going to have them over for dinner, her and her family. Break the news to them then."

"Do you think he would have waited to sign the will until after he told his sister of his intentions?"

At that question, Charles Atkins, who had been surprisingly transparent, grew more guarded. Seth guessed he was thinking he had already said too much.

"I can't say, but I do know that the two of them were not close, either in age or affection. That fact was no secret."

"One last purely legal question, Mr. Atkins. You say there must be two witnesses at the signing of a will in New York State. Can they be anyone?"

"Theoretically, anybody can sign except beneficiaries, though blood relatives can be a problem. And with a large estate, it would be wise to have it notarized as well."

Atkins rubbed his hands together as if washing them, "I wish I could be of more help to you and Rabbi Gellman."

If that last sentence were not a clear enough dismissal, the fact that Charles Atkins—courtly as he was—stood and looked at his watch made his intention clear.

When he returned to the car, Harriet raised questioning eyebrows, "Well?"

"Not much new. He said there was little love lost between Lawrence and Irene. Though he didn't say so, he implied that Gollancz would not have felt he had to talk to her before he signed the will. Gollancz might have signed it before the not-so-delightful dinner party. Or then maybe he was still looking it over and signed it the next day. And maybe it never did get signed."

Van der Berg nodded, "And one must wonder precisely where it is."

Chapter Twenty

Thursday

Alice Crandall's home health care aid had left a voice message on the church's landline late Wednesday afternoon saying, "Mrs. Crandall would look forward to the opportunity to be served communion, if Pastor Ludington is not too busy."

Pastor Ludington was, in truth, quite busy, though not with matters related to his duties as minister of Old Stone Presbyterian Church. Moreover, he was vaguely uncomfortable with the practice of home communion. In Presbyterian thinking, the Sacrament of Communion was understood to be intrinsically communal, not a private act. When conducted privately on account of the infirmity of a communicant, it was to be considered an extension of a communal celebration of the sacrament and was usually offered soon after such a communion service in church. He called Alice's aid back and asked if early that afternoon would be convenient for Mrs. Crandall.

"Of course, Pastor, about eleven, shall we say?"

All the theology surrounding home communion was quite lost on the housebound Alice Crandall, for whom the sacrament was both a bit of holy magic and a break from the tedium of chatting with her healthcare aide about the latter's troublesome children and the even more tedious tedium of daytime television. And she rather enjoyed having the handsome new minister visit her musty apartment, still decorated and furnished as it had been in 1982. So every month or so, with or without a reminder call, Seth found the little home communion kit that his mother had given him as an ordination gift, cut half a slice of Wonder Bread into a few little cubes, stuffed the other half in his mouth, filled the kit's tiny bottle with Welch's Grape Juice, and phoned Harry Mulholland. Home Communion protocol required an Elder be present in addition to the officiating minister.

Harry was not only an ordained Elder, but Old Stone's Clerk of Session, the highest lay office in a Presbyterian Church. He had also been a friend of Jim Crandall, Alice's late husband, since their Youth Group days at Old Stone. Harry knew that Alice was lonely, her less-than-attentive children having gone west to California to seek their fortunes in the land of tech, the present iteration of a gold rush. It was not clear what kept Alice Crandall, not yet eighty, housebound. Assorted medical diagnoses added up to ambiguity. Both Harry and Seth suspected abandonment and melancholy and said as much to each other as they rode the elevator to the woman's apartment.

The three of them stationed themselves in their accustomed home communion places in the apartment's parlor, as Alice named the room. Though invited to participate, the aide—a Roman Catholic, she said— absented herself politely. Harry read the Twenty-Third Psalm and First Corinthians 11, Paul's little reflection on the sacrament as practiced—or mispracticed—two thousand years ago. Seth then worked through the sweet and crusty words of the communion liturgy from Henry van Dyke's old *Book of Common Worship,* which he knew Alice favored. He passed around the little silver plate with the three tiny cubes of soft bread and then the shot glasses of deep purple, too-sweet Welch's Grape Juice. As he did so, he recalled reading that Mr. Welch, a teetotaler, had devised a method to forestall the fermentation of the juice of grapes in order to keep real wine out of church. Even though the polite little ceremony seemed to Ludington far removed from the original Last Supper, it pleased and comforted Alice Crandall.

* * *

After extracting themselves from her entreaties to stay for third cups of tea and more stale shortbread, Seth and Harry walked south down 3rd Avenue toward Old Stone Church and Harry's apartment. Aware that Seth and Harriet had their camel noses poked into the tent of matters related to Temple Beth Shalom, the retired cop dared a few questions. As a former professional homicide investigator, nosy amateurs naturally concerned him, even though their two prior forays into sleuthing had won them his reluctant regard.

Seth decided not to tell Harry quite everything. Everything—which ran to plaster castings of footprints, breaking into garages to find receipts for extension cords, oddly clean boots, and interviews with caterers, lawyers, and White nationalist antisemites—would only upset Harry Mulholland and win Seth another lecture on "letting the police do their work." But he decided to tell him about the Torah Scrolls the FBI had taken from his care, the altered will and the license plate. And, having had Harry track down that plate, he had to mention the sudden death of a member of Temple Beth Shalom, one Lawrence Gollancz in whose driveway he had photographed it.

"The story of Gollancz's death was on the news, Harry, but you may not have seen it. A gas generator was running all through the night of those storms, right under the guy's open bedroom window."

"I did see it. Not the kind of thing that usually makes local New York news, but he was the guy with the ice cream trucks, semi-famous."

"Ice cream trucks that made him a great deal of money and created some flak for him recently."

"Yeah, the news picked that up again. The politically incorrect tune the trucks used to play."

Mulholland paused, obviously fitting puzzle pieces together in his detective brain.

Seth said, "And there's the will, Harry. Long Island lawyer recently drew up a new will. It shifted most of Gollancz's estate to the synagogue. He says he delivered it to Gollancz at his home out on Long Island for him to look over and sign. It seems Gollancz told his sister and her family about the change at a Sunday dinner, the same day as the vandalism, a few hours earlier. It went ballistic. I mean the dinner."

"And that plate you had me run?"

"Belongs to the sister. We saw her poking around his house the afternoon after her brother died when I drove Rabbi Gellman out there. Seems the sister and her family had been the primary beneficiaries in the old will and much lesser ones in the second. But nobody knows if he signed it, or even where it is. All kinda makes you wonder, Harry."

"Wills often make you wonder, Seth. You have to guess the sister was at the house looking for something when you saw her. And you can guess what the something was."

Mulholland screwed up his face and said, "And the scrolls. They want them for fingerprints. That's what they're after, of course. What do they look like, these scrolls?"

Seth noted that there were three of them, each large, rather heavy, and bedecked in a velvet cover called a mantel. "And they have handles you normally use to carry them and unroll them when you read from them at services."

"What are they made of, these handle things?"

"Wood or metal. Both in the case of Beth Shalom's."

"If that's how you hold them, they'll find a slew of prints on them. From folks at the synagogue. Doubt they'll find anything."

Mulholland stopped walking and turned to his pastor. "But Gollancz's death was ruled accidental, right?"

"Yep. Doesn't look like anybody's much looking into it."

As they reached the corner near his building, Harry Mulholland offered Ludington a resigned smile and said, "I'm guessing somebody's looking into it. Just be careful, Seth."

When he arrived back at Old Stone, Seth found Harriet pacing back and forth in the hallway just inside the Parish House door. Harriet van der Berg was not a pacer, so he had to guess something had induced her to either agitation or excitement.

"Thank heavens you're back. Come with me to my office. Right now. I mean forthwith, please."

She had turned abruptly away from Seth as soon as he was in the door and led him to the staircase and up to their second-floor offices. Harriet was fit for a woman pushing eighty, and for a moment, Seth thought she might take the steps two at a time. She was barely winded as she parked herself in the chair in front of her computer.

"*Episode Three of The Gas Generator Mystery* has been posted. Early this morning. Dominie, I mean Seth. It hints at a major turning, assuming the girl's silly fiction mirrors reality."

Harriet already had YouTube open and *Episode Three* prepped to play. She tapped the play arrow emphatically with a bony index finger.

"Wait till you see this." Seth bent over to watch.

Chelsea appeared, clad in her trademark trench coat and deerstalker. She used the meerschaum pipe to point into the room of a house. It appeared to be a bedroom. Judging from the Foo Fighters and Imagine Dragons posters plastered on the walls, a teenager's bedroom. Or perhaps that of somebody who was a teenager in 2014. Chelsea entered the room and faced the phone doing the recording, doubtless mounted on a tripod. She began to speak in a theatrically sonorous voice, half an octave lower than her normal tone.

"Viewers of Episodes One and Two of the Gas Generator Mystery will recall that an extremely wealthy elderly gentleman named Larry Golden died under totally mysterious circumstances in New Jersey. He died from the fearsome effects of carbon monoxide that came from a gas-powered generator that was placed under the window of the bedroom in his incredibly huge mansion one night as he slept peacefully. In the last episode, we discovered that the night before his untimely death, he had informed his brother and his family that he planned to change his will toward his church in Newark, leaving his shocked family extremely distraught, as you can totally imagine. None of them was more super upset than the rich guy's extremely temperamental nephew. He ran out of the dinner, squealing his tires and leaving trails in the mansion's driveway. Well, there is a major new development, dear viewers. This nephew, a twenty-year-old with a history of doing lots of drugs, has gone missing—like totally vanished. He didn't come home last night, and no one has been able to contact him. As much grief as he has caused his family over the years, he's never just—you know—disappeared before. This is

your faithful sleuth, Chelsea Bun, reporting live from the distraught family's home in New Jersey. Watch for Episode Four of the Gas Generator Mystery coming extremely soon."

Chelsea Stark groped for the meerschaum pipe she had slipped into the trench coat's pocket after using it as a pointer. She found it at last and stuck it in her mouth upside down. She giggled and turned it right side up.

Harriet said, "The girl must tame her use of adjectives and adverbs. She employs far too many."

Seth raised an eyebrow and said, "Extremely true, totally true. So, Harriet, it would seem Hudson has gone missing. I doubt Chelsea would just make that up if it hadn't happened. I don't think she has the imagination."

"And it would seem the young man may have issues with drug abuse. Such drugs are costly, are they not?"

"They are indeed. And people who do them often go missing. But Hudson vanishing just now is worrisome. And odd. I suppose he could just be back at Hofstra, but Chelsea could find out if he were there easily enough. 'Missing' to her means he's not at home and not answering his phone. Yes, worrisome and odd, but I bet he'll show up."

Their speculation as to the whereabouts of Hudson Stark was interrupted by Ramon, the new very part-time church sexton, poking his head in the door and saying, "Mail" as he deposited a plastic tray with the day's yield of church equipment catalogues and flyers from non-profits dreaming of financial support from Old Stone Church. Little personal correspondence arrived by snail mail anymore. Harriet routinely went through the pile each day, gleaning anything she judged worthy of the pastor's attention and placing it on his desk.

Seth retreated to his office, leaving her to that task, so he might consider the sermon he'd be preaching in three days. He looked up the lectionary passages he had rather carelessly told Harriet to print in the bulletin for the coming Sunday and was reading them when the woman burst into his study without knocking, her customary formality abandoned. She held an opened five-by-seven bubble envelope in her hand.

"Well, you'll never—I mean *never*—guess what has come to us in the mail, overnight express mail." She reached into the envelope and pulled out its contents. Her face alive with excitement, she opened her hand to show Seth what it held. It was an iPhone in a black leather case, a newer iteration, Seth guessed.

Harriet said, "There is no return address on the envelope. It was addressed only to 'Old Stone Presbyterian Church' and posted from a place called 'Commack, New York.' I have no idea where that might be and I have no notion who sent us this device, but I can hazard a guess as to whom it once belonged."

Chapter Twenty-One

Thursday

The phone was dead, totally dead. It had doubtless been sitting somewhere for the last ten days and had not been charged by whoever sent it. Just where it had been sitting and who had express-mailed it to Old Stone Church was a curiosity. Seth rummaged in the left-side drawer of his desk to find the spare Lightning charger he kept there. He guessed the phone to be an iPhone XR. The charger fit. After he'd plugged it in, he looked at van der Berg and said, "We'll just have to be patient, Harriet. This'll take a bit." She responded with an impatient grunt and retreated to her office.

Ludington had one eye trained on the phone's battery icon—still red-orange—that lay before him on his desk. He had his other eye on the beginnings of a hand-written sermon outline that lay to the right of the phone. The phone and the sermon notes, he thought to himself, emblems of his conflicted callings. He castigated himself yet again for having told Harriet two days earlier to "just put in the lectionary texts for the day in this Sunday's program, whatever they are." It had turned out that the Gospel reading was one of several foreshadowings of the cross in Matthew. With antisemitism hanging in the air, any mention of crucifixion could carry a whiff of the blood curse business. The author of the first gospel would, a few chapters later, have the Jerusalem crowd call out to Pilate on the day of Jesus' trial, "His blood be on us and our children." That little nettle of a verse would later grow into theologized hatred of Jews.

The cross would not do, not this Sunday. On the other hand, the reading from the twelfth chapter of Romans could perhaps be preached faithfully to the matter that still lay painfully before the neighborhood and the church. In that section of his longest letter, Paul exhorts the little congregation in the imperial capital—probably a mix of Jews and Gentiles—to "let their love be genuine" and to "weep with those who weep." Old Stone, he thought, could stand to be reminded to weep with Beth Shalom. And some genuine love would help all around. He nodded in relief and jotted down a few rhetorical moves he thought might shape a cogent sermon on sharing grief and outrage. Maybe he'd end up with Paul's injunction to love. Outrage and love: Ludington knew they sometimes intersected in life. He put his Number Two pencil down and glanced at the iPhone next to his notes. The battery icon was green.

"Harriet," he called over his shoulder, rather too loudly and eagerly.

She was in his office in a flash. She pulled the chair across the desk from her pastor close, shoved a framed photo of Fiona and the twins gently aside, planted her elbows where it had been, and said, "Well then, I assume we believe this to be Lawrence Gollancz's device. Shall we hazard a guess that he used his customary four-digit access code, the number of his building on Park Avenue, to open his phone? Just as he used it at the doors of both his synagogue and garage?"

"Worth a try." Seth punched in the number, one-zero-zero-one, remembering it was also the number of Arabian nights Scheherazade managed to delay death by telling one cliffhanger after another. The phone popped open to a sea of app icons. He smiled in satisfaction and flipped through them to find the Ring app.

Harriet watched impatiently. Finally, she could restrain herself no longer and reached for the phone. "Seth, please, I have been online these last hours reviewing how one makes use of the Ring application. I believe I understand it." She did not say, "Better than you do."

It had not been hours, Seth thought to himself. Forty minutes at the most. He handed her the device, having come to regard the woman's tech savvy.

Harriet put on her glasses, poked deliberately at the screen, and said, "Eureka." Seth watched impatiently as she scrolled through what he hoped were short videos Lawrence Gollancz's Ring doorbell had captured. He hoped, even more, that she would find videos captured on the night of Gollancz's death. He could see that she had indeed schooled herself in the navigation of Ring.

Her eyes glued to the phone, van der Berg finally said, "There are dozens of videos taken the day after he died, of course. Look at this one. Irene Stark at the door. This is doubtless precisely when you and Rabbi Gellman spotted her as you were leaving." She continued to scroll through videos. "Here are assorted official vehicles passing by the camera. Here's the gurney with his body being wheeled out of the front door. How sad. Lots of you and Rabbi Gellman and that nice local policewoman we chatted with."

Seth, impatient with her methodical review, said, "Harriet, it's Monday evening and night that matter." He rose and pulled his wheeled chair around the desk to sit close beside van der Berg.

She found the several videos timestamped the evening before the night Gollancz died, turned the phone so he could see the screen and said, "You'll note that each is time stamped."

"Let's look at them in chronological order, Harriet. I think better chronologically."

"Agreed."

Harriet dutifully scrolled down to the first video of the evening. It was timestamped 6:13 PM. She punched the play arrow. The video showed a black Mercedes Benz G-Class pull up in front of Lawrence Gollancz's Eaton's Neck home and come to a stop. A woman clearly recognizable as Irene Stark emerged from the vehicle and walked around it toward the camera at the house's front door. They saw her finger loom huge as she moved to push the doorbell button just below the camera on the Ring device. They then watched her torso, intimately close to the camera, as it moved back and forth in a manner that seemed to signal anxiety. Then it disappeared from the camera's view, its owner presumably having been admitted to the house.

Harriet raised an eyebrow and said, "The redoubtable Mrs. Stark come for a visit."

The second video was time-stamped 6:36 PM. It captured Irene's generous backside as she left the house and returned to the Mercedes parked in front of the door. She was walking much faster than she had when she arrived.

Seth said, "She was in the house for twenty-three minutes. And note that she came and left before the rain began."

The third video of the evening captured a dark-colored sedan as it rapidly passed the front door on the circular drive, not stopping, at least not in the camera's range. The day's light was fading, so the video was not in color, but had gone to black and white. It was much less well-defined, rapid movement blurring the image further. It was stamped 8:38 PM.

"Looks like it could be Masterson's car," Seth said. I mean, it looks like it could be his Taurus. Hard to tell, but it's a dark color. His is a deep gray. It was raining by then. We know it was raining by then."

The fourth video was timestamped at 9:01 PM. It was short, and as the light had grown even poorer, less distinct, but the camera had caught what looked to be the same black Mercedes G-Class that had appeared in the earlier video. It drove by the front door, much more rapidly this time. It did not stop, at least not in front of the camera. At 9:05 PM, something seemed to trigger the Ring device, a brief blur, but no actual video recording of anything.

They gazed at each other, pondering the implications of what they had just watched on Lawrence Gollancz's iPhone.

Van der Berg said softy, "Firstly, I have learned that Ring cameras are activated by motion. They begin to record when they perceive motion within their range and continue to do so as long as they perceive any. And do so for a few moments thereafter."

Ludington nodded and then summed up what one particular Ring camera had recorded on the evening of the night Lawrence Gollancz died. "So, we saw two different visiting vehicles arriving after the rain started, one for a second time—a dark sedan of some ilk and the unmistakable Mercedes G-Class. And if a person in one of those two vehicles did move the generator to a position under the bedroom window as we suspect, I have a question, Harriet. Why is there no video recording of said person doing so? They would have had to pass by the front door while moving it, would they not?"

"Yes, they would. Unless, of course, said person were aware of the Ring device and wheeled the generator around the back of this house."

Ludington leaned back in the chair, pushed the errant forelock from his eyes, and thought for a moment, "Yes, I suppose you're right. If they moved it through the front yard, the Ring camera would have caught the movement."

Harriet turned her attention back to the phone, moving her index finger to scroll farther down the long file of time-stamped video recordings. Seth noticed for the first time that though her fingernails were beautifully manicured, they were not long, and she wore no polish.

She stopped scrolling and said, "There are several video recordings taken a day earlier, which would be the Sunday night of the dinner. Not of the dinner, of course, but of the comings and goings to and from that event, to be precise."

Harriet moved through them carefully, most recent to earliest. "Here we have Irene and Chelsea easing the wheelchair with their husband and father down the steps. Not his motorized one. This is in chronological reverse order, you understand. And here, let me see, ten minutes earlier, we have young Hudson leaving, and doing so very rapidly, I must say." She scrolled a bit more, back in time. "Here, three Starks are arriving for the dinner, only ninety minutes earlier, Irene and Chelsea drawing the wheelchair up the steps. Here is Chelsea ringing the doorbell. Only an hour and a half, hardly a leisurely dinner. Now, five minutes earlier, we have Hudson at the door. My, he is frightfully thin. And the last video, which would be the first chronologically, a dark sedan passes the camera, the vehicle in which one must assume young Hudson arrived. Seth, it would indeed appear the family Stark travelled separately, in two vehicles, that evening."

Their ruminations about Ring videos were interrupted by Ludington's cell phone blasting its Old Doorbell ring. He pulled it out of his blazer pocket and saw that it was Dan Gellman.

"Dan?"

"Seth, news, pretty good news. An FBI agent, guy named O'Reilly, just left my room. Seth, they've made an arrest, not for the fire, but for the vandalism. Seems there were fingerprints on the *aitzim,* the handles of the scrolls, you know. Only his prints and mine. Our Lena is a bit of a germaphobe, cleans the handles every Monday when she comes in. And believe it or not, they had the guy's prints on file from a previous arrest. And get this. A CCTV camera on 3rd Avenue caught what they have identified as his car. I'm assuming it was a guy. It was parked a couple of blocks down the street from the synagogue, both on the night of the vandalism and on the night of the fire. Both nights, Seth, both nights at almost the same spot. O'Reilly said the car doesn't belong to somebody who lives in the neighborhood. He said the prints and the car are enough to make an arrest for the break-in and the vandalism, but not for the fire. They seem pretty sure this person is also the arsonist, though. I mean, he doesn't live in Yorkville, so he must have come back that night, the night of the fire. Anyway, they think they have him for breaking and entering. As well as vandalism and hate crime charges. O'Reilly said the judge set the bail pretty high, and nobody's paid it, so whoever it is, they're still in custody."

"Who is it, Dan?"

"O'Reilly wouldn't say. Even avoided using pronouns. I mean, I asked him, but he said he was, quote, 'not at liberty to disclose the information at this point in an ongoing investigation.' He did say that they are 'continuing to interview the suspect.' But they won't say who it is, Seth."

"Dan, would it be okay if Harriet and I came for a visit? We've got some videos you might like to see. Maybe the three of us can watch them together. I mean, if you're up for it? "

"I'd fix popcorn if I could."

Chapter Twenty-Two

Thursday

Harriet, Seth, and Rabbi Gellman had just finished watching four brief and blurry Ring videos on Gollancz's phone and all three episodes of *The Gas Generator Mystery* on Harriet's iPhone, each of them twice. They were lined up beside each other on Gellman's hospital bed, Harriet in the center, holding both her own phone and the mystery iPhone.

Seth spoke first after both gadgets had returned to their home screens. Gollancz's, he noticed, was a shot of an ice cream truck, the Met on 5th Avenue rising behind it. Van der Berg's was a rather stiff photo or herself and Margaret. "Two facts," he said. "First, the FBI have arrested somebody for the vandalism, a somebody who's probably also an arsonist, second, Hudson Stark has gone missing. Chelsea may or may not know that he might have disappeared into FBI custody. They would have let him make a call, of course. A twenty-year-old kid would likely call his parents, but he may not have done so right away. And if he did, this mother and father might not have told Chelsea. But she does know he's gone. He's not at home and hasn't been for a day or two. From what I heard him and Chelsea say when they were sniping at each other in the kitchen at the shiva, he's a student at Hofstra, but he's been living at home for the summer, much to his sister's displeasure."

Gellman said, "I want it to be Masterson."

As do I, Dan. Still could be. Let's check. On the way down here in the cab, Harriet managed to track down his work phone number."

Van der Berg nodded and said, "He runs a little septic tank business in Greenlawn, 'George Masterson Septic Service.' Pumping them out, you know.

Seth smiled. "So let's us give him a little phone call and see if he's still on the loose and not locked up in Lower Manhattan."

He dialed the number Harriet had discovered and switched his phone to speaker. The three of them recognized the voice that picked up as George Masterson's, though all he spoke was a blunt "Septic Service."

Seth immediately hung up. Dan frowned and said, "Live and in Greenlawn, unfortunately. I was really hoping it was him."

Ludington slipped his phone back in his pocket. "But there's another reason I think it may be Hudson—the timing. Caterer told us the kid flew off in a rage just after the dinner at his uncle's house. That was early Sunday evening. He was incensed that some synagogue was going to end up with what he had always understood to be his money. The timing fits. He hears the name of the synagogue over dinner and heads into Manhattan to take out his wrath on both Beth Shalom and his treasonous uncle who loved the place."

Ludington was now counting deductions on his fingers. "And one more thing—there's drugs. Drugs usually mean money problems. And, well, maybe he was high on something less mellowing than grass that Sunday. Either at the dinner or after he ran off. Addicts tend to head for their drugs in a crisis."

Gellman nodded and added, "And then he comes back two days later to finish the job. More rage to vent."

"Maybe, Dan, maybe. But assuming he is the arsonist, I'm guessing the return trip into the City on Wednesday was made for a more practical reason. Remember Irene's visit to the house, not the one she made the evening before her brother's death, but the one we saw her make the day after he died, the day we were out there? That one got caught on the Ring camera as well. She had to be looking for something. Could well be it was the new will she was after. Maybe to make it disappear if Lawrence had signed it before he died. Assume she didn't find it and that she then told her family she didn't find it. Hudson hears this and guesses—wrongly—that it might be in the synagogue. So the kid ransacks the place he had broken into two days earlier—mostly your office—probably looking for the will, and then torches the building to cover his tracks. And maybe for a bit more revenge. All this is assuming he's both the vandal and the arsonist."

"But if he's not the arsonist, why would his car have been in the neighborhood that night?"

Seth nodded assent. "Exactly. I thought this through on the cab over here. I'm going to take a chance, a bit of a gamble, one which I think might be worth the risk. I'm going to call Irene Stark and offer to visit her son. I'm clearly jumping to a conclusion, but it's a chance I'll take. I understand clergy can finagle prison visits, though so far, I've not had the opportunity to visit any incarcerated members of Old Stone. Although you never know when the opportunity might arise. Anyway, I'm going to dare a guess that it's Hudson they've arrested and that he has called his mother. But when I make the offer, I won't say I'm willing to visit him in jail. I'll just say 'visit.' If I'm wrong about him being arrested, it'll be an odd offer for me to be making, but not as awkward as offering to visit him 'in jail.' If I'm right, she'll wonder how I knew. But I think I've got that covered."

Dan Gellman nodded, "She likes you better than me, Reverend WASP, so go to it."

Seth pulled his phone out of his blazer pocket and dialed Irene Stark's home number. He had memorized it and added it to his contacts when he and Harriet made the shiva visit. Irene picked up immediately, answering with an anxious double "hello." She seemed to have been waiting for a call.

"Mrs. Stark, this is the Reverend Seth Ludington phoning. I'm calling today as a pastor. If it would be helpful, I'm willing to visit with your son, Hudson, I mean." If he were wrong about the arrest, maybe she'd think he was just offering clerical council for an unhappy young man.

But he was not wrong. Irene Stark lapsed into incoherent sobs, struggling to find a word in response. She finally stiffened herself and said, "I can't believe this has happened. I know my boy. He's no vandal. He was raised with values, Reverend Ludington. Not that we forced him into any kind of organized religion, but we said grace at meals, sometimes. And he used to watch Mr. Rogers, when he was young, I mean. This is all wrong. I can't believe it. My son is being held at the detention facility at the Federal Courthouse in Lower Manhattan." Her defensive declaration was followed by a single sob that waxed to a near wail.

"This must be horrific for you and your family, Mrs. Stark. I am so sorry. So, if a visit would be of any help…?"

Irene Stark seemed to again pull herself together and managed to choke out a response to the odd offer, "Well, I suppose. Yes, I'm sure Hudson would be happy to see you. And Rev. Ludington, I fear Hudson may need a lawyer, a real lawyer, not some public defender. Would you happen to know any lawyers in the City who do this kind of work?"

Seth hadn't expected this. His brain raced to "lawyers I know." Most of the several attorneys at Old Stone were corporate or estate types, but he did hit on the name of a member he'd heard practiced criminal law. She was an irregular attender, but she had chatted him up at coffee hour last Easter. "I do. A member of my congregation. Criminal lawyer named Cecily Monroe."

He heard Irene moan as he spoke the word "criminal."

"I'll contact her if you wish."

"If you would, yes, yes."

Irene Stark paused, obviously thinking through this unexpected phone call and its offer more carefully. "Rev. Ludington, how did you know Hudson had been arrested?"

"Well, oddly enough, I have contacts in law enforcement." Which was true, though "contacts" should have been singular. His lone contact in New York City law enforcement was a retired cop named Harry Mulholland. And that contact had nothing to do with his having made a raw guess at Hudson Stark's arrest. Another entrance into the gray zone prevarication.

"Mrs. Stark, I'll try to visit Hudson as soon as I can. And I'll phone Cecily Monroe to see if she'll take his case."

Her tears now largely contained, Irene Stark offered Seth Ludington profuse thanks. "Please call me after you see Hudson. My boy did not do this, Reverend Ludington. I know my son."

Seth ended the call and looked at Dan Gellman, then van der Berg. Harriet smiled. The rabbi said, "Well, that was a good guess, Reverend Ludington. So, do you think it was Hudson who moved the generator under his uncle's bedroom window?"

"Well, that would be the ultimate revenge, I suppose. And it would have accelerated the kid's anticipated inheritance. Or he might have thought it would. He might be desperate for money.

Ludington and van der Berg rose to leave as Gellman stood, his right hand still bandaged. A broad smile across his face, he said, "They're releasing me Sunday. I cannot wait to be out of here."

By the time they'd gotten in a cab after visiting Gellman at Weill Cornell, it was well after five o'clock. But Ludington decided to call the Federal Courthouse's detention center anyway. His call was answered by a polite enough recorded voice suggesting he call during the hours of nine to five.

Chapter Twenty-Three

Friday

Ludington waited until exactly nine o'clock the next morning before phoning the lock-up he had learned was officially called the New York Metropolitan Correctional Center. This time he was greeted by the living iteration of the recorded voice of the day before. It informed him that he would have to be processed through the NCIC system (whatever that was) before he could visit Hudson Stark. And since Mr. Stark had not requested the visit himself, the prisoner would have to agree to it before it could be scheduled. The process would take several days. "It'll be Monday at the earliest, Reverend Ludington."

Ludington next called Cecily Monroe at her Midtown office. She was jarred into unlawyerly silence when Seth identified himself. He decided to address her as "Ms. Monroe," as they had met but once—and then briefly—at coffee hour after the Easter service some five months earlier.

"Ms. Monroe," he began, "a young man connected to Old Stone"—by a frayed shoestring, he thought as he said it—"is in need of legal representation. It's a vandalism charge." He had almost said, "Just a vandalism charge." He then added, a bit reluctantly, as he was afraid it would put her off, "and, well, probably also a hate crime charge, or so I understand." He knew the more serious matter of arson, perhaps even the murder, could surface in time, but at present, the boy was charged only with vandalism. He then told her he planned to visit Hudson Stark at the Federal Courthouse early next week, hopefully on Monday. Would she be willing to accompany him? Ludington assured her that her fees would be covered, but he sensed she agreed to make the visit mostly because she was intrigued that her pastor had somehow gotten himself involved in a vandalism and hate crime case—in a neighboring synagogue, at that.

Monroe ended the conversation with "That lockup down at the Federal Courthouse is an embarrassment. They ought to shut it down."

Seth slipped his phone into the pocket of his jeans, which he wore only on Friday, sermon writing day, as he would be confined to his study for the next eight hours. His homiletics professor at Princeton had suggested that preachers should figure on one hour of sermon preparation for every minute of a sermon's length. Ludington's sermons usually ran seventeen to twenty minutes, typical of Presbyterian sermons in the present day. This would mean two or three days of every week devoted to sermon research and writing. Not a chance, he had soon concluded.

Harriet had left several copies of the bulletin outlining Sunday's service on his desk, perhaps as a reminder to him that it was indeed Friday and he needed to get busy with his sermon. He opened one of the programs and saw that she had entered the three principal lectionary passages for the day, omitting the Psalm. Three was plenty of scripture for the last Sunday in August. All the passages were relatively familiar, but he read through them again, read them from the venerable Westminster Study Bible Moze Washington had given him when he left Philadelphia inner city mission work to take up pastoring and weekly preaching. He discovered that the assigned Old Testament reading was the first fifteen verses of the third chapter of Exodus, the story of the call of Moses, that pivotal tale replete with its burning bush and the disclosure of the enigmatic Divine Name. It could provide a firm foundation for a second sermon in as many weeks on the long and fraught relationship between Judaism and Christianity and yet another look into the ugly face of antisemitism.

The Moses story, a chapter of which was illustrated in one of Old Stone's stained glass windows, offered a wide door into a sermon on covenants, the crusty word used to describe relationships of mutual commitment between

God and humanity. Seth knew that the history of Christian thinking around covenants was another of the contributing factors in the development of antisemitism, perhaps every bit as much as the blood curse nonsense. Seth pushed aside the sermon notes he had made, fired up his laptop, and created a file he named "Proper 17, The Thing About Covenants." The words came quickly enough, though the sermon would need some buffing up before he preached it. He began with a personal memory:

"A few years ago, I went to hear Elie Wiesel speak at the 92ⁿᵈ Street Y up on Lexington. You know that's the YMHA, "Young Men's Hebrew Association. Wiesel was perhaps the greatest scholar of the Holocaust. His topic that night was the relationship between Jews and Christians. There was a Q-and-A time after his talk, and somebody asked him about Jesus. I'll never forget his answer. It went something like this, "Jesus was a remarkable Jewish teacher. He was born a Jew, lived and taught as a Jew, died as a Jew. I have the highest regard for Jesus. But what his followers have done to Jews over the last 2,000 years…, that's a different story."

So, here's the haunting question. If Jesus and all the disciples were Jews, and if Jesus' teaching is rooted in Judaism, why has the relationship between Christians and Jews been so troubled? Why the expulsion of Jews from Spain in 1492? Why the Cossack pogroms in Russia? Why the Holocaust? Why the Southern Baptist official who declared that God doesn't listen to the prayers of Jews? Why the murder of eleven worshipers at the Tree of Life Synagogue in Pittsburgh just three years ago? Why the vandalism and burning of Temple Beth Shalom, the synagogue four blocks from where you are sitting? Why the antisemitism that's still lurking under the surface in so much of the Christian world? The answer is complex. This morning I want to unravel only one thread.

Early in the history of the church, an idea took hold among a lot of Christians that's sometimes called "replacement theology." A fancier name is "supersessionism." It goes like this. Both Jews and Christians affirm that God made a covenant—a mutual commitment—with ancient Israel. Christians, of course, also believe that God later entered into a covenant with them, a new covenant in Jesus Christ.

Here's where it gets sticky. The story of the call of Moses you heard a moment ago is a turning point in the story of the covenant God made with the Jewish people.

With the call of Moses, the glue (I guess you could call it glue) in the relationship between God and Israel will become Torah, sometimes translated as "Teachings, or "the Law," though Torah is way more than rules. Anyway, the covenant itself reaches back deeper, all the way to Abraham, but the story of Moses and the burning bush begins the shaping of the relationship into one mediated through Torah. In this covenant, the people of Israel—later the Jewish people—are called to faithful obedience to Torah. Moses, remember, will receive the Ten Commandments a few chapters later. Those Ten Commandments will form the core of Torah. In return for their faithfulness to Torah, God offers them divine presence and unique purpose.

So, the question is this... if God has entered into a new covenant with us Christians in Jesus Christ, what happens to this old one between God and Israel? Replacement theology says it's been replaced—no good anymore. Supersessionism says the old covenant has been superseded—cancelled.

Back in the 1980s, Presbyterians wrestled with this exact question. They produced a remarkable document entitled "A Theological Understanding of the Relationship Between Christians and Jews." Here's a few quotes: "Jews are in a covenant relationship with God." "The living God whom Christians worship is the same God who is worshiped and served by Jews." The "theory of supersessionism or replacement is harmful..."

Brave as this document was, the folks on the committee that produced it were not the first Christians to call replacement theology a bad idea. During World War II, as the Holocaust unfolded across Europe, a little Protestant village in south-central France saved hundreds of Jewish lives. The name of the village was Le Chambon. Nearly all of its residents were Huguenots, French Protestants. In their understanding, the old covenant between God and the Jews had not been replaced or superseded. Like them, Jews were also a people in covenant with God. When a family of Jewish refugees knocked on a door in Le Chambon in the middle of the night, the villagers had a code to let each other know that somebody needing shelter had arrived. They would say, "Five Old Testaments are at my door. Do you have room for them.?" Later the villagers would sneak them over the mountains into Switzerland.

So, if we reconsider replacement theology, just as the report commends, just as the villagers of Le Chambon did, how do we think about the relationship between Judaism and Christianity? Well, the Bible has a response. Paul's long and often complex Letter to the Romans tackles the question. In its eleventh chapter, Paul uses an image the Presbyterian report would pick up two thousand years later. Paul said that Christianity has been engrafted into Judaism. This is an agricultural metaphor, of course. The image suggests that Judaism is a living tree and Christianity is an engrafted branch. Paul begins that eleventh chapter with a rhetorical question: "Has God rejected his people?" He means Jews like himself. His quick answer was "By no means." Then, later in the chapter, he tells the Roman Christians, most of them probably Gentiles, that they are 'a wild olive shoot' engrafted into the trunk that is Judaism, so they can, in his words, 'share the rich root of the olive tree.' The Presbyterian report uses this very image when it declares, 'The church has not replaced the Jewish people. Quite the contrary! The church...has been engrafted into the people of God....'

I'm going to end this sermon by pushing the point further. To do so, I have to tell you one last story. Some years back, when I was a student at the University of Michigan in Ann Arbor, I often attended First Presbyterian Church near campus. That church had three next-door neighbors—a sorority, a fraternity, and the Jewish student center called Hillel. Hillel was by far the best neighbor. Now, this Hillel had a very small parking lot. First Presbyterian had a big parking lot, actually two lots, one of which was right next to Hillel. The church and Hillel worked out an arrangement. The Jews used First Pres's parking lot anytime except Sunday morning, and the Presbyterians used Hillel's extra classrooms on Sundays. As you might imagine, sharing a parking lot in a Big Ten college town with limited parking was a diplomatic feat. I figured if they could manage it, maybe they could take on peace in the Middle East.

But the parking lot is just background to my story. The director of the Hillel was a guy named Michael Brooks. The minister of First Pres and Michael Brooks became friends, took turns taking each other out to lunch, and they talked about more than parking lots. Anyway, I once got invited to a lunch with the two of them at the Michigan Union. Brooks said something that day I've carried around for ages. Now, before I tell you what he said, there's something you have to understand about Michael Brooks. He's wicked smart and given to these koan-like utterances that you have to keep thinking about and then think about some more. So, over lunch, the three of us got to talking about today's topic, the relationship between Judaism and Christianity. Here's what he said: 'If Christianity hadn't come along, it would have been necessary for us Jews to invent it.' If Christianity hadn't come along, it would have been necessary for us Jews to invent it.

Now, the first twist in that enigmatic line is obvious—Jews did invent it. But it's the second edge of his sentence that has long intrigued me even more. What did he mean when he said it would have been necessary to invent it? Why necessary?

I didn't ask him that day, but I've been thinking about it for twenty years. Here's what I've decided he might have meant. Christianity was necessary because Judaism is not a religion that generally proselytizes. Jews don't much try to make non-Jews into Jews. Sometimes, but not so often. You're mostly born into it. Christianity is the opposite. We invite everybody in—doesn't matter what family or tribe you were born into. Christianity has always worked to grow, to expand across the lines of nation and class, breaking through the boundaries of race and language. Christianity was necessary for a lot of reasons. One of them is that it is God's way of expanding faith in the one God to all of humanity.

So, what does this matter to us, neighbors to a synagogue that was fire-bombed eleven days ago? What's the take home from all this theoretical stuff? Two take-homes, at least.

First, if we understand Jews to be our older brothers and sisters in faith in the one God rather than people God kicked out of the covenant, it will surely dampen the antisemitism that still hides in the dark corners, even the polite dark corners, of the Christian world. A branch dare not hate the tree. A younger sister is less likely to despise her older brother.

Second, understanding ourselves as having been grafted into a tree that is even older than our two Christian millennia reminds us of just how deep our roots go— how very, very deep they reach into the wondrous depths of God's long walk with humanity. They reach back to Jesus, of course, but then they reach even farther back, to Isaiah and Moses, and then they reach all the way back to Abraham and Sarah. They reach way, way back, far back—deep into the roots of the one tree.

He added the traditional formula he ended every sermon with: "In the name of the Father and of the Son and of the Holy Spirit. Amen."

Chapter Twenty-Four

Saturday

Seth tried to save Saturdays—at least a piece of them—for Fiona and the girls. Occasionally, conferences with couples who worked weekdays and needed to meet with the minister to plan their weddings intruded. And he usually went over his sermon again at some point every Saturday, either at home or in his church study. He knew he was done with editing when he found himself changing things back to the way they had been.

On this last Saturday of August, he had no pre-marital sessions and was planning to take his laptop to the room on the top floor of the brownstone that served as a cozy home office and study to fuss with the sermon in the afternoon while the girls were napping. So this sweet Saturday morning found Seth sitting on their brownstone's living room floor, playing with the twins and Fiona in the kitchen scrambling eggs when his cell phone rang. As he went to extricate it from the pocket of his Bermuda shorts, Ingrid, just mastering the art of crawling, started moving remarkably quickly toward the staircase that led down to the kitchen, mom, and food. He reached out to grab a chubby leg and slowed her progress, missing the call.

He picked up both girls, one under each arm, thinking they were indeed becoming an armful, growing both heavier and wigglier. He set them down in the playpen in the corner of the living room, at which infant incarceration they protested loudly, even though it was well stocked with toys. He then installed the baby gate they had just bought at the Costco up on 117th Street at the top of the back stairs. He had already pushed the living room's two red leather ottomans in front of the main stairway. Testing the baby gate to ensure it was firmly in place, he lifted Ingrid first and then Astrid from their baby prison and plopped them in the middle of the twelve-by-twenty Isfahan carpet that covered much of the oak floor of the living room. He stationed himself in front of the room's massive fireplace to guard that attraction from curious eight-month-old girls. Only then did he take a look at the "recents" in his phone's call log. It was Harriet who had called. Odd for her to phone him on a Saturday. He punched the number to phone her back. She picked up before the first ring ended.

"Seth, hello. I mean, I must sincerely apologize for telephoning you at your home and so egregiously intruding into your Saturday respite. I know you often do come into church for weekend meetings and final sermon preparatory efforts, so I presumed to come into church myself. In hopes of speaking with you, that is."

"Harriet, that was two adverbs and—let me see—two adjectives in two sentences. Take care, or you'll start to sound like Chelsea Bun."

"Well, that is precisely why I dared to interrupt your Saturday. I assumed you would wish to know—and to know forthwith—that she has posted yet another video. It offers no fresh intelligence about our case, but it does betray much about the young lady and her attitude toward her brother. I suggest you go to YouTube and search either "Chelsea Bun" or *The Gas Generator Mystery.*"

"I will, of course. And I'll be over to church this aft when the girls nap." Harriet clearly wanted to talk. There was no avoiding or postponing it.

"I'll doubtless see you then. I shall be interested in your appraisal of *Episode Four.*"

Seth was about to open his YouTube app when Fiona yelled up the back stairs from the kitchen a floor below, "Breakfast, Seth. Grab the girls if you would."

Fiona's scrambled eggs were invariably served in the Scots manner—atop a thick slice of buttered toast. He wiggled the twins into their high chairs and snapped on their new rubber bibs. Dining with the twins had become quite the show. At their last visit to the girls' pediatrician, she had recommended the girls begin to feed themselves—no utensils, just their increasingly dexterous little fingers. "No feeding them yourself. And the food you eat, more or less. Just cut it up." This was, they learned, the latest fashion in child-rearing. Seth guessed that, on average, some forty percent of the scrambled eggs he set on the trays of their highchairs made it into their mouths. But they were eating happily, albeit with egg on their faces.

Seth ate while his were still warm, but with a fork. "Perfect, Fiona. Thank you."

"Flattering my cooking will not dismiss you from culinary duties, my love."

Seth smiled, picked up the iPhone on the table before him, and punched the YouTube app.

He and Fiona watched the fourth installment of *The Gas Generator Mystery* together while the twins fished for bits of cold scrambled egg that had missed their mouths and fallen into the food-catcher pockets at the bottom of their rubber bibs.

Chelsea Bun, no longer in her trademark deerstalker and trench coat, was standing on the lower steps of what was clearly a massive government building, a row of towering columns looming behind her.

"Chelsea Bun here with Episode Four of The Gas Generator Mystery. You guys who are really seasoned true crime viewers know cops make mistakes, sometimes really major mistakes. Well, they've made a total screwup of their investigation of The Gas Generator Mystery."

The adolescent confidence that had characterized her earlier videos was much diminished. Her half-comic bluster, even stagy playfulness, were cracking. The girl's voice hinted at the tears that often come when rattled witnesses are interviewed for a news story and find themselves in front of a television reporter's camera. No open weeping from Chelsea Stark, but the kid was clearly distraught. She suddenly looked very young, younger even than her eighteen years.

"I am standing in front of the imposing U.S. Courthouse in Lower Manhattan.

This grand courthouse has a, like, detention center attached to it. You know, a jail called the New York Metropolitan Correctional Center. And the FBI, you know, the Feds, are holding a totally innocent kid in there." She turned her head to look at the courthouse and gestured theatrically, pointing an accusatory finger at the building. *"It's the nephew of the rich guy who accidentally died from that generator I told you about, the thing he stupidly put under his open window and got carbon monoxide poisoning. Now they arrested his nephew, without any real evidence, just because he got a little pissed when the guy decided to change his will to his syna...church. So, yes, the kid's a hothead, but it's all, like, utterly circumstantial. You guys know about circumstantial evidence. Stuff that's, you know, indirect and can be explained, like just getting angry at dinner and stomping off. Doesn't mean he killed anybody."*

Chelsea wiped her cheek with the back of the hand holding the microphone. There was no sign of the meerschaum pipe. Her voice starting to break, she concluded, *"So, that's it. I'm signing off. More to come, at least I hope there's more to come."*

"Seth, I thought you told me she despised her brother."

He took a sip of his coffee, "At one level, she does. But there's usually a deeper layer underneath even the most venomous sibling enmity."

Ludington could not but think of his own sister. He certainly did not hate her. In some elusive way, he still loved her, though he had come to realize he no longer respected her. Her aimlessness, her fleeting passions, her untamable fiscal extravagances which were milking her parents—his parents—for ever more and ever larger advances on her inheritance had dulled the shine of the love he had had for her when he was the handsome big brother she worshiped. Time had relentlessly eroded his residual regard for the silly little sister who had dropped out of Skidmore and run off to Marin County to be a yoga instructor, or maybe a potter, or an actress. She had become, Seth had finally and reluctantly conceded to himself, a cartoon of the spoiled rich kid. Which, of course, was the very thing he feared someone might think of him.

Fiona said, "Poor dumb kid, Seth. Does she have any idea?"

Realizing she was speaking of Chelsea, not his own little sister, Seth said,

"No, I don't think so. She's over her head, and now she's scared. But she seems to be thinking about more than vandalism. Even though that's all he's been charged with."

Fiona winced. "So you think she suspects Hudson might be responsible for the arson? Even Gollancz. Or maybe she senses the cops think so? I think she's in a state, Seth, more than distraught."

After helping Fiona get the girls down for their naps, he trudged off to church as he had promised Harriet. Together they re-watched the video in his office and decided two things were clear from what they saw. First, Chelsea Stark was suddenly afraid for her brother and had converted a maybe-murder into an unfortunate accident. Second, it was apparent she—and doubtless her parents as well—did not yet know about either Hudson's fingerprints on the *aitzim* of the synagogue Torah scrolls or the CCTV shots of his car parked down the street from Beth Shalom, on both the night of the vandalism and the night of the fire.

Harriet leaned back in her chair. "Seth, as Chelsea notes, both pieces of evidence—of which she seems to be quite unaware—could be called circumstantial. I mean, you could, by a stretch, explain them some other way. Maybe Hudson visited Temple Beth Shalom out of curiosity when he learned his uncle was planning to alter his benevolence. Maybe he snuck in without being seen and handled the Torah scrolls for some reason. Maybe he was in Yorkville those two nights to purchase drugs. Unlikely in the extreme, but not impossible."

Then Harriet made the same observation Fiona had an hour earlier. "Seth, do you think she suspects her brother of arson, perhaps even murder? Equally to the point, do the authorities? Do you?"

"I don't know. Fiona said the same thing." He leaned back and tapped the steeple he had made with his index fingers to his lips. "Fingerprints are direct evidence, Harriet. The CCTV videos are circumstantial, I guess. But even circumstantial evidence can pile up. And when it does, it can pile up into a conviction."

He leaned forward and looked his admin in the eyes, "Harriet, we can't just sit on what we know. We have to try again to get it to the cops, this time to O'Reilly. I mean the death threat letters, the boots and the prints and the extension cord, the Ring videos and Chelsea Bun, the whole Gordian knot. Suffolk seems to be ignoring it because the ME ruled the death accidental. The FBI have taken it as that…or maybe they haven't. Let's you and me and Dan have lunch at Lex after church tomorrow and figure out how to do this. They may listen to Rabbi Gellman even if they won't listen to you and me."

Harriet nodded agreement, though reluctantly, as she guessed it could well put an end to their own sleuthing. Seth read her mood, cast an apologetic smile, and phoned the rabbi.

Chapter Twenty-Five

Sunday

At a minute after eleven the next morning, the Reverend Seth Ludington stood on the top step of Old Stone's chancel to lead the congregation in the responsive Call to Worship. Before he spoke the first word, he scanned the sanctuary, barely a third full on the last Sunday in August. He was startled to see Cecily Monroe sitting four pews back on the east side of the center aisle with a man he assumed to be her husband. He'd seen her in church only once before—last Easter. He had pegged her as a church two-timer—Christmas and Easter. When he climbed into the pulpit twenty-five minutes later to deliver his second sermon on antisemitism in as many weeks, it was not animated by the anger that had accompanied him a week earlier. This time, it was more disappointment, disappointment in a humanity that—for all its vaunted progress—still managed to hate so stubbornly and irrationally. The sermon was, he knew, a rather teachy one. He hoped it would land well with those in the congregation who liked being taught, though probably less well with the rest.

After the service, Cecily Monroe waited until the line of hand-shakers had dwindled before approaching Ludington. She held out her own hand, commented favorably on the sermon, and then said, "I presumed to call the MCC myself after we spoke. I got both of us in for a visit with your vandal at 11:30 tomorrow morning. I'll pick you up in the firm's car. See you tomorrow at 10:45. It'll take a good half hour to get down there. Shall I call for you here at church or at your home?"

Seth selected home and gave her the address of their brownstone on 84th Street.

"I do know where you live, Reverend Ludington. Stunning renovation, I hear." She cracked a smile as she took her husband's arm and walked out of the church onto 82nd Street.

Fiona had fetched the twins from the church nursery after worship and brought them to coffee hour. She was reluctant to set them down on the floor of the Social Hall, so she held Astrid while Seth grappled with a squirmy Ingrid. Both parents were loath to admit it, but like most mothers and fathers, they loved showing them off. After twenty minutes of baby display, Ingrid decided to fuss, and Fiona went to fetch the double stroller. "Let me get them home, Seth. You go off with Harriet to meet Dan." She managed to give him permission to leave her at home with the children while he dined out with no hint of anger. Maybe there was just a whisper of martyrdom.

Nero had saved the banquette in the back corner for them. Dan was already there, sipping a glass of red wine with his unbandaged left hand. Nero brought Seth a stem glass of the same without being asked. Harriet ordered sauvignon blanc. The tall waiter returned, a wine glass in each hand and three menus tucked under his upper arm. They looked through them, though Seth and Harriet hardly needed to, habitués of the Lex that they were. Dan had already decided on a burger, and Harriet ordered one of her usual choices, the salad Nicoise. Seth, feeling rebellious, departed from routine and asked for pollo scarpariello, at which selection Nero jerked his head back in surprise.

Ludington opened the conversation with the subject they all understood to be the order of the day, "So Dan, Harriet, and I have been talking, and we think it's time we try again to get what we know to the attention of the authorities. I think that now means the FBI, Agent O'Reilly specifically." He paused before saying, "And we both figure you're the man to do it. I mean, you have a legitimate connection to this whole thing. It was your synagogue that was vandalized, your synagogue that was burned to the ground; Lawrence Gollancz was a member of your synagogue. And he was your friend. O'Reilly is much more likely to listen to you. I mean, you're a part of this, Dan. I'm just a nosy preacher from down the street. And Harriet, well, she's just…." He decided to let that last sentence dangle for fear of wounding the woman's feelings.

Gellman twirled the stem of his wine glass between the thumb and index finger of his good hand. "You're right, of course. But Seth, when I call him and tell him what we know and what we're guessing, there's no way to keep you two out of it. It was you who got Gollancz's phone in the mail. You opened it and found the Ring videos. You found his boots by the back door, and you took the plaster castings in the mud. You found the Lowe's receipt for the fifty-foot extension cord that's disappeared. You saw the Nazi bumper sticker on what's-his-name's car. You talked to the caterer and you talked to Gollancz's lawyer about the will. Besides the synagogue, my piece of this is just the altered will and those death threat letters Lawrence told me about. And it was you two who found Chelsea Stark's' video postings. You gotta understand that he'll know you've been meddling. And Seth, my guess is that he'll be pissed."

Seth nodded, "Well, he already is. But a lot of people have been put out with me in my life. Especially after I became a pastor. I'm getting used to it. I mean, I can take it." He glanced at Harriet, who was smiling blandly, and added, "What's he going to do? Arrest us?"

"I have no idea. But I guess there's no reason to put off the inevitable."

Gellman reached in his shirt pocket for his phone, punched a number from his contacts, and said to Seth and Harriet as it rang, "He gave me his cell number when he visited me in the hospital and said to contact him if I thought of anything else. Call anytime, he said. I guess this falls under the categories of both 'something else' and 'anytime.'"

He turned his attention to the phone as the ringing ceased, "Agent O'Reilly, this is Rabbi Daniel Gellman, Beth Shalom Synagogue. Yes. I'm fine. Out of the hospital in fact. You said to call if I thought of anything."

Gellman proceeded to rehearse the whole catalogue of oddities surrounding the death of Lawrence Gollancz that the three of them had assembled. The rabbi ended with a summation of sorts, "It may be connected to what happened to my synagogue. I mean, Mr. Gollancz was planning to alter his will in favor of my congregation, and his family was not happy about it. We know he had assorted visitors the evening of the night he died. The whole generator-under-the-window thing raises a bunch of questions. And his neighbor is a rabid antisemite. We just thought you ought to know this stuff."

Gellman's phone was not on speaker, so Seth and Harriet could not make out the words Agent Brian O'Reilly spoke in response following a moment of what was doubtless stunned silence. But they could certainly catch the tone of it. It rose in a bolero of fury, finally waxing so loud that Gellman moved the phone a few inches away from his ear. It subsided at last, and when it ended, Dan said, "Yes, sir. We'll be there."

"Gellman struck a theatrical pose of shock—jaw dropped and eyebrows elevated. He slipped the phone back in his shirt pocket and said, "He wants us in his office tomorrow morning at nine sharp."

Harriet said, "Whom does 'us' mean?"

"I think you're safe, Harriet. At least for now. You don't seem to be on his radar."

Van der Berg was clearly disappointed not to be on the FBI's radar. She said little as the three of them picked away at their lunches.

Chapter Twenty-Six

Monday

The Reverend Seth Ludington and Rabbi Daniel Gellman were in the Volvo the next morning at eight-twenty, off to the New York offices of the Federal Bureau of Investigation. Never could either have imagined that ordination to their sacred callings would bring them to this.

Seth's morning had been hurried and distracted. He had strollered the girls up to the House of Happy Little Ones at seven-thirty and then jogged over to the parking garage to fetch the Volvo, which had not yet been brought up when he arrived. He snapped at the attendant just before the car appeared. He had hoped to find a moment for a few needful phone calls, but such a moment had never appeared. Gellman was waiting in front of his building as Ludington pulled up. Ludington saw him glance at his watch just before he spied the Volvo, turning the corner. Seth was indeed ten minutes late.

Once the rabbi was buckled in, Ludington said, "Dan, I've got to give Harry Mulholland a call. I think I told you about Harry. Our Session Clerk, retired NYPD and all-around good guy. He'll be apoplectic when I tell him where we're headed. But after he vents, he'll tell us what kind of trouble we may or may not be in."

As he found Harry's landline in the car's list of contacts, he guessed the man would probably be drinking his second cup of coffee and leafing through the *New York Daily News.* Georgia would be tidying up after breakfast. Seth knew them that well. Their retirement lives had fallen into a felicitous routine, as predictable as it was comfortable.

Georgia picked up, and Seth said, "Morning, Georgia."

She said, "Why, good morning, Seth. You're up and about early on a Monday. It's your day off, you know. I imagine you'll be wanting to speak with Harry. He's right here, drinking his coffee."

Harry Mulholland already knew his pastor had his nose in the twin tragedies that had fallen upon the synagogue down the street, vandalism and then arson, as well as the sudden death of one of its members out on Long Island. He had warned Seth about his meddling, just as he had done twice before, first in the matter of the skeleton Ludington found in his brownstone and again when a member of their Scottish tour group ended up dead in a Neolithic tomb. His warnings had accomplished nothing in either case and would doubtless be equally ineffective this time. But he would issue them anyway. It was his duty as a cop, former cop. Ironically, the detective in Harry Mulholland had come to begrudgingly respect what his pastor and his secretarial sidekick had managed in both matters. God must watch over amateurs.

When Seth told him he was with Rabbi Gellman and where they were headed, Harry did his best to feign shock and offer more dire warnings. When Seth asked for his counsel regarding their approaching interview, Harry simply said, "Tell them everything, I mean everything." Seth had so far spared Harry Mulholland most of the details of "everything."

So when Seth asked what kind of trouble they might be in, Harry said, "He'll rant, and then he'll threaten, but there's probably nothing he can get you for beyond trespassing. And the FBI is not going to fuss with a trespassing case. Just be careful, Seth. I mean, this kind of hate, and the arson, and a questionable death…. There's a dangerous character loose out there."

Seth thanked his Clerk of Session for the advice, but made no promises. As Ludington worked his way through morning Midtown traffic, he said to Dan, "And I gotta call Cecily Monroe, you know, the lawyer. She was sending a car for me. At our place. No way we'll get back uptown in time."

Ludington punched in her number from his contacts on the Volvo's screen. When she picked up, he said, "Ms. Monroe, as it happens, I had to run downtown this morning, so I can just meet you there at the Courthouse if that's okay."

"Fine, how about at the corner of Pearl and Centre?" She asked no questions, and he offered no reason for suddenly finding himself in Lower Manhattan on a Monday morning.

Ludington looked at Gellman and said, "Providential that the FBI's offices and the Courthouse lockup are almost across the street from each other." As he pulled the Volvo into a valet parking garage on Reade Street, he winced at the sign alongside the entrance that read, "Hourly Parking Starting at $48.75."

The New York City offices of the FBI were at Twenty-Six Federal Plaza, an ugly mid-century office tower that loomed in haughty modernity above the cluster of graceful neoclassical government buildings that crowd much of Lower Manhattan. After they had cleared lobby security and were in the elevator riding up to the twenty-third floor, Dan said, "Seth, I think I should take the lead in this. You and Harriet have done most of the poking around while I was laid up, but I'm the victim, or one of them anyway. Like you said, it gives me more cred. He held up the bandaged hand, burned when he had rescued the Torah scrolls, and said, "I'll milk this. Maybe cool his wrath with pity."

If Agent Brian O'Reilly's wrath was cooled by pity, neither Dan nor Seth noticed. O'Reilly was accompanied in the interview by Willa Norton, the same agent Ludington had met when the pair had come to Old Stone for the Torah scrolls. It was she who, today, took notes and used a phone to record the interview.

Dan laid out their tale for the two agents with rabbinical thoroughness, though he often had to default to the passive voice—"a receipt for a fifty-foot extension cord was found, footprints were seen, a pair of clean L. L. Bean Duck Boots were noted—size eleven, a cell phone belonging to Lawrence Gollancz was received in the mail." At several intersections in the story, he had to turn to Seth for clarification and detail, which further betrayed the fact that it was not Daniel Gellman who had taken plaster casts in the mud or found the Lowe's receipt for the fifty-foot extension cord on the garage floor.

O'Reilly was a smart cop, and he understood exactly what was going on. It was only after Dan had unloaded the whole tale that the agent erupted in a display of righteous anger. Rage was followed by threats as to what would happen if their meddling were to continue. Seth was savvy enough to see that the threats—ominous as O'Reilly made them sound—were vague. There was no such crime as "meddling."

O'Reilly's anger—real or feigned—soon transitioned to curiosity. He was especially interested in the two witnesses who said they had seen Hudson Stark leave the Sunday dinner at Gollancz's house in a fury—Shar Conlin, the caterer, and his sister Chelsea Stark, as she had related in her second YouTube video. Hudson's adolescent anger and the squealing of tires that both of them recounted had occurred the evening of the synagogue's vandalism. It appeared that that crime, as well as the arson two nights later, were the Agents' focus.

At the end of the interview, O'Reilly added, almost as a footnote, "We'll be wanting that phone." Then he said, with as straight a face as the man could manage, "Those plaster castings of footprints, too." He seemed clearly bemused that a preacher had engaged in such a clichéd bit of detection. But these two requests, offhand as they seemed, encouraged Ludington. They suggested the authorities might at long last be interested in Gollancz's demise.

Seth could not help himself and blurted out, "I understand that what happened to the synagogue is your first priority, Agent O'Reilly, but, well…, Gollancz's death doesn't quite add up to an accident. I mean, not for sure, anyway. It seems to me—seems to us—that it might all be connected. I mean, the business of the changed will, and this sketchy guy next door—Masterson. There could be motive for both, right? And there's the generator, which looks like it was moved after the rain started." Ludington had grown more animated than he intended. In truth, he was put out—more than put out—by the possibility that nobody might be investigating the death of Lawrence

CHAPTER TWENTY-SIX

Gollancz.

O'Reilly almost rolled his eyes before saying, "The Suffolk County Medical Examiner has ruled Lawrence Gollancz's death an accident. The Federal Bureau of Investigation has been asked by the New York Police Department to investigate the vandalism and arson at Temple Beth Shalom. Because it's a potential hate crime, it merited our involvement. So you can cease with the Sherlock Homes schtick, Reverend." Then he stood and said, "Thank you, gentlemen."

With that dismissal, O'Reilly picked up the copious notes Agent Norton had made. She turned the recording phone off and smiled blankly. He merely nodded at Ludington and Gellman. No trace of a smile crossed his handsome face.

On the elevator ride down, Gellman said, "I like it that he used a Yiddish word."

"What would that be?"

"Schtick. Not quite accurate, though. It suggests a comedy act."

Ludington grinned. "Dan, I think they maybe are going to be looking into Lawrence Gollancz's death, even if they're not convinced the man was murdered. O'Reilly just doesn't want us to know."

Gellman left Ludington at the corner of Pearl and Centre and continued south to the Fulton Street Subway Station so he could catch a Lexington Avenue train back to the Upper East Side. Before they parted, the rabbi reached out to his friend with his good left hand for an awkward backhanded shake. He held on for a moment and looked Ludington in the eyes. "Call me after you talk to the kid, Seth. I want to know what he says, what he's like."

Chapter Twenty-Seven

Monday

Ludington was an hour early for his assignation with Cecily Monroe so he crossed Centre Street, found a free bench in Thomas Paine Park, and checked his phone. Fiona had texted to say that Ingrid was running a temperature and was banned from daycare, that she had been called and had to cab up to the House of Happy Little Ones to bring them both home. Now, the girls would have to spend the day with their nanny, who was on her way down from the Bronx, but would not arrive till noon, which meant that she, Fiona, would be missing a lunch meeting at her UN offices. She was gracious enough not to remind Seth that Monday was his day off, and were he not off on this quirky side job, he would have been home minding his daughters, and thus, their mother would not have missed her meeting. She didn't have to say it. Guilt, Seth Ludington's intimate companion, crept up and sat beside him on the bench in Thomas Paine Park. He texted Fiona back, "Sorry. Should be back in a couple of hours. What would you like for dinner?"

He slipped the phone back in his blazer pocket and decided to walk through Foley Square, the designated New York gathering place for protests of every description, ranging from pipelines across Native American land (no) to gay rights (yes). He walked through the small square and a few blocks further south toward City Hall. It was a graceful and perfectly symmetrical neoclassical building, smaller by a mile than the Capitol in Washington, but much the same vintage and style. This juxtaposition of the antique and stubbornly staid alongside the new and in-your-face edgy was one of the many things he was coming to love about New York. Everything was here, whether you wanted it to be or not—Italian restaurants run by Albanians from Montenegro, stuffy gentlemen-only and ladies-only clubs that still served lentil soup with sour cream and sherry. When he was interviewing for his position at Old Stone, one of the search committee members, hoping to sell him on the City, had said, "Where else can you run out and get cilantro at three in the morning if you need it?" On a Monday a few weeks earlier, he and Fiona had brought the girls to the Metropolitan Museum because they—he and Fiona, not the twins—had wanted to see the Temple of Dendur. Where else can you amble through a re-assembled two-thousand-year-old Roman-Egyptian Temple in air-conditioned comfort with a cappuccino in hand?

Seth's life had been lived in urbanish places. First, Grosse Pointe till he was eighteen, which was self-consciously suburban, though the city of Detroit was only blocks away. But the Detroit of his youth had yet to be reborn. It was still The Place You Didn't Go, and if you did, it was probably for some questionable purpose. Then, Ann Arbor for four years, a quintessential college town, though it thought of itself as a city. Locals joked that it was "a small, flat San Francisco with bad weather." Ann Arbor was followed by Princeton for seminary, another college town with attitude. He and Fiona had met and fallen in love after he graduated while both were in the Middle East on an archaeological dig. He proposed (or did she?), and she had followed him to Philadelphia after their Edinburgh wedding. He took up his first post-grad job working as an assistant (a "General Dogsbody," Fiona called it) for an inner-city non-profit. They were young with no kids. Seth worked, and Fiona went to law school. Both came to love Philadelphia, gritty here and elegant there. They lived in the gritty part. Then it was Seth who had followed Fiona to New York when she had landed a plum human rights lawyer job at the UN just two years earlier.

Toward the end of their ten years in Philadelphia, Seth had felt the first stirrings of a call to parish ministry. So it smelled of sweet providence when he learned that Old Stone Church in New York was looking for a pastor. The church was located on the East Side of Manhattan, not far from Fiona's UN office. The salary was pitiable, but money was not an issue.

The seven-person search committee was a likable bunch, so earnest and a bit desperate. (And you could get cilantro at three in the morning.) He said yes, though with reservations he did not speak of, not even to Fiona.

Their new city, they soon learned, was deliciously varied. It was a place of immigrants just like them. Old Stone and the Yorkville neighborhood boasted precious few native New Yorkers like Harry and Georgia Mul-holland. (And proud of it they were.) But most of the church and the neighborhood were immigrants, many from across the U.S., bright and ambitious young things from Glens Falls or Paduka. They came following their particular star as it settled over Wall Street, or Madison Avenue, or Broadway. Others were immigrants, or descendants of immigrants, who had been driven north by Jim Crow. And of course, there were the immigrants that come to most people's mind when they hear the word, also ambitious and bright, come from Puerto Rico or the Dominican Republic or Haiti or places Seth could not find on a map. It was like nothing anywhere. When people from back in the Midwest asked Ludington—often incredulously— what it was he could possibly like about New York, he had taken to answering, "the people."

Seth glanced away from the handsome façade of City Hall to check his Shinola Runwell. It was ten till eleven. He turned around and ambled back north to Foley Square. At eleven sharp, he watched a black Chevy Tahoe slow and stop at the corner of Pearl and Centre. Cecily Monroe stepped out and scanned the intersection, obviously looking for him. He rose from the bench and called across the street, "Ms. Monroe." She saw him and dismissed the driver with a wave. Seth could not but wonder how many criminal defense lawyers managed such perks as a black car at their disposal. Harry Mulholland had once told him they were a tough breed. "They get lied to for a living and get paid to exonerate people they despise, characters who, if they don't manage to exonerate them, are known to threaten bodily harm." Ludington's hunch was that the criminals whom

Cecily Monroe and her Midtown silk-stocking firm worked to exonerate were mostly accused of fiscal crimes, which seldom occasioned threats of bodily violence. Perhaps it was the novelty of a teenage vandal that had attracted her to the case. Or maybe it was the novelty of a Presbyterian minister—her personal Presbyterian minister—being somehow involved in such an unlikely matter. Seth imagined that defending duplicitous stock traders might grow tedious.

She was dressed in a dark gray pantsuit, perfectly cut and just the right weight for late August. A string of pearls about her neck and a sleek black leather attaché case completed the look of confident competence. Her narrow face was surrounded by auburn hair cut just above her shoulders. Seth had dressed for a prison call—gray slacks, dark blue blazer, and his clerical collar, the last of which might help ease his way into the Federal Courthouse lockup. It worked in hospital intensive care units. He had once worn it to see if it might work to dodge jury duty. It hadn't. Happily, he didn't get impaneled.

Monroe smiled when she saw him crossing the street. He stepped up and onto the sidewalk and she extended her hand for a handshake so firm it almost hurt. "We've got a minute, Reverend Ludington. Tell me what you know. Let's sit down."

Together, they crossed Centre Street and sat on the bench Ludington had just vacated. He began by telling her what they knew—that the authorities had arrested Hudson Stark, age twenty, on charges of the vandalism of Temple Beth Shalom, that his fingerprints were found on the *aitzim* of the synagogue's Torah scrolls, that CCTV cameras had photographed his car parked on a nearby street the night of the vandalism. Seth paused and said, "And one more thing. The FBI has CCTV footage of Hudson Stark's car in the neighborhood the night of the arson, too."

She raised an eyebrow at this bit of news, "Okay, a few questions. First, what's an *aitzim*. Second, does the kid live in the neighborhood of the synagogue? Third, is there any reason other than the vandalism that he might have been in the synagogue and touched these *aitzim* things?"

Ludington explained *aitzim*, adding, "And it seems they were cleaned after services the Sabbath prior. And the Stark kid lives on Long Island, and he was not a member of the synagogue." He paused before saying, "But his uncle was."

She jerked her head up to look at Ludington. "Uncle?"

Ludington realized there was no way to avoid telling her everything, or at least most everything. So, for the second time that morning, he walked someone through the labyrinth he and Harriet van der Berg had been exploring—Lawrence Gollancz dead of carbon monoxide poisoning, his ice cream truck jingle, the death threats, the altered will, the tumultuous family dinner, the storm and the emergency gas generator, the muddy footprints, the L. L. Bean Duck Boots by the back door, the extension cords of differing lengths, the cell phone with its Ring doorbell videos, Chelsea Bun's attempt at a YouTube true crime series, and finally, the neo-Nazi next door.

Cecily Monroe listened, carefully and without expression, nodding occasionally. Seth guessed she had heard wilder tales in her career. When he finished, she shook her head and said, "Good Lord, sorry, I mean, goodness gracious, Reverend Ludington, what the hell have you gotten yourself into?"

Chapter Twenty-Eight

Monday

Cecily Monroe had obviously visited New York's Federal Courthouse and the attached Metropolitan Correctional Center at 150 Park Row any number of times. She knew both its layout and security routines, routines which were, Seth discovered, vastly more onerous than those he had tasted when entering the FBI's offices a few hours earlier. The prison, a remnant of the 1970s' infatuation with brutalist architecture, had not aged well. It was, in fact, embarrassingly shoddy. It was not in the Courthouse building proper, but connected to it by several long skyways built over an alley. Traversing one of the skyways behind Cecily, who was moving at an impressive clip in her high (though not quite stiletto) heels, reminded Seth of Dante's descent through the layers of his Inferno.

When they arrived, they verified their respective identities to a bored official in uniform behind a mesh grill with bullet-resistant glazing. They told him they had an appointment to visit Hudson Stark. The guard checked his computer to verify both their credentials and reason for visiting Stark. He then pointed to a nearby alcove with a stack of lockers. "Keys and cellphones in a locker, please."

After obeying his orders, they waited. Leaning against a wall, Cecily said, "They're never close to ready, even if you're late."

Seth said, "I guess prison is always about waiting, even if you're not the prisoner."

Twenty minutes later, another uniformed correction officer approached, looked at Ludington and Monroe, and jerked his head for them to follow. He led them to an airport-style metal detection system. Just like at the airport, jackets and shoes came off for a passage through an X-ray machine on a conveyor belt. They were then each presented with a temporary ID on a lanyard to hang around their necks, led to an elevator, and escorted up to the third floor, where they were stopped yet again to double-check identities and to ascertain the prisoner's right to visitation. Finally, they were escorted to an interview room. It was maybe eight feet by eight feet with wire-glass windows on two sides. Inside was a rectangular table with metal legs, a chipped Formica top, and three molded salmon-colored fiberglass chairs.

"Wait here. I'll bring him in."

He was back in ten minutes with Hudson Stark, dressed in an incarceration-brown jumpsuit, its legs and arms far too short for him. The guard searched him head to toe before letting him into the little room. Hudson was tall, maybe an inch taller than Seth. He was a good-looking kid, but shockingly thin, on the cusp of anorexic. His eyes were hollow, dark half-moons resting under them. He was not cuffed.

The guard said, "Had to wake him up."

Hudson had seen Seth at the shiva at his parents' home. And the kid had granted permission for his visit—odd as it was—so he knew who Ludington was.

Seth said, "Hudson, this is Cecily Monroe. She's an attorney and, with your approval, will represent you. Your mother asked me to make the arrangements."

Cecily did not smile, but nodded slightly. Hudson was leaning back in his chair in an attempt at nonchalance, his long legs under the table, his feet poking out between the chairs Ludington and Monroe were sitting in.

He said in a near whisper, "Man, I can't believe this shit."

Cecily said, "Mr. Stark, Please tell me what happened that night, after you had dinner at your uncle's house on Long Island."

His head snapped up, "How do you know about the dinner?"

"We have a witness who was present that evening, at the dinner."

"Well, you might as well know…I already told the Black cop I did it. I mean, I told him I busted into my uncle's synagogue in the City and messed things up a bit. Yeah, I was pissed. Had a right to be. You would be, too. All I did was toss some stuff around and leave some comments on the walls. I signed their paper. I mean, I owned up to it because they told me they had no reason to think it was me who torched the place. They said if I confessed to Sunday night, they'd go easy on me with… anything else."

"Mr. Stark," Cecily said, leaning forward and folding her hands on the table in front of her, "Cops lie, prosecutors make promises they can't keep, promises they have no intention of keeping."

Almost whispering and leaning even closer, she said, "Listen closely, Hudson. Do not say anything more. Nothing. I mean *nothing*."

Suddenly, the kid looked rattled, his feigned insouciance cracking before their eyes. "Now they're asking about the night he died. I mean Uncle Larry. Where was I? Like it was murder or something. Stupid geezer put that gas generator thing of his right under his window. I swear, I haven't been near the place since his big reveal at that dinner. Can't believe this."

Cecily appeared not to be surprised by what Hudson Stark had just said. She leaned back and said, "Mr. Stark, do you want me to represent you?"

He looked at the ceiling as if it held an answer to the question, paused, and said, "Yeah, I guess so."

"Then hear me again, young man. Say nothing. Do not answer questions. Nothing. Nada. Zilch. Who has been to speak to you?"

"Just the Black cop. 'O' something. Smooth. Said somebody from the prosecutor's office would also be interviewing me. My mom's coming this afternoon."

Seth realized Hudson had twice called O'Reilly "the Black cop." He had to wonder what might lie behind such a racial focus. He could not but remember the hateful graffiti smeared on the walls of Beth Shalom. It was so viciously antisemitic, especially for a kid who said he just wanted to blast his uncle and who was himself Jewish, technically anyway.

Seth asked the question that was haunting him, "Hudson, how did you know about the SS insignia you painted on the wall of the synagogue."

The kid looked confused. "You mean those two lightening things? Internet. I Googled around on my phone and found stuff I figured would really piss the old fart off. And piss off the people who were gonna end up with our money. Not hard to find. That stuff is all over the internet."

"Hudson, you're Jewish yourself."

"Yeah, right." He seemed mystified by the thought.

If Monroe caught this, she said nothing. She was more focused on what the kid might say to the "Black cop." She said, "Hudson, say nothing to either of them. You do have a right to remain silent, hard as it may be. They told you that, I assume."

"Yep, read me my rights, they did. Just like on TV."

"Okay, I want you to tell me exactly what you told O'Reilly. Lay out your movements the day and night of the dinner at your uncle's house."

Hudson Stark muttered his way through a reluctant and doubtless abridged version of the evening—what his uncle told them about altering his will, his own anger in response—which he now named "disappoint-ment"—and, finally, buying a can of spray paint and driving into the City where he broke into the synagogue and "messed things up a little."

Monroe made a few notes on a sheet of paper that had not been taken from her and said, "Where were you Monday and Wednesday night of that same week, Mr. Stark?"

"You too? You expect me to remember where I was—like, what—two weeks ago?"

"You'd be wise to try to do so, Mr. Stark."

He looked back at the ceiling where answers seemed to lie. "I don't know. I think I drove into Hempstead one of those days, maybe both of them. To check on the apartment. I'm moving out of the dorm into my own place for next semester. Wanted to see if they got it ready."

"Did anyone see you while you were in Hempstead? You attend Hofstra University, I assume."

"Didn't see anybody. They'd already sent me the code for the apartment, so I got in on my own."

CHAPTER TWENTY-EIGHT

Monroe nodded and made a few more notes.

Speaking only for the second time in the interview, Seth said, "Hudson, I'm here as your, well, spiritual counselor." He almost choked on that presumptuous job description. "Your mother asked me to visit you…for that purpose. So, is there anything I can do for you?"

"Like pray? I don't think so. Just get me out of this hellhole."

They finished the interview in half an hour. Cecily rose and tapped on the glass for the guard. Hudson retracted his legs from under the table and stood. As he did so, Seth saw that he was wearing L. L. Bean Duck Boots. The laces had been removed, of course, so his feet slipped in them as he followed the guard out of the room. The correction officer frisked the kid yet again. To make certain his visitors had not passed anything to him, Ludington assumed. As they were led back to the entry room, Cecily said to Seth, "No talk till we're out of here. The walls have ears."

Once they were in the sunlight at the bottom of the steps in front of the courthouse—sunlight that felt cleansing—Cecily said, "First off, the kid's a cokehead. He's a cocaine addict in withdrawal. I've seen it with a dozen— actually a couple dozen—of my Wall Street clients. They always look the same. Anorexic, the sunken eyes, the sleeping, the anger, and the attitude. He wants his drugs, and he wants them now."

Seth nodded. He was not so much surprised as saddened. He was equally saddened by Hudson Stark's minimizing of the horrific vandalism he had wrought in Temple Beth Shalom. Ludington guessed the kid was doing his best to wiggle himself—psychologically, at least—off the sharp hook of guilt over what he had done. Hudson, as the son of a Jewish mother, was himself Jewish, whether he understood it or not. Ludington could not but wonder about some manifestation of self-hatred.

Monroe interrupted his reflections. "Second thing, they do think he's your arsonist as well. They're going to press him on that. Promise him all sorts of stuff, like hinting that they might or might not charge him for it, which would be a much bigger deal if they did. And you can bet they're going to look at Gollancz's death, even if Suffolk says it was an accident. And they may also use it as leverage, even if they don't have a case, even if they agree it was an accident. Best we can do is to limit his liability to the vandalism and dig up some extenuating circumstances, his youth maybe. He's not a minor, though. First offense maybe, but I'll have to check on that. You said they had his prints of file. That's a worry. And it's too late for a plea deal."

Seth said, "Thank you, Cecily," using her Christian name for the first time.

She nodded and said, "Where do I send the bill? I'll discount it, but this is not *pro bono*. Don't do *pro bono*."

"Send it to me," he answered, wondering if he was footing the bill for a pricey lawyer who just might get a vandal—perhaps an arsonist and a murderer as well—off a hook he richly deserved to dangle on. But even the guilty deserve a defense. That's how it was supposed to work.

Chapter Twenty-Nine

Monday

In answer to the guilt-induced question about dinner Seth had put to his wife that morning, Fiona had answered, an edge in her voice, "Seth, I really don't know. Whatever. Maybe that new pasta thing you did last week."

"That new pasta thing" had been linguine with speck. Ludington returned the Volvo to its garage on 96th Street and caught a yellow cab down to Grace's Marketplace so he could pick up some speck. There were grocery stores closer to their brownstone, but he knew that Grace's would have speck, the South Tyrolean version the recipe called for and Italians preferred. You could substitute smoked prosciutto, but it wasn't quite the same. He also found fresh rosemary and sage. Unsure of what iterations of pasta hid in their pantry, he bought a bag of high-end tagliatelle, a change from the linguine of last time. As he listed the ingredients in his head, he remembered having seen a block of parmesan, an onion or two, and some heavy cream in the fridge at home.

The dripping-wet heat of the last few days had finally broken, and the sun shone bright and dry, so he decided to walk the sixteen short blocks up 2nd Avenue, a bag of groceries in hand and a clerical collar about his neck. Even in heathen New York City, the latter garnered a smile or a nod once and again. It was almost three when he arrived home. Inez was in the living room, scrolling through her Facebook feed. She rose when he entered and told him she had just put the girls down for their afternoon nap.

Seth asked, "How's Ingrid doing?"

"The temperature she had, it is now gone I think. Mrs. Ludington asked if I could stay over the night and tomorrow. In case one of them has the temperature tomorrow and cannot go to school. It is okay. I can stay. German is not working tomorrow and he can be home for Brendan." German Reyes was Inez's husband, who worked as a security guard at a Walmart in the Bronx. The improbably named Brendan, the youngest of their three sons and the only one still at home, was a junior at Bronx Science. Seth had met the kid and judged him to be a star, a star closely guarded by his doting immigrant parents.

Seth decided to prep dinner while the girls slept, so he returned to the kitchen, chopped a white onion, and cut the sage and rosemary into small pieces. Then he sliced the speck into long, thin strips. "Cut them skinny, to make them like matchsticks," Walter had said when he shared his recipe after serving it at a dinner for six in June. Walter and Lydia were Old Stone members, he a rare Italian Protestant, the son of Waldensians from the Piedmont. She was Philadelphia Italian, raised Roman Catholic. She attended Old Stone with Walter, but did not formally join until both her parents had died. Walter was quietly proud of his religious forebears whose break with Rome had pre-dated the Reformation and who had hidden Jews from the Nazis. He was also a superb cook and had been happy to surrender his pasta-with-speck recipe, simple as it was, when everyone at the June dinner had clamored for it.

As Seth sliced the last of the speck, he heard one of the girls fussing, the sound of baby squawks amplified through the monitor sitting on the kitchen counter. Inez had one in the living room as well, so they marched up the stairs to the nursery in single file. Seth changed Ingrid's diaper while Inez did the same for Astrid. The girls were not identical twins, but looked much alike. He wondered how parents of identicals ever managed to tell them apart. He had had classmates in seminary who were identical twins. He did not know them well, and it had been just after Christmas break when he saw them together for the first time that he realized the person he thought was one was two.

He was back downstairs on the living room floor with the girls when his cell rang. He decided not to answer. It was his day off, after all. But he could not resist pulling it out of his pocket and looking at the screen to see who was calling. The screen read, "Stark." It had to be their home landline. He had saved the number in his contacts after seeing it on the wall phone in their kitchen when he and Harriet-Henrietta had attended the shiva. He took the call, "Hello, Seth Ludington."

The first thing he heard was a wail, inchoate and wordless. Then sobbing and finally a barely comprehensible, "Thank you, for answering my call. I was afraid you might not." Then more sobs and, "I can't believe this. It's a mother's worst nightmare."

"Mrs. Stark? Irene? Is that you?"

"Yes. Reverend Ludington. I don't know what to do. I don't know where to turn. I'm afraid of what I might do. Can I come see you?"

It was more the faux detective than the real pastor who answered the question. "I think it would be better if I came to you." The detective, Ludington, wanted to be in the Stark house again. Seth was realizing that his erstwhile resistance to, even embarrassment at the amateur sleuthing which kept knocking at his door was slowly morphing—albeit reluctantly—into pleasure. It was not merely his nagging curiosity and tiresome zeal to set wrong things right. He found himself enjoying the doing of it.

"Would you?" Irene said.

"Of course. And I'll bring Rabbi Gellman with me."

The phone was silent for a good five seconds, "Irene, you still there?"

"Yes, yes. Well okay. I mean, if you think you need to. But he must hate us."

"He's not a hateful man, Irene. I'll have to see if he can come. Tomorrow then? Ten-thirty, okay?"

Irene Stark's answer was another litany of sobs. Followed by, "Okay, ten-thirty." Then she managed to tell Ludington that her husband might not be there as he might be attending the day program for Parkinson's patients he went to several times a week. Ludington surmised that the woman was as distraught as she was because she had just returned from visiting her son and now knew he had confessed to the vandalism of Temple Beth Shalom. And he had probably also told her the FBI was pressing him about his whereabouts on the nights of the bombing and the death of her brother.

Seth understood that he was not Irene Stark's pastor, even though Irene seemed to have adopted him as such. And Dan Gellman was certainly not her rabbi. For either one of them to be making this visit was decidedly odd. But he wanted to do it, and he wanted someone with him when he did it. For two reasons. First, he never made home calls on women when they could be alone—unless they were well over eighty. Jack might not be in the house. And he had no idea whether Chelsea would be there. It was not what might happen if he visited a woman alone that induced such caution in most clergy; it was what someone might say happened. He had been taught this in a class on pastoral care in seminary. He recalled nothing else from the seminar, but he remembered that precautionary warning. Yet there was a second—and rather less precautionary—reason he wanted Dan Gellman with him.

Astrid was in his lap as he called down to Inez, who was in the kitchen making herself the usual afternoon cup of Constant Comment. "Inez, when you've got your tea, could you watch the girls for a sec?"

Relieved by Inez of day-off fatherly duties (duties he generally relished), Ludington climbed the stairs to his study on the top floor of the manse to make two phone calls. He called Gellman first and related the tale of his visit to the Hudson Stark with Cecily Moore that morning. He told him Hudson had confessed to the vandalism, and they were questioning him about where he might have been the nights of the arson and his uncle's death.

Gellman said, "Such hateful stuff, Seth. To the Temple, I mean. What's with him?"

"Dumb, nasty kid. Drugs, internet, greed. I'm not even sure he's an antisemite. I'm not sure he knows he's Jewish, even knows what Jewish is. But he wanted to hurt. And he found a way. Dan, this is asking a lot, but would you be willing to visit the Starks with me. Irene, I mean."

Gellman consented to making the curious visit to Irene Stark without a hint of the reluctance Seth guessed he harbored. He agreed it was singularly strange that Irene had called Seth at all and even stranger that she had consented to the rabbi of the synagogue her son had vandalized coming along. Ludington speculated that Irene was absolutely desperate and did not know where else to turn. Then he told Gellman both of the reasons he wanted him along. As he finished the call, Seth asked, merely out of curiosity, "I'm sure you visit your congregants, you know, in the hospital and at home. Do you call them pastoral calls? Rabbinical calls?" Not waiting for an answer to a question he suddenly thought inappropriate, he said, "Pick you up at eight-thirty?"

Gellman chuckled, "We call them all of the above. See you tomorrow, Seth, eight-thirty. I'll bring coffee."

Seth was dreading the second phone call he had to make. He phoned Harriet on her cell, assuming she would not be at Old Stone on a Monday. The call went to voicemail, but she was obviously listening in and picked up as Seth began to leave a message. He would have much preferred to leave his message.

He began by assuring Harriet that the information they had gathered had been shared with the FBI and that even though Agent O'Reilly seemed unhappy with him, he was happy with the information, even if he did not say so. Seth then rehearsed the tale of his and Cecily Monroe's visit with Hudson Stark, informing Harriet that the boy had confessed to the vandalism, and the FBI was now pressing him for alibis on the nights of Gollancz's death and the arson. Ludington hesitated before telling her the bit he dreaded. "Harriet, I won't be in tomorrow, but I'll get you the information for Sunday's program by the end of the day, or maybe early Wednesday, if that's okay."

Van der Berg was silent for a moment, "Well, I guess I'll just have to make accommodations."

She did not ask Seth where he was going to be all day, but he knew she guessed it had to do with "their case," as she named it. She had been put to the side Monday, and now it seemed she was to be sidelined on Tuesday as well. Seth could only surmise that she was not at all happy about it. She muttered only a curt, "Well, goodbye then."

* * *

Seth had set the table for two, plus the two high chairs. As soon as Fiona came in the door at six-ten, he tossed the tagliatelle into the pot of boiling water. In the past, they had often relaxed with a glass of wine before dinner, but Ingrid and Astrid Davidson-Ludington had put a stop to that. He then melted a couple of tablespoons of butter in the biggest frying pan they owned, added the rosemary, sage, and onion, plus a bay leaf. A few minutes later, he tossed in the slices of speck. Walter had said not to overcook, so as soon as the onion slices looked like they might be about to brown, he drained the pasta and added it to the skillet. That, plus a dash—actually three dashes—of heavy cream, a dollop of the pasta water, all topped with grated parmesan, and he called up the stairs to the living room, "Dinner."

Pasta with speck was a success again, even with the girls. They liked slurping tagliatelle noodles, thought it quite humorous, in fact. After dinner, Inez took them up to the nursery for a change of diapers and to get them into their jammies while Fiona and Seth cleaned up. As he scoured the frying pan, he told her about the visits with Agent O'Reilly and Hudson Stark. Then he stopped scouring, looked at his wife, and told her he and Dan Gellman were heading out to Speonk tomorrow.

"Crivvens, Seth, you've got a real job, you know, a job they're paying you for."

This was quite true. There was no defense, so he nodded, smiled as fetchingly as he could manage, and said, "I'll do the story tonight."

The story was usually two or three story books, the last of which was always *Goodnight Moon*. Seth judged that classic to be all about stalling, the bunny in the bed putting off the end of the day and the inevitability of sleep with a litany of "good nights." Seth Ludington understood stalling perfectly well. He had wanted to stall on telling Harriet van der Berg that he and Dan Gellman were off to Speonk without her as long as possible. But in the end, it had to be done.

Chapter Thirty

Tuesday

Rabbi Daniel Gellman was in a surprisingly chipper mood when Ludington picked him up in front of his building the next day. He wore new and less dramatic bandages on his right hand. "Hardly hurts anymore. Healing up nicely, the doc said. There'll be some scars, but not too bad."

Several times in his brief pastoral career, Seth had seen people fall upwards into a giddy happiness after weathering one of life's storms. It wasn't gallows humor; rather, it was a post-gallows comicality, the joy—or almost joy—that can bubble to the surface after you realize that you survived when you might not have. As Ludington eased the Volvo up the on-ramp onto the Queensboro Bridge, Gellman was becoming downright playful.

The rabbi lifted one of the coffees he had brought along from the car's cupholder, took an enthusiastic sip, a bit of which dribbled down his chin, and said, "Okay, my friend, boring drive ahead of us. Last night, I got this idea for a new sort of interfaith dialogue. Let's you and me test it out. I mean, here we are, the minister and the rabbi. All we need is the priest. For the joke, I mean."

Seth could not but smile. "I'm game."

"Okay, here's how it works. Each of us names one thing about his own religious tradition he doesn't much like, and then we each have to name one thing about the other person's faith we admire. So I would identify some aspect of Judaism that makes me a little uncomfortable and then something about Christianity I kinda like. Then you do the reverse."

Seth had to admit it was original. "Okay, Dan, but you gotta give me till we get on the Southern State before we start. I need to think about this a bit. And I know I can't theologize and navigate Queens traffic at the same time."

"Agreed, but I need to warn you, I've already been thinking about mine."

With that, Gellman retreated to his iPhone while Ludington considered what it was about Christianity he wished were different and what it was in Judaism he most admired.

Twenty minutes later, as the Volvo merged onto Southern State, Gellman looked up, saw where they were, slipped his phone into his shirt pocket, and said, "May I go first, reverend?"

Ludington nodded.

"Okay…I wish Judaism wasn't so, well, clannish. That's not quite the right word, though. What I mean is this. We're both a tribe, a people, and a religion. And sometimes that's a problem. It's complicated." Gellman laughed at himself. "Like the movie. So you've got atheist Jews; they're in the tribe but with no religion. And then you've got messianic Jews, Jews who follow Jesus. They want to be in the tribe—think they are—but with a rather different religion. Then you add in Israel, I mean the country, and it really gets awkward. The tribe has become a country, and those of us who are in the tribe but not the country, the country of Israel, I mean, we have this clunky loyalty. Even if we're unhappy with what they're doing over there, I mean with the Palestinians. Jews around the world get blamed for what some Israeli Jews are doing. It's actually a big piece of antisemitism, lumping us all in with Israeli hard-liners. All those rabid settlers on the West Bank, not to mention the ultra-Orthodox and their perks, we American Jews are supposed to zip our lips, at least publicly. Stay loyal even when your faith makes you uncomfortable with what some of the tribe are doing. I don't much like it, but I have no idea how to fix it. So, Seth, what don't you like about Christianity?"

Traffic was thin, so Seth clicked on the Volvo's adaptive speed control. "Several things, truth be known, but the one that nags at me the most is the strain—maybe stain is a better word—the strain in Christianity that seems to hate—and that's not too strong a word—seems to hate the physical, hates the human body, hates materiality in general. It sets up this good-bad dichotomy—spirit good, material bad. It can morph into a hatred of sex and then become blatant misogyny, hatred of women. Celibacy is only one corner of it. It's been defended as a way to let clergy focus on their work without the burden of family, but there's no denying that part of the rationale was the notion that to be really holy, you had to foreswear stuff and sex, because stuff and sex were somehow evil. And it's so ironic… I mean, for this kind of thinking to unfold in a faith the core of which is the Incarnation, the idea that the Divine took on human flesh, entered right into gross materiality. Which must mean it's good. I mean flesh and stuff must be good if God made it and then wore it. It's such an inconsistency."

"Okay, Reverend Doctor Ludington…"

"Sorry, Dan, no doctorate."

"I was using the term figuratively, Seth."

Gellman was having so much fun with this. It cheered Ludington to see it.

"Okay, Reverend Not-doctor Ludington, now we switch directions. I tell you something I admire about Christianity and you do the same with Judaism. So here goes." Gellman took another gulp of his coffee, now gone lukewarm. "So, I was going to say I really like your Christian clergy outfits, the stuff you Christian ministers and priests get to wear. Not you Presbyterians. You're basic black robe types just like us. Boring. I mean the R.C.s and the Episcopalians. Whoa!"

Ludington was aware that the rabbi was teasing. "I hear you, Dan. Sometimes I get chasuble envy too."

"What?"

"Never mind."

Gellman decided not to pursue chasubles and said, "Of course, that's not what I really admire about you guys." Gellman hesitated before continuing, "Seth, I gotta say that I'm fascinated with exactly what you ended with. I mean Incarnation. This nutty idea about God coming close to us, like in the flesh. Sometimes, our Yahweh seems so distant, unknowable, like he-she is hidden in a galaxy far away. I mean, I don't believe it, the Incarnation, I mean. I can't believe it, but while we're playing truth and dare, I have to admit that it, well, pulls at me, at part of me anyway. Now you go."

"Okay, Dan, I'm going to play your 'I was going to say' game, too. So, I was going to say that I admire Judaism for inventing ethical monotheism. Well, not exactly inventing. It came to you. It was given to you." Ludington took his left hand off the steering wheel and pointed upwards with its index finger. "Before your ethical monotheism, all we had was this herd of little 'g' gods. I mean, in all the old paganisms it was a gaggle of gods, often behaving rather badly. And they could have cared less about us mortals, much less right and wrong. Then, from who-knows-where, you give us this one God who can't be carved in wood or stone, this spirit, this God-of-all-the universe who's not just our tribe's personal deity. And more than that, this God you gave us cares about right and wrong and actually loves—that's a new theological word you gave us—loves humanity. It's all so fresh, Dan. And you gave it to us."

"But that's not what you're going to say, right?"

"Yeah, too obvious. What I *most* admire about Jewish tradition is slathered all over the Hebrew Bible, the 'Old Testament,' as we call it, as if it's a gallon of month-old milk past its date. The bigger thing I like about you guys is this—your ability to critique yourself. The prophets are all about critiquing Israel's bad behavior and then letting you have it with both barrels. But it's more than the prophets. There's Ruth and Jonah. Both books are subtle narrative critiques of the idea that God cares only about us, I mean just us Jews, you Jews. Jonah is supposed to care about the nasty Ninevites because God does, even though Jonah hates their guts. And Ruth is this total foreigner, but a gem of a woman who marries into the clan and then becomes King David's great-grandmother. And then there's Job. The Book of Job is one long and laborious critique of the notion that good things happen to good people and bad things happen to bad people. I know it's an oddly comforting idea. It's comforting because it means if you keep your nose clean, you'll be safe. You're in control. Job turns that idea—which Jews at the time loved—right on its head. What I'm saying, Dan, is this. Do you know how hard it is for people to honestly evaluate themselves, I mean to look hard at what they believe and how they act, and then say, 'We got it wrong, or partly wrong?'"

Gellman reflected on Ludington's words and said, "So Seth, you know this Saturday is the first Shabbat Beth Shalom will be worshipping in your building. The little transition committee has got the details all worked out. Would you come? Say some words of welcome?"

"Wouldn't miss it, Dan. Of course."

Signs for their Speonk exit started to appear just as their interfaith dialogue reached a peak in candor. Ludington changed the vector of conversation. He had decided it would be a good idea for him to go over the second reason he had asked Dan along on this latest foray to the East End. "If Chelsea's in the house, it might be a problem, of course. I should be able to keep the elder Starks occupied. That should give you enough time to do it."

Chapter Thirty-One

Tuesday

As the Volvo exited the Sunrise Highway and wiggled through the residential lanes of Eastport and into Speonk, Seth noticed something about the houses that he had missed on his earlier visit with Harriet, something the architectural purist in him found nettlesome. "Dan, look how many houses have a brick façade, but shakes or clapboard on the sides, and I assume the back."

Gellman nodded, "A way for builders to economize. You see it all over the Island. The zillions of houses that went up when Nassau and Suffolk exploded after World War Two. My parents' house in Islip has brick on the front and cheapo siding everywhere else. It's only a brick house if you look at it straight on. I grew up in the City, but my folks moved out when Dad retired. Long Island really is a place apart. There's the accent. You still hear it. Tract houses and colonial history side-by-side. Pretty villages like Northport and sprawling sixties shopping malls. Big money in this corner, fresh immigrants scraping by in that. And, let me tell you, it's so incredibly provincial. Lots of 'em never leave the Island, except maybe to go into Manhattan for a show once a year or to Miami in January. My dad says they think of the United States as consisting of three islands—Long Island, Manhattan Island, and the big island to the west." Still wrapped in his giddy mood, Gellman thought his father's witticism funnier than it was.

Ludington parked in the Stark's empty driveway with its cracked asphalt

"

flanked by mature azaleas that had long since finished blooming for the season. Beyond a basic orderliness, the Stark property was edging toward seedy. Yews planted around the foundation were overgrown and hid the bottom half of the first-floor windows. The grass was mowed, but sported brown spots everywhere in spite of the recent rain.

Gellman stood behind Ludington as the minister—sans clerical collar for this trip—pushed the doorbell. The Irene Stark who opened the door could hardly have looked more different from the one Seth had seen at the funeral and the shiva—no makeup, no Chanel suit, hair still wet from a shower and combed back. She was dressed in dark gray sweatpants and a blue Hofstra long-sleeve tee shirt. Her eyes were red and swollen.

"Oh, you've come." She threw her head back as if to commence keening. "My pastor has come to me in my darkest hour." With this theatrical declaration appointing Ludington to a new position, she backed away from the entrance to let the two men enter. Ignoring Gellman, she gave Ludington an inappropriately long hug. "Jack didn't want me to take him to his program, so he's here. But Chelsea's not. She's at a friend's house. She just had to get out. This has crushed her as well."

Ludington caught Gellman's eye at this latter and welcome piece of news. Irene, now the flustered hostess, finally said, "Come in, come in. Can I fix coffee?"

Both confessed to being coffeed out. Irene led them through the kitchen into the family room. Jack Stark was parked in his wheelchair facing the massive television screen. Irene grabbed the remote from him and turned the set off. He emitted a grunt of discontent.

"We have guests, Jack. You'll remember the Reverend Ludington. He was kind enough to attend Larry's service in the City." She paused, "And he visited with Hudson yesterday. And he has procured legal representation for our son. So we can put this behind us." The woman's optimism was surely a mask for her fear. She stifled a sob after declaring it.

Ludington looked at Jack Stark—gaunt, gray-faced, thinning colorless hair. Parkinson's or no, his face was a mask. The man seemed detached from all that was swirling around him, a resigned observer of the inevitable.

Irene swept her hand in the direction of the huge sectional couch that dominated the room, "Sit, please."

Ludington and Gellman sat next to each other on the longer arm of the L-shaped piece of furniture covered in ersatz leather. The short arm faced the television, leaving space for Jack Stark's wheelchair beside it. Irene settled her ample self on the couch near her husband. She reached out for his hand, resting hers on the black plastic arm of the wheelchair. He laid his atop hers, a movement he made with some difficulty.

Irene cleared her throat and struck what she doubtless meant to be a courageous pose. She said, "Tell me about my boy. I mean to say, tell me about your visit. And his visit with the attorney. What did he say?"

Unsure whether Irene was asking what Hudson or the attorney had said, he guessed at the latter, "The attorney is named Cecily Monroe. She is a member of my congregation, and I judge her to be highly competent. You saw Hudson yesterday after we did, so I assume he told you he has confessed to the vandalism of Temple Beth Shalom."

Irene nodded. A single tear wandered down her cheek.

Ludington said, "Ms. Monroe said a plea deal is probably not possible. Hudson has confessed, both verbally and in writing. She's hopeful that between his age and this being a first offense—if it actually is—she can make a case to the judge for leniency."

Gellman, perhaps seeking to justify his presence, or perhaps because he needed to unburden himself, leaned forward to speak. He sat on the forward edge of the deep couch, resting his hands on his knees and hiding the bandages on the one as best he could with the other. He spoke slowly and softy. "Mr. and Mrs. Stark, what your son did to my place of worship, what he did, by extension, to Jews everywhere, was horrific. It was a gross crime, one that cries out to heaven. Assuming he's guilty, he must be punished. But neither I nor my congregation desire vengeance. Can he ever be forgiven? Can I ever forgive him? I don't know. In time, perhaps. But know this, to forgive is not to forget. I will not forget what I saw in my synagogue, nor should I. And remember also that to forgive is not to trivialize. Sometimes when people forgive, they say, 'Oh, it was nothing.' That's often a lie. What was done to Beth Shalom was not nothing. Seth told me your son talked about 'just messing things up a bit.' It was much, much more than that. It was hateful, deeply hateful, and I cannot and will not minimize it. But perhaps, with time, I will choose to no longer bear the weight of my fury."

Ludington was unable to judge how Gellman's eloquence landed with the Starks. Save for a second tear descending Irene's cheek, they were both impassive, though Irene did look Gellman in the eyes as he spoke. Jack stared at the dead black of the television screen.

After his speech, Gellman rose and said, "If you'll excuse me, I have to check my phone. I must have left it in the car." He turned and walked through the kitchen toward the house's front entryway which also lodged the staircase to the second floor.

Ludington promptly fired the salvo he knew would lock in the attention of both Starks. He leaned forward, just as Dan had, and said, "I am sure you are aware that the Federal Bureau of Investigation, who are handling the case now, have asked your son about his whereabouts on the Monday night after the vandalism. That would be the night your brother died, Irene. And they are also asking if he has an alibi for the following Wednesday, the night Beth Shalom burned."

Jack's head jerked up. He looked directly at Ludington for the first time in their visit. Irene blanched, "What are you saying? That there's something suspicious about Larry's accident? That my son is an arsonist?" Before Ludington's eyes, Irene Stark's fear morphed into anger. "Hudson may have done something stupid and broken into Larry's synagogue. But those other things, never." She paused, looked at her husband, and said, "You may as well know. My brother was considering making some changes to his will, adding some bequests to his synagogue in the City. He mentioned what he was planning the evening of the dinner. It was, as you might imagine, a disappointment to Hudson." She did not need to say, "And to all of us." Those words hung in the air, unspoken. She seemed to deliver this news as if it might excuse the vandalism.

Before he had decided to make this visit, Ludington knew it would lead him to further needful acts of prevarication. He hoped their needfulness would justify them. "Mr. and Mrs. Stark, the FBI are aware that a vehicle matching the one you own, the black Mercedes-Benz G-Class, made three visits to your uncle's home around the time of his death. Two were made the evening of the night he died and another the next day. They have witnesses to those visits." He was implying the FBI had conveyed this information to him or to Cecily Monroe, when it was actually the other way around. Nor did he mention that the "witness" was a doorbell in the first two cases and himself and a doorbell in the third.

Irene went wide-eyed, rattled into temporary silence. The silence lasted just long enough for her to think carefully as to how she might respond. "Well, yes, of course. I called on Larry the day he died, early in the evening, actually, a bit after six. I wanted to talk to him more about his plans regarding his will." She hesitated before continuing, doubtless at a loss as to what to say next. She threw her head back and said, "And the day after he died, I went to his house because I had forgotten my... phone. Yes, my phone, I must have left it when I went to chat with Larry about the will the evening before."

Ludington had not mentioned that she was on camera for both those visits, but not the visit the G-Class made later that evening, the one timestamped just after nine. Nor did he mention the specific time. "Irene, do you know who made the second visit, the later one on the night he died? It was made by someone driving your vehicle." He hesitated, "That would be well after your six o'clock visit and conversation with your brother."

Irene Stark was one of those people whose facial coloring unavoidably betrayed their emotions. At Ludington's last question, her face went apple red. She said nothing for at least ten seconds. When she spoke, it was with a vaunted dignity meant to speak her indignation at being asked such a question. "Well, if you must know, I returned for a second talk with Larry." She rubbed her hands vigorously on the thighs of her sweatpants and said, "Jack has an appointment at his day program. I must drive him, of course. So, if you'll please excuse us."

She stood and began to forage in her immense purse, probably for car keys, mumbling to the universe, "Where are the keys to the Mercedes? They're not in my purse."

Jack Stark glanced away from the television screen, "Look in the drawer in the kitchen, Irene, where we keep keys."

"I almost never put them there, Jack. I always keep them in my purse. And the kids have their own."

Her hostess smile gone, she rose, a quick movement that clearly invited the man she had so recently elected her pastor to leave. She marched past Ludington and into the kitchen, opened a cabinet drawer, and said, "How odd."

Ludington showed himself out the front door and found Gellman sitting in the passenger's seat of the Volvo, looking pensive. He smiled wanly as Seth got in. Ludington pushed the start button and told Gellman all he had asked Irene about. Then he said, "I think she might be lying about it being her who made the nine o'clock visit. Said she went back to talk more about the will. Possible, but I sensed she was surprised by the second Mercedes visit. She's not much of a liar. Or then again, maybe she's a fine actress, talented at feigning surprise." He paused before adding, "How did you do, Dan?"

"Snuck upstairs and found what is obviously Hudson's room. Kid's a slob. Three pair of tennis shoes in a pile in the closet. All size eleven." Seth raised both eyebrows at that news and said, "Figures." It means, of course, that there are two pair of size eleven L. L. Bean Duck Boots in the story. One pair sits on Lawrence Gollancz's back stoop, and another is on Hudson Stark's feet in the Metropolitan Correctional Center."

Gellman nodded, "And both are big enough to get most feet into."

The drive back into the City was passed not in theological musing, but in speculation of a more mundane order. Seth said, "My guess is that the six o'clock visit Irene made to her brother was just what she said it was—another chat about the will, though I doubt 'chat' is quite the right word. And my guess is that the visit she made the day after he died, the one you and I witnessed, was to search the house for the will. I bet she wanted to see if he'd signed it. And maybe make it disappear if he had. But the nine o'clock visit when the G-Class flashed by and then, a few minutes later, the

little curious video when the camera goes dark, got recorded. That's the
interesting one."

Chapter Thirty-Two

Wednesday

Seth found Harriet ensconced in her cubicle when he arrived at Old Stone at nine-thirty the next morning. Seated with her back to him, she appeared to be adding several typed pages of Session minutes to the giant leather-bound ledger books long used by Presbyterians for the keeping of records for a posterity unlikely to ever read them. She did not look up as he entered. He said, "Morning, Harriet."

Neither turning to him nor using his name, she said, "It is indeed morning."

For all her self-discipline, Harriet van der Berg's anger was inevitably transparent. Ludington sat in the extra chair, squeezed into her office, sighed loudly enough for the woman to hear, and said, "I want to bring you up to speed on a few things. I mean, the FBI visit and the one with Hudson Stark on Monday, and then the parents yesterday."

She set the Session ledger aside and turned to him. "Do you really need to, Seth? You and Rabbi Gellman seem to have matters well in hand, quite by yourselves."

He said only, "Harriet." He did not need to explain to her why she had been side-lined these last two days. She understood it; she simply did not like it. It was he and Gellman who had been summoned to the offices of the Federal Bureau of Investigation, not her. And she could hardly have gotten herself into the Metropolitan Correctional Center for what purported to be a legal and pastoral visit. And to the Starks, he hardly needed to remind her, she was still Henrietta Berg, Lawrence Gollancz's final flame.

"I know, I know," she said. "But perhaps I should simply return to my merest secretarial duties. She waved a dismissive hand at the Session ledgers, "Typing and filing, you know, and politely answering the phone for you."

"Don't you quit on me, Harriet. You know I need you."

"For what?"

"You see things I don't see. You know things I don't know."

"Here at church, you mean?"

"Yes, and in our alternative efforts."

Ludington was able to bring her back on board by walking her through the details of his visits to various Starks, visits she had not been a part of, including the lace-less duck boots he had seen on Hudson's feet and neglected to mention when he had called her Monday.

Even though she feared she had become superfluous, Harriet could not tame her hungry curiosity. After hearing his summary, she said, "L. L. Bean Duck Boots, you say. And he was wearing them when you saw him, that strangely fashionable duck hunting footwear."

Ludington was pleased to see her softening. "Means, of course, that there are two pair of size eleven duck boots in the Stark-Gollancz world. And I'm guessing Irene may have been fibbing when she said she went back to visit her brother for a second time that night. Said she wanted to chat about the will some more. I suppose it's possible, but if you could have seen her face, Harriet."

"Well, you and Rabbi Gellman have doubtless discovered it on your own, but should you have not, you need to know that Chelsea Bun has posted a fifth episode of *The Gas Generator Mystery.* This news was offered triumphantly.

Seth was happy to tell her that he and Gellman had missed it, which pulled the woman back into the realm of the useful. She turned to her computer, found the video on YouTube, and said, "You'll see that she's both directive and bold."

Chelsea Stark was back in her signature trench coat and deer stalker. Ludington did not recognize the location at first, a sloping lawn leading to what looked to be the rear of a midcentury house. Then he knew. "Good Lord, Harriet, she's in Masterson's back yard."

"Precisely."

"Chelsea Bun here with Episode Five of The Gas Generator Mystery. And dear viewers, the plot has thickened. Really has. So, it turns out that the dead rich guy, you know, the one who got gassed by carbon monoxide, the guy whose family was in a state because he was going to leave his money to his church, well he was—get this—a convert. He was actually Jewish. By birth, you know. Anyway, the Keystone Cops who are investigating this case, they paid a visit to his brother and his family in Plainfield yesterday afternoon. They had all sorts of stupid questions about where the members of his family, like the dad and the mom and the son —the one they arrested—where they were the night the guy died. Really wanted to know about the son. And they took pictures of the family car in the garage. Well, as you might guess, they're thinking that maybe it wasn't an accident like I said last episode. That somebody put the thing under his window. And that it was, like, murder. Maybe they're right. Well, if that's the case, Chelsea Bun's got something to show you guys".

Chelsea stepped toward the phone and its camera, which must have been mounted on a tripod of some sort, took it in hand, and turned it toward the rear of Masterson's house. She walked closer to the sliding doors on the lower level, finally aiming the camera directly into a large finished room and the huge flag pinned to the opposite wall.

"That, dear viewers, is the Vinland flag. It's like a new Nazi symbol. And this house is right next door to the rich guy that got killed. Your faithful detective came snooping because I spotted an interesting bumper sticker on this guy's car a while back. ADL. Arian Defense League. Look it up. Neo-Nazis. And you know these wackos hate Jews, even if they convert. I hope the Keystone Cops see this episode. I know I've got some cop followers".

Harriet looked away from her monitor to her pastor. "I'm surprised she knows who the Keystone Cops are. Out of her generation's range, I should think."

Seth leaned back in his chair, stretching out his long legs to the right of Harriet's office chair. He clasped his hands behind his head and said, "It's become a trope—Keystone Cops, I mean. Even if you've never seen the old films. *Episode Five* is quite informative, Harriet, wouldn't you agree? The FBI—I assume they're the Keystone Cops—are indeed investigating Gollancz's death as a possible homicide. O'Reilly or somebody is taking our stuff a little bit seriously. They must have called on the Starks sometime after Dan and I left, and Chelsea must have been at home when they came. Of course, she's trying to deflect them away from Hudson and toward Masterson. Gotta hand it to her that she saw the bumper sticker on his car and had the guts to record right in the guy's back yard. My guess is that she filmed the episode late afternoon yesterday. After the Keystone Cops left Speonk and before Masterson got home from pumping septic tanks. She was smart enough to check, I hope."

"Seth, she could be right. Hate so often ends in death. And the dark sedan the Ring camera photographed driving speedily past was perhaps indeed him, Masterson that is. And maybe the second visit by the Stark vehicle was Irene, who had come to talk with her brother again."

"Maybe, Harriet, but why would Masterson have to drive over to do it? He could have walked."

"It was raining, Seth, raining hard. I took the precautions of emailing the Ring videos to myself before that FBI agent came for Gollancz's phone and my plaster castings of assorted footprints. I think I shall take yet another look at those recordings, especially the one of the dark-colored sedan."

Something else bothered Ludington about the Masterson theory, but he couldn't quite recall what it was. "Harriet, I know I've got to get the bulletin information to you. I know I'm late, sorry. He hoped that little apology, though about something else altogether, might dull the edge of van der Berg's irritation. He retreated to his office, leaving Harriet to her "merest secretarial duties."

He was debating his choice of the final hymn for Sunday when his cell rang. The screen read, "Monroe."

"Ms. Monroe," he said.

"Reverend Ludington, I just got a call from Hudson. He's frantic. Says they're threatening to charge him with his uncle's murder. From all you told me, the evidence looks pretty circumstantial. Motive, matching footprints, the family car at the scene at the right time. Those doorbell recordings, you know. But, I've got a hunch they're still not convinced they have a murder on their hands. I think they're trying to frighten the kid into copping a plea on the arson. If they do charge him for homicide I'm pretty sure I could get him off, unless there's more they're not talking about yet. It wouldn't be a hard one to defend. He's scared shitless, and he's in withdrawal. I'm going to try to see him again, today if I can, or tomorrow. Tell him again to keep his mouth shut." She paused, "But I doubt I can get you in again."

"I understand. Ms. Monroe, you should know that Rabbi Gellman and I visited Hudson's parents yesterday, a sort of dual pastoral call. And I need to tell you one thing. I don't think Irene knew about their Mercedes making the second trip to her brother's house that night. She said it was her, but I'm pretty sure she was lying."

"Well, that must have been one hell of a pastoral call. I mean, you, the minister visiting the Jewish family, and the rabbi whose temple their kid vandalized tagging along. A couple of clergymen pressing two doubtlessly distraught parents about visits to a crime scene. Jeez." She paused for a moment before saying, "Well, I just thought you should know about the possible indictment of the kid, since you're up to your neck in this. Another question, Seth. Why are you paying me to defend this jerk?"

"Even jerky kids deserve a lawyer, Cecily." This was quite true, of course, but Ludington had no desire to see Hudson Stark exonerated of anything. He wondered if the lawyer guessed he had hired her largely to keep himself on the inside track of the investigation of the cluster of crimes he thought were interrelated.

After Monroe hung up, Seth went into Harriet's office and told her the news. She said only, "Do you really think they're quite sure about Hudson? Have they not viewed the latest episode of *The Generator Mystery?*"

Not knowing the answer to either of those questions—in fact, not knowing the answer to a great many questions—Seth went back to his desk and decided on hymn number 49, "The God of Abraham Praise," for the final hymn for Sunday. He was not planning on yet another antisemitism sermon, but a hymn written by a Jew might keep the subject in the congregation's consciousness for another week. It was certainly stuck in his consciousness.

He emailed the details for the Sunday bulletin to Harriet. As he passed her office on his way out of the building, he said to her, "I'm off to Marco Polo for a slice. Can I bring you one?" Maybe pizza would mollify her. Van der Berg offered the slightest smile in response. "Yes, that would be perfectly delightful. Just cheese."

They ate their noon pizzas separately. Seth wanted to get a jump on the Bible Study he would begin later in the month. He officially called it "The Breakfast Bible Study," although almost everybody at the church called it "The Men's Bible Study." All were welcome—men and women both—but by some unspoken agreement, only men came—five of them on a well-attended Thursday morning. He had pointedly invited several women. They had smiled and said, "We'll see," which he soon understood meant, "Not on your life." Harry Mulholland, who never missed and always brought the donuts, had suggested they tackle the prophet Isaiah this go-around. Seth liked the idea. Christians often reduced Isaiah to little more than a predictor of the coming Messiah, a mere prelude to the gospels. The prophet was even more, and Seth was eager to usher the Thursday morning gents deeper into that even more.

It was four-thirty by the time he had finished brushing up on Isaiah and outlining the eight sessions of The Breakfast Bible Study. Harriet had already gone home, and he was eager to pick up the girls at the Happy House of Little Ones and get them home before Fiona arrived. He was shutting down his computer when his cell rang. He pulled it out of his pocket. It was Cecily Monroe again.

"Did you see Hudson?" he asked without thinking.

"No. I'm on for a visit tomorrow morning, not that I need to bother. So Reverend Ludington, as you might imagine, I've got my sources in local law enforcement. Just got a call from one of them. Reverend Ludington…can I call you Seth? Seth, you are not going to believe this. Irene Stark has confessed to the murder of her brother. Called the agent who visited them yesterday afternoon. They're on their way out there to bring her in for questioning."

Seth Ludington was shocked into atypical silence. Cecily Monroe broke it, "I gotta tell you, Reverend, this is better than *True Detective* any day."

Chapter Thirty-Three

Wednesday

The dinner party was Fiona's idea. It was last minute, the inspiration coming to her after Seth phoned to tell her that Irene Stark had confessed to murdering her brother. Not that Fiona wanted to celebrate either murder or a sibling's confession of it. Rather, she assumed this meant her husband's co-sleuthing with Harriet van der Berg and Daniel Gellman was at an end. She was pleased about this and decided it merited a dinner party. She left her U.N. office early, at three-thirty, calling her husband from the cab with her plans. Seth agreed to fetch the girls and have them home by four-thirty. Fiona told him she had phoned Dan's wife, Lilly, who said they'd be happy to come as long as it was okay to bring Zack. Harriet, who lived alone and never declined a dinner invitation, had said yes without hesitation even though she was still feeling marginalized. Even after three years, she had not grown accustomed to eating alone in front of the PBS NewsHour, though she really did like Judy Woodruff. The woman was so straightforward and unaffected.

When Seth arrived home, he plopped the girls in their playpen and opened a couple bottles of an exquisite 2009 Chianti riserva that had been hiding on the bottom shelf of the wine fridge. They needed to breathe. The wine was, he judged, just reaching its prime. Fiona had christened the evening "celebratory," though he was less confident that it was quite time to toast the sleuths. Sampling the Chianti, he said to his wife as she stirred spaghetti sauce, "Fiona, this is so sweet of you."

The table in the Ludington kitchen was too small for five plus the three high chairs, so Fiona and Seth set the dining room table, seldom used but plenty large. They decided to do spaghetti again, this time with Italian sausage, all beef. Fiona had picked up the sausage, two jars of Raos's vodka sauce, and three bags of a prepared Caesar salad at Fairway on the way home. Seth assured her that people would forgive the premade salad. This was eleventh hour, after all.

Though the dinner proved a success, no one chose to toast the sleuths. A sister having confessed to murdering her brother was indelibly tragic. If the meal was a celebration, it merely feted a return to normal routines for those gathered around the table, whether they welcomed such a return or not. No more drives out onto Long Island. No more confrontations with loathsome antisemites. No more scorching interviews with the FBI. No more descents into the Hades of the Metropolitan Correctional Center. Though Ludington did guess that he would probably need to make a genuinely pastoral call on Irene Stark at some point and perhaps another on her family. That is, if he was still deemed her adopted pastor.

As Seth and Fiona cleared the table, Dan Gellman sighed and said, "I figured it was Masterson. I really did."

Harriet looked at the rabbi, nodded, and said, "I had hoped so as well. I find Irene Stark rather a distasteful person, so ambitious to be what she is not, but I did not fathom her a murderess."

Lilly Gellman, who had been watching the unfolding tale for weeks, but from the sidelines, could only shake her head and say, "Simple greed, the consuming ambition to be someone else, and her sense that she had been cheated—by the new will, I mean. It all must have driven her to it. But then, in the end, the mother in her trumps all, so she confesses."

Dinner over and the table cleared, Seth was foraging in the freezer for the coffee ice cream he knew was there somewhere. Ice cream and a glass of something—Grand Marnier perhaps—would be a fitting punctuation to the evening. The hour was not late, just after eight, but babies needed their beds. His phone rang the moment he located the ice cream under an immense bag of frozen shrimp. He stood, ice cream tub in one hand, and pulled the phone out of his pocket with his other. It was Harry Mulholland, of all people. Church business, doubtless. But odd for him to call at home and in the evening.

"Harry, what's up?"

"Can I come over, Seth? Some news just came my way, news you'll want to hear."

"Sure, Harry, but the Gellmans are here, and Harriet."

"So much the better. I'll be there in ten."

Harry arrived in shirt sleeves and no tie, the first time Seth had ever seen the man without a jacket and necktie. Harry excused this sartorial indiscretion, saying, "It's warm outside, and we were just watching *Frasier* reruns when I got the call." Seth was surprised to hear that his Clerk of Session did not wear a tie for television viewing.

Harry agreed to the coffee ice cream but not the Grand Marnier. Seth pulled up a sixth chair to the table for him.

"You can all hear this," Mulholland began. "It's about the synagogue and that guy out on Long Island, I mean the gas generator death, and that kid the FBI arrested for the vandalism. I know you've been poking your collective noses into the whole thing."

None of the owners of the collective noses responded to his accusation. Harriet smiled blandly. It was clear to the table that Harry did not know that the kid's mother had just confessed to murdering her brother.

Mulholland took a sip of his water. "So, I got a call an hour ago, an old buddy from the precinct who's now FBI, guy named Jimmy Maddox. I had lunch with him last week and told him my pastor was snooping around what happened to the Temple on 3rd Avenue and that carbon monoxide death out in Suffolk. Told him that he—that would be you, Seth—had suspicions about it all. So anyway, my friend decided to give me a call when he heard some FBI office chatter. My buddy says he thinks O'Reilly—he knows the guy—was talking a murder charge with the kid—Jimmy used the word 'kid'— and that they were pressing him for a plea deal. Well, the kid suddenly remembered something. Said that he'd been stopped in Queens, I mean stopped by NYPD the night his uncle died. Said he'd been pulled over on Northern Boulevard for a busted tail light, but not really. Narcotics had set up a sting operation in back of a warehouse in Flushing, a spot they guessed was being used for drug transactions, dealers buying and selling, pills and cocaine mostly. Anyway, kid was there, so they pulled him over as he left and searched his car. No drugs, but they found a wad of hundreds under the front seat. They brought him into the precinct and grilled him for a few hours. They hadn't witnessed him break any laws, so all they could do was write him up for the tail light and let him go. But they had him for over two hours. Seems the kid remembered all this when the FBI started hinting about murder on top of vandalism. Kept quiet about his evening in Flushing until they started quizzing him about his uncle. What's his name, Seth? I mean the kid."

"Hudson, Hudson Stark."

"Point is, I thought you'd probably want to know that this Hudson Stark was in Queens getting grilled about drugs and cash under his front seat the night his uncle died. They didn't release him till after ten that night. Jimmy says the timing doesn't work."

Seth looked at his Clerk of Session and said, "Can't be in two places at once."

Fiona and Lilly had taken the three babies into the living room when Harry had begun his tale, so it was just Seth, Dan, and Harriet who found themselves staring at Harry Mulholland in silent incredulity.

It was Seth who broke the quiet. "What time did Hudson Stark manage to remember this, Harry? Do you know?

"Jim said it was yesterday afternoon, early."

It was Harriet who spoke the obvious, "Before his mother confessed to the crime."

Harry's head jerked back in surprise and cried, "What?"

"Harry," Seth said slowly, "Hudson Stark's mother has confessed to killing her brother, did so today. It would seem she did it after her son found his alibi, but before she knew about it."

Mulholland, the retired homicide cop, said. "Well, this is a first."

Seth nodded, "And Harry, one more favor. Would you call your buddy

Jimmy and have him call the Queens guys who brought in Hudson Stark and ask them a question."

"What do you want to know now?"

"See if you can find out what he was wearing on his feet when they brought him in. What kind of shoes, I mean."

"You're kidding, Seth, right?"

Nope. Harry, I'd really like to know."

Harry Mulholland answered with a shrug of the shoulders.

Seth decided not to share the hunch that had been taking shape in him since he had heard of Irene Stark's confession that afternoon—that she had done it only to protect her son. She had confessed before she knew Hudson had come up with a rock-solid alibi. Seth wondered when the cops would tell her. Probably not for a while. They hold what they know close.

Seth looked up from this reflection, aimed as it had been at the untouched glass of Grand Marnier in front of him. He could see Fiona and Lilly in the living room, jiggling sleepy babies in their arms. He saw Lilly kiss Zack on the top of his head and thought to himself, "Mothers are like that, even crazy ones. Do anything for their babes." Of course, this particular mother may have confessed in order to save her son and still be quite guilty. Even mothers who are willing to sacrifice themselves for a child might be driven by anger and greed to do unthinkable things.

Chapter Thirty-Four

Thursday

Cecily Monroe called Ludington at nine o'clock the next morning, just as he was wrestling the empty double stroller out the door and up the steps of the Happy House of Little Ones. "Seth, Cecily here. So why do you only send me clients who confess? I prefer the kind that maintains their innocence, even if they're guilty as hell."

"I assume Irene Stark or somebody in her family called you."

"She did. From the Suffolk County lockup out in Riverhead. Quite hysterical. The woman was barely cogent."

"You agreed to take her case?"

"Of course, too juicy to refuse. It'll be all over the papers, TV, social media. All publicity is good publicity. True for politicians and lawyers."

But not for clergy, Seth thought to himself. What he said was, "I assume you know that Hudson has an alibi for the night of the murder."

"The prosecutor's office told me. Exculpatory evidence. They don't dare sit on it. But how on earth did you learn that bit of news, Reverend?"

Seth enjoyed answering, "I have my sources, Cecily."

"Okay, okay. What else do you know, Detective Ludington?"

"Nothing that I haven't told you, except for a hunch I have. So, you know I paid a call on Irene and Jack Stark earlier in the week, a sort of pastoral call, me and Rabbi Gellman. She called me when they arrested Hudson. Seems she's adopted me as her chaplain. Though I may have been fired. I told her about the two visits their Mercedes made to her brother's place the evening of the night he died. We know she made the first. She's in the video, ringing the doorbell. The second was the fast drive-by, but it's their car. Well, she admitted to the first. Said she went to chat—that was her dubious verb—with her brother about the will business. But Cecily, I'm not sure she knew about the second visit the Mercedes made. She seemed taken aback when I mentioned it, then claimed she went back to talk to Lawrence some more. It's possible she was merely surprised that I knew about it. So anyway, that's my main hunch. My ancillary hunch is that she could be confessing to protect Hudson. I mean, she didn't know about his alibi at that point. Maybe she thinks it was him who made the second visit. Or then, maybe it was her that second time, and she waited to confess till they were about to charge her son."

"So, you're guessing the generator was moved under Gollancz's window by whoever it was in the Mercedes that second visit."

"Makes sense, though there was the other vehicle, the sedan that passed by half an hour earlier. I know, this is a lot of 'or maybes.' Oh, and another thing, not that it much matters anymore. Hudson wears a size eleven shoe."

"Well, young Hudson is off the hook for homicide. The kid's alibi is as airtight as they come. Seth, how do you know Hudson's shoe size?"

It was as much fun to say it the second time. "I have my sources."

Monroe was lawyer enough not to press anybody on the question of sources. "Well, Mr. I-Have-My-Sources, the prosecutor will eventually have to tell her about Hudson's alibi. And they'll have to let me know when they do. It'll be interesting to see if she retracts. So, I get hunches, too. My hunch is that they think they have their woman, Seth. The goofy pile of evidence you and your little old admin collected has gotten the FBI thinking that Gollancz was a homicide and somehow related to the vandalism and arson they were called in on."

"Well, I must say I am pleased to hear that somebody shares my—I mean our—suspicions. It's not that I need to be right. It's just that, well, justice is needful. Oh, and Cecily, I would not call Harriet van der Berg my 'little old admin,' at least in her presence. She would detest all three words."

"Understood. So, I'm going to visit Mrs. Stark later today, as soon as they bring her in from Riverhead. FBI is maintaining jurisdiction because they're guessing all these things—the vandalism, and the arson, and maybe Gollancz, are connected hate crimes. Not the same person, but maybe the same family. Though I still don't get the idea of Jews being antisemitic. I mean, Irene is Jewish right, which makes Hudson Jewish too?"

"Anything is possible, Cecily. With human beings, anything is possible."

"You don't need to tell me that, Reverend. I've seen it all."

After they ended the call, Seth agreed that Cecily Monroe, the criminal defense lawyer, probably had seen it all. He wondered if she carried the all of it home with her. It had clearly hardened her. But had it hardened all of her—the wife part and mother part, as well as the lawyer part? Fiona, the human rights lawyer, had seen it all, crimes crueler than any Cecily Monroe might imagine. Yet his wife managed to leave those horrors in her office at UN Plaza. Not always, of course. But mostly. He decided that sometimes you really do need to compartmentalize your life. He knew he did.

Seth worked away at his upcoming Breakfast Bible Study plans, remembering just in time that he had a noon meeting with the Worship Committee, such as it was. It had just three members, all retired. And they met only quarterly. Two of its members lived alone, so Seth decided they might welcome gathering over lunch at Lex.

He had come to understand that the priorities people brought to meetings varied dramatically. One type saw them as a vehicle to get things done— make decisions and implement them. They liked short meetings. Another type welcomed committee meetings as a social opportunity. Getting the business done mattered, but was often secondary. For them, the longer the meeting, the better. These two kinds of committee members frustrated each other enormously. Happily, his little Worship Committee consisted only of the second, social types. Lunch would be long, but Seth figured he could pay the bill and leave when business was accomplished. And he actually did have a piece of Worship Committee business to conduct.

The matter he set before the committee as they sat around a four-top near the front window at Lex was whether to serve wine rather than the customary grape juice at communion. The coming Sunday was the first of the month and by tradition a communion Sunday. He posed this question just as Nero set three glasses of Chardonnay and one of cabernet in front of him and the Worship Committee. The discussion unfolded much as he anticipated. He pointed out that wine, not Welch's, had been served at the Last Supper, indeed that unfermented grape juice had been an impossibility prior to Mr. Welch devising a method to pasteurize it. He did not mention that, in his opinion, the stuff tasted sickly sweet and that it was so, well, faux. The counter-argument offered by two committee members was equally predictable. "What about alcoholics? Would not they be tempted?" Seth said, "We'll offer grape juice as well, just as we do gluten-free bread." In the end, there was little passion for the question around the table, save for his own. Seth guessed that the stronger motivation for inaction was simply inertia. "We've always done grape juice." In the end, Martha Nickerson moved to table the matter so that members of the committee might ask around the church to see what people thought. They adjourned the meeting proper and proceeded to enjoy their luncheon—the food, the fellowship, and the wine.

On his way back to church, he stopped at Fairway and bought a loaf of bread and a large plastic bottle of Welch's Grape Juice for Sunday. As he paid for it, he thought of T. S. Eliot's line in *Ash Wednesday*, "Teach us to care and not to care."

Chapter Thirty-Five

Friday

Friday was sermon writing day, though this Friday was actually to be a sermon re-writing day. Seth Ludington had not been preaching long enough to have collected much of what ministers call "a barrel," that library of former sermons you could reach into and pull out an oldie-but-goodie for the Sunday looming ahead of you. Any sermon he had preached at Old Stone in his nearly two years there would be too recent. People sometimes do remember sermons.

Fortunately, Seth had served as a guest preacher several times in his decade doing social and advocacy work for New Philadelphia Ministries. He remembered that one of those sermons had been based on Matthew 18:20, *"For where two or three are gathered in my name, I am there among them,"* the last verse of the lectionary Gospel reading for the coming Sunday. If he recalled correctly, the sermon had affirmed the Divine Presence that can be incarnate in communities, even very small ones. This particular Sunday fell on Labor Day weekend, and a significant portion of Old Stone's members would be away in what New Yorkers generically call "the country," where they would not, of course, be laboring. There would be more than two or three gathered in His name at Old Stone come Sunday, but not that many more. So Ludington did not feel as guilty as he otherwise would have about reheating an old sermon. But as he worked through it, he realized how much his preaching had changed, indeed how much he had changed, in the nine years since he had first preached it at the Wayne Presbyterian Church in suburban Philadelphia. By eleven o'clock, he found himself rewriting an old sermon he now found to be earnest but callow.

He had opened it back then with a long—too long—quotation from Robert Putnam's study of the disintegration of community, *Bowling Alone.* The quote fit, even if its tone was starchily academic, but Putnam's book was now twenty years old. So he chased down an essay he had recently read in the *Times* on what the piece had named "the epidemic of loneliness." He shaped the sermon around the truth that human beings are built for life together, and without community of some kind, souls whither. *"In community, we don't just find each other, we find ourselves, and often we find God as well, right there, in the midst of us."* He decided to keep the richly ironic story of St. Simon Stylites he had used a decade earlier. *"Simon was the bizarre fourth-century Christian mystic who had chosen to live his life on a platform atop an ever-higher pillar—ultimately perched fifty feet off the ground—in the Syrian desert. "Simon's initial hope,"* Seth wrote, *"was to be radically alone with God. But soon, hundreds of visitors called on him every afternoon to ask for his counsel and prayer. Dear Simon was so wrong in what he sought, but so blessed in what he found."* Ironically, Seth thought to himself, he would be preaching this sermon about community to souls who had gotten themselves up and out of their beds on a Labor Day weekend and gone off to church to be together with other souls, all endangered by the epidemic of loneliness, but having done something about it.

He had largely finished writing what was, for the most part, a new sermon by three o'clock when he heard a soft knock at the door. It was Harriet's usual trio of quick taps. He called out "Come in." Van der Berg was dramatically apologetic for the interruption. She guarded her pastor fiercely on his sermon-writing day and loathed doing what she attempted to prevent anyone else doing.

"I am so terribly sorry for disturbing your sermonic cogitations, Seth, but I was certain you would want to know."

He turned away from his laptop and offered a forced smile. "No problem, Harriet."

She came around his desk to face him across its oaken expanse and said, "Long Island *Newsday* has run an online story about Irene Stark, that is to say, a story regarding her confession to having murdered her brother. You'll need to come into my office to view it on my computer screen. I was certain you would wish to know of it forthwith, even though I observe that you are in the midst of your hermeneutical preparations for Sunday." She nodded at the sermon on the screen of Seth's laptop.

"I'm pretty much finished, Harriet. No apologies needed."

He followed van der Berg into her cubicle and sat on the extra chair at the end of her little desk. She remained standing, tapped a few keys on the keyboard and turned the monitor so Seth could see the *Newsday* story that popped up on its screen. It was not on page one, but in the Suffolk section a few pages in. *"Sister Confesses to Slaying,"* the headline read in a medium-sized font. The three columns of the story outlined the case without offering any speculation as to the crime's motive, but paid heavy attention to the novel means by which Irene Stark had ostensibly brought about the death of Lawrence Gollancz. It noted that Irene Stark's son, one Hudson Stark, age twenty, was also under arrest, he in New York, charged with the vandalism of the late Mr. Gollancz's synagogue, Temple Beth Shalom, which had burned to the ground two days later. The piece was punctuated with a three-word passive voice sentence, "Arson is suspected." Nice prose touch, for a journalist, Seth thought.

"Nothing we didn't know, Harriet."

"Precisely. Do you believe Mrs. Stark will retract her confession when she is told of Hudson's alibi?"

"We shall see, and soon I would guess. Irene can retract her statement, of course. But the prosecutor could still press the case. There's evidence, though it's as circumstantial for Irene as it was for Hudson."

Ludington went back to his study to polish the sermon a bit, only to be interrupted a second time a bare hour later, this time by a call from Cecily Monroe. "Seth, this just gets curiouser and curiouser." Ludington wondered whether Cecily knew she was making a literary reference to *Alice in Wonderland.* Perhaps she had seen the movie.

"What's happened now, Cecily?"

"Another alibi, believe it or not. A friend of Irene's saw a story that ran in the online *Newsday* late this morning and called the FBI offices in Manhattan. She finally got to O'Reilly and told him… are you ready for this, Seth? She told him that Irene Stark could not have been in Asharoken committing murder that Monday evening because she was walking on the beach with her in Speonk at the time. O'Reilly, God bless him, shared her statement with me, almost immediately after he took it. He just sent it over. Again, it's exculpatory, and they tell you pronto. Anyway, the woman's name is Muriel Gross. She and Irene are neighbors and friends from way back. She says they often walked the beach together and were doing just that on the evening of the night Irene's brother died."

"Unbelievable, Cecily. You might also want to remember that I send you not only clients who confess, but also clients with alibis."

"Right. Anyway, this Muriel Gross said she knew Irene was going through a rough patch. So, she called her that Monday night at a little after seven and suggested they take one of their strolls. She recalls the time because she hoped they might catch the sunset Then she drove over, picked Irene up, and they went to a little public beach access in Speonk. They walked the beach, went east toward Westhampton. It was raining a bit, Muriel said, but nothing like the deluge they got on the North Shore. They even got a peek at the sunset. Muriel says she had brought along a big golf umbrella, and they sat under it and talked for a good hour. Says Irene poured out her lament about Lawrence cutting her and her family out of his will. Lots of tears, as you can imagine. Muriel's story might be iffy except for this. She took a selfie of the two of them, and it's dated and timestamped 8:42 on that Monday. No way Irene could have gotten herself to Asharoken by nine or so when the Mercedes G-Class arrived at Gollancz's place."

Seth chose not to tell Cecily that he had guessed from the beginning that the confession was false, that Irene was lying to protect her son.

"But Seth, how could Irene think this confession of hers would hold up? I mean, she was on the beach with Muriel at the time. She had to know that the woman would eventually come forward with the story. Could Irene be so discombobulated?"

"No, not really, Cecily. You see, I never told Irene the exact time the family Mercedes made its second visit. I just said that it was later, sometime after she had called on her brother, that first Mercedes visit. Could have been midnight, for all she knew. Irene may wear her passions on the outside, but she's not stupid. I can only assume she thought she could have had enough time to go for a stroll on the beach with Muriel, gotten herself home and into the Mercedes, and up to Eaton's Neck in time to do what she thought Hudson had done."

"So, what the hell, Seth? Everybody's got an alibi."

"Not quite everyone, Cecily."

After Monroe rang off, he called the rabbi with the news, "Dan, it's like we guessed." Seth generously used the first person plural even though both men knew that the guess was Ludington's alone. "Irene was fibbing to save her vandal of a son. Some friend she was walking the beach with that night came up with an alibi just as air-tight as Hudson's."

Gellman sighed loudly enough for Seth to hear it over the phone, "It's gotta be Masterson. I just know it. Let's you and me pay him another call. Tell him we have a Ring video of a car that's not the Stark's passing by Gollancz's front door at…what time was it exactly, Seth?"

"8:38."

"Tell him we know it's his car. Maybe we even tell him that we recognized him in it."

"You are becoming as willing to prevaricate as I am, Dan."

"For a good end. I'd just like to see his reaction. Frankly, this is as emotional for me as it is logical, Seth."

"So, when do you want to go?"

"How about just after our Shabbat service tomorrow? You'll be there, right?"

Telling van der Berg about Irene Stark's out-of-the-blue alibi was easy. She was happy to hear it because it meant they were not done with sleuthing. She smiled slyly when Seth unfolded the tale and said—her response edging to the precipice of flattery—"Well, you were right again, Pastor."

Seth decided to delay telling her that he and Gellman were off to Long Island the next day. Without her.

Chapter Thirty-Six

Saturday

The Gothic revival interior of Old Stone Presbyterian Church, with its aspirations to the Medieval, was presently serving as a temporary nest for Temple Beth Shalom. The space was unaltered save for the large screen hiding the cross. Projected on the screen from the rear was one of Marc Chagall's several depictions of the story of Joseph, this one of his brothers pulling him out of the pit after changing their minds about murdering him. Dan had told Seth he was planning to match biblical Chagall images—of which there were a great many—with the focus of his sermon each week for a while.

Beneath the screen and toward the rear of the raised chancel rested the new portable ark the synagogue had purchased. The three Torah scrolls, recently returned by the FBI, were hidden behind its richly decorated curtain, which Dan had named the *parochet*. Old Stone's communion table was just where it usually was, at least since Seth had insisted that it be pulled away from the back wall. When the Worship Committee asked him why, he said, "Because it's a table, not an altar, and you don't push tables against the wall." This not-an-altar communion table would now do double duty, serving every Saturday morning as the synagogue's bima. Dan had asked carefully about using it as such. Seth had said, "Not a problem. Furniture is not sacred, only what happens around it."

Temple Beth Shalom's first Shabbat service since the fire was reasonably well-attended. Dan had told Seth he expected more than a few curiosity seekers, drawn by the novelty of a plucky synagogue that had been burned out of its building, making do with Protestant space. Beth Shalom's service was mostly in English with just a bit of Hebrew injected at the right intersections in the liturgy. The part-time cantor had a remarkable voice. When the Old Stone Session had met after church a few weeks earlier, they had eagerly voted to accommodate Beth Shalom. Veritably the only events that ever happened in the church's worship space on Saturdays were weddings, and they were seldom in the morning. As Ludington found a seat toward the front of the sanctuary so that he could rise and offer a word of welcome when Gellman called on him, he noticed Harriet van der Berg sitting alone, tucked in a pew toward the rear.

Dan's first sermon after the fire was based on the climax of the story of Joseph and his brothers. The cantor read the first fifteen verses of Chapter 45, then the rabbi rehearsed the entire Joseph cycle, condensing the last fourteen chapters of the book of Genesis, into seven minutes. He began by saying to his congregation, rather optimistically, *"You know the story, of course, but a reminder won't hurt. You'll remember that Joseph, a bold dreamer, was the youngest son of Jacob and the favorite of his father. This latter truth was made painfully obvious to his eleven big brothers when Dad presented Joseph (and him alone) with the infamous coat of many colors. Jealousy soon fermented into plans for fratricide. But the brothers hesitated when an opportunity for murder came. Instead, they stripped the kid of his fancy coat, threw him in a handy pit out in the desert, and sat down to lunch. When an Egypt-bound caravan happened by, they fished Joseph out and sold him for twenty pieces of silver.* Gellman turned and looked at the projected image behind him and to the right of the pulpit in which he stood. *"That's the moment the artist, Marc Chagall, captured in the painting you see before you."*

"Once in Egypt, Joseph ends up a servant in the household of the Pharaoh. He's good at dreams, very good, and as the years pass, he rises to become the grand vizier of all Egypt, no less. Meanwhile, back at the ranch, a famine has risen in Canaan, and Dad sends the eleven brothers on sequential trade missions to Egypt to buy grain and save the clan from starvation. The story slows and gets complex

here, but it culminates in the incredible scene Beth just read to us. The brothers find themselves standing in front of the baby brother they had thought to murder but instead sold into slavery, a fate perhaps even worse than the death they had planned. They've been accused of pilfering a silver cup found hidden in one of their sacks of grain. That's another story, but the point is, the boys are in deep trouble, and they know it. Little brother Joseph, risen from slavery and ascended to number two potentate in Egypt is standing there, arms crossed, all done up in eyeliner and Egyptian royalty duds, probably talking Hebrew with an Egyptian accent. The brothers don't recognize him, but he knows who they are."

Gellman paused and scanned the congregation. Ludington recognized the same playfulness that had animated their conversation on the drive out to Speonk earlier that week. This unassuming rabbi was an engaging preacher.

Gellman punctuated his rhetorical pause by resting the elbow of his undamaged left arm on the still-bandaged right hand. He was trying to hide the bandages, just as Ludington had seen him do before. He might have strategically milked his burns for sympathy with Irene Stark and Agent O'Reilly, but he wasn't going to do so with his congregation. He then touched the raised index finger of his right hand to his lips and tapped them several times—a sign that words of weight were about to be spoken. *"Right there, right there, Joseph has all the power. He can do whatever he pleases. His brothers' knees are knocking. What is he going to do?* Another pause. *Now, if you've read the book of Genesis up to this hinge point, you know the whole saga that comes before is marked by one payback after another. It's tit-for-tat all through Genesis. And if you know that, when you come to this intersection, you're expecting the mother of all paybacks, the big tat. They certainly deserve it, those crummy brothers. But what does Joseph do?* Another pause. *Joseph weeps. He breaks down and he weeps. He weeps for all the jealousy, all the greed, all the sorrow, all the hatefulness in the world, weeps over all that has estranged him from his brothers. He throws his arms around their rotten necks and weeps until eyeliner is running down his cheeks. He had a good cry with his crummy family."*

Gellman paused yet again, his eyes scanning the congregation. He had them in the proverbial palm of his hand, and he knew it. *"Yes, they have thought to murder us. Yes, they have thrown us into pits. Yes, they have sold us into slavery. And like Joseph, I choose only to weep. I choose to weep for the hatefulness we as a people have known over the centuries. Like Joseph, I can only weep for the hatefulness we as a community have experienced in these last weeks. Justice must be done, of course justice must be done. But like Joseph, I do not choose paybacks. No tit-for-tat. No reciprocal hatred. I choose not to carry the burden of it. I choose to get on with life."*

Ludington noted that the rabbi had never spoken the word forgiveness. Too soon for that, perhaps. He also realized that Dan had not unpacked Joseph's declaration to his brothers at the end of the last chapter of Genesis: *"You intended to do harm to me, but God intended it for good."* That twist on the mysteries of providence was a sermon for another day.

Seth discovered that Reform Jews stood around and drank coffee after worship just like Presbyterians. A gaggle of well-wishers surrounded Rabbi Gellman at the far end of Old Stone's Social Hall. The coffee tasted just like Old Stone's, but Beth Shalom's treats were better. Harriet van der Berg found him with a paper cup of coffee in one hand and half a bagel with cream cheese in the other. She nodded to him and said, "I noted your Volvo automobile parked on 3rd Avenue. At least, I must believe it to be yours. I observed the two child safety seats in the rear."

She knew he never left his car on the street. Parked near the synagogue as it was meant that it was about to go somewhere. Her statement was a question, and he could no longer stall answering, "Dan wants to confront Masterson. He wants to drive out to Eaton's Neck today. I called the guy's landline this morning, and he picked up. Told him we'd be stopping by."

"Bold, I must say. How did he respond to your promise of a visit?"

"Said he was going to call the Asharoken cops and complain. About trespassing or harassment, or something. I'll be surprised if he does it, though."

"Well, it should be an interesting visit for the two of you." With that, she took a sip of her coffee and walked away.

The most resolute of Beth Shalom's coffee drinkers had finally had their fill by one-fifteen. Freed at last from surrounding congregants, Dan caught Seth's eye and nodded his head toward the door.

They climbed into the Volvo after Seth pulled a parking ticket from the windshield. Too close to a fire hydrant. Saturday traffic was light as they drove down 3rd Avenue. Freeing himself from the left lane, which was blocked by a double-parked box truck, Seth said, "That was one fine sermon, Daniel Gellman. Well done."

"Thanks. I made kind of a daring leap at the end, though. I mean, when I said, 'They thought to murder us, threw us in pits, sold us into slavery, yada, yada. The "they' in the Joseph story is his brothers, his own family. The 'they' I was talking about is the non-Jewish world with its antisemitism. But I'd defend the move because there really are no Jews yet in Genesis. Abraham and the Patriarchs and Matriarchs right down to Joseph are not exactly Jewish yet. I mean, this is before Moses, before Torah. Arabs and Muslims consider themselves children of Abraham. Even Christians, by extension, see themselves as children of Abraham. I'm being defensive, I know. But the analogy let me make the point about weeping over the hatred, about refusing to hate back. And doing it with a story I love. Do you love the story, Seth?"

"I love the whole big dysfunctional Abraham family. You're so right about the paybacks. The Book of Genesis is stuffed with revenge and jealousy and deceit, the occasional theft, and a few rapes and murders thrown in. Such a human tale, so honest, and yet impregnated with the Divine." Seth sensed that his relationship with Gellman had reached a level of trust that allowed the most delicate topics. He said, "My friend, I hope we are at a point in our friendship where I can ask you this. Where do you think antisemitism comes from?"

Gellman leaned back in his seat, looked out the window, and watched several lanes of traffic compressing themselves into the narrow approach to the Queensboro Bridge. "It's not just Masterson and the loony right. I mean, the Nazis didn't invent antisemitism. They presided over what is doubtless its most horrific manifestation, of course. And you Christians didn't invent it either, although you have presented it with some handy Biblical and theological justification. I read your sermons of the last two weeks. Online, you know. You nailed it both times. Anyway, there's antisemitism on the left, too. Marx was an antisemite, did you know that? Crazy right -wing stuff leans toward racial purity bullshit, displacement theories. That would be displacing the likes of you, Reverend WASP. Then there's the world domination stuff. You know, international cabals of rich Jews, *The Protocols of the Elders of Zion.* On the left, it's sympathy—often quite appropriate sympathy—with the plight of the Palestinians. But underneath that, the left tends to see the world ever so neatly divided between the oppressed and the oppressors. We Jews used to be among the former, but the left has recently promoted us to the latter."

This was clearly a subject Daniel Gellman had thought about deeply. He rested for a moment as Seth kept silent, hoping his friend had more to say. He did. "But deep down, deep, deep down, I think at the black heart of it lies the human proclivity to hate people who are, well, different—people who refuse to conform, people who aren't—or won't be—like us. And we Jews are different. That's what we're about. We wouldn't go along with Caesar worship in ancient Rome. Wouldn't get baptized in the Middle Ages. Spoke Yiddish or Ladino and wore funny outfits. Haters hate the Other. And as long as we are being frank, Jewish success stokes that hatred. We Jews tend to do fairly well wherever we find ourselves. My dad used to say, "When they're always after you, you learn to run fast and think quick.""

Ludington said, "Dan, it's more than that. You value education, have a major work ethic, strong families, all the things tending toward prosperity, Jewish or otherwise."

"Yeah, and then we pay for it. You know about the scapegoat, don't you, Seth? I mean the original one. Book of Leviticus. Aaron, the maybe-brother of Moses and the original Jewish high priest, takes two goats, rolls the dice to see which one is sacrificed and which one is turned loose in the desert after he has laid all the sins of the community on the head of the poor creature. This second one came to be called the escape goat, then the scapegoat. Jews didn't invent this goat idea; it's way older. My point is that humans hanker after a scapegoat—somebody or some group of somebodies on whose head they can lay everything that's wrong in their world, and then send them out into the desert to die, because they're the source of the problem, not me, not us. It's them."

Seth said, "And time and again, you've been the scapegoat."

"True, my friend. And when it happens, beware. We're like the canary in the coal mine. The first to catch the poison in the air. But never the last."

They rolled onto lovely Eaton's Neck just as this dark conversation ended, rolled up to a pleasant and well-kept suburban high ranch house. Such an unlikely home to the oldest hatred. Seth stopped the car in Masterson's drive just as his phone rang. The caller's identity appeared on the Volvo's screen—"Harriet."

He raised a surprised eyebrow as he took her call, hitting the speaker button so Gellman could listen in. "Afternoon, Harriet."

"Indeed. As I was aware that you are paying a visit to our Mr. Masterson, I thought I should inform you of a discovery I have made. I do hope I have caught you before you arrived."

"Just pulled into his driveway."

"Very good. Well, as I indicated, I have carefully reviewed the Ring doorbell videos of the evening of the night of Mr. Gollancz's demise. I examined the brief recording of a passing automobile made by the camera at 8:38 with especially close attention. That would be the one showing the dark-colored sedan moving by rapidly. I shall presently email it to you, but what I noted upon a reexamination is that there appear to be two persons seated in the front. If indeed it is Mr. Masterson's automobile, he seems to have had a passenger with him. You may also wish to examine the video again to see if any of the discernable design details of the passing vehicle correspond with those of Mr. Masterson's auto. The video was made during a period of heavy precipitation in near-total darkness, but you might perhaps be able to determine if it is indeed similar to the one driven by Mr. Masterson."

Seth ended the call after thanking her and looked at Gellman, who said, "She's a wonder, your Miss van der Berg."

"You don't know the half of it, Dan."

Chapter Thirty-Seven

Saturday

Ludington parked in Masterson's driveway alongside the man's older gray Ford Taurus. Hoping that he had not seen them pull up, Ludington and Gellman watched the Ring video Harriet had emailed, a brief recording of a dark sedan passing quickly by the front door of Lawrence Gollancz's home at 8:38 the night he died. The car was indeed moving fast, and the night was as dark as Hades. The storm had extinguished the neighborhood's power, so there was no outdoor lighting for the camera. And in the drenching rain, no moonlight either. They watched the video twice, then looked at Masterson's Taurus parked next to them. The car was all rounded corners. "Like a bar of used soap," Dan said. It also had an unusual crescent-shaped rear quarter window. Seth pointed to the phone's screen and then at the car parked next to them and said, "You can just glimpse the small window in front of the C-pillar as it goes by. Moon-shaped." He nodded toward the window of the car parked next to them.

Gellman said, "C-pillar?"

"I grew up in Detroit. Some of it rubbed off. What car guys call the pillar between the back side window and the rear window. C-pillar."

"I can guess which ones are A and B. Yes, it does look the same. Not exactly definitive, but a strong probable." Gellman pulled Seth's phone even closer to his face. "And yes, I can see the second head. I mean, you can see it when you look for it. Just barely, but Harriet's right."

Seth nodded. "These are interesting little factoids we can present to Mr. George Masterson."

Mr. George Masterson did answer the door when they knocked. They had been afraid he might not. Again, the man glared at his callers through the screen door, then he smiled and started humming a ditty of a tune. He was dressed in jeans and a dark blue Under Armour hoodie, no shoes or socks on his feet. He was unshaven, but his thinning hair was neatly combed. Seth guessed this to be the man's post-shower, day-off attire. He looked Ludington in the eyes and said, his voice dripping venom, "Get off my property, the both of you." He did not make eye contact with Gellman.

Gellman stepped closer, "Mr. Masterson. We know the authorities have spoken with you about the leaflets you recently distributed in the neighborhood." This was a guess, but one about which Gellman was confident. "I'll bet they would be interested to know you paid a visit to one specific neighbor, a Jewish neighbor named Lawrence Gollancz, and that you made the visit on the night he died."

"I did no such thing."

"We have proof, Mr. Masterson, and we plan to forward the evidence we have of your visit to the FBI. You should know that they are now investigating Mr. Gollancz's death as a possible homicide. He had recently received antisemitic letters threatening his life." Gellman paused and then stepped closer to the screen door. "What were you doing in his driveway that night? We have photos of your car passing his front door." Gellman turned and nodded to the Taurus in the driveway. Even as he said this, Ludington guessed Masterson had probably already been visited by Agent O'Reilly and that the FBI knew about him and the leaflets. He also assumed they had viewed the Ring videos on the phone Seth and Harriet had passed on to them.

Masterson blanched and took a step back. He seemed to assume that further denials would be in vain, so he retreated, blurting out, "I just went over to check the culvert. He said he was going to clean it out. It gets clogged up with leaves and grass clippings, and then when it rains, water backs up all over my back yard. Just like I told that Black cop."

Gellman glanced at Ludington, a crack of a smile on his face to indicate that one point had been settled. George Masterson had been there that evening and the FBI knew it. It was indeed his car that passed before the Ring camera at 8:38, well after the rain had begun, the rain which poured down the gutter, pooled at the corner of the Gollancz house and formed the tell-tale mud where the generator sat.

Seth spoke next, "Who was in the car with you that night?"

At that question, the color completely drained from Masterson's face. He slammed the door in their faces. Seth looked at the rabbi, "That would seem to be a touchy subject."

Seth backed out of Masterson's driveway, turning not back to Northport, but toward the Gollancz estate. "Might as well check the clogged culvert story while we're here."

He parked at the top of Gollancz's sloping driveway, well out of range of the Ring camera mounted by the front entrance. They got out of the Volvo and walked along the top of Gollancz's property near the road toward the back of Masterson's house. Dan saw it first, pointing it out to Seth. "There's a low spot at the bottom of his yard, Masterson's yard, I mean. I suppose water could collect there." They walked closer, treading on grass as dry as it had been saturated after the deluge three weeks earlier.

"And there is a culvert," Ludington said. "Corrugated metal. Looks like it runs from the low area on Masterson's property, under that little ridge, and empties onto Gollancz's front yard. Another mud-maker."

Gellman grimaced. "Masterson certainly thought quickly to come up with the I-was-checking-the-culvert story."

Ludington did not respond at first. Then he said, "When Masterson saw us at his door, he started humming something. Strange reaction."

Dan shook his head. "That something was the ditty of a tune that got Lawrence in hot water, at first with the left and then with the right when he dropped it. And Seth, it was gas that killed Lawrence. Such a perverse echo of the Holocaust."

Their attention was diverted from that horrific thought and the potentially exculpatory culvert to the flashing light atop the marked Asharoken cop car that had pulled up behind Ludington's Volvo at the head of Lawrence Gollancz's drive.

Seth said, "Let's just hope it's Officer Marge Anderson."

It was. She stepped out of her vehicle as the two men walked across the lawn toward her. Anderson was leaning back on the door of the cruiser, arms crossed, as Ludington and Gellman reached her.

"Reverend Ludington, Rabbi Gellman, fancy finding the two of you out here on Long Island yet again. Station just got a call, an anonymous call about two sketchy guys trespassing on this property."

Gellman spoke first. "It may well be my property. Well, not mine exactly, but the property of the synagogue I serve."

"That's interesting. Asharoken PD was contacted by the guy's sister, Mrs. Irene Stark, a couple of weeks back, asking us to keep an eye on it. Said she had inherited the place and was still figuring out what to do with it. Worried about it, she said. Sitting empty and all, though she said she was going to be checking on it once and again."

Seth nodded, not at all surprised by what Anderson had said. "Officer Anderson, you might not know that both she and her son were detained by the FBI in connection to Lawrence Gollancz's death. But alibis have surfaced for both of them. Hudson Stark is still facing vandalism and hate crime charges, though. Point is, the feds do suspect something, even if Suffolk is still thinking tragic accident. What's the sports euphemism they use when they suspect an unknown something, that term to cover all the possible bases of malefaction? Foul play?"

Anderson looked at Ludington and then toward the corner of the house where the generator had been. It was not there. She said, "Foul play, indeed. You'll both be happy to know that Suffolk is no longer sure about it having been an accident. They don't want to be caught with their pants down on this one, especially by the Manhattan office of the Federal Bureau of Investigation. I know all this because they quizzed me about those antisemitic leaflets that showed up around here a few weeks ago. Well, we did get some local folks to share Ring video shots they got of the guy who was passing them around. Taken in the dark of the night, of course, and in a hoodie, but we were still able to ID him. She nodded toward Masterson's house. We're going to try to prosecute him for putting non-official material in people's official mailboxes. Like I told you, against the law, even though people do it all the time. Hardly ever enforced. A fine, I would guess, but it'll be public. I'll make sure it gets to the media. He'll be outed for what he is."

Gellman pulled the question hanging in the air down to earth, though he hesitated before asking it. "Do you think they suspect him of moving the generator, Officer Anderson?

Before she could answer, Ludington added, "I mean, we do know he was there that night. And I have to guess the FBI knows it as well."

The woman shrugged her shoulders. She didn't ask Ludington how he knew Masterson had been on Gollancz's property the night the man died. Nor did she ask how he guessed the feds probably knew it as well. And because she didn't ask, Seth Ludington could only assume she knew exactly how he knew. It was then that he was certain who had overnighted Lawrence Gollancz's iPhone to Old Stone Presbyterian Church nine days ago.

Chapter Thirty-Eight

Sunday

Ludington was still not happy with the reheated sermon he was supposed to preach in an hour and a half. Yes, it was Labor Day Sunday, and the congregation would be sparse, but they deserved better. He was leaning into the laptop on the desk in his study as if physical proximity to the words on its screen might unravel their convoluted logic. He deleted an entire section and added an illustration that had come to him the night before. He was still less than satisfied when he heard Harriet van der Berg's trinitarian knock at the door between her office and his, "Knock, knock, knock. Father, Son, and Holy Ghost. " Or if you're liturgically trendy, "Creator, Redeemer, and Sustainer."

Instead of his routine, "Come on in, Harriet," he shouted, "Harriet, can it wait?"

But he was too late. She was already through the door and in his office, flushed with excitement, gripping her iPhone in front of her face.

"Harriet, I've got a sermon to preach in what…?" He looked at his Shinola Runwell, "Eighty-three minutes."

"Seth, I have made a most important discovery, most important, I must say. Regarding our case, that is."

He spun around in his chair and said, "Let me and Fiona take you to lunch after church, Harriet. It just has to wait. I've got a sermon to rewrite."

She didn't say it, but her face betrayed what he knew she was thinking—

"Rewriting a sermon at this hour?"

What she did say was, "Alright then. I shall meet you there. Have you made a reservation?"

He rolled his eyes, to which she responded, "I shall make one, for three adults and two high chairs, *n'est-ce pas?*"

She wisely beat a quick retreat. Seth poked away at the laptop until he was marginally satisfied with a sermon on the life-and-death importance of relationships to human beings. He printed it out and then fished his rabat, tabs, pulpit robe, and green stole out of the closet in his study. He vested, lifted the ten double-spaced pages of sermon out of the printer, and headed down to the one third-full sanctuary of Old Stone Presbyterian Church.

Harry Mulholland cornered him at coffee hour after the service. Seth felt he had to make a coffee hour appearance, even though he did not like them in general, and was dying to know what Harriet's important discovery "regarding our case" might be. Harry waited till he and Seth were standing alone before he said, "Jimmy called me last night. He called the guys at the 109th in Flushing who picked up the Stark kid in the drug surveillance a couple of weeks ago. Anyway, they did remember what he was wearing that night. A pair of cargo shorts and those black Nike flip-flop things all the kids wear. They remembered because he crossed his legs and kept trying to balance one of them on his toes during the whole interview. He dropped it about ten times. Kid was nervous. Seth, one of these days, you'll have to tell me why this matters."

"I promise, Harry. I will." Seth thanked his Clerk profusely. Because it did matter.

Harriet was guarding the banquette at the far back of the Lex when Seth and Fiona arrived with the girls in their immense double stroller. There was no room for the thing in the compact restaurant, so they did what New York parents trustingly do. They left it parked outside by the entrance door. After wiggling Astrid into one of the high chairs Nero had brought, Seth squeezed his lanky frame into the banquette to sit next to Harriet. Fiona had indulgently consented to sit at the other end of the table with the girls and watch them work pasta with olive oil and parmesan into their mouths so Harriet could tell Seth the news that was so burning hot she had dared to interrupt him just before church on a Sunday morning.

"So," Harriet van der Berg began, as she often did when about to offer a conclusion or to outline the summary of some matter. "So yesterday, while you and Rabbi Gellman traveled together to Long Island… And yes, I am eager to hear what the two of you may have learned. But first, I must tell you of the technical discovery I have made." She assumed her "woman-triumphant" look and continued, "Yesterday, while I was here in the City alone, I travelled by taxi cab to the Costco store in Harlem. It's on 117th near the river, you know. Did you know one must be a member of their club to shop in their stores? Well, I had to join. Sixty dollars for a basic membership card. I've never heard of such a thing, but I knew they sold just what I wanted to purchase. Seth, I purchased a Ring doorbell, the basic kit. I tremble to tell you what I paid for the device. Perhaps you and Fiona will have use for it. I certainly don't, as I have a doorman. At least, I no longer have any use for it."

Nero set a glass of the house cab before Seth and glasses of white in front of both Fiona and Harriet, all without their having ordered. Van der Berg thanked the waiter, ever mannerly as she was, even in the thrall of a tale about to burst from her.

"So, I set up the Ring doorbell camera system in my apartment kitchen. It includes the doorbell camera unit itself and also the receiver, a device which needs to be plugged into a nearby electrical outlet. Not especially difficult. I programmed it to my iPhone, though should you wish to purchase it from me, at a slight discount as it is now used, I can reprogram it to your cell phones."

Since his recent descent into Ring world, he and Fiona had thought about getting one of the things for their brownstone. He was about to consent to buying it from Harriet, but she cut him off. "Seth, you will recall that for all the virtues of our apartment, it has no windows in the kitchen. Something Margaret always lamented. She insisted there should be a window over a kitchen sink. My point is this—if I close the door from the kitchen to the dining room and extinguish the kitchen lights, the room becomes very dark."

Seth suddenly saw where this was going and said, "Dark like Lawrence Gollancz's front yard the night of the storm with the power out."

"Precisely. My kitchen was not totally dark. Some light seeped in around the closed door to the dining room. Once I had assembled the system and mounted the doorbell with its camera on the refrigerator, I commenced to experiment. I walked past it several times at different speeds. Then I approached it from the side, snuck up on it, you might say, and placed my finger over the camera lens. It's just above the doorbell button which you push to make the receiver unit ring. By the way, I programmed in the Old Doorbell ringtone. I thought you might like that, should you choose to purchase it."

Van der Berg finally stopped to take a breath, and Seth was able to edge in a word. "We'll buy it, Harriet. Retail."

"I thought you would. Back to the point. Placing my thumb over the camera did indeed activate the device and induce it to record, but only for a flash. Then it remained dark." The several—six to be precise—video recordings I made in my kitchen with my thumb over the lens are all precisely like the recording made by Mr. Gollancz's Ring device several minutes after the recording of the Starks' large Mercedes vehicle passing by, the one timestamped 9:01. Seth, it appears quite clear to me that someone wished to blind the Ring camera—as it were—so that it would not document some action."

Seth took a sip of the cabernet and said, "Like wheeling a gas generator past the front door."

Van der Berg nodded. "Precisely."

"That's three."

Three what?"

"Never mind, Harriet. I just wanted to observe that one could hardly move a generator while holding his or her thumb over the lens."

Van der Berg nodded again. She then fished in her purse and brought out a roll of black electrical tape. She said nothing, took her phone off the table, went to the Ring app she had just installed, punched the screen a few times, and turned it toward Ludington. "Behold my experimental video number seven, in which I cover the lens with an inch-long piece of this tape. It's called electrical tape, though I have no idea why. I purchased it at Costco as well. Though, I had to buy a pack of eight rolls. Don't know what I'll do with them. I selected it because it appeared to be totally opaque."

"Aren't you Miss Marple *revivitus*, Harriet van der Berg?"

She smiled her satisfaction at that. "Well, Miss Marple was Margaret's favorite. And do remember, Seth, that there was no similar brief blinding video like this after the dark sedan passed by at 8:38."

Nero approached their table quietly, said nothing, but was clearly ready to take orders. He had brought the girls their regular pasta as soon as they had settled in, but adults need to make choices, even if they were quite predictable. Back to chicken Milanese for Seth, salad Nicoise for Harriet, and salmon for Fiona.

Nero retreated, and Seth continued, "Now, my news. Dan and I were able to confront George Masterson yesterday, if briefly. And we were able to take a look at his car, his Ford Taurus. First off, he admitted he drove into Gollancz's driveway that night. Dan and I took a close look at both the 8:38 video and the guy's car. Looks to be a match. He said he went to see if Gollancz had cleaned out a culvert. If it's plugged up, it sometimes floods his back yard. Dan and I checked, and there is such a culvert. But when I asked him who was in the car with him that night, he slammed the door on us. Obviously, something he did not wish to talk about."

"That could be interesting, could it not?"

"Maybe. Officer Marge Anderson—you'll recall her, smart Asharoken cop you met at the beach—well, she happened by. Said they'd gotten an anonymous call about a couple of trespassers. It was Masterson who called, no doubt. Anyway, I told her we had IDed his car as being at Gollancz's that night and that he admitted it. And that there were two heads in it. She didn't even bother to ask me how I knew that. Harriet, she knew how I knew because she assumed we had gotten into Gollancz's phone and accessed the Ring videos. She didn't ask because she sent it to us, of course. Remember that she said she found it on Gollancz's nightstand and accessed an emergency number, Irene's number. I'm guessing she put it in her pocket and forgot about it. Then she found it and figured that getting access to it legally was going to take an age, even if they could. So she overnighted it to us."

"Van der Berg nodded and said, "Precisely."

He paused, sighed deeply, and said, "But Harriet, there are a couple of things that point away from Masterson. First, your Ring discovery—I mean, the fact that the thing looks to have been blinded just after the Stark's G-Class drove by for the second time. It points at whoever arrived in the Mercedes then. But there's something else, something that's been bothering me about the idea that Masterson might have pulled the generator around the back of the house to dodge the Ring camera. I finally remembered. Harriet, the tracks I told you about, the ones Dan and I saw, those wheel tracks in the wet grass? We both saw them, saw them the next day when we were out there. They had to have been made by the generator. They went directly from the driveway in front of the garage, across the lawn, right in front of the camera, to where the thing ended up. Harriet, I do wish it were Masterson. But I don't think it was."

The twins happily distracted by oily linguine, Fiona had been able to listen closely as this conversation unfolded. Her lawyer mind clicked, and she interrupted, "All this clearly suggests that whoever blinded the doorbell camera moved the generator. And is obviously the killer."

Seth smiled at his wife and said, "Exactly. And one more bit. Harry was able to learn that Hudson Stark was not wearing his L. L. Bean Duck Boots the night the cops were grilling him in Queens, so his pair was presumably at home in Speonk that night, available to anybody in the family. He hadn't moved into his apartment at Hofstra yet."

Van der Berg absorbed these several bits of memory, information and deduction and found the logical conclusion to which they pointed unhappily inevitable. She looked solemnly at her pastor, "This would all rather suggest that a young true crime aficionado may have slipped into committing a true crime herself."

Chapter Thirty-Nine

Monday

The next day, Seth Ludington found himself depressed by the thought that an eighteen-year-old girl, little more than a child—and one who impressed him as a consummate naïf—had murdered her uncle. Like the two before, this latest "case"—a term that still made him wince—was leading him and Harriet van der Berg into another dark valley, a veritable "valley of the shadow of death." Again, it was a place that demanded excruciating choices. He was at home on his day off with his own girls. He had just loaded them into their stroller and was headed to Carl Schurz Park along the East River. The day was sweet, and the twins would soon be ready for their afternoon naps. Perhaps they would sleep while he stared across the river and pondered this death and what it asked of him.

He found a free bench facing the water. He turned the stroller toward him so he could watch his girls, covering each of them with their favorite blankets. The afternoon sun shone brightly, but the day was cool, with an east wind blowing across the water. He was soon looking over their heads at the lovely Blackwell Island lighthouse on the northern tip of Roosevelt Island and not so lovely Astoria on the far side of the East River. Ingrid was already asleep. Astrid was fighting it as she often did. She always wanted just a little more of everything, waking life included. Chelsea Stark had once been an eight-month-old baby, doubtless doted upon by her parents, perhaps dotted upon by her childless uncle as well. It was all devastatingly sad. He was conflicted about what he and van der Berg should do with what they knew and what they surmised. He could phone O'Reilly. He should phone O'Reilly. That call would doubtless earn him another verbal thrashing. Maybe the cops would figure it out on their own, in fact he guessed they probably would. Probably. O'Reilly was smart, and what Marge Anderson said suggested that Suffolk had opened the case. Seth Ludington had to think.

His thinking was interrupted by his cell phone vibrating in the pocket of his polo shirt. He had turned off the ringer so as not to wake the girls. He pulled it out and looked at the screen. It was a 631 area code number. Long Island. He answered with an inquisitive, "Hello?," the way you say the word when you don't know who's calling.

"Reverend Ludington? It's Marge Anderson, Asharoken PD."

"Officer Anderson. Hello, hello. How can I help you?"

"Actually, I'm going to help you, but you might not like my help. So, I just got read into the FBI and George Masterson business. Seems they've had a chat with him already. About the flyers and the synagogue in the City and his relationship with Gollancz. Some of it's in our jurisdiction as we investigated those flyers, so they brought us in, not that they had to. They found Masterson at his place of work this morning. Runs a septic service outfit in Greenlawn. They pressed him hard on his whereabouts on the night Lawrence Gollancz died. I'm guessing they also got access to the Ring footage on Gollancz's phone. Can't imagine how. Whatever, they told him they had evidence he was on Gollancz's property mid-evening. Evidence they have thanks to you, Reverend."

Ludington could not restrain himself, "And you, don't you think?"

She chose not to respond to the question. "Masterson admitted to being there that night. He got the time right. Eight-thirty or so. Said he drove over in the rain to see if the drainage thing that runs from his back yard to the front corner of the Gollancz property was open. It was fine, he said. They asked him if he was alone. At first, he said he was. So then, the FBI Agent—O'Reilly is his name—O'Reilly tells him they know somebody else was in the car with him that night. Masterson suddenly remembers that he had picked up a friend and that they had dinner together in Huntington. O'Reilly was able to get the name of the friend out of Masterson by hinting at a murder investigation and the virtues of having an alibi. The friend is named Morton, Terrance Morton. This is the part you are going to love, Reverend Ludington…. The name rang a bell with me, so I called a guy I know in Suffolk Vice and flew the name by him. You ready for this? He's a local rent boy, a prostitute. They nabbed him in a sting last year. I'd read about it at the time, which is why I remembered the name. So, your Take America Back, Arian Defense League white power macho honcho buys his sex, same-sex sex. This is not likely to get out, but if it did, my guess is it would severely damage his reputation with the ADL crowd. That's the good part. The bad part is the jerk has an alibi."

Ludington was not surprised that George Masterson had produced an alibi, though he was taken aback by the nature of it. If it weren't for the blinded Ring camera a half later and the wheel tracks across the lawn, Seth might have suggested Terrence Morton as an accomplice. But he said nothing to Anderson to betray the fact that he had already decided that Lawrence Gollancz had not been murdered by his antisemitic next-door neighbor, his one-man alibi or no.

After she finished her Masterson story, Anderson said, "Alibi's everywhere, Reverend Ludington. I do wish this were my case."

"So do I." But he did not tell her where cruel logic was leading him and Harriet van der Berg. After all, it was not Anderson's case. Nor was it exactly his. It belonged to Agent Brian O'Reilly. He thanked her for the call.

Both girls were sleeping soundly in the afternoon sun. They slept especially well when the stroller moved, so he decided that instead of calling van der Berg to tell her about George Masterson's alibi, he'd walk over to her apartment. Thinking about this case alone was not as good as thinking about it together. He did call her, though, and asked if it was okay to come over with the girls.

Harriet van der Berg had never had children, and though she adored Astrid and Ingrid, she felt awkward around them, not knowing quite how to pick them up or just how to hold an infant. They were still sleeping when he arrived, all the more soundly after having been strolled a few blocks up 2nd Avenue, so Seth and Harriet had a chance to talk while watching the girls doze in Harriet's overheated living room.

Seth told her what Marge Anderson had related to him in her call, not reminding her that he had already guessed that George Masterson was innocent—not in general, but of this one particular murder. When he mentioned the specifics of his alibi, van der Berg said, "Hypocrite." He assumed she was referring to the inconsistency between the man's politics and his sexual orientation. Though she and Ludington had occasionally spoken of her and Margaret's fifty years together, van der Berg was of a generation that tended to eschew direct speech about same-sex relationships.

The unpleasant topic of George Masterson exhausted, Harriet said, "Seth, I have a confession to offer you. Not as my pastor. I have no need of clergy to confess my sins. Rather as a friend and—dare I say?—colleague."

Ludington looked away from his slumbering babes to van der Berg and said, "Confess away, my child.

"Well, I did not tell you this because I gathered you rather disapproved of my assuming the identity of Henrietta Berg, inamorata of the late Lawrence Gollancz. Nevertheless, I felt that doing so might well advance our investigations."

"Inamorata?"

"Yes, discrete word, don't you think?"

"Humm."

"So, my confession. I have been in telephonic conversation with Chelsea Bun since her second posting of *The Gas Generator Mystery.* Beginning two days after that posting, to be precise."

Ludington was not especially surprised to hear that Harriet had done such a thing. He was surprised she had not told him.

"Seth, I must also confess that I was jealous. I was jealous because you were working so closely with Rabbi Gellman. I felt overlooked, 'side-lined' as they put it in the world of sport. Such feelings have been something of an issue for me much of my life. As a woman and as a secretary to men, many of whom were—to be quite frank—not precisely my intellectual or moral superiors. All the old emotions came back these last weeks. I am sorry. Not for what I did with Chelsea Bun, but for not speaking to you about it. I needed a role to play."

"No apologies needed, Harriet. And I am sorry you felt set aside. I really am."

Apologies made and accepted, Ludington's curiosity devil was suddenly perched back on his shoulder. "Harriet, how in the world did you present yourself to Chelsea Stark when you called? And how did you get her phone number? In order to be in "telephonic communication?'"

"I simply told her I was a great fan of her YouTube mystery series because they were so very well done. I introduced myself as Harriet van der Berg, a Los Angeles producer of true crime documentaries. You can imagine her response to that little prevarication. We were never introduced at the shiva, and I never spoke directly with her that day. Anyway, people of my age are quite invisible to people of her age."

"Even people of my age are probably invisible to eighteen-year-olds."

Trust me, Seth, you are never invisible."

"At any rate, the girl craves attention for what she names 'her work.' She told me she has been accepted into New York University's film school. She has also informed me—and this is perhaps germane—that she did not receive the scholarship she had been counting on. How did I get her cell number? Online at Whitepages.com. Cost me a pittance. What I can't figure out is how she thinks I got Chelsea Bun's number. The number is listed as Chelsea Stark, Speonk, New York, of course. Maybe she simply assumes that famous California film producers have the resources to discover most anything. So far, I have spoken with her three times, on each occasion offering laudatory reviews of her productions. In truth, I have been shamelessly fawning. She basks in the praise and asks no questions. She has aspirations to cinematic greatness, and she is young and so terribly naïve. And I think she may be quite desperate for funds to cover the cost of tuition. Seth, do you know how much tuition costs at New York University? I checked online. I must say that I was shocked."

"Motive," Ludington whispered. "So, what's next?"

"Well, I have been giving it thought, a great deal of thought, following our conclusions of yesterday. It all does point toward her, Seth, unhappily it does. By this, I mean the cascade of alibis exonerating other suspects, our recently ascertained fact that a pair of duck boots like those which made the muddy prints seem to have been available for use in the Stark house, those wheel tracks in the wet grass across the front yard of Gollancz's house you saw, the family's unique vehicle visiting just after nine that night, and then a few minutes later, the odd little flash of a Ring video which I duplicated in my kitchen with electrical tape."

Ludington sighed. "It does seem inescapable. Harriet, we have to call O'Reilly, even though my guess is they have most of this figured out. It'll be unpleasant. I'll do it, Harriet."

"I must say that I find it ever so regretful that we should be required to fade into the background after all the investigative work we have done. I firmly believe it is our moral obligation to bring this matter to its conclusion, however agonizing the denouement may be. We should make one last journey to far Speonk to do so. We began it; we must end it."

Seth hesitated before responding. He guessed that motives older than moral obligation were spurring the woman's reluctance to back away. "But Harriet, there comes that intersection in most cases when we amateurs must summon the professionals. Harriet, I'm going to call O'Reilly right now. Are you okay with it?"

Van der Berg pursed her lips several times in reply and frowned at the floor.

The FBI agent's cell number was in Ludington's contacts. Seth punched it and O'Reilly answered on the second ring. "Afternoon, Reverend Ludington." His number was obviously in O'Reilly's contacts as well. "What can I do for you?" Ludington rehearsed all they knew and had concluded, the labyrinthine trail of evidence leading to a teenage true crime fan.

The agent listened carefully, went silent for a moment after Ludington finished, and said, an edge to his voice, "We are not stupid, sir. And yes, we know about the boots. Got some soil samples from them." O'Reilly seemed to bite his tongue after that confession, then asked, "Tell me about that business with the Ring camera again, that flash after it recorded the vehicle passing at 9:01." Seth rehearsed the tale of Harriet's experiments with electrical tape in her darkened kitchen. O'Reilly hummed what might have been admiration and barked, "Do I have to remind you yet again to stay out of this?".

Ingrid woke her sister up with a sudden screech. Seth recognized the cry, one meaning, "I want out of this stroller, and I want out now."

He unbuckled his slightly younger daughter and took her in his arms, at which point big sister Astrid offered a like complaint.

"Harriet, would you hold Ingrid?"

Not waiting for an answer, he handed the angry child to the angry old woman who held her uncomfortably, unaccustomed to infants as she was. But Ingrid did not know that, and finally snuggled her head against Harriet's breast. The child seemed to relax. Seth could not but wonder if van der Berg was thinking what he had thought a few hours earlier about an infant Chelsea Stark in her uncle's arms. But he knew for certain she was unhappy about the call he had just made.

Chapter Forty

Tuesday

Seth was in his study the next morning prepping his information for Sunday's worship bulletin when he heard Harriet's tripartite knock on his door, not soft, but loud and insistent. "Come on in, Harriet."

She wore a neatly pleated gray skirt, a brilliantly white blouse with a high collar, and her most resolute face, "Well, Chelsea has finally contacted me. You'll recall that I admitted to placing several duplicitous phone calls to her. It seems she had indeed misplaced her phone last evening and was unable to respond, as she only received my last voice message this morning. She said she listened to it as she and her mother travelled to Lower Manhattan for some matter regarding her enrollment at New York University's film school. Dormitory accommodations, I think, she said. She was profusely apologetic for not having gotten back to me promptly. She said she and her mother will soon be returning to Speonk to meet me, the version of me who is a Los Angeles true crime documentary producer, that is to say. I had asked if we might meet."

Ludington rolled his office chair around to face her. "Harriet, we have to bow out of this. We've done what we could. I mean it, seriously."

Twenty minutes later, he walked into her cubby with a copy of his notes for Sunday's worship bulletin. The office was empty. He set the notes down on her desk and said to himself, "Gone home to pout." He went back to his office to put in another hour on his upcoming study of the prophet Isaiah for the Breakfast Bible Study. Just after noon, his cell rang.

"Dominie, I mean Seth." Then silence. The woman was clearly rattled.

"Harriet, is that you?" A needless question. No one else ever addressed him as Dominie. And that person had generally stopped doing so at his pleading.

"I find myself at the Remsenburg-Speonk Long Island Railroad Station."

"You found yourself there, Harriet?"

"Metaphorically speaking, I found myself. I confess that in spite of your admonishment, I decided I would keep my assignation with Chelsea Stark. As my Hollywood true crime television producer persona, that is to say. But in the latter part of my railroad journey, I decided that you were correct, that it would be wiser to allow the proper authorities to attend to their duties and bring this matter to conclusion. I just wanted to let you know where I was and why I was not at my desk attending to my responsibilities. There is a train scheduled to return to New York in several hours."

Harriet van der Berg was seldom indecisive and never as shaken as her voice hinted. "Harriet, stay there. I'll fetch the car and come pick you up."

Midtown traffic was light at midday. He crossed the Queensboro Bridge without a wait, wiggled his way through Long Island City to Queens Boulevard, which route the Volvo's navigation system had determined to be the quickest to the Long Island Expressway on this September afternoon.

About five miles shy of the William Floyd Parkway exit, his cell rang. The Volvo's screen identified an unrecognized 516 Long Island number. He took the call. It was Irene Stark, perhaps more hysterical than she was the last time she phoned. Oddly, she spoke softly, almost in a whiper. "Reverend Ludington. Thank God you answered. It may be happening again, I cannot believe it. This is unreal." The woman stifled a sob, then moaned theatrically. "You need to call Ms. Monroe. She has not returned my call. And I need your counsel."

"What's happened, Irene?"

"That horrible FBI agent, the one that falsely accused Hudson of murdering Larry, well, he contacted me as we were about to leave the City. Wanted to know where Chelsea was. I'm so afraid, Reverend Ludington. I'm terrified, petrified that they are about to accuse her of the same crime. I mean, if it was a crime. I haven't told her about this yet. But why else would he want to know where she is?"

"Where are you, Irene?"

"We're in the car. On our way home. Chelsea's asleep. She has a meeting with a television producer. From Hollywood. Such an opportunity for her."

Irene ended her call with another moan and a second whispered plea for him to call Cecily Monroe. Seth did so and got Monroe's voicemail just as he pulled into the parking lot of the Remsenburg-Speonk Station. Van der Berg was waiting for him outside. She marched up to his car with a sheepish look on her face, a rare expression for Harriet van der Berg to wear.

"Thank you, Seth. I am so sorry about this. As you know, I seldom change my mind about anything. I had thought this visit through, but not quite thoroughly enough, it would seem. While on the train, I received a voice message from Chelsea. It induced more than a little remorse at my duplicity."

She fished her phone out of her bag and played it for Ludington. *"Miss van der Berg. It's Chelsea Stark. Chelsea Bun, you know. My mother and I are in major traffic, I mean, major. The Williamsburg bridge is, like, totally closed. An accident, I think. We're going to try another way to get onto the Island, the Midtown Tunnel probably, but—well—I'm going to be a bit late for our meeting. I am so sorry, I really am. I called my dad. He's at home, and I told him we had a meeting. He's in a wheelchair, but he can let you in. I am so sorry. Super sorry. I am so totally looking forward to meeting you, and my mom is too, but I probably won't be there for a couple hours. New York traffic. Ugh. You have traffic in L.A., don't you?"*

Van der Berg said, "She's so young."

Ludington nodded. "And so dumb."

He did not pull out of the parking lot, but eased the Volvo into a free space. He drummed his fingers on the steering wheel as he stared through the windshield as if the answer to his question lay somewhere in the parking lot of a Long Island Railroad station.

Van der Berg watched him, growing curious. "Seth, are we not headed home to the City?"

"I don't know, Harriet. Not quite yet. There's something I think I want to try, I mean just in case." He slipped the car in reverse. "Let's head over to the Starks one more time."

It was almost three in the afternoon when Seth parked the Volvo on the street in front of the Stark residence. He turned to Harriet and said, "The only person in the house is Jack Stark. There is no easy way I can explain you to him, Harriet. I'm going to play the family pastor. And that's a role I have to play solo."

He got out of the car, leaving van der Berg fidgety and unhappy in the passenger's seat. He walked to the front door and pushed the button on the Ring doorbell. A voice he presumed to be Jack Stark's said, "I'll buzz you in. I'm in the family room, down the hall, and through the kitchen to the right."

This particular Ring doorbell system was obviously equipped with an optional remote door locking and unlocking feature. He heard a series of clicks as the door's deadbolt retreated to open position. Ludington gave the door a push, entered the front hall of the house, and walked toward the family room at the back. As he passed through the kitchen, he admired its large center island, surrounded by a row of stools on one side. He and Fiona had thought about adding a kitchen island, but the brownstone's kitchen was too tight. As he scanned the Stark's island and the cabinets across from it, Seth Ludington was flabbergasted by a sight which instantaneously changed everything. It changed what he and van der Berg had surmised about the death of Lawrence Gollancz. And it made what he had already planned to do vastly easier on his conscience.

Jack Stark clearly recognized him. The man in the wheelchair did an almost comic double take, "What are you doing here?" The accent was on the pronoun. "I thought it was the California woman come to see Chelsea."

Ludington stepped down into the sunken family room and stood near Jack Stark, seated in his wheelchair. "Mr. Stark, I come with some very unhappy news. I am here because your wife has come to consider me something of a pastor to her, perhaps to your family. You and she will doubtless be wanting pastoral care, so I presumed to make this call. They will be here soon, your wife and daughter…." He hesitated before saying, "As will Agent Brian

O'Reilly of the Federal Bureau of Investigation." He knew nothing of the sort, of course. Lies were coming to fall off his tongue with frightening ease. "Mr. Stark, when they arrive, your daughter will be arrested and charged with the willful murder of Lawrence Gollancz. I have been informed that they have visual and physical evidence which clearly implicates her. I thought I should be here." Then he said even more cruel words, words intended to provoke. "Mr. Stark, do you know what it will be like for Chelsea? In prison, I mean. Such a pretty young thing. You watch a lot of television. Maybe you've seen a few episodes of *Orange Is the New Black*."

Jack Stark's already pale countenance blanched wan at Ludington's words. He sat still as death in his wheelchair for what seemed an age. Then, he emitted a long and demonstrative sigh as he cast a glance into the kitchen toward what Ludington had noticed when he passed through the room. Jack Stark braced himself on the arms of his wheelchair, grasping them tightly, and pulled himself to his feet. He was a taller man than Ludington had thought. He then walked easily and steadily into the kitchen. He found what Seth had seen, namely the glass of what looked to be whiskey with fresh ice, a glass that rested toward the back of the stool-height counter, out of the easy reach of a man in a wheelchair. And above it, even higher and definitely out of reach of a man in a wheelchair, high on the top shelf of an open upper cabinet stood the fifth of Bullet Seth had also seen.

Stark returned to the family room and sat, not in his wheelchair, but on the sectional. He motioned Ludington to sit and took a long gulp of whiskey. "Chelsea didn't kill her uncle. I did. I have a hunch you know way more than you are pretending to know, Reverend. I moved that generator he bought. Pulled it across the lawn and put it under his window. Did it in the pouring rain. Wasn't a hundred percent sure it would work, but it did." Stark smiled and took another sip of the whiskey. "Figured it would look like an accident. He deserved it, you know. I hated him for what he was going to do. You probably won't agree here, but he had no right to leave family money to some synagogue in the City. I mean, Irene has a right. What he told us he was going to do with the money was wrong, plain and simple wrong."

Seth Ludington looked Jack Stark in the eyes. "Do you have Parkinson's

Disease, Mr. Stark?"

"Yes, I got it, but what I really got was screwed. Screwed by the school district, screwed by the damn board, screwed by my boss. Then I got diagnosed. So I just decided to die, sit in that chair, and watch *Game of Thrones* over and over until it was all over. I mean me. And drink a little." He raised the glass toward Ludington, now half empty. "There's no point in it all. No point at all. But I won't let this happen to Chelsea, I mean take the fall for what I did. Beyond that, I don't give a shit."

"So you can drive?"

"Oh yeah. It's slow for me, Parkinson's, and I'm a great faker. My dad had it. I watched him close for ten years."

"Does Irene know? Do your son and daughter know? I mean, do they know you're feigning symptoms you don't have?"

"They don't pay much attention. Nobody does. They're gone all the time, most of the time anyway. They hate looking at me." He looked Ludington in the eyes and drained the last of the Bullet, then swirled the ice around in the glass.

Ludington and Stark both turned as they heard the door into the kitchen from the garage open. Seth stood, assuming it would be Chelsea and her mother. It was an out-of-breath Harriet van der Berg. She entered the kitchen triumphantly, a long, coiled, heavy-duty extension cord draped over her shoulder. "Dominie, I found this in the garage. It's precisely fifty feet in length."

Ludington looked at Harriet and her extension cord, then at a dumb-founded Jack Stark, and back at van der Berg. "You might want to display it to Mr. Stark." He nodded toward the man, who was seated not in his wheelchair but on the sectional couch.

"Jack Stark has confessed to me that it was he who moved the generator."

Harriet van der Berg stuttered in disbelief, "But he has Parkinson's Disease. He could hardly drive a vehicle, nor could he wheel a heavy gasoline generator across a wide expanse of lawn."

In response to that observation, Stark stood and walked into the kitchen past van der Berg and reached for the bottle of Bullet high on a shelf to pour himself another two fingers. He leaned against the counter near the sink, took a sip, gave van der Berg a smile dripping cynicism, and said, "Who the hell are you?"

"Oh my," she said, "Sound logic seems to have misled us."

They all turned as they heard the front door open. Irene and Chelsea moved through the entry hall and into the kitchen. Chelsea raced into the room ahead of her mother. She saw only Harriet and said, "Miss van der Berg, I am so honored that you are here, and all the way from LA." Only after Harriet shook her head did the child scan the kitchen and see Ludington and her father, standing on his feet.

It was impossible to tell which sight confused Irene the most, the presence in her kitchen of Henrietta Berg, the Reverend Seth Ludington, or her husband erect and leaning against the sink with a glass of whiskey in his hand. She simply said, "Miss Berg, Reverend Ludington," and finally, after a long look that grew confused, then comprehending, and lastly furious, "Jack," At which word she promptly fainted, sinking gracefully into a pile between the wall oven and the center island.

Irene Stark recovered quickly, as she usually did, and was escorted to the sectional by her daughter and Harriet. Her husband did not move to help. He merely watched the scene, as if from a great distance. When it was clear that Irene Stark would survive her trio of astonishments, Ludington stepped outside and called Agent Brian O'Reilly, whom, he discovered was just leaving the City, bound for Speonk to question Chelsea Irene Stark.

"Glad you're coming, Agent O'Reilly, but you need to know that her father has just confessed."

After silence as dumbfounded as Jack Stark's, O'Reilly said, "Traffic is still backed up. A bridge closure. I'll call some locals."

The two beat cops from Westhampton Beach arrived a bare twenty minutes after O'Reilly called them. They took a now-inebriated Jack Stark into custody, willing and uncuffed. Only after Irene had regained something approaching composure and Chelsea had come to understand that no California true crime producer was pursuing her talents, did Seth ease into his pastoral mode. He sat with the two women, mother and daughter, absorbing growing fury at their husband and father. Their rage seemed aimed as much at the man's long and egregious deception as at the homicide he had committed.

As the day edged toward evening and Chelsea turned on lights in the family room and kitchen, Harriet asked the question Seth wanted to ask but was afraid to put to either Irene or Chelsea. "Irene, Rabbi Gellman, and Rev. Ludington were at your brother's home the day after he died. They mentioned to me that there were footprints in the mud around the generator." Here, she hesitated, as the question on her lips was about to betray the fact that she knew too much. "Those footprints seem to have matched a pair of your brother's boots as well as an identical pair owned by Hudson."

Chelsea answered, though no question had been asked. "Uncle Larry gave them to Hudson on his last birthday. Uncle liked them so much he also bought a pair for himself." She paused, then looked first at van der Berg and then Ludington. "Dad's a size smaller."

It felt graceless, leaving mother and daughter alone, but at seven-forty, all that could be said had been said, and Seth made motions signaling that it was time for him and Harriet to leave. He felt he had to ask, so he did. "Irene, would you like me to pray with you before we go"?

To his relief, she said no. He would pray for them, but later and alone.

As the Volvo found its lane among the six of the westbound Long Island Expressway, van der Berg said, "I cannot but consider Occam's razor. How does it go?"

"You never cease to impress me, Harriet van der Berg. 'The simplest explanation is usually the right one.' Something like that. But his case might be closer to Sherlock Holmes."

Van der Berg finished the reference for him. "Margaret's favorite, quoted it to me all the time. 'When you have eliminated all which is impossible, then whatever remains, however improbable, must be the truth.'"

Chapter Forty-One

Tuesday and Wednesday

It was nearly eleven o'clock by the time Ludington dropped van der Berg at her building and got the Volvo to its garage. He walked home to find Fiona in bed, awake and waiting up for him. He planted an appreciative kiss on her lips and told her the whole tale. He did not sleep well.

* * *

The reason for his restlessness was made clear to him when he phoned Dan Gellman just after eight the next morning. He told the rabbi the same story he had told his wife the night before, including the bit about seeing the glass of booze with fresh ice sitting on a high counter and the bottle from which it was poured perched on a shelf far too high for Jack Stark to reach in his wheelchair. "I had a hunch, Dan, and had already decided to play it. But it was confirmed when I saw that out-of-reach glass with fresh ice and then the bottle up there. Made it easier for me to goad him. People fake disease—not often, but sometimes. It can be a way out of life. Just giving up is an exit. A slow suicide."

If Gellman agreed with this bit of psychological speculation, he did not say so. The rabbi went silent for a moment before saying, "Irene confessed to save her son, Seth. Crazy mother, but she loved her kid enough to do that.

Crazy father, but he might love his daughter just as much."

Seth now understood what had caused his restive night, "I am totally sure Jack Stark confessed to save Chelsea. Dan, I have no doubt that's what he did. I pushed him to it. Deliberately."

"Seth, the question is not why he confessed, but whether he did what he confessed to doing."

Ludington nodded into the phone. "But Dan, O'Reilly will ask him for details. I mean the exact time he was there, the locations of the generator before and after it got moved, the two extension cords, how he blinded the Ring camera, what he was wearing on his feet."

"He'll do just that. But Seth, those are all things Chelsea Bun, our little true crime maven, could have told him."

"After she did it, you mean? A little family conspiracy?"

"Possible, Seth, not likely, but possible."

"This does not comfort me, Rabbi. Talk to you later. I gotta get the girls to school."

Ludington wheeled the twins up 2nd Avenue, pondering the depth of his love for his own daughters. He supposed he would do just about anything for them. He dropped them off at the Happy House of Little Ones and walked down to Old Stone, pushing the empty stroller before him. He hoped van der Berg would be there when he arrived. He needed to unpack these fresh doubts with her. He had to wonder if they had risen to trouble her night as well.

Harriet was in, seated at her desk, a restless mien about her face. Seth told her that he'd had a night of fitful sleep. "I was so tired, Harriet, and sad of course, but I couldn't put my finger on what was troubling me until I talked with Dan this morning." He related the conversation he'd just had with the rabbi. "Honestly, I found Jack Stark's confession totally convincing. It just never occurred to me that he might be lying to save Chelsea."

"Well," said van der Berg, "it occurred to me. It occurred to me as I was about to fall into sleep at eleven-forty. At ten minutes after midnight, I arose and prepared myself a cup of hot Ovaltine. That usually works, but I still couldn't sleep."

Ludington struck a sad, crooked smile and looked at van der Berg, "Harriet, what troubles me most is that we may never know."

"Well, Seth, I cannot live with never knowing. I simply cannot."

Ludington nodded agreement. "And there's one more thing, Harriet—Gollancz's clean-as-a-whistle duck boots by his back door. I assume he put them on when he set up the generator in his driveway, ran the long cord to the junction box, and plugged the thing in. Wouldn't they have gotten muddy?"

Van der Berg pushed her chair away from the desk and said, "Well, that query had me up last night as well." She smiled slyly and looked her pastor in the eye. "So upon waking this morning, I telephoned LILCO, the local Long Island power company, to inquire as to precisely when power was lost on Eaton's Neck that night. I was at long last connected to a person who could answer my question. It occurred at 7:11 PM. The gentleman seemed intrigued with my inquiry and then related a second and consummately relevant point—electrical service in the Northport area where their large facility is located was actually lost some ten minutes before the storm passed over Eaton's Neck. So Dominie, Mr. Gollancz's home was without power before the rain commenced."

Ludington grinned for the first time in two days. "So when Lawrence Gollancz's house lost power and he set up his new generator, the ground was still dry."

"Precisely."

One quandary resolved, Ludington spent the balance of the day as ill at ease as he had been the night before, struggling to focus on the Isaiah study and finishing up a report he was going to make on behalf of the Mission Outreach Committee of the Presbytery of New York City. He was a member of the committee, but not the chair. The chair, who would normally make the report at the coming Presbytery meeting in Brooklyn, had emailed him a few days earlier, confessing that she was vacationing in Italy and pleading with Seth to fill in for her.

His cell rang just before five. He pulled the insistent thing from his jacket's breast pocket and looked at the screen. It was Agent Brian O'Reilly. He took the call just as it was about to go to voicemail.

"Listen, Reverend Ludington, I'll make this quick. I have resented you and your admin—and the rabbi—for poking your noses into these cases we were called in on, the vandalism and the arson, and then Gollancz. I resented it, but have to admit that your nosiness did help us wrap up the Gollancz part. You know, Reverend, I read all the Father Blackie Ryan books—the whole series back when, so I thought I owed you a call. In his honor."

Ludington had no idea who Father Blackie Ryan was. "Okay..."

"So, you should know this. We've been waiting on a bunch of court orders to get us cell phone tracking data. It's new, and it's becoming a big deal in police investigations. In short, you can tell roughly where a certain cell phone was at a given time. The location is not that precise, but it doesn't always need to be."

Ludington thought, but did not say, that here was yet another tool of detection available to the authorities but not to the amateur.

"Anyway, yesterday we finally got court orders for all four of the Stark cell phones and Masterson's too. Got the data this morning. Hudson's phone was pinging a tower in Flushing all evening. No surprise. Irene's pinged a Westhampton Beach tower. No surprise. Masterson's was busy pinging a tower in Northport. No surprise. Jack Stark's phone was also pinging the Westhampton Beach tower, a bit of a surprise there. But he told us he left his iPhone at home when he went to Eaton's Neck. But this is the one you might want to know about... Chelsea. Her phone was active that night, pinging the same Westhampton Beach tower as her mother's. Chelsea was at home all that night, Reverend. Told us she was in her room binge-watching some true crime show and texting with a friend who was also watching it. We checked with the friend, confirmed her story. Even got screen-shots of their back-and-forth texts. All time-stamped, of course. Her father isn't lying for her, Reverend. Thought that might worry you, too. O'Reilly hesitated before continuing, "Frankly, I'm not sure we could have pulled a case together without the confession you wiggled out of him. I have to say, I've developed some regard for your Protestant Blackie Ryan act. So, well, thank you, Reverend. "

Ludington reciprocated thanks, rather too profusely perhaps, ended the call and sprinted into van der Berg's office with the liberating news that Chelsea Stark was in her bedroom watching true crime television the night her uncle was murdered. Then he called Dan Gellman and told him.

Only then did he dash up to the Happy House of Little Ones, arriving ten minutes after closing and smiling fetchingly at the two employees who had to stay late because of him. He was billed ten dollars for each minute he was late, times two, of course. He didn't much mind, but hoped the two women got a cut. He wheeled the girls home to Fiona at a record pace. He fixed macaroni and cheese with hot dogs for dinner, and he and Fiona tucked the girls in with yet another reading of *Goodnight Moon*. Seth and Fiona went to bed early after a celebratory half-inch of Grand Marnier on ice in front of the cold fireplace. He slept well for the first time in three weeks.

Epilogue

Thursday

Thanksgiving is perhaps the only holiday Jews and Christians can comfortably keep together. It is as secular as it is religious, and of course, giving thanks to God is common to both traditions. The sparse congregations of Temple Beth Shalom and Old Stone that gathered in the latter's sanctuary in the early evening of the fourth Thursday in November were less sparse when together.

Dan had asked Seth and Harriett to join him at the Lex for post-worship drinks. Nobody was hungry, the Gellmans and the Ludingtons having separately feasted that afternoon, the latter joined by Harriet van der Berg and two other singletons from church Fiona feared would otherwise find themselves alone.

After Nero set their drinks before them, Dan raised his glass of Scotch and said, "I wanted you both to know the insurance settlement finally came through, rather better than we'd hoped. So we shall rebuild, but not the old monster. It'll be smaller. Right-sized," he said with a grin. "But we're genuinely going to miss Old Stone." He raised a glass in Seth's direction.

Seth had floated the idea of the two congregations permanently sharing Old Stone's building and found himself disappointed at this news. But he understood the longing for a uniquely Jewish space unadorned with Christian stained glass and hidden crosses. He clinked Dan's neat glass gently with his own stem glass of cabernet and said, "I am happy for you,

Dan, and I am pleased for Beth Shalom."

They took their requisite sips and went silent until Seth said, "So I talked to Irene this morning. As her chaplain, I guess. She still thinks of me as such. I called her. Thanksgiving Day and all. And, well, curiosity. Seems she's bought a huge pile of a place on the beach in South Hampton. Looked it up on Zillow. It was listed for eleven million. She's living there alone. She did her best to sound chipper, but I think she's perfectly miserable. She said that Chelsea's loving NYU. She didn't mention them, but I imagine Hudson's not much loving Rikers Island, nor is Jack enjoying life in Ossining."

They had known for two months that a copy of Lawrence Gollancz's revised will benefiting his synagogue had been found locked in his home wall safe. It was unsigned, so Irene Stark had inherited her brother's fortune. As soon as the will had cleared probate, she sold the soft serve business and the houses in Asharoken and Speonk so she could ascend to her aspirational life in the actual Hamptons.

Harriet took a delicate sip of her Chardonnay. "It is consummately unfortunate that no one was ever charged with the arson." She said this knowing that the three of them—as well as Agent Brian O'Reilly—were confident the vandal and the arsonist were the same. The surmise was that Hudson Stark had returned to the synagogue in search of the new will after his mother had failed to find it in her brother's house the day after his death and had torched Beth Shalom, perhaps out of anger or maybe to cover his tracks. Or both. As with so many lost synagogues in history, the cause of its destruction was unproven, and no one was ever held accountable.

Seth said, "The next-to-the-worst thing about all of this was Jack Stark faking Parkinson's. It seems he does have it, but it's not that debilitating. What he was doing was such an insult to all the people who struggle bravely with it. People who are not faking.

Harriet picked up on that last word. "So much of this matter was about faking. I mean to say, this case was very much about the grave perils attendant to pretending to be that which you are not."

A Note from the Author

The various places that figure in our story are all quite real—Northport, Asharoken, Eaton's Neck, Speonk, and Westhampton. They represent the little-known but often charming and always wild diversity of Long Island, a unique place in the American landscape. The several restaurants visited by our characters are also real, and all well worth a visit. Neither Old Stone Presbyterian Church nor Temple Beth Shalom exist outside our imaginations. Any similarity of our characters—except for Nero—to real persons is quite unintentional.The story brings our protagonists to consider both the long history and tragic contemporary reality of antisemitism.It is not intended to be an academic or exhaustive exploration of the topic, though we hope that it might bring readers to consider and to read more deeply about this oldest of hatreds.

Acknowledgements

We both offer thanks to our patient spouses and children who indulged our regular retreat to our laptops while writing this book. We express deep appreciation to Rabbi Meir Bargeron and Dr. David Lundquist for sharing their considerable expertise on Judaism and antisemitism, as well as to beta readers Fred Hasecke and Terri Lindvall, and to Susan Whitlock for her thorough copy-editing. And again, thanks to Joe Veltre, our literary agent at Gersh, and to the remarkable Dames of Detection at Level Best Books.

About the Author

M. M. Lindvall is a father-daughter writing team. Madeline Lindvall Radman is a writer, producer, and director of non-scripted television, specializing in investigative documentary series. Michael Lindvall is a published author of several volumes of accessible theology and two novels.

SOCIAL MEDIA HANDLES:
   https://www.facebook.com/profile.php?id=100088633655692
   https://www.instagram.com/m.m.lindvall

AUTHOR WEBSITE:
   https://www.mmlindvall.com

Also by M. M. Lindvall

Ashes to Ashes by M. M. Lindvall

Earth to Earth by M. M. Lindvall

The Good News from North Haven by Michael Lindvall

Leaving North Haven by Michael Lindvall

A Geography of God by Michael Lindvall